T0146605

A MAN LIKE HIS
GRANDFATHER

Other books written by R. Jack Punch

White Treasure
The Barrister

A MAN LIKE HIS
GRANDFATHER

R. JACK PUNCH

A MAN LIKE HIS GRANDFATHER

iUniverse books may be ordered through booksellers or by contacting:

iUniverse
1663 Liberty Drive
Bloomington, IN 47403
www.iuniverse.com
1-800-Authors (1-800-288-4677)

ISBN: 978-1-5320-3552-4 (sc)
ISBN: 978-1-5320-3554-8 (hc)
ISBN: 978-1-5320-3553-1 (e)

Library of Congress Control Number: 2017918519

Print information available on the last page.

iUniverse rev. date: 12/08/2017

People do kind things. Whether they perform kind acts habitually because their parents taught them to be kind or they need to work to be kind, their kindness changes the world. No matter how bad a person may be, one kind act can be wonderful. A good person uses kindness to enhance other people's perceptions of the world.

This book is dedicated to anyone who performs some type of kind act.

My brothers and sisters are, in my mind, perfect examples of kindness. We must have had truly wonderful parents and ancestors. My children make me proud, and I thank them for becoming the adults they are. I am grateful to my grandchildren and great-grandchildren for showing me that their kindness will continue to make the world a better place. Thanks to my siblings for their support and help in writing this book, and thanks to anyone who tells stories about the way things were. Thanks to my wife, Jane, who supported me and tolerated my obsession with this story. Thanks to my brother Jim for his help in getting me started on this book.

CONTENTS

FAMILY TREE OF DONAHEES IN AMERICA

			Born	Died
First Generation				
Raymond Donahee	Mathew	William	1800	1851
Isla	Ryan		1807	1847
Second Generation				
Mathew	Jack	Karl	1825	1898
Jade Malloy	Ross	Lydia	1831	1909
William	Son	Daughter		
Mary	Daughter			
Ryan	Frederick			
Eileen				
Third Generation				
Jack	Son		1859	1920
Felicity Flynn	Daughter			
Karl	Son		1862	1919
Gwen McKeon	Son			
Ross	Odessa	Helen	1869	1911
Trina	Hunter		1871	1911
Lydia	William		1871	1961
Zachariah Smith			1865	1917
Odessa			1886	1961

Fourth Generation					
Hunter	Megan	Luke		1892	1967
Margaret O'Reilly	William			1891	1948
Fifth Generation	Megan	Michael	Scarlett	1919	1999
	Austin Brown				
	Luke	Hannah		1921	2001
	Penny			1925	2015
	William	Jade M	Catherine	1923	1984
	Donna	Peter William	Patrick	1923	2012
		Tristan Hunter			

1847: LEAVING IRELAND

Matt Donahee was six feet tall, and at twenty-two years old, he attributed his body's sinewy mass of muscles to his hard life working on farms. The Irish evening sunshine sparkled on Matt's damp suntanned skin and brown hair. Matt loved the smell of the sea, but today he detested the smell of the sea mixed with produce and livestock. The farm odor filled the air around the loading dock. Matt felt sorry for the tired men who loaded the beans, corn, and butter that filled the hold of the giant ship while English soldiers pompously supervised activities on the dock. Matt felt tired and angry as he herded the last of Macintyre's fine cattle to the dock. Matt feared his growing anger toward the injustices the English bestowed on his fellow Irishmen.

Matt knew those cattle had provided milk, butter, and meat to many hungry people in County Cork. Matt was angry that the 1846 repeal of the Irish Corn Laws meant Macintyre could no longer afford to feed his cattle. As a result, Macintyre had sold them to an English farmer. A saddened Matt knew that tomorrow Macintyre would use the money from his farm and cattle to buy passage to America, where, apparently, work was abundant. Matt was becoming angrier and more frustrated, though the reason was not clear to him as he watched his fellow Irishmen suffer the economic plight.

Matt witnessed the exportation of food to the greedy English merchants while his Irish brethren suffered the Great Hunger. Matt was happy his year of employment had ended, leaving him with a year's pay, which would help his family survive. Matt was thankful that Macintyre fed his help well, but as the feed for the cattle had become scarce, so had the food for the help. Matt's thoughts of home, family, and Catherine, his fiancée, filled his mind. Matt's thoughts provided the energy to start the long journey home.

Matt noticed a lifeless fog that crept over County Cork as he started walking the wearisome two-day journey to Malloy in North County Cork. Matt knew his family waited for him to bring the benefits of his laborious job away from home back to them. Matt recalled that Macintyre believed the fog brought a curse that caused the potato crop to fail. Others thought the smoke from the new train system was to blame. Matt thought the blight was a punishment from God, but he did not know what the sin was.

Matt thought of his two brothers. Ryan was the youngest at seventeen years old, and a year older was William, or Will, as he was called. Matt felt guilty for leaving Ryan and Will to help their father, Raymond, work the farm. Matt thought of how Ryan was always devising methods or tools to make the work easier. Ryan's favorite device was a wooden pole with a concave carved into one end. The pole negated the need to bend over to push bean seeds into the ground at just the right depth. Matt was more traditional and used his brute strength to accomplish tasks.

Macintyre had hired Matt to learn the cattle business in the city of Cork. At first, Matt was homesick, but the work occupied both his body and mind. Still, Matt spent every leisure moment thinking of home, family, and Catherine. Stories of the potato blight reached Matt near the waterfront in Cork, where Macintyre's livestock farm was located. Matt hoped the money he'd managed to save while working for the past year would help his family through the Great Hunger and give him and Catherine a good start. The memory of the beautiful Catherine, his betrothed, was foremost on his mind.

Matt heard voices coming through the fog on the road. He saw silhouettes of unknown people who sounded distressed and afraid. Matt listened carefully, trying to recognize any voices that might be familiar. Parts of conversations enlightened Matt as to the severity of the Great Hunger. Matt heard some people talking of death and disease. Matt figured that others were too hungry, poor, and depressed to journey with those along the road to Cork.

Matt heard a gray silhouette say, "Mary was too young to die."

Knowing a Mary, Matt bellowed, "Mary who?"

No answer came. Matt felt an unusual anxiety. Instant and uncomfortable warmth came over him. He must have moved too fast toward the voice, because the silhouette became a real person who stepped back as Matt approached. Matt did not understand where his desperation came from, but he apologized immediately and, with a calmer voice, said, "I am sorry for startling you, but I have been gone for a long time."

More relaxed, the stranger said, "Where are you from?"

"Malloy."

"We are from Kildee, just a few kilometers from Malloy. Be prepared for the worst, but pray for the best. Malloy and Kildee are both badly affected by the Great Hunger and the sickness."

Matt noticed a frail woman with the man. They were carrying many belongings and looked like the people he had seen in Cork waiting for passage to the Americas.

"Thank you, and have a safe journey," Matt said. He barely heard their reply. Matt started walking faster, using the adrenaline his anxiety had created at the conversation. Malloy was a long way off.

Matt noticed that others' silhouettes and voices seemed alike, as if his mind were repeating the same dismal conversations. The road quieted down as night's dark blanket fell upon the land, except for the occasional sounds of tired snoring from travelers sleeping off the sides of the road. Matt could not sleep while worrying about home. He just kept moving and thinking. The fog turning from charcoal black to dreary gray signaled that day was approaching.

The fog lifted, revealing the beautiful green trees, rolling hills, and fresh air. More travelers passed by Matt, but now they had faces. Matt looked at each face for recognition without success. Matt had not slept or eaten, yet his energy was as strong as if he were gliding along with wings. On the top of a hill, Matt could see Malloy close to the west. Just at the bottom of the hill was a fork in the road: left to Malloy and right to the Donahees' farm. The beauty of the Irish country reminded Matt of Catherine.

Matt figured Raymond and Will must have recognized his energetic gait approaching the farm. Will ran toward Matt, leaving their father walking a steady stride. Matt and Will took turns asking several questions without providing the other time to answer. Matt saw Ryan heading toward him from behind the house. Matt figured Ryan had heard the commotion and left the project he was working on to meet Matt and Will. The happy reunion ended when Matt asked how their mother was. Matt's heart jumped at the silence. Raymond arrived just in time to answer the question.

Matt's fear grew when his father took a moment to either catch his breath or prepare for the words that inevitably came: "Mother has died. The sickness got her last month."

Matt felt as if his knees were going to abandon him. Matt struggled to walk as the four Donahee men walked back to the farmhouse, each holding his emotions deep inside. Matt's father had taught his sons that real men didn't show despair, but while no tears developed, despair was in the air. Matt's father broke the silence as they reached the farmhouse.

"We could not afford to buy a proper stone for her grave. Ryan made one. It is beautiful."

Matt finally spoke. "I want to see her grave."

Raymond told Will and Ryan, "Go inside, and prepare supper. Matt looks starved."

Matt walked with his father slowly up the hill behind the farm. No words were spoken. The stone was well made and neatly marked:

Isla Donahee
Born 1807, Died 1847
Beloved Wife and Mother
Now in Heaven

Matt felt angry as father and son stood motionless, looking at his mother's grave. Matt knew it was a sign of weakness to show a tear, and he wanted to prove his manhood to his father. Matt struggled to hold his emotions inside. Looking down at the grave, Matt saw a small splash on the ground in front of his father. *Was that a tear?* Matt thought. Matt made the sign of the cross to signal that he was done and turned away from his father so neither could see the welling of eyes.

They started downhill to the farmhouse in silence. Then Raymond said, "You'd better go see Catherine before dinner."

"Is something wrong?"

"She is a strong fighter. She's fighting the sickness."

Matt had planned on getting cleaned up and looking his best before visiting Catherine. Now he could not run fast enough. Without a word, he left his grieving father. His pace increased as he ran down the hill, past the crops, and by the farmhouse.

Catherine Holden lived two kilometers to the east. Matt was there before he could think or feel his exhaustion.

Matt knocked on the door, and when it opened, he was too out of breath to talk. He was ushered into the house and saw his Catherine lying on a bed with her mother holding her hand. Kneeling beside her, he could say only her name. Catherine opened her eyes and smiled at him. She held up her hand for Matt to hold. Matt took her hand, and before he could tell her that they would get through this sickness, she closed her eyes and took her last breath.

Matt knew he could not hold his emotions inside. He hugged Catherine's mother as her tears started flowing freely. He shook hands with Catherine's father and hurried out the door. Tears of fire exploded from Matt's eyes. He cursed the sickness, the Great Hunger, and Ireland. He cursed God and himself.

Matt appreciated that Ryan had become a talented carpenter, as evidenced by his repairs on the house and the donkey cart he'd built to haul produce to the market. Matt agreed that Will had become a competent farmer as the Donahee farm expanded into beans and the new American corn. Matt learned that there was plenty for the family to eat, but little went to the market. Matt's family, the Donahees, were proud Irishmen and shared much of their crops with less fortunate neighbors. Matt and his brothers had been taught to read and write by Isla, their mother. Matt's father had never learned to read, but he worked hard, providing a good example to Matt and his brothers. Matt's loving mother, Isla, had lectured that literacy was key to the Donahee boys' successes.

Matt's emotions were out of control. He felt that without Catherine, there was nothing left for him in Ireland. The look on his face was a combination of grief and anger. He wanted to run away from all the problems and felt guilty. He mentioned going to America, and to his surprise, his father agreed that it was a good idea. He said Matt should send money home so that his brothers could join him in America. Raymond told Matt that he'd heard there was much money to be made in America. Matt's father had farmed all his life, and Matt believed he could survive working a smaller farm without his sons. Matt vowed that he would send for his father too.

An unhappy Matt decided that after Catherine's funeral, he would leave the farm, Malloy, and Ireland.

Catherine's family had no money and not much farmland. They decided to bury her next to Matt's mother. Matt, his father, his brothers, the Holdens, and other neighbors did not have a dry eye among them. They lowered Catherine into the ground and said their goodbyes. Mathew Donahee never had known physical love, and it did not matter that he never would. He made a promise to himself to bring his family to America. He would not fail. Matt feared that the sickness was breaking hearts over all the land.

Matt accepted some corn bread and dried meat from his father to take on his journey to America. Matt felt guilty when he took enough money to pay for passage on the ship to America, but he told himself that it was for the good of his family. Still, Matt left what he could with his father to help with the farm. Matt's work for the year at Macintyre's had yielded enough money for passage for one to America with little left for the family farm. Still, Matt believed the farm would likely survive. As Matt left his family to walk to the city and docks of Cork, he remembered and feared the despair in those he'd passed when he came home a few days ago.

Matt was angry and sad and knew he would never be loved again. But he conceded to leave his despair behind him. Matt walked slowly and forced a smile and a cheery hello to all he met on the road to Cork. Matt saw an English merchant going in the opposite direction to acquire produce to send to England. Matt heard the merchant yell obscenities and saw him use his whip to get people out of the way as he met them head-on. Matt felt the rage inside him leap out uncontrollably.

Matt walked straight toward the merchant, grabbed his whip with his left hand, and punched the donkey, because it was closest, before he attacked the merchant. Three men the merchant had swung his whip at pulled Matt off the badly beaten merchant. Matt knocked the donkey onto its side, and the cart tipped over behind it. Matt looked at what he'd done and felt afraid of his own anger—anger he'd never experienced before. He heard the merchant mumble, because the merchant could not talk clearly in light of the damage Matt had done to his face. Matt understood the merchant mumble that the English military would find him and make him pay for what he had done.

Matt looked around, expecting thanks for what he'd done to the merchant. All he saw was fear. Matt knew others were afraid of the big Irishman who could not control his anger. He increased his pace to leave those fearful of him behind. Matt justified that the merchant deserved what he'd gotten, as did any greedy English coming to Ireland for big profits. Still, Matt knew he needed to control his unexpected rage.

Matt hurried to make it to the docks in the city of Cork. The familiar odor reminded Matt of the increasing poverty in Ireland. Matt felt relieved when he procured immediate passage to America because he had the money to pay full fare. Fear left Matt when he managed to get on the ship despite the many English soldiers posted around the docks. He was relieved to be on the ship and avoid the trouble that the badly beaten merchant could have caused. However, he soon discovered the meaning of the term *coffin ships*, as the passenger boats were called. Matt's ship was larger than the cattle ships that went to England, but space was extremely cramped. He was aboard an American ship called *Washington*.

People had to sleep sitting up in the tight space provided for them. A woman asked Matt, "Kin ya hold one of me children for me? There is no room, and I be afraid they get hurt or stepped on if I leave 'em on the floor."

With arms out, the child smiled innocently.

"Sure." Matt took the young boy and felt warmth go into his heart. He thought of Catherine and how she'd hoped for children. Catherine had loved all people, especially children. Matt felt his insides soften while holding the boy. Rage left Matt Donahee for the moment. "What's your name?" he asked the child.

"Peter."

"Well, Peter, my name's Matt."

"And dis es me sistar, Eve." Peter pointed to the little girl in her mother's arms.

"Hello, Eve," Matt said as Eve shyly hid her face in her mother's shoulder.

"I'm Abby," the mother said as she held out a single finger to shake. That was all she could muster with her hands full.

Matt patted her hand rather than giving a proper, firm handshake. Matt began looking at the Irish faces cramped in the ship. Generally, he liked people and enjoyed talking and listening to others. The noise of the engines, the low whisper of voices, and the loud cries of children made it impossible for Matt to consider a dignified conversation with anyone.

Matt believed the conditions aboard the American ship were bearable. He was glad when, on the second day, passengers were moved about so they had more room to sleep. Matt's passage fee, like that of the other passengers, was to include food, but none had been served. Matt's compassion demanded that he share the food his father had packed for him with Abby and her children. He rationed the food and ate little so that he would not run out for a while. Still, the food would not last for the month-long journey. Food came that night, and Matt was disappointed because it was poor quality.

Matt had paid triple what the cost used to be. He felt cheated and believed the other passengers had been cheated as well. He recognized that the benefit was that the steamship was faster than the wood ships that sailed to Canada. Matt thought about his brothers and father when passengers shared stories of how the British ships lost one out of five passengers to typhoid or malnutrition. Matt surprised himself when he prayed for the many who were buried at sea or simply thrown overboard, thus the name *coffin ships*. Conditions improved on the *Washington*. He'd heard promises that food was better quality on the American ships, but no one had said anything about food not being abundant. Matt shared his satisfaction when Abby and her children settled into a berth with another family. Matt had to sleep in a large hold with many other single men. He needed air and sunlight. The confinement warned him that the rage was coming back.

Matt asked a crewman if he could go on deck. The crewman seemed friendly but explained that below-deck passengers were not allowed above deck. Matt felt that was unnecessary. A few hours later, the crewman came looking for him and told Matt that the captain wanted to make the trip in less than three weeks and was looking for coal shovelers to feed the large boilers. Matt jumped at the opportunity to be useful. There was no pay. Food and water were plentiful for the coal workers. Matt found his strength improve due to the hard work, and the rage lessened.

The *Washington* made the overseas trip in three weeks, but it seemed like an eternity. Matt was ready to stand on solid ground. A large newly built immigration office was at Barge Island in New York Harbor. It took two miserable days for Matt and other passengers to depart the ship and traverse the red tape at the immigration office. Matt noticed that many immigrants could not read the signs or the forms, which slowed the process. Matt followed a separate line for literate passengers. The literate line moved much quicker. Matt was happy his mother had made him study hard and learn to read. Matt Donahee was processed on June 17, 1847, at twenty-two years old.

Outside the immigration office, Matt watched men who sought workers for various jobs. The first company Matt came to was looking for coal workers to go to Pennsylvania. Matt felt he had done enough coal work and wanted to work outside on a farm, not in a dark underground mine. Matt followed the line of Irish immigrants looking for work and a new life. He saw three big men push Abby to the ground and hold her down. Her children had been knocked on the ground and were crying. Matt had compassion for the brave Irish who made the dangerous journey to America, but it was not compassion that made Matt act.

RAGE

Matt didn't think. He jumped toward the large man standing over Abby, put his left hand on the man's shoulder, and spun the attacker around. The man was smiling until Matt's right uppercut caught him on the chin. The big man hit the ground hard. Matt turned his attention to the other two. Matt was the oldest of three brothers, and he'd learned how to fight without hurting his younger brothers. These were not his brothers, however, and the fight was not a fun shenanigan. Rage negated any playfulness. The second attacker went down, while the third got ahold of Matt's arm. The first attacker was on his feet and grabbed Matt's other arm. The smallest of the three bullies got to his feet and came at Matt while the other two held him tightly. The smaller man had an evil face and a twitch in his left eye. That evil look contributed to more rage, allowing Matt to twist his body and duck as the smaller man's fist came toward his face. The move broke his arms free from the two who were holding him. Skill, physical ability, and rage left Matt standing over three badly beaten men. A whistle blew a short distance off.

New York Police Officer O'Doul was a large Irishman with a calm demeanor. He smiled at Matt. "What happened here?"

Commotion provided several explanations from onlookers who were helping Abby to her feet. A voice from somewhere in the crowd said, "I'll take care of this."

O'Doul turned to the voice, saying, "Good day, Mr. Corning. Do these men work for you?"

"The three men who look like they got the worst of it are here to get workers for my businesses."

O'Doul turned and walked away.

The well-dressed businessman looked sternly at Matt, held out his hand, and said, "Erastus Corning."

"Mathew Donahee," Matt said, shaking hands. Matt heard Mr. Corning converse with his three employees to find that they'd offered Abby a job in the red-light district. Matt smiled when they told him that Abby had started punching the men. Mr. Corning called Abby over to apologize for his men's' indiscretion. He told Abby that he had a contact at the Mercy Orphanage in the city. He could get her respectable work there. Abby looked at her children. Mr. Corning assured Abby that her children would be with her, but the job probably would not pay much. Abby said all that mattered was that she was with her children and that they would not go hungry. Mr. Corning assured her and ordered his thugs to see to it that Abby and her children were taken safely to Mercy Orphanage.

Matt liked Mr. Corning for his actions. Abby nodded a thank-you to Matt as she left for her new life. Matt watched briefly as Abby and her children left, knowing he would never see them again.

"As for you, young Donahee, you are not in this country for an hour before you are in a fight and have your first run-in with the police. If I weren't here, you would be on your way to prison for fighting."

"Yes, sir." That was all Matt could respond as he thought that the rage could take control of his life at any moment. Matt was shocked at what Mr. Corning said next.

"I can use a man of your special talents. I am building a railroad through the countryside to the north of New York City. Are you looking for work?"

"Yes, sir!"

Mr. Corning explained that he could teach Matt how to

control his rage. Matt was happy for the opportunity. What resonated in Matt's mind was the word *countryside*. Work was simply a part of life that Matt was willing to accept. After an hour in New York City, Matt was ready for the country.

Mr. Corning told Matt to be at the Mohawk Hudson Railway Station by seven o'clock tomorrow morning. "Follow this road into the city to find the rail station," he said.

Matt was to report to Mr. Webster at the station. Matt thanked Mr. Corning. He looked around and quietly said goodbye to the immigration area, and in his mind, he wished the other Irish immigrants good luck.

Matt headed in the direction Mr. Corning had pointed out to the rail station. His emotions were conflicted as he observed a mix of wealthy New Yorkers and impoverished people. The rage still burned in his veins. At the same time, his compassion stirred a desire to help the unfortunate men, women, and children who were in the streets, begging for food. While Matt had found work, it was obvious that many others were not as fortunate. Matt's thoughts went home.

A large window in a shop showed a plethora of writing tools and papers. Matt entered the store and found several fancy writing tablets. He found a less expensive writing tablet and a two-pack of pencils. Matt knew pencils were hollowed-out dowels with graphite inside. Carrying a pencil would be easier than carrying an ink fountain and dip pen. Matt purchased the writing supplies and packed them carefully in his bag. He left the store, and his eyes met the glare of Officer O'Doul.

"Well, lad, where might you be off to?"

"I'm off to the Mohawk Hudson Railroad Station to report for work." Matt was surprised at how Officer O'Doul's glare turned to a friendly smile.

"Good for you, lad! You're most fortunate to have earned the favor of Mr. Corning. The rail station is just ahead about a mile."

"Thank you, sir."

Matt liked Officer O'Doul now that he was free from trouble. Matt noticed that the officer had the uncanny ability to scare a person with his sternness or to show compassion to make a person feel relaxed and safe. O'Doul could control his rage, and Matt wondered whether he could do the same without having to resort to violence. Matt thought of how other people might see him. *Special talents* was the term Mr. Corning had used to describe the favorable attributes that had led Matt to his job. Matt wondered how building a railroad and fighting might be related. He reached the rail station with a resolve to control the rage.

Matt would do whatever he could to make enough money to bring his father and brothers to New York. He found a bench under a strange-looking light. The light was not a candle and did not smell like whale oil. A worker explained that the rail station was one of the first places to have gas piped into the lights to burn all night. Matt had never seen gaslights, but the new gaslight provided ample light for him to write a letter home. He wrote the letter to his father, even though he knew his brothers would have to read it to him. Matt dozed off while reading his carefully chosen words.

"What's that in your hands?"

The voice woke Matt. He looked up at a man wearing a long coat and a fedora and said, "Paper and pencil. A letter to my father."

"So you can write?"

"Yes, sir."

"How are your deciphering skills?"

"Good. I kept records of cattle weight and feed quantities at Macintyre's farm in Cork."

The conversation was friendly, and Matt was happy to talk to someone. The man introduced himself as Ken Webster of the railroad company and told Matt to call him Ken. Ken was tall and burly, with thick brown hair. Matt liked his willingness to be helpful. Matt was excited to tell Ken that Mr. Corning had sent him to meet a Mr. Webster at the rail station, and he asked, "Are you that Mr. Webster?"

"I certainly am."

"I'm to meet you at seven this morning."

"You are two hours early."

"I am eager to start work."

"I spoke to Mr. Corning last night and was expecting a typical thug. You are literate and don't look so mean."

"I assure you that I am a good worker."

Ken smiled and said, "I can believe that."

Matt asked Ken where he could mail his letter, and Ken sent Matt over to a post window and explained that postal services might be rare where they were going. Ken waited while Matt paid for the letter with the last of his money. Matt walked with Ken over to a massive steam locomotive connected to a large coal car followed by several mixed-type cars. Matt noticed men busily loading the freight cars. The new gaslights made the night work possible. Matt told Ken he was ready to start loading with the other workers. Matt was surprised when Ken told him he would ride in the luxury car at the end.

"But I'm here to work."

"And you will."

Matt went with Ken back to see the luxury car. The car had many windows and red tapestries on the walls. A dining area was in the rear; sleeping quarters were on the side in the front of the car. Matt was surprised and asked Ken what type of work he would be doing. Matt's answer was that his job would be to handle problems that arose while setting up the rail work. Matt realized that his fighting rage was his so-called special talent, and he was somewhat disappointed. Matt's confusion was obvious, so Ken offered to let him ride up front in the locomotive with him. Matt agreed instantly.

Matt studied a map of New York railroads and discovered that the Mohawk Hudson Railroad was far to the north, and they were on the Hudson River Railroad's west-side track that ended north of the city. A dotted line continued up to Peekskill and on to Schenectady. Places Matt had only heard of were on the map, which showed a thin line all the way to Niagara Falls. There were dates printed in small red numbers on the map. Matt guessed the dates were completion times to get to that point on the map.

Mohawk, New York, had a date of September 1831. Peekskill had a date of 1849, but what intrigued Matt the most was the Albany date: April 1847. Matt had several questions to ask Ken. All Matt's thoughts ended when a loud horn blew. He watched people start boarding the train. The man with the horn was on a horse and seemed to take a position in front of the locomotive. Matt saw Ken headed for the locomotive and followed.

The process of moving the train filled with passengers and the steel track loaded by the night crew was slow. Ken explained that the man on the horse was called a west-side cowboy and that he had nothing to do with cows unless one got in the way. The train would travel between three and four miles per hour. Matt had to convert miles to kilometers in his mind. Outside of town, the train would increase speed up to fifteen miles per hour. Scenery started to remind Matt of Ireland as the train left the heavily populated New York City.

Matt wanted to help shovel coal but was entwined in conversation with Ken. The train came to a stop long before noon.

The Stone House Hotel was next to where the train stopped. Ken suggested he and Matt go inside for a meal. Matt told Ken he was out of money and would scrounge about for some wild berries. Ken laughed and told Matt that Erastus Corning took good care of his men as long as they earned their pay. The meal would come out of something called an expense account.

The Stone House Hotel was busy. Ken and Matt found an empty table and sat down. Matt watched as a dark-skinned man in nice clothes came over. Ken looked up at the man and said, "Coffee and pork with potatoes."

The waiter wrote down the order and looked at Matt, and in uncertainty, Matt said, "I'll have the same."

"Yes, sirs," the waiter said as he turned and walked away.

Matt asked Ken if the man was a slave. He thought Ken laughed a little too loudly, but Ken explained that he'd never seen a slave. The dark-skinned men were free working men who had an uncanny ability to work hard. The slave trade had been abolished fifty years ago, but slavery still existed in some of the southern states. Matt was pleased that he'd ended up in the northern part of the United States of America. An old emotion added to Matt's feelings: pride.

The dark-skinned waiter brought the coffee first. Matt had never tasted coffee before but liked the hot beverage. The pork and potatoes came before they'd finished their coffee. Matt had not eaten since he arrived in this new country. He devoured his meal before the waiter brought a silver pitcher and refilled their coffee mugs. Matt counted twelve pennies for the meal when Ken paid the bill.

Matt watched several of the passengers come into the hotel, but most passengers seemed to disperse in different directions. From the hotel, Matt watched the train maneuver so that the car with the steel rails was in front of the locomotive. The train accomplished this task by backing into parallel tracks and unhooking cars before it pulled back onto the first track to go ahead. Then the train would move specific cars until the desired positions were accomplished. Matt was able to understand the complexity of the arrangement well.

Matt followed Ken over the tracks and down a hill to the boat dock. They boarded a small steamship called the *Traveler*. The *Traveler* was similar to the *Washington* but smaller. Matt found it hard to believe that he'd gotten off the ocean ship only yesterday. A famous man of wealth from New York City owned the *Traveler*. His name was Vanderbilt. The ship was steam powered and had two large paddle wheels, one on each side. The upper deck had fancy staterooms for wealthy travelers. They were full. Matt shared a smaller bunk room, or berth, with Ken.

Matt put his canvas bag in the berth with Ken's larger leather case. He did not want to spend another voyage in a cubical and was elated to find that he had the freedom to go anyplace on the ship. He put on a clean shirt and left the berth to find Ken talking to a man on the deck. The man was the smallest of the three from the dock in New York. Matt walked up to his new friend Ken.

"Matt, this is Stony."

Stony held his hand out.

"We've met." Matt did not accept Stony's hand.

Ken recognized Matt's rage brewing. "You two will be working together. Stony is not too bright, but he is a good man in a pinch."

Matt remembered Father O'Sullivan's sermon on how forgiveness was good for the soul. He held out his hand and shook Stony's.

Stony proclaimed, "I will be happy to work with such a tough Irishman."

Forgiveness worked. Matt felt the rage diminish. Still, he would keep a close eye on Stony. Stony excused himself, saying he was tired and going to his berth to sleep. Ken told Matt that sleep was a good idea, but he was happy when Matt looked around and said, "Sleep is not a good option when I can see this beautiful country."

The steamer left the dock and headed north, exposing to Matt more beauty with every turn the ship made. Matt went to the bow so he would not miss anything. Ken followed. They talked about Matt's meeting with Stony and the other two men. Matt listened to Ken describe the value of using tough thugs. Matt resolved that he would not use force when he could talk his way into a favorable situation. Deep inside, he knew the rage was available if needed.

Great green hills rose above the lively river as they moved north. A cool breeze added comfort to the journey. Matt noticed that the birds were different from those in Ireland. He listened intently as Ken tried to name the bird species with much success. Two deer were drinking water from the river on the west side.

Matt enjoyed Ken's explanation of how the railroad was expanding to the west. The Mohawk Hudson Railroad traveled along the Erie Canal. The Erie Canal had been completed in 1825 to bring wheat from western New York. Western New York was called the breadbasket of the world. Wheat was shipped east on the Erie Canal and then down the Hudson River, where it was loaded onto ships going to other parts of the world. Corning's Hudson Railroad bypassed several canal locks, which made it easier and less expensive to ship the wheat. Matt couldn't wait to see all the places described by Ken.

Matt would be part of a survey team that would work to expand the railroad farther west. Stony was an excellent horseman who would ride between the surveyors, passing information. Matt would do everything else, including carrying a musket to hunt game. The job sounded like heaven to Matt. A distant noise ended Matt's conversation.

Matt and Ken walked to the starboard side of the ship to see what was coming. Two larger steamers were side by side and catching up fast. The *Traveler* slowed and hugged the shoreline when the ships came close. The larger ship had the name *Oregon* painted on the side. Men were carrying beautiful mahogany furniture from the staterooms to the boiler room. The other ship had gold lettering that read *C. Vanderbilt* on the cover of the port paddle wheel. Everyone on the *Traveler* was standing on her starboard side, watching the two ships chaotically traverse the river.

Matt saw that the town of Ossining was in sight on the east bank. When the ships were perpendicular with the town, the *Oregon* made a turn to port. The *C. Vanderbilt* misjudged the turn and ran into the port paddle wheel of the *Oregon*. A steam whistle that hurt everyone's ears blew on the *Traveler*. The *Oregon* was heading right for Matt on the starboard side of the *Traveler*. Matt watched people leave the side of the ship and hide in their rooms. He saw rocks protruding from the shallow water beside her, and there was no escape from an inevitable collision. The *Traveler* reversed its engines, throwing Ken up against the low forward railing. Matt realized Ken was about to go overboard, so he grabbed his arm, keeping Ken from the path of the oncoming ship's paddle wheel.

The quick maneuver by the *Traveler*'s captain brought Matt and Ken so close to the bank that they could have reached out and grabbed a maple tree's limb. Matt thought of doing just that when the grinding of the *Oregon*'s paddle wheel came arm's length from hitting the smaller ship. Matt watched the *Oregon* pass by close but without hitting the *Traveler*. The captain of the

Traveler came out of the pilothouse and ordered the crew to check the water in case anyone had fallen overboard. All was well, and the *Traveler* maneuvered back to deeper water as the *C. Vanderbilt* passed a safe distance away.

Matt saw Ken holding his chest. "Are you okay?"

"I just hit the railing a little hard," Ken said. "Thanks for catching me. You saved me from falling overboard. I'll be all right."

Ken stood up straight, and he and Matt watched the town of Ossining go by. The captain was still on the deck above outside the pilothouse.

"Rich men and their toys." He cursed and went back to the pilothouse.

Passengers came out of their hiding places to stare at the racing ships. Before long, the journey once again was peaceful. An hour passed with Matt and Ken sitting on the deck at the bow. Matt was mesmerized by the tranquility of the Hudson River. A crew member walked around the ship, announcing that the dining room was open.

Matt and his new best friend, Ken, had eaten once, but Matt stood up, realizing he was hungry again. Matt saw Stony sitting alone in the dining area. Matt and Ken went to his table, and Ken asked Stony if they could join him. Stony was friendly, and looking at Matt, he said, "My pleasure."

There was no menu; the threesome ate what was brought to them. Matt enjoyed the long meal, especially the coffee. Stony told stories of giant moose with antlers larger than the front of a locomotive. Silent black bears that would steal food were a menace to the survey team. Matt was both apprehensive and anxious to see such amazing animals. Stony's accounts of rattlesnake encounters scared Matt the most. For a moment, he thought of Saint Patrick and was homesick for his youthful days in Ireland. This was a new world, as evidenced when the server brought a dessert: a mixture of sliced apples, sweetened bread, and sweet cream. Matt was truly living the American dream. Matt enjoyed the rest of the steamboat trip, especially the colorful scenery. He kept his eyes on the shoreline, looking for the giant creatures Stony had described. Many brown deer, some with large antlers, and wild, mangy-looking coyotes appeared. Large birds called turkeys traveled in a line on the shore. The line made them look as if they were one large serpent. Matt lost count of the different species of birds. Some were blue, others were yellow or red, and many black or brown birds decorated the shoreline. Peculiar sounds seemed to come from somewhere deep in the woods beyond the shoreline.

Matt slept well despite Ken's loud snoring. He woke early in anticipation of the adventure to come that day. Matt and the *Traveler* arrived in Albany just after breakfast. The Hudson Mohawk Railroad workers left the ship to travel on the railroad. Others left for various parts of Albany, and some, with a longer journey, boarded a mule-drawn boat to travel the Mohawk River and the Erie Canal. The railroad was faster, but the government would only allow freight in the train cars. Matt, Ken, and the other railroad workers could ride the train because they worked for the Hudson Mohawk Railroad. They rode in the freight cars.

Several railroads existed that branched away from the Erie Canal. The Hudson Mohawk changed its name to the Albany Schenectady a month after Matt started work. Railroads went to Utica and Auburn, from Geneva to Canandaigua, and from Canandaigua to Rochester. Matt would be working on a direct railroad line from Syracuse to Rochester. He would work with the survey and acquisition team, while Ken would follow, clearing the way. Twenty-five years ago, the area had been quite desolate. The building of the Erie Canal had brought people and work, and many small towns had developed along the canal. The areas were booming with farming and farm-tool manufacturing. The Erie Canal was successful financially. The railroad was faster and cheaper.

After disembarking from the long ride, during which the men had sat on crates of supplies in the hot freight car, Matt heard a loud explosion, and the earth shook. Matt thought the earth had crashed into the sun for a moment, until he heard Ken's roaring laughter.

"I'm home! We rode here on crates full of dynamite."

Matt was speechless.

"You'll be working with the surveyors, and I'll be right behind you, making the path flat."

"Isn't working with dynamite dangerous?"

"Not if you know what you're doing. I can teach you."

"I'd rather wrestle with giant moose and bears."

"I don't blame you. This is where we part for a while."

Matt shook hands with Ken and thanked him for his friendship. They promised to find each other when the survey team and the clearing teams met. Matt went ahead to catch up with Stony, who seemed to know his way around. Matt followed Stony to a tent and was introduced to the rest of the survey team. Mark and Tom were obviously expert surveyors as they studied maps laid out on a makeshift table. They greeted Matt professionally and then started showing him the maps and asking him questions. They were testing Matt to see how much he understood about cartography, the fancy name they used for map making. Matt understood much but asked as many questions as Tom did. Matt passed the test, as evidenced when Tom looked at Mark and said, "He knows some."

Mark replied, "He seems eager to learn."

Tom smiled at Matt. "You'll do."

Matt spent the next hour with Mark, who took him to various tents where Matt was provided new boots, a musket, powder and balls, and a canvas backpack to carry his supplies in. Stony was talking to a gentleman near a horse area when Matt and Mark approached him.

Mark and Stony shared greetings. Matt's pride showed when Mark told Stony that Matt had passed the test and would be working the front trail. Stony confirmed that he'd known Matt would. Stony reached behind his back, pulled a sheaved knife out, and handed it to Matt.

"A gift for forgiveness of my poor actions at the dock in New York."

Sincerely, Matt said, "All is forgiven."

"You'll need one of these anyway."

Matt went back to the tent with Mark. He put the knife on his waist belt first and then put on some clean socks and his new boots. He emptied his travel sack and carefully packed the new canvas backpack. He got out the cleaning kit they'd given him with the musket. He had hunted in Ireland for food with an old flintlock musket. Matt felt eager to encounter a bear with this new Whitney percussion rifle. Stony promised to help him get some practice shooting before he needed to use the gun.

Matt heard the rapid clattering of horse hooves moving fast. The sound stopped in front of the tent. Matt jumped to his feet while Tom smiled and said, "Stony's ready."

Matt left the tent and saw Stony sitting on a wild-looking mare that seemed to be irate because it had to stop running.

"Meet me at the trail west of the tents in a half hour. Bring your rifle."

Matt did not have time to reply. He stood in amazement as Stony's horse galloped between rows of tents to an open area in the direction of the canal. Matt put the powder and balls in his backpack, picked up the musket, and set out to get used to his new boots. At the west side of the tents, Matt found a large open area with a hill to the north. Stony was there, walking his horse.

Matt observed as Stony tied his mount to a small tree and pulled his musket out of a saddle holster. They spent the better part of an hour loading and shooting. Stony could shoot a small rock off a tree limb. Matt's aim was true enough to hit the target, but he knew he needed much practice to be able to load the musket as fast as Stony could. Matt learned fast and improved much.

Matt and Stony walked out to the clearing and set up some stones to use as targets. They came back, and Stony introduced Matt to his horse. The horse was large and coal black. Stony simply called the horse Black. As Matt and Stony were shooting, they moved closer to Black. Matt knew this was to help Black get accustomed to the sound of the muskets. Black did not flinch when the musket noise blasted. Matt reached up to rub Black's snout, and Black tried to bite his hand and then reared up and tried to kick him. Matt's fast reflex saved him from getting kicked. Stony reached up and rubbed Black's snout and said, "Good boy. Black is a one-man horse, and no one but me gets near him."

Stony apologized for Black. He told Matt to stand back and watch as Stony loaded his musket and put it in the saddle holster. Stony's evil smile reminded Matt that Stony was a skilled thug. Matt listened as Stony explained that Black might not be friendly but made up for his personality with skill. Stony jumped up on Black, gave a hoot, and kicked his heals into the horse. Matt saw Stony as a little awkward and even clumsy, but he was astounded while watching Stony in the saddle of Black. Matt backed away as Stony raced to the open area, drew his musket, and hit the first rock target. He reloaded as Black raced for the next target. Stony continued until he'd fired five shots—and hit five targets. Matt could not help but admire Stony on the back of his horse. Stony was anything but awkward. He appeared like a wild animal with purpose and skill. He was vigorous and nimble. Matt respected and feared Stony's talent. Black came running at Matt and stopped in an instant five feet in front of him. Stony leaped off and landed on his feet with his musket in his hand. He looked as if he were as imposing as Black was. Stony walked with Black's reins in his hands to let the horse cool down slowly. Matt knew Stony could kill if he wanted to. Matt felt the rage deep inside as he walked to the surveyor's tent.

The next morning, Matt and the surveyors gathered maps, books, and papers. Matt loaded their survey equipment onto a horse-drawn cart. They headed east. Matt saw Ken loading dynamite onto another cart, but he was too far away to speak. Matt waited for Ken to see him and waved a distant hello to him. Ken saw Matt and waved back. The sun shone through the bright shades of green trees. The canal glistened. Matt's work began.

Tom, the lead surveyor, had Matt carry some of the heavy equipment east through the woods. Matt would then go ahead to see what problems might exist—human problems. The surveying was a slow process, so Matt could take his time traversing through the wooded area. A few times, Stony rode up close to check that Matt was okay. Matt would wave his hand, and Stony would disappear back to the surveyors.

Matt could hear the trickle of a stream downhill from his position. He decided to follow a deer path to get some cool water from the stream. The stream was farther away than he'd thought. He got there, bent down, and was rinsing the sweat off his face, when a noise on the trail startled him. He stood up and turned but saw nothing. He thought it might be Stony checking on him. Matt remembered Stony telling him to never let his musket out of his hands. Matt looked at the tree where he'd leaned his musket and decided to pick it up. He wiped his hands dry on his shirt before reaching for the musket.

Matt heard the sound again. Someone was stalking him. He picked up his musket and checked that it was ready to fire. He could hear his own voice reverberate when he asked, "Who is there?"

He received no answer.

"I have a gun."

He heard a growl.

A black bear appeared from the woods and stood five feet in front of Matt. Matt fired. The bear became angry and dropped down to all fours. Matt backed into the shallow stream. He did not have time to reload the musket. The bear reared up on its hind legs and was about to charge. Matt reached for his knife and charged the bear. The bear must not have expected Matt to charge. The collision knocked the bear down. Matt stabbed the bear in the heart, lungs, and throat. The bear did not want to die. The bear could not get up, but it looked into Matt's eyes. Matt apologized to the bear, but he knew it was either him or the bear. The bear died with its eyes open.

Matt stood there looking at the bear with the bloody knife in his hand. He did not hear the clatter of Black's hooves or Stony walking down the path.

"We'll eat well tonight."

Matt looked up and saw Stony standing on the stream bank and looking at Matt standing over the bear. Matt was thankful Stony had heard the gunshot and come to check on him. Matt thanked Stony. Stony got some rope from his saddle.

Matt figured that gutting a bear was the same as gutting a stag that he'd hunted in Ireland. He went to work on the bear while Stony got the rope. It was a hard job to drag the bear up the path. Black got wind of the bear and was acting nervous. Stony led Black away, tied the long rope to his saddle, and helped Matt fashion two thin logs together before they loaded the bear onto the log sled. Stony waited for Matt to reload his musket and reprimanded him for not doing so sooner. Matt kept the sled from digging into the ground while Stony walked Black toward the camp.

The sun started to hide behind the trees that Stony, Black, and Matt walked out of. Matt's pride showed as Tom and Mark came and marveled at the bear. Matt did not have a scratch on him. Work was finished for the day. The survey team headed back to their camp. Tom and Mark built a fire to make coffee. Matt skinned the bear under Stony's supervision. He listened to Stony complain that the skin would have made a good winter coat if it hadn't had so many knife stabs. Matt quartered the bear's meat under Stony's tutelage. Matt wished Ken had come with the crew that came to check on the survey team. The crew was excited to take the bear meat back to their camp. Their cook would make salted jerky from the meat and send some back. Matt kept enough bear meat to make his famous stew. He watched Stony make a stretching rack for the bearskin and hang it to dry. Matt and the survey crew ate and slept well that night.

Matt heard the rainfall in the night. The rain was quiet at first and then hard and fast. The sound lulled Matt to sleep. He and the survey crew had work to do, rain or shine as long as the surveyors could see each other and the equipment they worked with. Matt went ahead with his musket close by. The rain became gentle and hid the normal sounds of the woods. That morning, Matt heard a new sound. He approached a clearing and heard human voices ahead. A father and son were clearing land to farm right where the railroad was going.

It was too late to go back for Stony, as was the plan when Matt came to populated areas. The farmer spotted Matt and demanded, "What are you doing here?"

"Scouting for the railroad."

"Ain't no damn train comin' through here. We spent all spring and summer clearing dis land for farming."

Matt smiled and leaned his musket up against a tree stump. He walked over as the men started working a stump out of the ground. Matt stepped in and helped until the farmer's horse pulled the stump clear. Matt explained that the survey crew would be there in a few hours, and they would know exactly where the tracks were going to be laid. Matt looked around and asked the farmer why he was clearing that area, when it looked like there was better farmland next to the new field.

"In the unlikely event that the tracks are going here"—Matt spread his hands like a proud Irish farmer—"will you be happy if we clear that better land for you?"

"I'll think it over."

"Good enough. Maybe I'll see you again soon."

Not sure he'd handled the situation well enough, Matt headed back to the surveyors. Stony seemed to sense when Matt was around. Maybe Black smelled Matt. Stony listened carefully as Matt explained about the farmers. Stony told Matt that he'd handled the situation well and that he would ride back to tell Ken about the situation. Matt continued on the trek, avoiding the working farmers.

Matt went back to the surveyors for lunch and progress reports when the sun was at its highest. Matt got back as Tom was making the coffee, and Mark was dishing out some new salted meat. Stony was not around. Matt had his coffee and tried the meat. It had a strong flavor and took some chewing. Mark watched Matt's face as he tried the meat.

"Never ate bear before?" Mark asked.

"This is bear? My bear? Best I've ever eaten," Matt said.

They all laughed.

The sound of Black was unmistakable, but he was moving slower than usual. Matt thought it sounded as if two riders approached. Stony was riding Black, with Ken riding another horse behind him. Matt was happy to see Ken. Ken thanked Matt for the bear meat and asked him how it tasted as Matt chewed on a big bite of the bear. Ken then asked how far it was to the farm as he got off his horse.

"About a mile."

Matt sat with Ken and Stony by the fire and drank some coffee and chewed some bear jerky. Ken told Matt, "Go to the farm, and tell the farmer that you will send my crew in the morning after the survey is checked. Do you see any trouble?" Matt described the farmers' hard work and told Ken that he saw no problem. Stony would, of course, be there if needed.

As he'd promised Matt, Ken showed up with a team of twelve workers and six horses. Matt, Stony, and the farmer and his son sat and watched for a while before all but Stony jumped in to help. Matt was happy Ken's horses were much stronger and more capable to pull stumps. The farmer's wife brought cold apple cider for all the workers. By the end of the day, Matt and the railroad crew had cleared more land than the farmer had cleared all year. The farmer was ecstatic. Stony was impressed with the way Matt had handled the situation without violence or even the threat of it.

Matt was skilled at handling the farmers. Maybe the skill was derived from his empathy for hardworking farmers. However, a town would prove a much different situation. Matt entered the town of Newport, which was a new town that had formed after the Erie Canal was built. The town was clearly a shipping port where farmers brought their crops to ship to parts of the world they would never see. Stony was always close but let Matt handle any problems with diplomacy. Matt would look around the town to find the greatest advantage the railroad had to offer. Mostly, the benefit was simple economics, and that was easy to deal with. The idea that a farmer might someday be able to get on a train and see the world was a psychological factor that gave the hardworking farmers and farm-related business workers a dream.

Word of Matt Donahee's negotiation skills reached high places in the railroad industry. People were getting filthy rich from railroads. Others would lose fortunes. Matt would help clear land, lay track, or do whatever task was needed. Matt was well liked by everyone he met. His rage was gone. The railroad company agreed to send half of Matt's pay to his family in Ireland. He put most of the other half in a bank. Matt kept enough to mail letters and splurge on the occasional restaurant in the small towns he encountered. Mail came to Matt through a railroad address.

Matt received a letter in the summer of 1851 informing him that his father had passed. He was buried next to their mother on the hill behind the farm. The letter was four months old. Matt read that Ryan Donahee had left to work in Liverpool, building houses, while William Donahee was growing flowers on the farm. With the money they saved and the money Matt sent home, they were planning to move to America.

Matt was no longer homesick. There was nothing left for him in Ireland. He prayed for his father and made peace with God. Two months later, he received a letter from Boston. The return address was Donahee Construction Company. Matt read the letter slowly. It explained that Ryan had partnered with Will, and they were building homes in the northern area of Boston. Ryan was designing the homes, and Will was designing landscapes. Matt had hoped they would come work with him on the railroad, but he was glad they were doing well. Matt was needed at the railroad company, and he wanted to see the project through to completion.

ROCHESTER

Matt knew that the survey team was far ahead of the clearing and track-laying teams. Matt was about to enter Rochester, New York. Rochester would be a huge challenge because of the effect the railroad would have on many businesses, homes, and government buildings. The railroad put Matt up in the Savoy Hotel while he evaluated positive and negative negotiation strategies. The hotel was located near the Auburn Railroad Shed, where the new track would merge with other railroads. Matt enjoyed the hustle and bustle of Rochester, the Flour City, as it was known because of all the flourmills on the Genesee River, which ran through the middle of the city.

Matt woke up early feeling excited. He was to meet with Erastus Corning and other railroad officials. Matt made his way downstairs to the entrance of the Savoy Hotel, where guests were served coffee. Outside and around the corner was a newsroom. Matt had seen and read old newspapers since his arrival in New York. He bought a copy of the *Rochester Daily Advertiser*, a newspaper that provided local and global news stories. The paper was dated with that day's date. Matt enjoyed reading the advertisements that offered the sale of all kinds of goods. Those advertisements would help and were crucial in his research leading to the future benefits of the railroad. Matt went back to the hotel to enjoy some coffee and read the paper.

"Hello, Matt."

"Ken!" Matt said with excitement. He put the paper down and listened to Ken describe the progress of the rail construction. Matt was happy Ken was going to the meeting to report on that progress. Matt described a story about the new direct line from Syracuse to Rochester and the advantages it would give the city of Rochester. Matt was proud of the story because it was based on his written reports he'd filed with the railroad. Ken told Matt he was hoping to beat the 1853 completion date that Matt's newspaper reported.

Matt and Ken walked to the Auburn Railroad Shed for the meeting. Matt saw several well-dressed men at the meeting. Erastus Corning introduced Matt and Ken to a gentleman named Cornelius Vanderbilt. Ken shook hands with Vanderbilt. Vanderbilt held a finger up to Matt to show recognition and that he wanted to talk to Matt in a minute. He congratulated Ken on his work. Ken seemed happy, but Matt saw his mind working. Matt remembered the steamboat collision and the name on the careless vessel: C. Vanderbilt. He knew Ken was thinking the same.

"So you're Mathew Donahee?"

"I am."

"I'm looking forward to your speech."

Matt was shocked that Vanderbilt expected a speech. Matt had never given a speech. Vanderbilt left to talk to another man. Erastus Corning saw Matt's expression and knew that Matt was startled to think he had to give a speech. Corning explained that Matt and Ken would give an oral report about their progress. Ken, who was smiling at Matt's dilemma of speaking in front of all these people, now shared his distress. Matt and Ken excused themselves and went outside, where they could prepare and practice their speeches.

Not listening to each other, Matt and Ken paced the boardwalk next to the railroad, practicing talking to imaginary groups. Erastus came out to announce the beginning of the meeting. With much anxiety, Matt took his seat next to Ken on an inside passenger bench. Vanderbilt was the first to speak. Matt thought his speech was long; it covered railroad expansion throughout New York and the rest of the country, including out west. Other speakers followed with shorter speeches. In one short speech, Corning introduced Matt's friend Ken Webster. Ken's speech described what he was doing and accomplishing. Ken received a round of applause when he announced that he was ahead of schedule by three months. Ken finished and sat down next to the nervous Matt.

"Good speech," Matt said.

"Thanks."

Erastus Corning was up front and introduced the next speaker as Mathew Donahee. It was all Matt could do to stand up, because he was extremely nervous. He remembered killing the bear with his knife and thought about that incident when he reached the front of the group. His mind shifted to all the people he'd satisfied by negotiating the advantages of the new railroad. As he looked at the group of individuals in front of him, his mind went blank. He hesitated. He forgot the speech he'd practiced outside.

Matt looked at Erastus Corning, who simply gave him a nod. Matt stopped looking at the group as a group of railroad executives and imagined all the people he'd helped to accept the coming of the railroad in a group in front of him. Matt started his speech with an explanation of how everyone in the room appreciated the men who worked so hard. He continued by saying that all individuals had goals and explaining how the railroad would help them achieve their various goals. He described his methods for extracting information and determining how the railroad would help people. Then he convinced them that the railroad was a benefit that only the railroad developers could afford to make happen.

Matt did not get the applause that Ken had gotten. Instead, he got questions. Members of the group had specific examples of dealing with dissension, which Matt was able to respond to with examples from his experience with the Syracuse-to-Rochester direct line. Matt's confidence grew as he answered the questions. Vanderbilt returned to the front of the group to announce the meeting would adjourn for lunch. He then turned to Matt and asked him to join them for lunch. Matt told him he planned to have lunch with Ken. Vanderbilt said, "Good! Bring him with us."

Erastus, Matt, and Ken joined Vanderbilt and two other railroad executives at the Canal Side Café for lunch. Matt was pleased to be included in the private lunch meeting, which disclosed secret negotiations to merge specific railroads. The New York Central was buying the smaller privately owned lines that branched throughout the state. Vanderbilt said, "The days of using thugs to convince people are coming to an end." Looking at Matt, Vanderbilt proclaimed, "You will be a valuable asset to our mergers."

Vanderbilt offered Matt a job as chief negotiator. Matt did not know what to say. He felt he owed his loyalty to Corning. Erastus Corning told Matt that after the merger, he would become a stockholder, and he assured him that his work for Vanderbilt would help him greatly. Matt agreed to think about working for Vanderbilt's New York Central (NYC) as long as Corning approved. Vanderbilt told Matt that if he invested part of his new larger pay in NYC stock, he would become a wealthy man. Corning mentioned that after Matt stopped sending half his pay to his family in Ireland, he started putting the money in savings at a bank in New York. Matt's money would have a greater return if he invested it in the railroad now. Matt was willing to take risks, so he agreed to buy the stock in the New York Railroad and accepted the job.

Matt was excited about the new job as a chief negotiator and wanted Ken Webster to share his good fortune with a better job as well. Matt mentioned that idea. Vanderbilt and Corning looked at each other.

"If that is what I need to get you on board, then so be it," Vanderbilt said to Matt. Vanderbilt then stated that a new station house was to start construction and be completed before the Syracuse-to-Rochester line reached Rochester. Looking at Matt, he offered Ken a job as the new station manager.

Vanderbilt told Ken and Matt that they weren't needed at the rest of the meeting until before dinner at five o'clock. Matt and Ken agreed and left. Matt asked Ken to go for a walk with him along the west side of the Genesee River to talk. The first subject of their conversation was the steamboat race. They agreed that the "rich man's toy" indeed had been the steamship *C. Vanderbilt*. Matt reminisced about the boats' reckless collision and their journey with the railroad that had brought them to Rochester.

Ken thanked Matt for getting him a better job. Matt was surprised when Ken told him that now he could get married. Matt knew Ken had met a girl in a canal town on the way to Rochester. The name of the town was Newark, if he remembered right. Matt had not known how serious the relationship had become. Ken was glowing.

"You'll be my best man."

Matt agreed, even though Ken's offer had come out as a command rather than a request. Ken would give the details of the wedding to Matt after he told Emma the good news. The friends spent the rest of the afternoon examining the flour mills along the Genesee River and the other businesses they passed. Matt had an idea how the railroad would help all the businesses they saw. Matt enjoyed his afternoon with Ken. He thought Ken was lucky to make Rochester his home. Matt would probably continue traveling. His thoughts soon escaped to Ireland and his Catherine.

Matt left Ken to meet with the manager of the present railroad station and plan for the new transition when the current stationmaster retired next year. The stationmaster had told Ken he was moving to a smaller house in Charlotte, north of the city. His big house on First Street was for sale. Ken agreed to look at the house and considered buying it. Ken would keep it a secret from Emma for now. Matt was pleasantly surprised when he learned that he would have an office at the train station with Ken. He would train others on how to gather information and would travel only for larger negotiations.

Matt's meeting lasted much longer than Ken's had, and darkness fell before he left the traditional gaslights of the rail station. Matt was provided with a standard of how to dress for work and the means to acquire some new clothes. Matt found Ken drinking a cup of coffee at the Savoy Hotel. Matt suggested they go out for some dinner. Ken agreed. Matt acquired a tinge of new personal importance and felt good.

The newly promoted railroad workers left on foot to go to a restaurant called the Public Cookery. Matt had seen the restaurant on their earlier walk. Only a few gaslights illuminated the street corners on the way. Voices came out of a dark alley on the way. Matt listened carefully but could not make out the conversation. Two other hidden dark areas convinced Matt that there was a secret and maybe dangerous nightlife in the city. No one tried to rob them. Matt felt the rage increase for the first time in a long while. He controlled the rage but was ready to let it escape his control if needed. They made it to the restaurant safely.

A dark-skinned waiter brought the menus, which were the size of books. Matt ordered coffee, while Ken ordered tea. Ken told Matt, "I have to become more dignified if I am to marry." Matt laughed and said he really liked his coffee. Ken agreed that coffee tasted better after he tasted his tea. They spent much time looking at the menu. Ken was first to decide on lamb chops with fresh bread and butter. Matt ordered a beef pie, not knowing what it was. The food came. Their conversation continued but was about the food rather than the railroad. After dinner, both ordered coffee. Matt was pleased that Ken went back to drinking coffee rather than tea.

Ken described Emma as a pretty girl of twenty years, almost half his age. Her father was a blacksmith from Newark. Matt remembered talking to her father about the potential jobs and customers the railroad would bring to his business. Matt learned that Emma taught school and was active in current affairs. She believed in the abolitionist movement to make southern slaves free. The waiter appeared out of nowhere with a coffee pitcher and filled their cups. Matt was a little embarrassed at knowing that the waiter had heard the conversation about abolitionism. Ken said that Emma loved to talk, and he liked to listen.

The friends left the restaurant and headed back to the hotel. They passed the spot where they'd heard voices and looked into the dark. It was dark, but Matt felt that someone was watching. They almost walked into a man blocking their path. Ken stepped back and readied himself for a fight. Matt felt threatened, which brought the rage on instantly.

A bright white smile kept Matt from striking out. The man was asking for food for his family. Matt's eyes were becoming accustomed to the dark and followed the man's gaze to the dark alley. Matt's heart went out to a little dark-skinned girl holding the hand of a younger boy. Matt was angry at the speed with which his rage had come on. He had not experienced his rage in a long time. Matt pulled his money purse out to give the man some money. The man said the money was no use, because the restaurants open at night could not serve dark-skinned people.

Ken stayed and talked to the man while Matt went back to the restaurant. Matt found the waiter who'd served them earlier and explained that he wanted food for a poor dark-skinned family outside. The waiter told Matt to meet him at the back door and walked away. The path to the back door was so dark that Matt had to step slowly to avoid racks and other hazards on the way. At the back door, the waiter gave a sack of food to Matt. Matt tried to pay for the food. The waiter would not take the money and made a strange request instead.

"Give the money to the railroad. They need it more."

Matt did not understand the statement, but he would not forget it. Matt brought the food to the dark-skinned man, who was genuinely appreciative. The two small children were standing with Ken and their father. When Matt handed him the sack, the man's wife and two other children came out of the darkness. Matt had been hungry before and recognized the need for food. Still, before eating, the family lowered their heads to thank God for the food. They also thanked God for the two strangers who'd delivered the food. Matt realized he'd stopped praying when his mother and Caroline died. He thought to God and prayed. *Thanks for my work, my skill, and my friend.*

Controlling the rage made Matt mentally exhausted. Ken was leaving early to go back to clearing land and laying track. Matt decided not to tell Ken about the formal dress rules railroad executives had to adhere to. He told Ken he was scouting out new types of business, which was true, because Matt had never been to a tailor. Matt had trouble sleeping that night and wasn't sure why. He got up, dressed for the day, and went to get his paper. Ken was getting coffee when Matt came into the hotel. They enjoyed the coffee together. Matt said goodbye when Ken left for the stable to get his horse and go back to the railroad and to Emma.

Matt read the news stories in the *Daily Advertiser*. An article by Fredrick Douglass discussed what people could do about slavery. Matt did not believe slavery was right, even though he'd never before experienced slaves or slave owners firsthand. Matt turned to the advertisements and found a tailor, a cobbler, and a milliner. Matt had never heard of a milliner but figured a milliner made hats, based on the pictures in the paper. Matt was done shopping early in the afternoon, even though he would have to go back to the shops to pick up his goods later next week.

Matt went to the railroad station to find that the stationmaster had set up a makeshift office for him. Matt even had special railroad mail on his desk, addressed to him personally. He opened a letter to find that fruit farmers were complaining that the railroad could not deliver fruit in the spring, because a hot spring day would damage the fruit. Matt dove into the problem and found that salt and ice would cool a special railroad car. Within four months, the railroad had some ice cars and a series of icehouses to keep ice in the cars. Matt personally supervised the loading of the first icebox car. He felt it was not the best solution and made a note to recheck the issue at the end of the year.

JADE

Matt received a letter from Ken telling him that the railroad was getting close to Rochester. The letter stated that Ken and Emma were coming to the city in two weeks. Matt was happy to hear from Ken. He had moved into a boardinghouse that housed several single male railroad workers. The Savoy Hotel was where Ken would stay. According to Ken, Emma would stay with a friend. Matt wrote back, telling Ken how much he was looking forward to seeing him again and to meeting Emma. Matt was busy with negotiations that would continue railroad tracks to Buffalo and to Niagara Falls. He had traveled to Buffalo, New York, and was in the process of writing several letters to confirm the merger of the Rochester-to-Batavia railroad and the Batavia west railroad that went on to Buffalo. He was looking forward to going to Niagara Falls to establish rights for a railroad to connect Niagara Falls to Rochester.

Two weeks later, in Rochester's cold February 1852, Ken brought Emma to meet Matt. Matt realized Emma was everything Ken had said she was. She was talkative. She was petite and barely came up to Ken's chest. Her light brown hair peeked out of a broad bonnet. Emma told Matt she planned to meet a friend she would be staying with. The friend was taking Emma to an abolitionist meeting later that day. Matt was surprised at her boldness when she asked, in a way that demanded the right answer, how Matt felt about the slavery issue. Matt simply proclaimed that slavery was immoral, and he hoped that was the correct answer. It was, as evidenced by Emma's continuous babble.

Matt invited Ken and Emma to his office. Ken accepted, but Emma gave Ken the look and stated that she wanted to wait outside for her friend. Matt was disappointed when Ken stayed with her. Matt went to his office and finished a letter to the main office for the New York Central Railroad about his progress with the Buffalo expansion and his plans to go back to Niagara Falls the next month. Matt came down to find that Ken and Emma were gone.

Matt looked around the station and the street for them and noticed a well-dressed woman standing by herself. It was unusual for a woman to be unescorted at the railroad station. She started walking toward Matt and appeared to be looking for somebody. She had light-colored skin and dark brown hair. Her dress showed curves that aroused Matt's emotions. Matt walked toward her. She looked at him with deep brown eyes and spoke with an Americanized Irish accent that sounded like the voice of an angel.

"I'm looking for my friend who's coming from Newark via Canandaigua."

"Is her name Emma?"

"Yes. Is she here?"

"She was awhile ago. She's here with my friend Ken Webster."

She smiled and relaxed when she found out that Matt knew Emma.

"I'm Mathew Donahee." Matt's heart melted at her smile.

"My name is Jade Malloy."

Matt saw Ken and Emma coming from the Savoy Hotel up the street. He was looking over Jade's shoulder. She noticed Matt's eyes shift slightly. She turned and saw Emma walking ahead of Ken toward her. Matt noticed the smell of her hair. He wanted to taste it. Jade and Emma met between Ken and Matt and hugged each other. Matt had not thought of Catherine for a long time. He realized that his memory of Catherine was fading. Ken walked past Emma and Jade and stood next to Matt. They both looked at the women talking in the street. Matt thought Jade looked older than Emma and seemed to have a manner of wisdom. Ken broke the silence by telling Matt he was ready to see his office. Matt's office was small but neat. Matt had cleared his desk, hoping to spend time with Ken. Obviously, Ken wanted to spend time with Matt, but he was in Rochester to talk to a priest, Father Sullivan at Saint Patrick's Roman Catholic Church on Franklin Street. Matt knew where that was. It was a beautiful newly built stone church.

Matt had had the good sense to reserve one of the railroad's four-by-two coaches and a driver. Matt told Ken to keep an eye on the women while he went to the stables for the coach. Matt and the black-lacquered coach pulled up in front of the station. The coach had four wheels and was pulled by two horses. The coachman wore a black suit like the one Matt was wearing. Matt opened the half door and stepped out. Even the women stopped their chatter and came to inspect the new coach with plush burgundy velvet seats.

Matt introduced Thomas, the coachman, to the women and suggested Thomas give them a little tour of the city. Emma was excited and had Ken hold her hand while she climbed into the coach. Jade stepped up to climb in. She turned to Matt, smiled, and held out her hand for Matt to help her in. Matt held her hand a little too long. He had never felt anything so soft and delicate, yet there was something strong about the woman. Matt made a good living reading people and dealing with them. He'd never dealt with a woman like this and was confused by his lack of ability to read her.

Emma asked Ken if he was coming. Matt explained that he

and Ken had some business to take care of. Matt assured the women that they were in good hands with the coachman. The coachman spoke loudly and explained, "We will start up State Street. If you have any questions or want to stop, just pull the rope on the wall next to the door." The rope was connected to a bell by the driver's seat. The coachman yelled, "Clear!" and cracked a whip. The coach hurried forward. Ken seemed glad to be away from Emma's chatter, but Matt sensed that he missed her already. Matt led Ken back to the railroad station and upstairs to his office. He opened a curtain that revealed a small closet in his office. Matt reached in and carefully picked up a hanger with a black suit on it.

"Standard railroad wear," Matt explained. "I hope I got your measurements right."

"I never wore a suit before."

"It's just like the one the stationmaster is wearing."

Matt was getting out a white starched shirt, some new shined shoes, and a black tie. Matt offered to help Ken take his new uniform to the hotel. Matt suggested that Ken get cleaned up before the women got back. Ken told Matt that Emma and Jade were going to hear a man named Frederick Douglass speak at the Corinthian Hall at six o'clock. Matt's heart jumped when Ken asked him to join them.

Matt felt something stir as he thought of an evening with Jade. He agreed to come along as long as the women seemed to desire his company. Ken laughed and reminded Matt that he always did what he wanted and would make people want his company. Matt confided that he could not quite understand Jade—or Emma, for that matter—but the thought of Jade's company excited him. Ken told Matt he'd felt the same way when he first met Emma.

Hanging around railroad men, Matt had found something that was almost as good as coffee. He took two cigars from his jacket pocket and gave one to Ken. Ken did not hesitate. He'd smoked cigars in New York City and had not had one since. A light snow was falling when the coach delivered the women back to the railroad station. Matt could see the women from his office window. Matt and Ken were still smoking their cigars when they got to the coach. The coachman had the coach door open and was helping the ladies out.

Matt noticed Emma's shocked look when she saw Ken wearing his black suit. "Where did you get that suit?" she asked pleasantly. Ken simply explained that all railroad executives, borrowing the words from Matt, wore black suits when not in the field. Matt noticed a stern look on Jade's face. Ken mentioned to the ladies that he thought it would be nice if Matt joined them for the evening. Emma smiled, but Jade spoke her mind, looking at the cigar in Matt's hand.

"Not with that thing."

Matt dropped the cigar in the street and squished it out with his foot.

"Better."

"It would be an honor to escort you to Corinthian Hall and to dinner tonight."

"I accept."

Matt told the coachman their plans: they would be going to Corinthian Hall for a speech at six. The coachman suggested they leave by five. Five o'clock was an hour away, which gave the coachman time to tend to the horse team. Matt suggested a walk around the corner to see the construction of the new station, Ken's station. They agreed. It was a five-minute walk around the corner to Front Street. The construction was already three stories high. Matt told them his office would be on the third floor. Emma was quick to ask Ken where his office would be. Ken shrugged because he didn't know. Matt was quick to tell Emma that the stationmaster would occupy the big office on the first floor, with his staff in smaller offices around him. Ken smiled with humility. He looked at the huge building, and Matt knew Ken was eager to start working there and start his new life with Emma.

The coach was ready when they got back to the railroad station. The weather was getting miserably cold, with the blustery wind whipping snow across the streets. Matt was accustomed to the cold and considered the beauty made by the white blanket of snow on rooftops, streets, and the trees. Fresh snow glistened in the gas-powered streetlights, while the blowing snow brightened the area but limited how far they could see. The coachman navigated the streets skillfully yet slowly. They could hardly see the top of Corinthian Hall through the snow as the coachman pulled into the entrance circle at the front of the massive building.

Walking to the stairs, Matt noticed something at the side the building—something black that gave Matt a chill. It was a man wearing a bearskin coat and a tattered black fedora. He kept his head down, either hiding his face or shielding it from the snow. Matt turned to Ken and told him to take the women inside; he would catch up in a moment. Matt turned back to go confront the man. He was gone.

Corinthian Hall was large, exquisitely decorated, and comfortably warm. A podium was on the stage in the front, positioned so everyone could see the speaker. Matt sat next to Jade. He delighted in her radiant warmth and flowery smell. Jade gently put her hand on Matt's hand, which was resting on his knee. She asked, "Have you ever heard Douglass speak?"

"No, but I read about him the *Rochester Daily Advertiser.*"

"Good. Tonight will give us something to talk about later."

She patted Matt's hand before sliding her hand away. Matt

wanted her hand back. He wanted to hold her hand, to smell her hair—Matt wasn't even sure what he wanted, but he knew he wanted it more than anything he'd ever wanted before. Matt thought about what later would be like.

Matt had become quite comfortable speaking on a stage. His job provided many opportunities. Frederick Douglass proved to be a powerful, informative, and worthy speaker. Matt thought maybe he was a bit too dramatic, but he realized the speaker earned empathy for slaves, as Douglass himself had been one. Matt gained a better understanding of the abolitionist movement, and he confirmed a personal opposition to owning slaves. When Douglass had finished, Matt felt there was more going on than abolitionism—maybe a hidden agenda that was not quite clear.

Emma was busy telling Ken what she thought about the speech. Jade turned to Matt, but rather than telling Matt her feelings, she asked for his. Hearing her ask with her angelic voice, Matt looked down into her eyes. He thought he saw desire sparkle in her eyes as he evaluated the speech to her. He yearned. As they walked out the front door, he questioned how the government could create such a law as the new Fugitive Slave Law. The Fugitive Slave Law demanded that any citizen report runaway slaves, making every citizen a slave catcher.

Their coach was easy to spot in a line of coaches. The wind had slowed down, leaving a few white snowflakes dancing in all directions. The coachman had an oil lantern lit on the side and back of the glowing black coach. The light seemed to control and organize the snowflakes' chaotic falling. Matt had the coachman take them to a restaurant that overlooked the Erie Canal aqueduct. Matt and his friends enjoyed a leisurely dinner. They discussed Ken and Emma's upcoming wedding. Matt was elated at the fact that Jade would be walking down the aisle while he waited with Ken at the altar.

As dinner was coming to a close, the foursome planned activities for the next day. Matt had some work to do in the morning, while Ken was meeting with the stationmaster. Jade was taking Emma shopping. Ken wanted to meet Emma at one in the afternoon. Ken and Emma had a meeting with Father Sullivan at five. Matt suggested they go to the Canal Café after Ken and Emma's meeting at the church. He looked at Jade when he made the suggestion. Jade smiled warmly.

Matt went out into the cold to let the coachman know they were ready. Thomas thanked Matt for the dinner he'd eaten in the back dining room and left to ready the coach. Matt recognized Black secured to a hitching post across the street and north a ways. He figured Stony was around someplace. He wondered what Stony was doing in Rochester. When the survey team had finished the route to Rochester, Stony had told Matt he was going back to New York City.

The night was still, and only a few flakes of snow were floating in the air. Matt listened to Jade give directions to the coachman to get to her house. An oil lamp inside the coach took the bite out of the winter cold as the coach made its way down the streets of Rochester. Jade lived with her father in a modest home on Lake Avenue, on the north side of the city.

Ken walked Emma to the front door while Matt slowly escorted Jade behind them. Jade told Matt there was a meeting at the Presbyterian church near the railroad station tomorrow afternoon. She did not have to ask him to escort her to the meeting. Matt declared that the meeting sounded interesting. He was thinking about spending more time with Jade. Jade warned Matt that Isaac Post was a little out there. Matt understood.

Jade introduced Matt and Ken to her father, Michael Malloy, at the front door. It was a short meeting because, as Michael declared, the cold air was filling the house. Matt thought of his

father when he met Michael Malloy. Matt and Ken hurried back
to the warmth of the coach when the women were safely in the
home. Matt asked Ken about Stony and declared his suspicion
that Stony was in Rochester. Ken had not seen him since the
survey team left for a new assignment in Pennsylvania. Matt
had the coach drop Ken off at the hotel. Matt rode back to the
railroad station and told the coachman he would walk home. It
was a short walk, and Matt wanted to think about Jade while he
walked.

Halfway home, Matt saw Black tied to another hitching
post. His thoughts of Jade faded. He respected Stony for his
outdoorsman skills but still did not trust him. Stony was hiding
in a dark doorway and stepped out in front of Matt. He was
smiling.

"How was the speech at Corinthian Hall?"

"Have you been following me?"

Stony briefed Matt that he'd become a slave catcher, and he
warned Matt that he seemed to be traveling in bad circles. Matt
realized Stony was telling the truth. Even though slave catching
was a despicable occupation, Stony was within the law. Matt
noticed a bulge under Stony's coat. Stony saw his eyes checking
him out and then thanked Matt for the bearskin coat. Then Stony
bluntly asked Matt what he knew of the Underground Railroad.
It was easy for Matt to answer that he knew nothing about the
Underground Railroad other than what he'd read in the papers,
because it was true. Stony pulled his coat open to show the pistol
he carried under his coat.

"You'd better not be lying to me."

"I've no reason to lie."

"Your new friends might get hurt if they are hiding slaves."

Matt took Stony's comment as a threat and felt the rage. He

tried to control his emotions, but the look on Stony's face drew the rage out. "Don't threaten my friends."

Stony moved his hand for the gun. He was fast. Matt grabbed the gun with his left hand. The skin between his thumb and pointer finger blocked the hammer from hitting the percussion cap. Matt's rage, directed at Stony for trying to kill him, provided a powerful right hook that laid Stony on the ground. Matt and Stony still had their hands on the pistol. Matt swung his leg around Stony's arm and dropped to his knee. Stony cried out in pain as the bone snapped. The gun came out of his hand. Matt tossed the pistol to the ground and readied to pulverize Stony with his fists. The pistol fired. The ball grazed Matt's leg before splitting Stony's shoulder. The fight was over. Matt slowly gained control of his rage.

The loud eruption of the pistol echoed down the street, alerting a night watchman on horseback. Rochester had formed an organized police organization the year before. The night watchman looked the situation over before getting off his horse. Matt watched the night watchman help Stony to his feet and offer to get him to a doctor. Stony was in a lot of pain and was bleeding from the left arm. Stony told the watchman that Matt was interfering with his work.

"What work is that?"

"Slave catcher."

The night watchman handled Stony a bit roughly after he heard his occupation. He asked Matt what his name was and where he could find him in the morning. Matt told the watchman that he worked at the railroad station and said his name was Matt Donahee.

"I'm not finished with you, Matt Donahee," Stony mumbled.

The watchman swung up onto his horse and led Stony down the road. Matt was alone in the cold, fighting his rage.

He wanted to pull Stony back off his horse and pulverize him. The watchman took the fired pistol with him. Matt took a few steps toward home and thought about Jade. His new feelings for Jade and the rage created a skirmish in his heart that created a sleepless night.

Matt was in his office early the next morning, when a uniformed day watchman came to the railroad station. The day watchman said a belligerent Stony had pulled a knife on the night watchman. Stony's arms were too badly hurt to damage the watchman, and he would be spending some time in the new Rochester jail. The watchman wanted to be assured that Matt was uninjured, and he let Matt know that his fight with the night attacker made Matt somewhat of a hero.

Matt thought about his father after the day watchman left. Raymond Donahee had been a strict man who believed that fighting solved moral discrepancies. The name Donahee meant *hero*. Matt did not feel like a hero. Stony was not too bright but was a hard and skilled fighter. Matt felt as if he'd betrayed a friend. Nonetheless, Stony was a slave catcher. Slave catchers were on the side of the law, and Matt determined that any law that would return men to a life of slavery was undeniably immoral.

The hunting knife Stony had given Matt was hanging on the wall in Matt's office as a reminder of his days with the survey team and with Stony's protection. An image of the bear was fresh in Matt's mind when he took the knife off the wall and put it in a desk drawer. Matt picked up a copy of the *North Star* news flyer and read the stories on abolishing slavery. Frederick Douglass was not liked by mainstream Americans. Matt believed that Douglass's tenacity in working for a moral goal made Douglass a real hero.

Matt met Ken at noon after Ken's meeting with the stationmaster. Matt described his encounter with Stony. Ken was silent and listened to every detail outlined by Matt. When Matt finished, Ken told him that he must tell Jade about Stony stalking them. Matt told Ken he did not want to trouble the women with such news, because it might frighten them. Matt thought for a moment and decided that if Stony had an accomplice, Jade could be in danger. Matt kept looking for the coach with Jade and Emma in it.

The coach was coming down the street. Emma and Jade had spent the morning shopping. Emma stepped off the coach. Matt asked her where Jade was. Emma's face took on the look of a woman years older as she told Matt they'd left her at her home with their wares. Matt suggested Emma go inside so Ken could explain. Matt asked the coachman to wait for him. Thomas, the dark-skinned coachman, said, "I's at your service."

Ken explained to Emma about Stony the slave catcher and said he might have an associate working with him. Emma assured the men that all had been quiet during the night and that Jade's father had helped carry the shopping supplies into the house. Matt decided to go at once to Jade and her father. Ken and Emma would continue their day as planned but on foot. Matt left in the coach.

Matt thought the wheels might fall off the coach as Thomas cracked his whip and barked encouragement to the team of horses. The coach slid easily on the snowy streets, which probably saved the coach from rolling over and smashing to pieces. Matt wondered if he were naive; everyone seemed to have a secret he or she kept from him. Matt thought of Jade. Thomas slowed down on Lake Avenue. He went past the Malloy residence. Matt demanded an explanation.

"Patience, sir," Thomas said.

Matt realized that even Thomas was aware that something secretive was going on and that discretion was imperative.

Thomas took the coach down an alleyway that led down a hill and to the back of the Malloys' house. A single horse-drawn buckboard with a canvas cover was at the back of the house. Matt got out of the coach just as Thomas's feet hit the ground. Matt relished the agility the old dark-skinned man demonstrated. Matt walked up to Michael Malloy, who was standing at the back of the cart, tying the canvas closed.

"What are you doing here?" Michael spoke in a tone that was more fearful than threatening.

Matt saw the desperation on Malloy's face and told the truth about his run-in with a slave catcher. Matt was interrupted when a voice in the back of the buckboard declared, "Thanks for the food the other night."

The black man's children were giggling under the canvas. Before Matt could tell the man it had been his pleasure, Michael ordered the cart to move out. Matt looked toward the house to see Jade standing by a back door with an antique blunderbuss pointed directly at him. Matt was scared—not for himself but for Jade, because the hundred-year-old gun might explode. He took a step toward Jade.

"I know how to use this," Jade said.

Matt had seen many people transform their personas in the last few hours, but none was as impressive as Jade Malloy. He had spent much time thinking of her as a soft, gentle woman with a passion for justice and for moral people. Now he was looking over the large barrel of a dangerous gun and directly at her eyes. His heart beat fast, not in fear but with desire. The strong, fierce woman stirred an animalistic desire that Matt had not realized was possible. His desire was stronger than for the gentle girl he knew Jade could be.

"He's okay, Miss Malloy."

The calm voice came from Thomas, who was standing next

to Matt. Jade acknowledged Thomas by lowering the rusty gun. Matt watched as Michael put his hand on Thomas's shoulder, thanked him, looked around, and told him that it was best to leave for an hour. Thomas climbed up onto the coach and slowly maneuvered the coach away. Michael told Matt that he had much explaining to do and motioned him inside. Matt smiled at Jade.

Inside, out of the cold, Matt described the incident with Stony. Matt concluded by saying he wanted to help slaves obtain liberty. Michael decided to trust Matt and filled him in on his part in the Underground Railroad. Matt listened as Michael explained. In the summer, Michael and Jade helped runaway slaves board ships on the Genesee River. It was too cold in the winter for boats, so the slaves followed a west route along the southern shore of Lake Ontario, often working for fruit growers along the way. Normally, the runaways left at night. However, an apparent slave catcher had been seen lurking around the city and openly seeking support to find slaves. Varying the departure times had become necessary. Michael wanted to lie low for a while, but the runaways just kept coming for help. Jade had demanded that they do more to help.

Matt looked at Jade's father and saw a man so dedicated to his daughter that he would do anything for her, even when what she wanted negated keeping her safe. Matt thought he could keep Jade safe. He watched Jade get up and look out the front window. Then she looked out other windows that gave a view of the Genesee River in the back and Lake Avenue in the front. Trees were on each side of the house, which made it easy to hide in the house or outside the house. After her surveillance of the neighborhood, she announced that it looked safe outside. She reprimanded Matt for taking a chance that someone might have followed him. Matt assured her that no one could have followed the way Thomas drove. Jade told Matt that Thomas thought slave catchers were watching him.

Matt asked Jade, "Do you feel safe here?"

"Doesn't make a difference."

Jade's bold answer made Michael shrug. Somehow, Matt understood Michael's dilemma as Jade's father. He also understood his own emotions, which were driving his mind and body insane. He was instantly in love with Jade. He knew he would never have a traditional life with Jade, but that did not matter. He wanted her. She drove him insane. And it felt good. Jade stood up. She recognized the sound of the railroad coach coming down the road. She looked out the window and announced, "Good. It's Thomas driving the coach."

Jade softened. She walked over to Matt and reached out for his hand. She told Matt that she was eager to hear what surprise Ken wanted to show Emma. She suggested she ride back with Matt in the coach. Matt felt like saying no just to egg her on, but he looked at her father and simply agreed with Jade. She went upstairs to change. Michael told Matt that she was twenty-six years old and had never found a man who could tolerate her modern ideas. He wished Matt luck, exposing that he recognized Matt's feelings for his difficult daughter.

Jade came downstairs wearing a light blue dress that was small in the waist and tapered out before dropping straight to the floor. The neck had a yellow lace collar that matched the ends of the sleeves. She'd put her dark brown hair neatly in a bun with a red ribbon accenting her brown hair. Matt thought her eyes glowed as he stared at her, impressed, and her father simply looked surprised at her dress. Jade put on a winter wrap, and they left in the coach to look for Ken and Emma.

Matt saw Emma sitting inside the railroad station, reading the *Rochester Daily Advertiser*'s advertisements. Jade hurried to

Emma and asked, "So what's the surprise that Ken wanted to show you?"

"We bought a house!"

Matt listened as Emma excitedly babbled on about the house on State Street. Matt wanted to ask where Ken was but decided he could find him before he had a chance to interrupt the feminine chatter. He found Ken busily going over the intricacies of running a railroad station with the current stationmaster. Matt congratulated Ken on his new home. Ken thanked Matt but was clearly busy. Matt went to his office on the third floor. On the way, he checked in on the girls. He reminded Jade that they were going to another lecture.

"Oh, I can't possibly go now. Emma needs me to help decorate her new home."

Matt sadly went to his office to read and respond to some letters about the merger of the Buffalo rail line. Sidetracked, his mind organized the events of the past day. Hours passed before Ken came to Matt's office to let him know that he and Emma were leaving to meet Father Sullivan. Matt walked him downstairs. Jade looked lovely and glowing. However, she arranged for Ken and Emma to drop her off to check on her father. Matt said his goodbyes and was disappointed that he would not see more of Jade that evening. When Jade got to the coach, she turned and kissed Matt on the cheek. Matt watched the coach disappear down the street with his friend, his friend's fiancée, and Jade. Matt was lonesome for the first time in years.

WEDDINGS

Matt could not take a railroad coach unless it was for railroad business or with a group involved with the railroad. He bought a horse and buggy. For a small fee, he kept his horse at the railroad livery station. Matt could walk to work and take the railroad anywhere he needed to go. He bought the horse and buggy to see Jade more often. While Matt tried to adhere to the Victorian courtship rules of only seeing Jade at her house under the supervision of her father, she insisted on what she called "getting some fresh air." On weekend outings, Matt would let Jade take the reins of the buggy.

Jade seemed to relish the freedom that driving the buggy provided. Matt had to keep his emotions under control. His rage used to bring about violent actions, and he was afraid his desire for Jade might also lead to inappropriate and uncontrollable actions. Matt was scared to be alone with Jade.

In March 1852, Rochester was warm. The snow melted early that year, creating streets of mud. Matt's buggy seemed to throw mud in all directions. Fortunately, the railroad coaches were available for Ken and Emma's wedding. Another advantage of March was that the crocuses were popping out through the leftover snow. The sight of the first flowers was a welcome sign that summer was coming. Matt knew change was inevitably coming.

Ken started his new job working as the stationmaster. Matt enjoyed helping Ken at the station. He also helped Ken work on his new house when they had the time. Emma came to the city with her parents. They stayed at Ken's house while Ken put a cot in Matt's small room until the wedding. Ken spent time with Matt and hardly saw Emma, since she was there to meet with Father Sullivan. Matt figured it was going to be a perfect wedding.

A sunny March 6, 1852, in Rochester marked an unofficial beginning of spring. Matt kept busy with helping Ken because several friends of Emma's family had come into the city from Newark. They took over in preparing Ken and Emma's house for a wedding reception after the church ceremony. Matt noticed that the railroad station was abuzz with people making plans to go to Ken Webster's wedding. Jade was with Emma, directing the placement of flowers in the church. Ken was ordered to stay away from the bride, so he stayed at work until Matt told him they should head for Saint Patrick's in Matt's buggy. Both of the railroad coaches were being used at Emma's pleasure because the wedding was related to railroad business. Matt thought of Jade.

Matt's jobs were to make sure Ken got to the church by noon and to keep Ken sober. Ken, like Matt, did not drink except at business lunches or dinners. The groom and best man were both nervous and thought a couple of whiskeys would help calm their nerves. The whiskey did its job. Matt and Ken enjoyed a conversation about nothing and everything. The owner of the Oak Street Tavern was tending bar.

"I hate to see you gentlemen leave, but haven't you got someplace to be?"

Matt looked at the clock and then at Ken. They polished off their whiskey in a single gulp, stood up, said goodbye to the barkeep, and staggered to the door. Matt provided a wild buggy ride to the church. The cool air refreshed their alcohol-laden brains somewhat.

Matt was pleased that the church service went smoothly despite the slight scent of alcohol. Matt saw Ken and Emma off for the reception in the first railroad coach. The parents of the bride rode with Jade in the second coach. Matt drove the buggy with Jade's father, Michael Malloy. Michael had a flask of whiskey that he shared with Matt. Their conversation quickly went from the wedding to the Underground Railroad. Matt learned that more runaway slaves were showing up in Rochester. Occasionally, slave catchers hung around the rail station, but no runaways were seen, so the slaver catchers would leave. Matt thought about Stony and the danger the slave catchers created. They were in the area, creating danger for those who helped the runaways. He knew Jade could be in danger.

The reception was an emotional event for all. Matt thought of Jade constantly now. Emma's parents loved the house Ken and Emma had bought to make their home. Ken had worked for the railroad for twelve years and saved enough money to make a sizable down payment on the house. The old stationmaster held a note on the rest of the cost. Emma used much of the money Ken had left to decorate the house with modern amenities. Matt had saved a considerable amount of money and thought he could make Jade happy.

One such modern amenity was the new water closet that Ken and Matt had worked on with the help of a potter from New York City Matt had found. The women at the wedding were enthralled with the water closet and spent much time running up and down the stairs just to see it. Ken had left the old outhouse in the backyard. The men had to use that outdoor facility. A water tub made of copper had a gas-fired copper coil next to it that heated the water for bathing.

Whiskey, ale, and wines were available for guests, as well as a large table with dozens of various food creations. Emma introduced Matt to her family and friends from Newark. Matt in turn introduced Emma to Ken's workers at the station. People ate and drank to their hearts' content.

Jade was happy. A couple of glasses of wine encouraged her to confront Matt about the liquor that Emma had told her she smelled on Ken's breath. Matt took pride as a negotiator in always telling the truth. He did so now by confessing to having been as nervous as Ken before the wedding. Matt thought Jade dropped the subject because she respected the truth. He was correct.

Matt took Jade to the front porch, where there were fewer people. They sat next to each other on the steps. Jade put her hand on Matt's hand and confided in him that the wedding, the Underground Railroad, and he were too much and that she just wanted to run away like the slaves. Matt wanted to wrap his arms around her and protect her from her uncertainties. Matt tried to assure her that things would settle down. More wedding attendees coming onto the porch interrupted their conversation.

Guests were leaving. Jade left with her father but made Matt promise to come to her house tomorrow. Matt thought it was a bad idea to see Jade so soon, because he needed time to control his desire for her. Matt went inside and announced that Ken and Emma needed some time to get used to their new home together. He shook Ken's hand, gave Emma a kiss on the cheek, and left.

Matt slept well that night while in control of his emotions. The next morning, he wanted to avoid seeing Jade, so he hitched up the buggy and went to Ken's house. Emma's parents were still there, along with some straggling wedding guests from Newark. They were going to leave for Newark on Monday morning after a day of rest. When Matt drove the buggy up the path to Ken's horse stable, he found Ken in back of the house with a shovel.

"Those darned women plugged up the sewage system."

Matt knew right away what Ken was talking about by the

stench emanating from the ground. Matt spent the better part of the morning helping Ken fix the system and do some other chores around the house. Emma's parents were helping fix a supper from the wedding leftovers. Friends of Emma's parents were loading more food on buckboards with secret destinations. Matt had talked to Ken about the Underground Railroad and knew that Emma's parents were as involved as Jade and her father. The subject was never discussed with Emma's people, because secrecy was imperative when it came to runaway slaves. Matt perceived that many of these people from the countryside were involved.

Matt thought about Jade. He went home to wash up and change out of his sewage-soiled clothes. Clean and smelling good, Matt headed for Jade's home. He pulled the buckboard around back, as was his normal routine now. Michael met him at the back door and invited him in for coffee. While Matt and Michael drank their coffee, Jade came up from the basement. She scarcely said hello to Matt while she nervously looked out the windows. Matt looked at Michael, who nodded, confirming Matt's suspicion that there were runaway slaves in the basement.

The Malloys brewed coffee to hide the pungent smell associated with the Underground Railroad. Jade's rusty blunderbuss was ready on the kitchen table by the back door. The cart came in the back alley. Jade took her place as watch from the house while Michael opened the cellar door and beckoned their guests to emerge from the dark. Matt met the cart and farmer while studying the surroundings.

A dark-skinned man with three dark-skinned ladies emerged from the back of the house. They carried old sacks containing all of their belongings. Matt's heart went out to the runaways as they quietly crawled into the cart. With a nod from the farmer, they were gone. Matt followed Michael into the house. Jade was not there. Neither was the blunderbuss. A commotion on the front porch caused Matt to leap to the door. Jade was pointing the old musket at a fox that was chasing a rabbit. The rabbit made an eerie sound. Embarrassed, Jade hid the gun from view and backed into the house, looking around.

They went inside. There was no more conversation about the runaways. Instead, they talked about the wedding, the water closet, and the problems from too many people using it. The subject of the wedding was tense because it brought out Michael's feelings of missing his wife and Matt's secret feelings of desire. Finally, Michael stood up and put his coat on. He said he was going for a walk and would be back in an hour. Matt jumped up and asked to join him. Matt was terrified to be left alone with Jade, because his desire was strong. Michael told Matt that he needed to be alone and walked out the door.

Matt looked at Jade while he grabbed his overcoat.

"Where do you think you're going?"

"I can't be trusted alone with you."

Jade stood up, smiled, and hurried to stand in front of Matt. Matt always was able to control a confrontation, whether verbal or physical, but not this time. The rumble was fierce. Jade flew into Matt; they hit the floor with Jade on top. Her arms were wrapped around Matt's neck, pulling his lips to hers. Furniture was being shoved and falling over. The side window curtain was yanked off the rods holding it up. They grabbed at each other's clothing, pulling and pushing. Matt's desire was all that existed in him, and it seemed that Jade's desire was as strong. Jade's hand guided Matt into her. A moment later, he exploded.

Matt rolled off of Jade, and they lay next to each other on the floor. It took a few minutes before Matt tried to apologize for his actions and lack of control. Jade said, "That's okay. You'll do better this time."

She sat on Matt, causing his physical desire to mount again. They lost themselves in each other. When their emotions calmed down, Matt looked at Jade nestled into his arm as they lay on the floor. He wasn't aware they'd become completely naked. He skin shined with perspiration. They were lying in a pool of sweat from their lovemaking, but they did not move. Finally, Matt slid his arm down and pulled her waist toward his. The desire that had built up over so many days and nights would not go away. Matt rolled on top of Jade. She wrapped her arms and legs around him and accepted him into her.

It was dark outside when they woke. They were covered with a warm quilt, and a fresh fire burned in the fireplace. The only thought on their minds was that they were still together. Their desire took over again. The smell of coffee woke them in the morning. The sun was brightening the living room. They heard rustling noises in the kitchen.

"Daddy?" Jade's weak voice asked.

"I want a grandson before I am too old to teach him how to fish."

Matt looked at Jade. Surprisingly, neither was all that embarrassed. They'd broken all the rules of Victorian courtship, common decency, and what they'd expected of themselves. Their lips met. It was worth it.

Matt and Jade planned a small wedding with Ken and Emma as witnesses. They never spent a night apart after their first night together. However, they did sleep upstairs in a bed after they spent a week recovering from aches and pains from their rumble on the hardwood floor. Matt had moved into the Malloys' home. When Jade asked her father to give her away at a traditional wedding, he laughed and said, "I already did."

And indeed he had. Matt figured that Michael had recognized the agony his daughter felt whenever Matt left her. Michael liked

Matt and was happy that Matt liked his daughter as much as he did. Matt loved Jade and didn't just tolerate her causes; he supported them with her.

Michael was even a little proud of the way he'd orchestrated their getting together. Michael Malloy realized that for a marriage to work in those modern times, two people had to find each other and fall deeply in love. After all, his daughter was getting old. He also hoped that once they were married, the house would stop shaking at night. He was afraid the house would fall apart. Matt married Jade in a small, private wedding.

RELATIVES, FRIENDS, OUTLAWS, AND ENEMIES

The winter of 1853 was cold and blustery. Matt bought eighty acres of land on Lake Avenue to build a home on. The land had several old maple trees, so Matt called it Maplewood. The New York Railroad was growing as Matt negotiated mergers with other railroad lines. Matt knew there were many more possibilities for the railroad to grow. The telegraph lines and faster postal systems made possible by the railroad contracts that Matt negotiated allowed Matt to spend his time in his Rochester office. Matt was happy to be able to be home with Jade every night.

The cold weather slowed down the work of the Underground Railroad. Matt spent much time chopping wood for the fireplaces at the Malloy home, his home. Matt saved half his pay and used it to buy the land. The other half of his pay bought stock in the New York Central Railroad. The stock was doing well and increased in value impressively. After six years in New York state, Matt was a wealthy man.

Matt was pleased when Ken had a new son and named him Mathew Kenneth Webster. Matt and Jade were disappointed that Jade had not conceived a child, but they kept busy with their other activities. Letters from Matt's brothers, Will and Ryan, were coming less often. Donahee Construction was keeping them busy. Matt's youngest brother, Ryan, had gotten married in the fall. It had been a quick marriage, and Matt had not had time to make arrangements to travel to Boston for Ryan's wedding. Will was getting married in June, and this time, Matt was making arrangements to take the railroad to Boston with Jade for Will's wedding.

Matt met with an architect to start the plans for his new house. He was interested to know when the construction would start and at what point money would be needed. His original plan was to sell some of his New York Central Railroad (NYCR) stock to build the house. Matt received a response from the railroad's fiduciary department that described a loan that would cost less in interest than Matt was making on his stock. Matt decided to take advantage of the program and borrowed the money from the railroad. It was simply good business.

Matt looked out his window and saw the two slave catchers who frequented the railroad to seek runaways who might be traveling by train. Slave catchers seemed to show up at the railroad regularly. Matt turned from his office window and thought he saw a familiar form. The man seemed to be missing an arm. Matt stepped into the shadow of the center of his new larger office to keep the one-armed man from seeing him. It was Stony, and he was checking the railroad station out. His eyes went from window to window, so Matt felt he did not know which office was Matt's. Matt knew Stony could find out easily enough.

Ken's office was huge. Ken left his double doors open so that he could see what was going on in the depot. Matt walked in and saw Ken's big smile as he talked to an employee. Ken was happy with his new job and did it well. The new station was in full operation, even though some carpenters were still adding the final touches. Ken held up his finger to Matt, demonstrating that he'd be with him in one moment. Ken finished with the employee, who left smiling.

"I just saw Stony," Matt said as he sat across from Ken at the desk. Matt told Ken that Stony looked to be checking the new station over and was walking toward the two slave catchers who often watched the station. Matt knew that Ken had some people dedicated to the abolitionist movement who would keep an eye on Stony. Matt thought that was a good idea. Matt mentioned that Stony only had one arm. Ken gave Matt a worried look and warned him that Stony would seek revenge.

Ken called a trusted employee into the office. He asked him to go out to see whether the slave catchers were still outside. The man must have been watching them, because he looked at Matt and explained that the slave catchers had met with a one-armed man and left walking east down State Street. Matt knew Ken was relieved, because he lived west on State Street. Matt decided to go for a walk.

Matt went back to his office upstairs to get his coat and hat. He left the station, going up Front Street to Main Street. While going east on Main Street, he came to a gunsmith shop. He went inside and bought a Colt pocket gun. The gun was a .31-caliber five-shot revolver. Like the muskets Matt and Stony had carried on the railroad, the revolver was a percussion gun that was easy to load and fire.

Matt bought a black leather holster that tucked the gun under his coat so that people could not see the bulge of a gun. The gunsmith provided a back room for Matt to fire the weapon in so he could get accustomed to the feel of the gun. Matt and the gunsmith were surprised at how accurate the gun was. Matt loaded the gun and put it in the leather holster. He slid his trousers' belt into the holster and made sure it felt comfortable. It did.

At the railroad station, Matt had to be careful whom he asked about the slave catchers and how he asked. Some people were on the slave catchers' side, the side of the law, while others believed slavery was wrong. Matt lingered outside to watch for any signs of the slave catchers or Stony. Matt was vigilant but worried more now that Stony was back and out of jail.

At the end of Matt's workday, Matt packed up his architectural plans to take home. He needed Jade's approval before he could make any decisions. He did not tell the architect that, because it was unusual for a woman to review a man's plan to build a house. Matt enjoyed Jade's input on domestic matters. It was a little early to leave when Matt stopped at Ken's office. Matt knew that Ken was always eager to go home to his Emma and the new baby. Ken always walked the short distance to his house. Matt offered him a ride in the buggy, and Ken accepted, knowing trouble might be close.

There was no sign of trouble on the way to Ken's house. Matt told Ken about the Colt pocket gun he'd purchased and was carrying. Ken warned Matt to remember that the law was on the side of the slave catchers. Organized speeches by Frederick Douglass and a newcomer to the cause, Susan B. Anthony, only brought awareness of slavery's evil to people. Matt considered morality first and the law second. Changing times meant changing laws. Matt wondered what he could do to change the law.

Matt got home, unhitched his horse, and stabled it before going inside. He called to Jade when he closed the back door behind him. There was no answer. He walked into the living room and saw that Michael had been beaten and tied up on the floor. The smell of gunpowder worried Matt as he looked around for Jade. "Jade!" he called.

Stony walked out from the shadow by the foyer at the front door. "So that's the bitch's name who tried to shoot me." Stony was holding an older pistol and pointing it at Matt. Stony's eye twitch was evident when he told Matt how hard it was to tie knots with one arm. Stony muttered as he pointed to Michael on the floor.

Matt moved between Stony and Michael, thinking Stony was going to shoot Michael for spite. Matt noticed the blunderbuss on the floor by the front door. It had exploded. "Where is she?" Matt demanded.

Stony told Matt he'd get to her when he repaid Matt for his arm. Stony pointed the gun at Matt. He laughed and started to say something as he put his finger on the trigger. Matt took advantage of Stony's belligerence. He drew his Colt and fired. Stony's gun fell to the floor as he cursed his other arm. Matt saw Jade running from the woods beside the house. Stony said, "I'll be back for your girl an—"

Stony never finished his sentence. Matt fired another shot at Stony's heart. Stony looked at Matt and died, falling to the floor. Jade came rushing through the front door. She took in the scene and looked at Matt holding the gun. Matt slid the gun back in the holster, concealing it again. He turned to untie Michael. Jade tended to a gash on her father's forehead. Other than that, Michael was okay.

Matt waited until Jade had her father settled before reprimanding her for the blunderbuss. Matt had never believed the old gun was even loaded. Jade had black powder all over her face from firing the antique weapon. She had not considered herself until now. Matt examined her face closely. "Still beautiful," he proclaimed as he kissed her blackened face passionately.

A knock on the open door startled them. Matt guardedly opened the front door wider. It was the same night watchman who'd attended to Stony last year. He looked the situation over and asked whether everyone was okay. He looked at the bulge caused by the Colt on Matt's hip and asked Matt to hand the gun to him. Matt did. The watchman carefully decocked the gun, handed it back to Matt, and told him that he didn't want Matt to shoot himself in the foot. The officer bent down and felt for breathing or a pulse from Stony.

The watchman declared that Stony was dead, and he looked at Matt and asked if there was anyone else in the house. Matt shook his head, and the watchman slowly asked Jade and then Michael the same question. The watchman told Matt that he assumed the man had held a grudge against Matt, and that was why he was there. Matt agreed persuasively. The watchman told them he would go get some help to get Stony's body out of the house, and he'd be back in an hour. Matt thanked him.

The watchman said, "You realize that this man is a slave catcher and protected by the law. Obviously, this was personal. You sure nobody else is in the house?"

Matt perceived that the watchman knew that the house was or could be part of the Underground Railroad. Matt knew he was warning them not to have any slaves there when he got back. Jade went down to the cellar to clean up any trace that there'd ever been anyone hiding in the basement. Matt, his wife, and Michael were ready when the watchman came back with a carriage and four other armed watchmen. Matt watched nervously as they searched the house from top to bottom. Satisfied that there were no runaway slaves in the house, the watchmen loaded up Stony's body and drove away. The three runaway slave women had nearly frozen to death by the time the watchmen left and Jade called them in from the woods.

Matt had thought Jade and Michael might object to his carrying a pistol. After that night's incident, no one commented. Jade took some food to the basement before they ate dinner. They were more determined than ever to hide the runaways, and they were vigilant for strangers. Matt, Jade, and Michael looked over the architectural plans for the new house calmly, as if nothing had happened. Matt was restless that night. Jade knew what to do to put him at ease, and she enjoyed doing it.

Matt knew Jade was an amazing woman. She knew how to please him, and he was easy to please. She was as loyal to Matt as she was to her father. Her heart poured out to anyone suffering. She was especially congenial with Susan B. Anthony's ideals of women's liberation. Matt respected her and gave her the liberty she needed, while in public, she provided a more socially acceptable atmosphere of the current expectations of the modern woman. Matt never ordered her around or even asked her to fetch anything for him. They were in love with and lusted for each other. Compromises came easily.

Summer 1854 came, and Matt was sad that Jade still had not conceived a child. They confided in a doctor to see why they could not get pregnant. Doctor Blanco was well renowned for having good and professional relationships with the medical community, including midwives. The Donahees met with him together. He spent some time gathering information. Finally, he told Matt and Jade that he would interview them separately. They assured him that there was no need to separate them. Matt and his wife had no secrets from each other.

The doctor asked how often they had intercourse. Jade blushed a bit when the doctor asked that question. Matt was quick to answer, telling the doctor usually once or twice and sometimes three times. The doctor asked if that was per week or per month.

Jade was quick to respond, as if she were insulted, and clarified: "Per day."

The doctor seemed shocked at first, maybe by the woman's honesty, but he composed himself and continued by explaining to Matt that he was not sure this approach would work, but often, couples went a month without intercourse. After the probationary period, they conceived a child. Matt and Jade looked at each other, and with great hesitation, they agreed to the trial. They agreed to start that night. Matt had to sleep on a rug in the living room. He was almost asleep, when the blanket was flung off him. Jade pounced on him like a wild mountain lion.

"We can start tomorrow," she said.

That night was like their first time. At one point, they talked about starting their abstinence from each other at the end of the month, which was two weeks away. Then Jade suggested that they could start then as long as her cycle was done. Jade needed physical love when she was menstruating. Matt knew many husbands who would not touch their wives at that time of the month because it was dirty. Matt thought that was crazy and that those men were missing a great thing. They were back in bed together every night. Jade's cycle did not come. She was with child.

Later in life, Matt would look back at 1853 as one of the best years of his life. Jade accompanied him on a trip to Niagara Falls. It was a business trip; however, the trip was as much for pleasure as for business. Matt and the railroad executives came from various parts of Ohio and Illinois. The restaurants and hotels of Niagara Falls provided entertainment that included the history of the area. Newspapers from all over the world were available at one newsroom near the falls. Some were not that old.

Matt suggested a stroll by the great gorge, which put Jade in a romantic mood. Matt was content that he made Jade happy with her life. The house began construction and was to be completed by Christmas. Michael made a new fishing pole, knowing that Matt's baby would be a boy. Work was going well, and next month, as long as Jade was up to traveling, Matt was taking Jade to Boston for his brother's wedding.

Matt was disappointed when Franklin Pierce was elected as

the new president of the United States. Pierce was adamant about enforcing the Fugitive Slave Act in order to satisfy the southern states. There were more slave catchers in Niagara Falls than Matt had seen in Rochester. They were easy to spot because they carried long guns and often were accompanied by the police.

On Matt and Jade's return to Rochester, the Underground Railroad was busy putting runaway slaves on freight ships on the wharf in the Genesee River. The ships would take them to Canada. Matt witnessed slave catchers taking slaves south on his railroad. He was appalled when he saw the slave catchers use iron shackles on ankles and wrists, with heavy chains to prevent the slaves from running away again. The slaves rode as freight because it was cheaper.

Matt perfected control of his rage. He addressed the inhuman quandary of slavery as a political problem of society. Politically incorrect Matt no longer tried to hide his stance on abolitionism. His Colt revolver was always on his hip. Matt studied newspapers and spent time talking to travelers to gain an understanding of the American political system.

Jade and Matt went to hear speakers, including Frederick Douglass, Susan B. Anthony, and Isaac Post. Matt thought Jade was right about Post being a little strange, but his message was clear. Matt made arrangements for the trip to Boston. He had not seen his brothers in six years.

Jade insisted on shopping for a wedding gift for William Donahee's wedding. Matt happily agreed to let her handle the task. Emma was more than happy to accompany her. Jade found an appropriate gift and bought a new trunk from the Pritchard store. She wrapped the present, which filled the trunk. A Pritchard trunk was known for quality and price, and the one Jade picked out was beautiful leather with strong brass hinges and locks. She told Matt what the present was, but he wasn't listening. His mind was on the danger of the Underground Railroad and leaving Michael Malloy behind alone.

First-class travel by railroad was luxurious. Matt had a double berth for them to sleep in, and it had large windows to see the countryside. Matt showed Jade the area where he'd killed the bear, and he described the survey team he'd worked with on his way to Rochester. She was attentive and enjoyed his stories along the route. Matt was happy to show his wife a piece of his past. Jade was starting to show the growth in her belly. Still, they enjoyed the cramped sleeping quarters because the rocking of the train made their lovemaking sweet.

Boston was a big city. Jade had never seen the ocean, and Matt was interested to visit the waterfront with her. Matt was excited to see William and Ryan waiting at the train station when the train pulled into the Boston railroad depot. The brotherly reunion was emotional. Ryan looked as though he had grown taller since Matt saw him last. William seemed healthy and strong. The brothers freely hugged each other. William finally looked at Jade and said, "And who might this lovely creature be?"

Matt proudly introduced her as his lovely wife, Jade Donahee. He introduced William and Ryan to Jade. The three brothers loaded the couple's luggage onto the top of a four-by-four coach. It was larger than the railroad coaches and displayed the name Donahee Brothers Construction and Landscaping Company in rich gold letters. Matt enjoyed the ride to William's and Ryan's new houses because it took them to the edge of the north side of the city. William and Ryan had built new houses next to each other and down the road from their construction company.

They passed a large business with several outbuildings, including one made of glass. The coach stopped in front of the grand enterprise. A large white sign with the name Donahee Brothers painted in gold letters with black highlights was on an arch spanning the width of the roadway entering the business. Matt asked William and Ryan to bring them back to the business for a tour later. Matt was impressed when the coach pulled up in a circle at Ryan's house. Jade was impressed with the large garden of flowers in full bloom that lined the walkway to the front of the house. Matt knew he would need flowers at his new home in Rochester. Inside the house, Matt saw that the home was small but well decorated. It had running water and, as Jade was quick to discover, a large room with a copper tub and a water closet with a comfortable round wood seat on a coffer funnel. A hand pull above delivered water to flush the water closet after use. Ryan's young wife, Eileen, who was showing that she too was with child, gave Jade a tour of her home and explained that customers would come into the house to see the modern amenities as Ryan designed their houses. Matt hoped his children would grow up knowing their distant cousins. Jade, who was an only child, was glad her baby would have a cousin, even though they were far apart.

Matt and his brothers brought the luggage into the guest room where Matt and Jade were to stay. Matt and Jade were left alone to freshen up and change after the train trip. Next, Matt was going to William's house to meet his fiancée. Jade, of course, was taking mental notes of things she would have Matt add to their Rochester house.

They went next door to William's house, which was different but had similar modern conveniences. William's backyard had a garden filled with various flowers and a trellis with big red roses that rose up the sides and covered the arch on top. Through the trellis was a grassy area where the wedding was to be held.

Matt practiced his skill at remembering names as he was introduced to both William's and Ryan's in-laws. William's fiancée was named Mary, and she had red Irish hair and freckles.

Matt thought she was adorable. Matt, his brothers, and their women took the coach to a restaurant by the beach. The four large horses pulled the full coach with ease. Matt determined that Jade was impressed with the large waves breaking on the shore. Large ships were entering and leaving the busy harbor in the distance.

As promised, Ryan and William gave Matt a tour of the business. At four in the morning, a fast rapping on the door woke Matt. Jade went back to sleep while Matt dressed in some work clothes that William had left with Ryan. Matt was happy to be there for William's wedding day. Success in business meant hard work, and the Donahee boys had grown up working hard.

Ryan was busy in a noisy building, cutting wood planks out of cut trees. Matt helped William load a buckboard with various plants and bushes. They headed farther away from the city to a newly constructed house. The sun had barely risen above the ocean before Matt was working up a sweat turning dirt over along the front of the house. Matt planted the bushes and flowers. When all the flowers were in the ground, William stepped back and looked the garden over. Matt joined him as William proclaimed, "Perfect."

Matt and his brothers hurried back to prepare for the wedding. A telegraph had come from the railroad for Mathew Donahee. The telegraph was from Ken and stated, "Come home at once."

Matt had been planning to spend a week in Boston with his brothers, but after the wedding, he told Jade to pack her things. They watched William and Mary open the trunk with the wedding present. William examined the fine craftsmanship of the trunk, while Mary loved the blue-and-white china set that was inside. Matt and Jade regretfully said their goodbyes and left for the rail station. The train home was available in regular passenger class only. There were no sleeping cabins available. Matt and Jade wondered what could be so urgent.

Ken was waiting for Matt at the railroad station in Rochester. Matt insisted on getting to the point of the emergency. Ken told him Michael Malloy had been shot in the leg while fighting slave catchers who'd caught him escorting a slave to a ship on the Genesee River at midnight. Michael's house had been burned to the ground. Michael was doing fine and recovering at Ken's house. The police were waiting to arrest Michael for slave trafficking. Matt tried to think about what to do as he and Jade hurried on foot to Ken's house. Emma greeted them at the front door and escorted them to Michael. Jade seemed relieved to see her father smiling. Matt was clearly upset.

"You should see the other guy," Michael said to Matt.

Jade gave her father a hug and examined his wounded leg. Matt's rage emerged, but there was no action to relieve his rage. A knock on the door startled Matt. He went to the front door and opened it. Two police officers stood there. They said they were there to take Michael to the jail. One patted down Matt to see whether he was carrying the pistol they knew he owned. Matt had left the pistol in his office drawer when he'd left for Boston. The other officer examined Michael's leg and determined that Michael needed a few more days to recover.

"You won't run if we leave you here, will you?" the officer asked.

Michael looked at his leg and said, "I'm afraid my running days are over."

The officer looked at Matt and apologized for having to arrest Michael; he explained that the law made everyone either a slave catcher or a criminal. The officer suggested Matt find a lawyer for Michael. A lawyer would help Michael in court. Matt worked with several railroad lawyers. He would see one right away. Matt left Jade and her father with the pregnant Emma and headed back to the railroad.

Mr. Maxwell was a lawyer who worked for the railroad. Matt worked with him often on railroad dealings. His office was on the third floor of the railroad building, a few doors down from Matt's office. Matt ran into Ken on his way to Maxwell's office. Ken told Matt that he and Jade were welcome, along with Michael, to stay with them. Matt thanked him and accepted his offer.

Maxwell was a foot shorter than Matt but seemed like a giant when he talked. He was aware of Michael Malloy's problem because railroad gossip was abundant, and the newspaper had published a rendition of the incident that morning. Maxwell assured Matt he could get Michael a shortened sentence in the county jail. The problem was not just the issue of Michael's helping slaves but the assault charge Michael faced. Maxwell said the police hated to arrest people for such crimes, but the judge favored the slave-catcher laws.

Michael Malloy was sentenced to thirty days for aiding a runaway slave. The judge dismissed the assault charge because of Michael's injury and the fact that his house had burned down mysteriously during the skirmish. Matt was carrying his pocket Colt again. He was on the lookout for any slave catchers.

A week after Michael's sentencing, Matt answered a knock on his office door. The man at the door introduced himself as the slave catcher who'd shot Michael. Matt thought about shooting the man, but the look on the man's face negated such action. Neither man offered to shake hands. The slave catcher spoke next.

"I need your help."

Matt was shocked at the request but heard the man out. The slave catcher could not return the slave to her owner. He explained to Matt that the owner beat and raped her. Matt said, "You shot my father-in-law and burned down our home."

"I can't possibly apologize enough for that, but I am sorry for shooting the man. He put up a hell of a fight. The fire was an accident."

The man seemed heartfelt. Matt thought of his Colt but decided that a violent beating would make him feel better. Another knock on office door preceded Jade's entrance. Matt told her to leave. She demanded an explanation. Matt clenched his fists and looked at the slave catcher. Jade was more scared by the rage she saw in Matt's eyes than by the stranger.

Jade asked the man to sit down and explain himself. Matt said, "This is the daughter of the man you shot."

Matt saw a side of Jade's persona that was far beyond the intelligent and compassionate wife he knew. She listened as her father's shooter explained that he'd fallen in love with the slave and needed help getting both of them to Canada. His story was so outrageous that Matt believed him. Matt asked where the slave was. When the slave catcher told him she was curled up and packed in a trunk in the railroad station, Jade went wild.

"You are a slave catcher—no one will question you with a runaway in irons! Get her out now."

Jade led the man and Matt downstairs. The man went to the trunk. Jade opened the lid. At least it was not locked. The girl was scared but climbed out of the trunk when Jade ordered her to stand up and get out of the box.

"Are you in love with this man?" Jade asked.

"It jus' happened. He was kin to me, and ah fell in luv wid 'im."

Jade was beside herself. She started to order Matt to take them to the house, but she remembered that the house had burned down. She then started to tell him that her father would know what to do, but she realized he was in jail.

"Get that slave in my office now."

Matt heard Ken's commanding voice. Matt took the slave catcher and the slave to Ken's office. Ken told Matt he'd overheard the conversation, as had everyone in the station. The slave catcher had tossed his shackles into a river, so Matt had Ken give the slave catcher some rope to tie up the slave. Matt went to the stable to find Thomas, the dark-skinned coachman. Ken opened his door and yelled at the slave catcher to get the slave to the freight train. Matt was impressed with Ken's action and thought that Emma would have been proud of Ken. Thomas came in with Matt's explanation of the situation. Thomas drove the couple away as they hid in the back of the carriage. The situation ended for Matt. Thomas would never declare what he'd done with the couple, but he did say that they were married before they left for Canada.

The Donahee house was competed in December 1853. Matt felt guilty for crowding his friend's home and did as much as possible to lighten the inconvenience. Jade helped Emma around the Webster house for another week. Emma gave birth to a baby girl. The house was really crowded, and all were happy when Matt and Jade could move into their new house. Michael was out of jail and was to live with Matt and his daughter at Maplewood Manor.

Jade's mother had been buried in back of their burned home years ago. Matt and his family cleaned up the rubble left by the fire. They donated the land to a Catholic cemetery that would become Holy Sepulchre Cemetery. Maplewood Manor was a large house with four upstairs bedrooms and one bedroom on the first floor. Michael slept in the first-floor bedroom because he needed a crutch to get around, even though his leg had healed. The house had a large basement.

Matt's Christmas traditions involved a short workday so that the family could spend time together. Matt started a new personal tradition of evaluating family, work, and society after Christmas. He kept a personal journal. His entries for the end of 1853 included time when family was important. He wrote that his father's strong work principle had provided a guide for him and his brothers that led to success. Isla Donahee had used that hard-work standard to teach the boys how to read, write, and decipher numbers. Unlike their father, the Donahee brothers took calculated risks.

Matt made a note in his journal to teach his child the same standards. Jade persuaded Matt to read a play from 1839 by Edward Bulwer-Lytton. One line in particular stood out from the play: "The pen is mightier than the sword." Matt made a note to put his writing skills to better use, especially in times when the rage wanted to take over.

Matt saw that injustice could be fought with words rather than violence. Jade could not vote in elections because she was a woman. Matt could not vote because he was an immigrant from Ireland. While some states had alien voting rights, New York had done away with the ruling in 1804 Matt made a journal entry that he wanted a son. A son born in the United States would have the right to vote. A son would be a part of the rapidly expanding economy of Rochester.

The winter of 1854 brought usual amounts of snow to Rochester. Matt bought a sledge—or, as he called it, a sleigh—to make navigating the city streets easier in the winter. The sleigh was bright red with black runners, and without the sleigh, winter travel would have been impossible. The sleigh was open to the air, so Jade and Matt had to wear layers of warm clothes. Michael worked on the northern fruit farms in the summer, which freed him to shovel snow in the cold Rochester winters. Michael's wounded leg was bothering him much less now.

Jade would ride into town with Matt to stay with Emma and help with her babies. In some spots, the horse pulled the sleigh through dark tunnels of snow piled by snow shovelers.

One March day brought only a single train to the railroad station. Frozen passengers debarked the train and huddled near the massive fireplace in the station. Snow kept falling. Despite the lack of trains, Matt and Ken's workers kept busy shoveling snow. After they cleared one side of the station, they would have to start over.

When the snow reached two feet in the streets, Matt decided it was time to get Jade and get her home. She was due to give birth soon. After Matt pulled the sleigh in front of Ken Webster's house, he had to walk through a snowdrift that was up to his chest. While Jade was getting her warm travel clothes on, Matt shoveled a narrow path from the street to the front door. As soon as he put the shovel down on the front porch, the door opened, and Jade emerged from the warmth of the house into the cold. The temperature increased during the day, which normally brought large, heavy snows in Rochester.

Driving the sleigh was difficult for Matt. The high snow piles on the sides of streets made the streets darker than normal. The light, cold wind was still allowing the snow to fall straight down. The horse balked at pulling the sleigh when the snow was up to the horse's waist. Matt was in a line of sleighs, carts, and pedestrians that trudged through the high snow. They were three of the four miles home, when the sleigh hit a large piece of ice. Jade let out a yelp.

"What's wrong?" Matt bellowed worriedly.

"I think the baby is coming."

The horse stopped from the strain of the invisible ice under the snow. Jade assured Matt that she was feeling labor pains and that she would be all right as soon as they got home. A man with a snow shovel helped Matt clear the chunk of ice. He told Matt that he shoveled snow for the city, and they'd sent people home because they could not keep up with the storm. Matt could not encourage the horse to pull. The horse had had enough of the snow as well. Matt had to get off the sleigh and pull the horse to get it to move.

An abandoned sleigh caused the snow to pile high around it. There was a silhouette of the sleigh covered with white. The snow got so deep that Matt and the horse could barely move the sleigh. The sleigh moved easier in some places than others. Snow blinded Matt's eyes, and he did not even see Jade slide off the sleigh and start pushing.

Matt heard Jade cry out in pain again. He was horrified to see the sleigh empty. He walked to the back of the sleigh and found a hole in the snow. He fished Jade out of the snow. She had another labor pain. Pushing the sleigh seemed to make it worse. Matt helped her back onto the sleigh, when a single horseman stopped in front of Matt's sleigh horse.

"My wife is having a baby!" Matt said.

The rider got off his horse and walked up to Jade. He smiled at her and asked how far apart the pains were.

"Every five bumps."

"I'm Dr. Goldman. Where're you going?"

Matt told the doctor they were another half mile from home. The man had Matt tie his horse to the sleigh horse. Two pedestrians came up from behind. The doctor told them to help push the sleigh. The doctor looked at Jade and said, "It's too cold out here to have a baby. You'll just have to wait."

Jade was feeling better as Matt and the doctor pulled the horses while the two men pushed the sleigh from behind.

Another man going in the opposite direction on foot turned around and helped after seeing Jade in the sleigh. Then another two men joined in pushing. Michael was shoveling a path when the procession turned into Maplewood Manor. Matt raced to Jade, and despite her petulant cry that she could walk, Matt picked her up in his arms and started for the house. Jade let out a sound like that of a wild wolf.

The doctor accompanied Matt to the house and upstairs to the bedroom. Michael had the three men who'd pushed the sleigh help unhitch the horses and put them in the stable. The men explained the obvious to Michael. He brought them all inside out of the cold. Matt was boiling water on the wood-burning stove when Michael came in. An ear-piercing scream resonated throughout the house. Then there was silence. An instant later came the sweet sound of a baby's cry. The doctor's voice sounded from up the stairs.

"I am ready for that hot water and some towels! You'll want to bring some wood up here and start a fire in the fireplace."

Matt ran up the stairs with a kettle of hot water. Jade's father gathered an armful of firewood.

"It's a boy," Dr. Goldman said.

Matt was speechless. He was worried about Jade. The doctor did not give Matt time to ask how Jade was. Matt stood outside the bedroom door with Jade's father, waiting for news. Time seemed to stand still as the men in Jade's life nervously waited for the doctor. They heard voices inside the bedroom. Jade was talking to the doctor. The door opened, and the doctor told Matt to come in and meet his son.

Matt looked at Jade lying in the bed with their new baby in her arms. Jade's father was still holding an armful of firewood. Jade handed the baby to Matt and said, "Meet Jack Patrick Donahee."

Matt thought Jade was pleased with herself. Matt held his

new son and counted his fingers and toes. The doctor told Matt
that he had a healthy son. "And you have a very lucky wife."

Matt stared at his son until he heard the crackling of fire in
the fireplace. Jade's father came and looked at his grandson. Jade
asked for Jack back, and Matt carefully put him in her arms. The
doctor suggested Matt stay with Jade until she fell asleep.

FROM HELL TO HEAVEN

Michael Malloy led the doctor downstairs to the kitchen, where three Good Samaritans huddled around the woodstove. Michael offered to cook them some dinner, but the doctor was anxious to continue home before the snow piled up too high. After congratulating Michael on his new grandson and being assured that Jade was all right, the group bundled up for their journeys. Michael bundled up to help get the doctor's horse out and see them off. They got as far as the back porch.

Another foot of snow had fallen as Jack Donahee entered the world. Dr. Goldman; Charlie and Dominic, the snow shovelers; and Billy, the cook at the Lunch Box restaurant downtown, became overnight guests. Michael explained that he was going to cook dinner so that Jade could have something when she was ready. Billy was happy to offer to cook, and Michael was happy to let him.

Michael took Billy downstairs to the fruit cellar to gather food for a stew. With Jade's pregnancy and the slave catchers watching, there were no more runaways coming to the basement. However, Jade had enough food to send a thousand runaways to safety.

Billy picked out some potatoes, carrots, and salted pork for a stew. He eyed some fermented peaches in glass jars. Michael helped him carry the food to the kitchen. Billy took over and had Dominic peel potatoes while Charlie sliced carrots. Dr. Goldman brewed coffee while Michael listened for sounds upstairs.

The scent of coffee roused Matt's senses. Jade was asleep, as was little Jack in Matt's arms. Matt gently put Jack in his crib and quietly snuck downstairs. Everyone congratulated Matt in quiet whispers. After introductions were made, Matt's eyes stopped at Dr. Goldman, who was sitting at the kitchen table with a cup of coffee. Matt poured himself a cup and sat with the doctor. The conversation led to politics.

Matt had planned on having Emma stay with Jade when the baby came. There was no way that was going to happen. The doctor informed Matt that normally, he would not even have seen Jade, because a midwife would have easily handled the birthing. Matt proclaimed to all the men eating Billy's peach cobbler that he was grateful to them. The men stayed until the storm settled three days later. Matt pampered Jade, but she wanted Emma. The snow stopped falling and started melting. Jade was moving around and taking care of the baby well.

After three days, Matt finally went to his office at the railroad. Ken was not there. People congratulated Matt on the birth of his son. The snow shovelers had spread the word of their adventure as fast as the snow had melted. They were proud of their part in helping bring baby Jack into the world, and rightfully so, Matt reckoned. Matt was filled with pride that his son, Jack Donahee, was the most popular person in Rochester that morning.

Matt saw Ken when he finally came in. Ken heard about the birth of Matt's son and left to take Emma and his sons to see Jade. The railroad was busy with delayed trains carrying passengers eager to tell their snowstorm stories. Matt helped Ken by carrying luggage for passengers and rerouting them to their destinations. It was a busy day. Melting snow was causing the Genesee River to rise.

Certain areas of Rochester often flooded when the snow melted. Such was the case in the spring of 1854. Floodwater filled the streets fast in the low area north of the railroad station. The water was frigid and pushed dangerous debris along the river.

People on the third floor of the railroad station could see the river overflowing its banks. Matt had just settled in his office and was writing a letter to the main office in New York City, when people running downstairs caused a commotion.

"There's a child in the river!"

Matt thought about his son for a brief moment and leaped to his feet, sending his inkwell and quill flying to the floor. Matt moved fast and made it past a group of gawkers and saw the child. Matt took his boots and coat off while heading for the water.

"Are you crazy?"

Matt heard the statement from somewhere in the gathering crowd. Matt thought to himself that his chance of surviving if he jumped in the water was slim. The child's chance was getting slimmer. Matt heard a frantic voice from a woman upstream: "My baby! My baby!"

Matt ran through the shallow floodwater on the road and bank and dove behind a floating tree. The frigid water made Matt gasp for air. The child screamed for help, and the current swept Matt into the floating tree. Matt rolled his body over the branches and swam as fast as he could to catch up to the boy, who was holding a piece of wood to keep himself afloat. The current pulled Matt under the surface five feet from the boy. Matt kicked hard and pulled with his arms to get to the surface.

Matt needed air. His chest hurt when he sucked the cold air in and reached for the boy after a shallow breath. The boy was no longer calling for help and did not even see Matt. The boy let go of the board and slipped underwater. Matt had a hand on the boy and pulled him up to the surface. The crowd was out of sight, as the current had carried them toward the high falls on the river. Matt pulled with one arm and held the boy with his other arm. Matt knew they would not survive the waterfalls.

Matt's hand felt something under the water. His feet started kicking the ground where the bank once had been. Matt made it to his feet and carried the boy to dry land. Matt dropped to his knees and laid the boy on the dry ground. Matt was nearly unconscious and ready to fall to the ground.

"Thank you, mister."

The faint voice of the young boy brought Matt back to being able to think reasonably. He stood and picked the young boy up in his arms. Matt looked around and did not know where he was. The sound of violent water falling over the falls let Matt know he had traveled a mile in the river. Matt was thinking clearly and moved toward the street. No one greeted them when they reached the street. A woman ran toward Matt and the boy. She was a distance away with a horse carriage following her.

"Mommy!" the boy cried.

Matt put the boy down and watched him run to meet his mother. The carriage driver put them inside. Matt was shivering and shaking uncontrollably when he got into the carriage with the mother and son. Matt did not recognize his surroundings when he woke. The boy's mother was in a chair next to Matt, talking to her boy in the bed next to her. Matt was in a hospital. Dr. Goldman came in and asked Matt if he was ready to go home. Matt thought about his son and Jade. He asked what time of the day it was. He was shocked to hear that it was five in the evening. Dr. Goldman told him he'd been in bad shape that morning when they'd brought him to the hospital.

"I guess I'll go home, but I need to let my friend Ken know I'm all right."

"Already knows."

Matt recognized Ken's voice in the hall outside the hospital room. Ken peeked into the door and told Matt, "Your carriage awaits, sir."

Matt was released from the hospital and said goodbye to the boy and his mother. The boy was going to spend the night at the hospital because he was coughing badly. Dr. Goldman assured Matt that everyone would be fine. Ken took Matt home to Jade. Matt and Jade slept in each other's arms that night.

Rochester survived that spring and the flooding. Jack Donahee was healthy and growing. Matt ran into the shovelers who'd helped the night Jack was born. They were always friendly. Dr. Goldman invited Matt to the newly formed Republican Party meeting in the spring of 1856. Matt agreed, as the party wanted to support John C. Fremont, a western explorer with abolitionist views. Despite the Republican Party's efforts, Democrat James Buchanan was elected in the 1856 presidential election.

Matt followed newspaper articles religiously. He learned that Buchanan did little to help the United States reconcile differences between the North and the South. The South organized, and seven southern states seceded from the Union. The succession was due to slavery issues. Strong leadership was needed. Matt understood that without such leadership, civil war was imminent.

Matt's son, Jack Donahee, was five years old and already reading a little. Matt and Jade took turns reading to him, and he loved to hear their voices transform the written word to speech. Matt and Jade were content that they would not have any more children. Matt was thrilled when Jade became pregnant in 1859. Karl Donahee was born in the summer of 1859. Jack was happy to have a brother.

In October 1859, Matt read about an abolitionist named John Brown, who'd attacked an arsenal in northern Virginia. Brown's intent was to collect weapons and arm a slave rebellion. Many northerners were excited by his act. Matt saw it as a seed for war.

Matt read that the 1859 Democratic Convention was chaotic. Matt saw opportunities for the Republican Party, as delegates had walked out of the Democratic Convention without selecting a presidential candidate. New parties were formed with different candidates. Matt and his newly formed Republican Party campaigned heavily for their candidate. Some Republicans portrayed their candidate as a poor farm boy who had risen to success. Matt was excited that a hardworking farm boy could grow up and run for president of that great country. Abraham Lincoln's main objective was to preserve the unity of the country. The party opposed the institutionalization of slavery in the new territories while not interfering with the southern states' slavery issues. Matt opposed slavery no matter what, but he knew from his negotiations that Lincoln was moving in the right direction.

Four candidates vied for president, but Matt's candidate won. Lincoln won both the popular vote and the Electoral College. Matt had high hopes when Abraham Lincoln became the sixteenth president of the United States. Matt read that southern states began withdrawing from the Union. Matt agreed when Lincoln simplified the problem by stating that the South thought slavery was right, while the North thought it was wrong. That was the difference between the United States and the Confederacy. The Civil War started in April 1861. The political differences were so closely related to the amorality of slavery that Matt wanted to be involved. The Emancipation Proclamation, enacted in January 1863, opened a floodgate for rage. By that time, Matt's rage was lurking somewhere inside him.

Matt followed news about the war closely, starting with the Confederates' attack on Fort Sumter in April 1861. Matt felt strongly enough about the moral aspects of the war to put his rage to work and fight in the war. As a professional negotiator and mediator, Matt knew how to examine the economic side of problems. The South depended on slavery for an economic advantage. The North was accustomed to putting immigrants to work. Businesses grew with the invasion of cheap labor from overseas.

In the summer of 1862, Matt went to the Lunch Box restaurant, as he often did. Billy, the cook, felt like an uncle to Jack after the snowstorm birth. War was an apparent conversation. Two young ruffians entered the restaurant. They heard Matt's conversation about freeing the slaves and walked over to Matt's stool.

"You have no right to dictate how southerners make money," one said.

"I do when southerners enslave people for profit," Matt said.

They pushed Matt, making him spill his coffee. Matt recognized the rage and let it take over. By the time Billy came from around the counter, the two southerners were in a heap on the floor. Matt knew Jade was worried he might join the army. News of the fight got out, and Matt was considered a hero for beating the boys from the South.

Captain Hiram Smith was recruiting a United States regiment. Matt enlisted in the 140th Infantry, known as the Rochester Racehorses. Matt was not certain what he was getting himself into. He left September 19 to serve in the Provisional Brigade, Casey's Division, Defenses of Washington.

Jade had been right to worry that Matt would go fight. However, Matt was one of the lucky ones. He returned unscathed in June of 1865. The war had been hell.

Matt did not take time to write to Jade that he was coming home. He simply showed up one afternoon while Michael was fishing with Jack and little Karl. Jade was home alone. They never made it to the bedroom. Nine months later, in February 1869, Ross Donahee was born. Ross was a sign that the war was over and that Matt had a good life.

Matt went back to work for New York Central in his old job as a negotiator and contract writer. His stock had fallen in value during the war, but it increased steadily after the war. Matt never discussed his wartime quest, but he was proud of his part in the war. Still, Jade recognized that his rage was only concealed. The assassination of Abraham Lincoln weighed heavily on Matt's mind. Again, Matt had to struggle with his rage.

With three sons—Jack, age seventeen; Karl, age twelve; and Ross, age two—Matt and Jade were thinking about grandchildren when Jade gave birth to a little girl. Lydia Donahee was born in January 1871. Jade was forty years old and had an easy birth. Matt thought she was getting too old to care for another child. Jade was so thrilled to have a daughter that she surprised Matt when she found a new energy in caring for her little girl. Lydia's brothers were protective of her, especially Ross.

Jack went to work for the railroad. With a little pull from Matt, Jack became a railroad engineer. Karl hung around the docks on the Genesee River after school. He always had his fishing pole with him. Ross was Lydia's best friend and always reflected her best interest. Ross would see that no harm ever came to Lydia.

In 1878, Matt's oldest boys were showing signs of success. Jack was engineering the train from Rochester to Hilton and west to Yates and beyond. Karl was interested in anything mechanical and went to work for William Kidd and Company, building steam engines. Lydia begged Matt to take her on Jack's train, and finally, he agreed. Matt and Jade decided it would be a fun adventure for Ross and Lydia. The trip was from the State Street railroad station to Niagara Falls and back. It would be an all-day trip.

"Ho!"

Matt was proud when his son Jack yelled as the train started to roll. There were several freight cars and only one car for passengers. The train followed Lake Ontario to the west but was far enough away that Lydia and Ross could not see the lake, but they could smell the lake air. Matt enjoyed seeing his younger children excited as the train moved slowly and crossed several trestles. Jade had packed some food for the trip, and when the train stopped in Hilton, the Donahee family got off and enjoyed some dried beef. The best part of the snack was the bunch of cherries Matt bought at a market next to the railroad.

Matt imagined what kind of a man Ross would become. Ross enjoyed watching workers unload wood barrels made by Lovecraft in Rochester. Then cherries and peaches were loaded into the boxcars. Lydia was looking for the lake. Matt asked Jack where the best place to see the lake was, and he said at Yates, one could see a sliver of the dark blue water. Travel from Carlton would be easy, but the Oak Orchard River was noted for rattlesnakes, especially at its mouth. North of Carlton was probably not a good area to take the children.

The train was about a mile from the town of Yates, when the smell of something burning filled the passenger car. The steam whistles blew as the train came to a halt. Jack and his crew carried canisters to a spot on the train where a brake had caught on fire. Matt, his family, and a half dozen other passengers got off the train to watch the excitement.

The train would need to stay still for a while until the wheels cooled down. One of the passengers decided to walk the mile to the Yates train station. Some other passengers thought that was a good idea and followed. Matt told Ross and Lydia that it was too far for their mother to walk. Jade looked at Matt and wanted to race him to the station, but she realized he was the one who was too tired to walk.

Matt waited patiently until Jack got the train moving, and they got to Yates right after the walking passengers. A large farm wagon brought a load of grain to the railroad station. The farmer heard Lydia's desire to see the lake and offered to take Matt and his family to see the Yates Pier. Jack had to work on the burned wheel and brake. Matt figured there was plenty of time to go see the lake before the train was fixed.

Matt, Jade, Ross, and seven-year-old Lydia climbed onto the empty buckboard to make the trip to Lake Ontario. A mile north of Yates was a pier that extended out 275 feet into the lake. Matt did not understand Lydia's desire to see the lake, as she had seen it several times from the Rochester Pier.

The driver yelled, "Hold on!"

The horse reared up and nearly broke away from the buckboard. Matt grabbed Lydia just in time, but Ross rolled off the back of the buckboard. When Matt saw what had startled the horse, he handed Lydia to Jade and jumped from the fast-moving buckboard. The bear that had scared the horse was on its hind legs and looking down at Ross.

Matt ran to Ross, scooped him up, and set him on the edge of the road. Matt turned to face the bear. He'd quit carrying his gun after the Civil War. His knife was in a drawer at home. He clenched his fists, because that was all he had. The bear was tall on its hind legs and looked down at Matt. Matt smelled the bear's breath as he was moving from side to side, getting ready for a fight. Fear for the safety of his son replaced his old rage. The bear must have sensed no danger from this puny little human, because it turned around and, on all fours, walked slowly into the woods.

"You're the most courageous of fathers," Ross said.

"Wouldn't have been my first fight with a bear."

Matt thought that if the rage had come, he surely would have attacked the bear—and lost the fight. Matt took his nine-year-old son by the hand and escorted the lad back to the buckboard. The driver had the horse calmed down. Jade looked at Matt with admiration, hugged Ross, and smiled at Matt. Lydia was telling everyone that she thought the bear was cute.

Jade enjoyed the green trees and golden wheat fields. Now the tree lines seemed to have eyes. Matt had the family compete to see who could see the animals first. They saw a red-tailed hawk, a bobcat, some raccoons, a deer, and various other wild animals. Jade was still holding Lydia, but she was standing so Lydia could see more. Then Lydia started chanting, "I see the lake! I see the lake!"

Matt and Ross were quick to look in front of the horse. Lake Ontario was right in front of them. A fresh, cool breeze from Canada filled their nostrils. Strangely, there were people around, doing everything or nothing. The farmer got off the buckboard and helped Lydia and Ross off the back. He offered a hand to Jade, who accepted it gratefully. Matt was a little slow in sliding off the back. He was embarrassed by the soreness he felt from jumping off a moving buckboard.

"Name's Bob," the farmer said.

"Matt Donahee. Thanks for bringing my family here."

"I want to shake the hand of a man willing to go fisticuffs with a bear."

"Twern't nothin," Matt said in some strange old Irish accent. He wondered where it came from, but it sounded tough. At fifty-three years old, Matt did not feel quite so tough. Then, with a touch of honesty, he said, "Too old to run! Had to fight."

They had a good laugh. The farmer went into the Botsford Customs and Café for a drink, while Matt joined his family at Gilbert's Pier. Several men were loading a large sailing barge with lumber. At the far end of the pier were men fishing. Matt felt guilty that they'd left Jade's father at home. He had not felt up to the trip.

Lydia wanted Matt to let her watch the men clear land

near the pier. Matt learned they were going to build a vacation hotel there: the Shadigee Hotel. Lydia liked the name and kept repeating it. The large oak trees were being dragged back to Yates to a water-powered mill to be turned into usable lumber. Lydia said, "I'm going to come back and stay at the Shadigee Hotel when it's finished."

"That sounds enjoyable."

Matt thought of Jade when he said that. He led Lydia back to where Jade and Ross had found a spot on the shoreline to watch the activity. Ross and Lydia took off their shoes and played at the edge of the water. Farmer Bob came back and told Matt that he had to get back to his farm. They climbed into his buckboard and headed back to the railroad in Yates. They said their goodbyes and boarded the train for Niagara Falls.

Matt watched Lydia and Ross as they snuggled next to Jade and fell asleep. It was dark outside, but the sky was full of bright stars. Staring at the guiding North Star out the window, Matt fell asleep as well. He dreamed that heaven was Shadigee and that he lived there with his family forever. Matt's dream ended when he woke up as the train stopped at the Niagara Falls station. Passengers got off the train, and more got on for the trip back to Rochester. Matt proudly stood with his son Jack as freight was unloaded and loaded.

"Ho!" yelled Jack, and the train headed out and turned back toward the east.

Ross poked Matt when the train stopped at Yates, waking him. Matt woke from a dream and thought the bear, wearing a Confederate uniform, was looking in his window. He hugged Ross and realized he'd been having a nightmare. Jade was awake and cuddling the sleeping Lydia in her arms. Matt got off the train with Ross and had enough time for a visit to the outhouse.

The train moved on, and despite Matt's warning, Ross's voice woke Lydia. The sun rose and shined in Matt's face just before the train stopped in Hilton. Lydia wanted to get out to see the falls. She did not understand that the train had moved all night while she'd slept. Matt heard that Salmon Creek ran through Hilton. A short walk from the railroad station was a gristmill on a small waterfall.

Near the gristmill was a bakery. Matt thought that bread had a unique and appealing smell in that quaint little town. Jade bought fresh, warm bread to take home. Matt bought cherry tarts for Ross and Lydia. Matt and Jade ate a new light cake made with baking powder. Jade never used baking powder at home. Matt suggested she should from that day forward.

The train ride to Rochester was comfortable with the passenger car's windows open. Jack was off for two days before making the two-day run again. He told Matt that he was looking for a house and making preparations for his wedding to Felicity Flynn. Ross was afraid Jack would move too far away, but Jack assured Ross that he would be close to home. Hearing that made Matt smile.

Matt hitched his horse to the carriage and was happy that there were no bears in Rochester. They left for Maplewood. Jade had become proficient in driving the carriage, and she insisted on driving home. Matt rode with Ross in the back, while Lydia, proud of her mother, rode up front next to Jade.

Jade pulled the carriage up to the stable. Matt was surprised that Jade's father did not come outside. Michael always greeted the carriage and tended to the horse when they came home. Jade left Matt to bring in the children and the bread and fruit they'd bought on the trip. Jade's father was in bed and having trouble breathing. Matt left to get his old friend Dr. Goldman.

The doctor had patients in his office and told Matt he would be at Maplewood in an hour. Matt hurried back and told Jade the doctor was coming. He went to Michael's room and found Michael sitting up with his pants and a clean shirt on. Matt helped him put his shoes on. Michael insisted on going to the living room. Matt helped Michael, with Jade reprimanding them both. Michael told Jade to relax.

Dr. Goldman examined Michael carefully. He told Michael to get as much rest as possible. Matt walked the doctor to his carriage. The doctor told Matt that Michael's heart was failing him. Matt's own heart sank when the doctor told him that Michael would only last maybe a day or a week; it was hard to tell. The doctor promised to stop by on his way home tomorrow. Matt thanked the doctor.

Matt helped Jade put the children and Michael to bed. Matt and Jade sat on the front porch to talk about her father. Michael did not have much time left in the world. Jade and Matt told stories of her father. He'd lived a good life and been an important part of Matt's family.

Two weeks later, Matt came home from the railroad and found Jade in the arms of Dr. Goldman. She was crying too much to talk.

Dr. Goldman looked at Matt. "Michael died peacefully."

Michael Malloy was buried in Sepulchre Cemetery next to his wife. They were together again at their old home. Michael had donated his land to the cemetery after his house burned down. Ken Webster was at Matt's side, while Emma helped with Lydia and Ross. Jack and Karl seemed to remember stories that shocked Matt. Michael had been good to his grandchildren, but it seemed he'd liked to take them on fishing trips in dangerous and secret places. Matt figured the memories were a good thing.

Matt held Jade all night. Even without intercourse, it was the most intimate night he could remember. Matt woke in the morning to the smell of freshly brewed coffee. Jade was already up and dressed. She was in the kitchen, fixing breakfast before Jack and Karl left for work. Her sons were hardworking, complacent, well-mannered men. She was glad they reminded her of her father. Matt thought of his own father and brothers. His sons were complacent like his father, and they lacked the fight that he and his brothers had needed to build successful lives in the United States of America. Still, Matt was proud of his boys and knew they would do well enough.

ROSS DONAHEE

Ross walked Lydia home from school at Saint Patrick's Catholic Church every day. On Monday, they took a shortcut down the alley behind the schoolhouse. Two sixth-grade boys stepped out in front of them and started harassing Lydia. Ross was in the fourth grade, and he thought of his father's readiness to fight a bear. Ross was going to make his father proud. He clenched his fists and stood the way his older brothers had taught him.

Eddie Panchen was a full head taller than Ross, as was his partner in crime, Tom. Eddie laughed at Ross, calling him a runt. Ross had learned to fight for fun with his brothers, and they were much taller than these two boys. Ross stepped inside the reach of Eddie and hit him fast with six short jabs. Eddie stepped back and took a right hook in the eye that knocked him back so fast that he fell over backward. Tom charged Ross, knocking him down on the gravel. Ross rapidly threw a leg over Tom and escaped his grip. Ross stood over Tom and said, "Get up, and fight like a man."

Tom did. Ross went inside with quick jabs and was able to easily block Tom's fists. A left uppercut knocked Tom over Eddie while Eddie was getting up. The sixth graders were left lying on the ground.

"Ready for more?" Ross asked.

The boys looked at Ross's readiness and confidence, which caused the two harassers to get up and run away. Ross turned to Lydia.

"Mom's gonna kill you for fighting," she said.

"Mom doesn't have to know."

"How ya goin' to explain those cuts on your face?"

Neither of the boys had landed a punch on Ross, but he'd gotten cut when he hit the gravel. Ross would tell his mother the truth: he'd fallen in the gravel on his way home.

Lydia was done teasing Ross and slipped her hand around his arm. "My hero!"

They walked home quietly. Ross did not feel rage, as his father Matt did. Instead, he felt a new emotion. Ross was proud. He'd fought with the skill that his brothers had taught him and the courage that his father had demonstrated on the bear. Jade cleaned Ross's cuts and seemed to believe his story about falling in the gravel while racing Lydia. Ross was relieved that he got away with his story.

At dinner that night, Karl asked, "What does the other guy look like?"

Lydia did not give Ross a chance to answer. "There were two of them, and they were sixth graders."

The dinner table got quiet. Ross looked at his father. Mathew Donahee was gleaming with pride, but he kept his mouth shut. Karl congratulated Ross. Jade sent Ross to his room.

"You'd better not be smiling," Jade said to Matt.

Matt tried to hide his elation. "Of course not. I'll deal with him after dinner."

Karl was smiling at his father, but he stopped when Jade looked at him. Lydia felt guilty that her big brother was in trouble for protecting her. Lydia asked to be excused from dinner to do homework. Jade did not wait for Matt to answer; she told Lydia to go do her homework, knowing and angry that she had not gotten the truth from her children.

Matt took his belt off on his way up the stairs. Jade finally smiled. Matt went into Ross's room. Ross saw the belt in his father's hand and stood up to bend over and assume the position.

Matt told Ross to sit on the bed. Matt sat next to his son and asked if there had been any way to avoid the fight. Father was proud of his son, but Jade was waiting. Matt whipped the bed with his belt while Ross pretended to yell out in pain.

Ross had a busy evening. Jade delivered a mother's wrath on the evil of fighting. Karl came by to hear about the fight. Lydia came to apologize for Ross's whipping. Ross felt loved and respected. Ross was becoming a man.

Tuesday morning, Ross's cuts were hardly visible. The school had two classrooms. Ross was in the same room as Eddie and Tom. When the teacher saw the black eyes and bruises on Eddie and Tom, she questioned them as to how they'd gotten their injuries. Ross thought he was going to be in trouble, but the boys explained that they'd fallen out of a tree. Ross was relieved. Ross and Lydia would never have to worry about older boys harassing them again.

Ross got a job working for John Boyd Jr. at Lake View Spring Ice and Cider Manufacturing on Lake Avenue. He and another ten-year-old shoveled sawdust onto large squares of ice cut from the lake and nearby river. The sawdust acted as an insulator to keep the ice from melting in the spring. The icehouse was nearly full, but much of the cut ice was loaded onto ships and sent to other parts of the world that did not freeze the way Rochester did.

Ross worked at Lake View part-time in the winters and full-time in the summers. Ross developed massive arms and enormous strength by the time he finished the sixth grade. Ross had less time for Lydia. She began playing with a neighbor girl called Trina Kelly. Lydia and Trina started teasing Ross because of his large arms. Ross loved his little sister and accepted the teasing without recourse.

One day Ross was cutting ice on Braddock Bay. There were

eight men cutting the ice and three teams of two men each dragging the ice blocks to load onto carts to take back to the icehouse. It was February 1885. When Ross and his coworkers started cutting at six in the morning, there was no wind, and the temperature was fifteen degrees. By noon, the air temperature had reached sixty degrees, which made cutting ice a wet and grueling chore.

The sound the ice made when it cracked was louder than thunder. West Creek and Salmon Creek joined together a mile inland of the bay. The warm air and sunshine brought water from melting snow under the ice, making the ice float upward and cracking the ice along the shore. The men dragging the ice put wood planks down to strengthen the area where they dragged the ice.

Ross and the cutters continued cutting until a five-foot stream replaced the east side of the floating ice. The ice became too dangerous to work on. The workers decided to quit cutting early and go back to the icehouse to stack the large squares of ice. When Ross started across the plank over the water, the ice where the plank rested gave way. Ross slid back toward deep water and under the ice.

Ross was wearing a safety line so the others could pull him out of the water in case he fell in. Ross's line got caught in a crack in the ice, and his crew pulled until the rope line broke. Ross was trapped under the ice. The water was frigid, and Ross was losing feeling and cognitive ability. Ross found himself lying on the lake bottom, looking up. He thought about fishing with his grandfather.

A voice in his head told him to move. He looked at the footprints in the slushy ice above him. He followed the footprints and found the edge of the ice. He saw figures of men through the water. He swam for the figures. His coworkers pulled him out and removed his wet clothes. Ross stopped shaking and became unconscious. The crew wrapped a canvas ice-wrapping blanket around him. Ross's home was closer than the icehouse. They delivered Ross home unconscious and white.

Jade had the crew put him in front of the fireplace and sent the crew for the doctor. Lydia was working at the Henry Likly Brass and Trunk Company as a bookkeeper. Ross woke up to find that someone had placed heated rocks under his blanket. His mother and Lydia were asleep in living room chairs. Trina was awake, tending to the hot rocks and holding a warm towel on his forehead.

"What's happening? Why am I here?"

His voice quickly woke Lydia, who woke her mother. The doctor and Ross's father came in from the kitchen. Ross could smell cigars. Everyone started talking at once. The doctor quieted all and asked Ross a series of questions. Ross thought the questions were trivial but answered them anyway. The doctor announced, "He's going to be all right."

Ross thought his mother looked older than he remembered. So did Trina. Ross felt well enough to go to work the next day, but he enjoyed Trina's caring for him and decided he needed another day to recover. Ross would fall asleep thinking about his close call with death but wake up thinking about Trina. While Ross slept, Trina sat in a chair and read a book. Ross was embarrassed because he would wake sexually aroused.

That afternoon, Ross was getting house fever and had to get outside despite the fact that cold weather had returned to Rochester. Trina insisted on going with Ross. Trina reminded Ross of Lydia because she did not stop talking. He thought her voice sounded like music. Ross would be going to work the next day and knew he would miss Trina.

Trina stayed for dinner at the Donahee house that night.

Lydia insisted Ross stay home while she walked Trina home. Trina made her interest in Ross clear. She explained to Lydia that a man with arms the size of Ross's would make a good husband because his strength would allow him to work hard and therefore be a good provider.

Lydia hurried back home. The family was relaxing in the living room. Water was heating on the kitchen woodstove.

Lydia looked at Ross. "Ross, why don't you come to the kitchen and help with the dishes?"

Ross's mother looked at Ross and said, "Times are changing. Men need to learn how to help women with their chores."

Ross's father looked up at Ross and smiled. With a nod of his father's head, Ross knew he had to help with the dishes. With the Donahee children grown up, Jade was becoming active in a women's rights organization. Ross knew his father let Jade enjoy her cause for women's rights and was thankful it wasn't dangerous, as was the Underground Railroad. Jade had been taking Lydia to hear speeches on women's right to vote. Jade had been involved since she was a young woman, for almost forty years now.

In the kitchen, Ross felt guilty about his feelings for his sister's friend. He figured he was about to get a lecture from his baby sister. He did.

"Do you like Trina?"

"If it's a problem for you, I'll not see her again."

"Do you like Trina?"

"Of course I like Trina; she's your friend."

"Don't make me ask again! I can see that you like her."

"Okay! I like her much, and if that is a problem for you, I will not look at her again."

"Trina is my very best friend, but we are different. I work, and I intend to vote one day. Trina wants to dedicate her life to a husband."

Ross was a little shaken at his sister's bluntness. He liked Trina but had not thought of marriage. He was only sixteen years old.

"You are my brother, and there is no one better for my friend than you."

"So I have your blessing to court Trina?"

"Yes! And she is expecting you to meet her parents at seven o'clock on Saturday evening."

"Really?"

"Really. Get cleaned up, wear your tan shirt with the brown tie, and for goodness sakes, take her mother some flowers. Now, finish these dishes while I go talk to Mother."

Lydia left the room as if she were on a mission. Ross's father came in and reminded Ross that he never did dishes. Ross suggested his father help. Matt Donahee put on his jacket and told Ross, "I'm going out in the cold to chop wood like a man."

Matt left, laughing. Ross's thoughts turned to Trina. His pay had been going to the family to help keep Maplewood going. He did not have enough money to get married. And Trina couldn't have cared less about women's rights. Still, he was excited about seeing Trina on Saturday evening.

"Go out and help your father chop firewood."

Ross turned to his mother's stern face and was thankful to go do man's work, even though he'd just done the last dish. Lydia was right behind their mother. She seemed much older than fourteen and seemed to be pretending she was her mother. Ross was happy to be outside by the woodpile.

Ross's father had taken up smoking cigars. He never smoked inside or around Ross's mother. Matt Donahee was smoking a cigar and splitting wood. He looked up at Ross and said, "So you are growing up."

"I guess so."

Ross's father gave him a cigar. Ross tried smoking it, but after five minutes, he became so sick he could barely lift the ax. Ross sat on the woodpile next to his father and vowed never to smoke again. Ross was surprised when his father bought up the subject of sex. Ross admitted that he knew nothing about sex. Ross's father explained that sex was a gift from God that rewarded a couple for being good to each other, the church, and all of God's children. He said, "You must respect each other, and under no circumstances can you have sex before you are married."

Ross sensed a little bit of sarcasm from his father. Ross had grown up hearing his mother and father carrying on for hours in the bedroom. He'd always wondered what was so great that his parents carried on so. Ross was afraid he would not know what to do. He asked his friends at the icehouse, but he got such a variety of answers, laughter, and advice that he figured nobody knew anything about sex. He would not talk about sex again.

Saturday evening arrived. Ross did as Lydia had said: he cleaned up and went into the water closet with his father's razor. Ross had a little fur on his chin and thought it manly to cut it off. He had watched his father shave many times and was able to remove his fuzz from his chin without bleeding.

"Get rid of that thing."

Lydia's voice was demanding. Ross looked at her and realized she was staring at his trousers. He had been thinking of Trina.

"I can't. It won't go away."

Lydia ran downstairs and put on her winter coat and boots. She ran to Trina's house to warn her that Ross had physical intentions. Trina was pleased to hear that Ross was excited to see her in such a way. Trina explained to Lydia that her father was going to be with them the whole time. Trina's father had explained to Trina why men got big down there, and he'd said a woman could easily control a gentleman. If Ross was no gentleman, then Trina's father was there to prevent anything bad from happening. Lydia would be waiting for Ross to come home and would rush back to hear details.

Ross and Lydia passed each other going between Trina's and their houses. Ross had his Sunday best on, including the tan shirt, and was carrying a bouquet of fresh summer flowers that his mother had helped pick from her garden. Lydia looked him over and gave him a "Humph" before hugging him. Whatever was about to happen was out of Lydia's control. Ross was a perfect gentleman, and that was what he told Lydia when he got home.

Ross's ability to outwork any two men landed him the job of delivering blocks of ice to wealthy Rochester homes. Cold closets or iceboxes were made of wood for aesthetics. They were modern pieces of kitchen furniture that kept food cold, making it last longer. The heavy block of ice usually went in a top compartment, while the food went in a storage area under or next to the ice. Ross made regular trips to the homes with iceboxes. When cold weather came, homes did not use the ice, so Ross continued as an ice cutter during the cold season.

Ross used his experience under the ice to teach workers both safety on the ice and how to deal with the emergency of a worker who happened to find himself under the ice. Ross saved half his money while contributing the rest to his family. Ross saw Trina every Saturday evening and on Sundays for church. He remained a gentleman. It was not easy for Ross, especially when Trina tormented him so provocatively.

Trina's father allowed Ross to take Trina to a church luncheon as long as Lydia was with them. Ross took the family carriage with Lydia. Trina was ready. Ross liked her new dress and noticed she was getting larger in the bust area. Lydia saw him smile as they stopped the carriage in front of Trina, and she scolded him for the way he looked at Trina. Lydia and Trina rode together in the back of the carriage, while Ross sat alone at the reins. Ross felt like a coachman transporting important people. His sister and Trina were important people to him, so he didn't mind his role.

At the luncheon, Trina kept holding Ross's hand, causing Lydia to scold him. It seemed like a game that they played, with Lydia playing the mother and Ross and Trina playing the naughty children. However, Ross was on his best behavior. Ross's brothers, Jack and Karl, were there with their female friends. Everyone was watching each other. The Donahee boys proved to be gentlemen in the year 1885.

That summer brought two weddings to Maplewood. Ross's brother Jack was married in July to Felicity Flynn. Ross was sad when Jack and Felicity moved into their new house the night of the wedding. Ross would go over to help Jack paint and repair some areas of the house.

Karl married Gwen McKeon in August. Ross liked Gwen and was happy when Gwen moved in with Karl at Maplewood after the wedding. Karl planned on building a new house. His father offered him part of the Maplewood land, and Karl accepted.

Gwen took much of the burden of house chores from the Donahee women. Ross was confused at his mother's political activities. Jade had more time to attend and participate in the women's rights movement. She often took Lydia with her. Susan B. Anthony had spoken actively for the abolitionist movement during and before the Civil War. Anthony worked with a woman named Elizabeth Cady Stanton. The Women's State Temperance Society lobbied to the New York state legislature in 1860 to gain women's rights to own property and engage in business.

Jade's three sons, including Ross, could vote, while she and Lydia could not. The National Women's Suffrage Group brought hope for changes that would empower women to live equally with men. Ross's father treated his wife as his equal, but she never felt equality. Lydia told Ross she felt sure that such equality was soon to be achieved. Lydia often talked to Ross about the differences among their mother, herself, and her brothers' old-fashioned wives.

Ross was serious about Trina. Lydia talked with Trina about the women's political movement. Ross enjoyed the fact that Trina had a simpler outlook on life. She felt a woman must be obedient to the church, her husband, and the good of her children. When Lydia asked Trina about being obedient to her husband, Trina explained that she would be a part of something much larger than herself. She was willing to support Ross's decisions unquestioningly.

Ross knew his sister and girlfriend respected each other's different views. Lydia thought Trina's philosophy about life would certainly make life easier for her brother. Ross felt comfortable that Lydia wanted to make sure her brother treated Trina as an equal. Lydia considered Ross to be trustworthy, gentlemanly, and fair. Those qualities would allow Ross to appreciate a woman like Trina.

Ross was offered a plot of Maplewood land to build a home on when he was ready. He continued working hard and saving money. Ross would go out of his way when he saw a house being built to observe how the house was built. Ross realized he could build a house cheaply by only building the parts he needed. He could add on as his family grew.

Ross brought up his idea of building a house room by room to Trina.

Trina asked, "And whom are you building this house for?"

"Us."

"I don't remember saying yes to a proposal."

Ross turned red, showing his embarrassment. Trina giggled at his discomfort. Mr. Kelly told his daughter that it was late and time for her to go to bed. Trina was obedient and said good night to Ross. Mr. Kelly stepped outside with Ross. When he was sure Trina could not hear, Mr. Kelly asked Ross what his intentions were with his daughter. Ross explained that when he could afford a home for her, he planned on asking Mr. Kelly's permission to marry her.

"You will have my permission when I see a house being built."

"Thank you, sir. I hope to start next year."

Mr. Kelly was then free to speak candidly of Ross's plan to build the house piecemeal. He told Ross that spending the rest of his life building a house was no life for a family man. Mr. Kelly worked putting slate roofs on large buildings. He told Ross he was also a pretty fair carpenter. He told Ross to show him the plans for the construction of the house. When Ross told Mr. Kelly he had no plans yet, Mr. Kelly smiled and said, "We'll talk about that next week. Run along now."

Ross walked home and thought about the house. He thought about Trina. The quicker the house was built, the sooner he could be with Trina. He promised himself that he would not sacrifice quality work for time. He would dedicate his time away from his job at Lake View Spring Ice to building a grand house for Trina.

Ross worked ninety hours a week all winter to save enough money to build a house. He and Trina drew pictures and plans for a modest home. Ross shared his plans with his father and with Trina's father. Ross saved enough money to have the basement dug and cellar walls placed. He figured that if he did the work himself, he could build a shell with a roof.

In March 1886, Ross and Trina decided to accept their fathers' recommendations for a larger kitchen and a front and back porch. Ross was between cutting ice and delivering with the pony cart. The ground was softening after the cold Rochester winter. Ross had the area marked out for digging the basement. He borrowed his father's spade and pickax.

Two friends from the icehouse showed up with shovels. By the time the sun came up, the three workers had the ground broken for the outline of the house. Ross heard a lot of commotion coming from his father's house. He looked up and saw many carts and buckboards. Trina's father was there with a large four-horse wagon filled with something that looked like finely cut sandstone.

The next hour was chaotic as Trina's father started barking orders. Mr. Kelly brought a crew of stoneworkers who used pulley and lift systems to unload cut stone. Ross's brothers and their friends showed up at the same time. Karl had the house plans and kept measuring and remeasuring the work.

A series of wheelbarrows and planks allowed the workers to move dirt from the area where the basement was to be built. By noon, there was a giant hole in the ground where the house was going to be. Trina and Lydia brought food and water for the workers. Ross's and Trina's mothers were at the Donahee house cooking all day. They must have fed fifty workers.

After lunch, the diggers left the hole and were replaced with stoneworkers. The diggers could barely keep up moving stone to the lift systems built by the stoneworkers. They dug a ramp down to the bottom of the soon-to-be basement. The basement began to take shape. The sandstone, which came from west of the city, was a beautiful brown color. Ross thought the stone was so beautiful that a whole house built of the stone would be nice.

Many helpers left to have dinner with their families. The stoneworkers kept going by oil-lantern light. They were determined to finish the basement before the end of the day. Ross was still moving stone but at a slower pace. Building the stone foundation was similar to stacking blocks of ice but much warmer. Mr. Kelly and a handful of his workers looked over the completed foundation and basement. Ross was nervous.

For the first time that day, he thought about the expense of the basement. Ross was hoping to get the basement dug that weekend and was going to order some limestone for the foundation. Ross shared his concern with Trina's father.

"How much do I owe the stoneworkers?"

"The stone quarry owed me a favor."

"I may not have enough for the quality job they did."

"It'll cost you a cow."

"Is that a metaphor?"

Trina's father laughed, as did the nearby workers. Trina's father explained that after the house was built, Ross would have to roast an ox to feed all the men who'd helped build the house. Ross was still worried about the cost of the stone. The stoneworkers finished putting a sandstone floor on the basement. They showed Ross how to make steps where the ramp came down. The stone workers loaded up their tools and left. Ross was alone at the building site, and he fell asleep on a mound of dirt.

Ross dreamed of coming home from work to find Trina waiting for him on the front porch of the new completed house. Ross woke in a strange place. He was inside a small building. Someone had wrapped a blanket around him. Not sure where he was, Ross sat up and looked over the low wall that surrounded him. The mound of dirt was beside the wall of lumber.

Someone had piled two-inch-by-ten-inch planks neatly around him. They'd moved him from the dirt mound and put him on a makeshift bed of lumber. Ross could not figure out who had moved him or how he'd been moved without waking. He was looking at the lumber and wondering where it had come from, when Lydia's voice startled him.

"You're late for church."

Ross was in a daze and just looked at Lydia.

"Your brothers have unloaded your lumber and are dressed for church, and look at you."

"What's wrong with me?"

"You're covered with mud, your clothes are a mess, and you smell."

Ross held out his arms and asked Lydia for a hug. He chased Lydia all the way home, threating to hug her. Lydia was screaming. Ross's parents were boarding their carriage to go to church. Lydia climbed onto the carriage and said, "Mother, help me! I'm being chased by a wild pig."

"Stop acting like children! Both of you."

Ross stopped by the carriage. "I just wanted to give my little sister a hug."

"Lydia, give your brother a hug."

Matt Donahee yelled, "Go!" and the horse separated the grown siblings. Ross was left standing in the yard, dripping with mud and holding his arms out. He knew his sister was smiling. Ross's mother was a stern woman, but she had a sense of humor. Ross went to the house to clean up. He seldom missed going to church with Trina and hoped she would understand his absence that morning.

A WOMAN'S WRATH

Trina was sitting on her front porch, waiting for Ross. Ross had figured she'd gone to church with her father, but he'd been wrong. Ross cleaned up and put work clothes on. He planned on going to work on his house. A little knock on the front door startled Ross. Trina had her Sunday best on, but her face was, well, ugly.

"I've been waiting for you."

"I fell asleep at the work site."

"That's no excuse."

"Everything I do I do for you. You are all I think about."

Ross wrapped his big arms around Trina. He drew her into him and kissed her lips. Trina melted in his arms and kissed him back. Ross was ready to take her right there on the front porch. Trina pushed him away and ran. Ross chased her with his arms out. He stopped chasing and watched her run away. It was the second time in an hour and in Ross's life that he'd chased a woman—his sister for fun and Trina out of frustration. Ross put his arms down and went to work on the house.

Ross went to the new foundation for his house. He studied the new plans his father had drawn for the three-bedroom house. The foundation and basement walls had to be level and meet specific measurements. Ross's family came home from church. Ross's brothers started putting the first-floor joists in place.

Ross had saved $1,100 to start building the house. He talked to his father about the foundation and tried to figure how much more he could build before he ran out of money. Ross's father told him not to worry about the cost; he would hold a note so that the house could be completed.

Ken Webster came to the Donahee house with Emma and their children. He brought a man from the railroad station. Ross's father looked at the stranger.

"Come meet your uncle from Boston," Matt said.

Ross knew he had relatives in Boston, but he'd never met them.

"I came early to make sure the foundation is laid properly to the specifications that I sent you." Ryan said.

Ross was introduced to his uncle Ryan Donahee. Professional greetings and firm handshakes were passed around. Ken helped unload some large trunks and take them inside the Donahee house. Karl came from the building site. He was introduced to his uncle Ryan. Ryan opened his trunk and removed some tools. Ross led them to the foundation. Ross learned that Karl and Ryan had been writing to each other since Ryan had bought a steam engine to run his sawmill. Ross helped Uncle Ryan spend an hour measuring and inspecting the foundation.

Ross's brothers had the joists in place and had started nailing them together. Ryan had them stop and told them to make double joists at the east and west ends. Ross and his brothers discovered that their uncle Ryan knew a lot about building houses.

Joists were in place, and there was nothing more they could do. They went to the house for supper. Ross learned that his brother and uncle were collaborating on building a house for Karl. Uncle Ryan explained that Donahee Brothers Construction was experimenting with a new way to build homes.

Plans had been carefully made, and he'd written a sixty-page instruction book so that anyone who could use a hammer could build a home. All the material had been cut at the mill in Boston to specifications. Windows and doors had been constructed at the shop in Boston. The house kit had everything needed to build a house, including the nails. The foundation and joists had not been included in the kit, because the cost to ship those items on the railroad was too high. Still, everything else was there. Ross's house was ready to ship.

Uncle Ryan explained what would be needed as far as carpentry work, framers, flooring, and roofing. They drew a time table that showed the house could be assembled in less than a month. Uncle Ryan would go back to Boston after spending some time with his brother and family. His son, Ross's cousin Frederick, would come with the house kit, as he called it.

Frederick would evaluate the construction to make sure it was done correctly and that the kit houses were practical. Ross was grateful. Matt and Ryan Donahee sat on the front porch and smoked cigars and talked well into the night. Uncle Ryan left the next morning with Ross's father. He took a train back to Boston. Jack made arrangements for the boxcar to be left by the wharf on the Genesee River. That would be the closest place to unload Ross's house kit.

Monday, after work, Ross went to see Trina to give her the good news. She was too busy to see him. Trina's father sat on the front porch with Ross. They talked about the kit house and the fact that the home should be finished by September. Ross finally said, "I would like your permission to marry Trina, if she'll have me."

"You have my blessings."

The front door flew open, and Trina ran out. She flung her arms around Ross. They kissed as Ross lifted her off her feet. When he put her down, she turned back toward the front door and told Ross she was still mad at him. She went inside and slammed the door. She did not say yes and left Ross confused. Trina's father said, "Women! You sure you want her?"

"Yes, sir."

Ross walked home. The boxcar came on Friday. Frederick interviewed friends and workers and started organizing the construction. On Saturday morning, a parade of men and various borrowed horse carts unloaded the house kit. Frederick organized the layout of the materials. By Saturday night, the walls were built on both the first and second floors. Trina was in Lydia's bedroom, watching out her window. She was still mad at Ross for not picking her up for church last Sunday.

The following Sunday morning, Ross showed up with a bouquet of flowers. Trina opened the door.

"Love of my life, I know I am not worthy. I beg for your forgiveness," he said.

"Yes."

"Yes, I'm forgiven?"

"No! You're not forgiven. Yes, I will marry you."

The Donahee house was full with all the family there, including Cousin Frederick. Lydia egged Ross on about not being forgiven by Trina. Finally, Trina felt sorry for Ross and said he was forgiven. After all, he was only trying to make a life for her. Monday morning was a return to normalcy. The Donahee men and Lydia went to work. Frederick had chosen some good construction men and continued building the house.

People from all over Rochester heard about the kit house being built at Maplewood and came to see the construction. Cutting boards was a time-consuming part of building a house. Because all the wood had been cut at the sawmill, the house was ready for the roof in three weeks. Trina's father and Frederick orchestrated the laying of a slate roof. The house was painted tan with white trim. It was time for Ross to pay. Ross's father paid all the bills. Ross worked out the payments. Frederick gave a huge discount because it was a new concept in house building. "A successful concept," Frederick admitted with a sense of pride.

The cow was agreed on with Ross's helpers. A Sunday afternoon in late July was set aside for the house-building party. Cousin Frederick went back to Boston but promised to come back for the party. He would bring his father, Ryan, and his uncle Will with him. Lydia and Trina started making arrangements. One of Ross's ice customers offered to bring two kegs of beer. Mathius Kondolf owned the new Genesee Brewery in Rochester.

An ox was donated by a Hilton farmer who of course wanted to see the house. Ross had to build a fire pit large enough to hold the enormous beast. Karl had some friends at William Kid and Company build a spit to hold and turn the cow. Ross's father readied the cow. He remembered how to butcher a cow from his days in Cork.

Firewood was gathered, and the cow was prepared. The women busied themselves baking bread, pies, and other summer foods for the party. People brought chairs and tarps in the event of rain. The sky was blue. Ross, Jack, Karl, and Frederick stoked the fire and took turns rotating the cow on the spit. They planned on thirty hours for the cow to be cooked.

The Genesee beer was delivered on ice. People came. The cow cookers enjoyed the cold beer after turning the cow on the hot fire. Trina and her father were ready to give tours of the house. Ross's mother estimated that two hundred people showed up. The cow roast was the event of the year. Frederick sold six houses at the event.

Ross drank too much beer while he was cooking the cow. He climbed up a maple tree and fell asleep on the intersection of two branches. Trina was looking for Ross as the party was winding down. Ross's brothers told Trina he was napping by a maple tree in the back of the house. Trina understood that Ross had not slept for two days while he cooked the cow. Trina was content visiting with Lydia and meeting partygoers.

The cow and other foods were being divided up, and people wanted to say goodbye to Ross. Trina said, "I know where he is. I'll get him."

Trina went back by the maple tree and did not see Ross. She called his name. A loud thrashing noise came from above. Ross appeared on the ground in front of Trina.

"Are you all right?"

"I don't think so."

Trina called for help. Jack and Karl came. They looked Ross over and saw no broken bones. They helped him to his feet. He walked behind the tree and retched.

"Oh dear! What is wrong with him?" Trina said.

"Too much beer."

Ross's fall worried Trina. There would be time to scrutinize the situation and punish Ross later. Jack and Karl helped Ross to his new house and left him on the parlor floor, where he slept for the night. Ross's condition made Trina decide one thing for certain: there would be no beer or other alcohol at the wedding.

The next day, Ross agreed with Trina on no more drinking alcoholic beverages. Ross took the pledge. Ross thought he had a weak constitution, because he could not smoke cigars or drink alcohol. However, he had not gotten hurt falling out of the tree and was able to work hard. The wedding was being planned for early September. Ross was happy that the women took over planning his wedding. The wedding was going to be at his new house.

Ross was able to concentrate on his work at the icehouse. The Genesee River's current slowed down in late summer. Before loading his pony cart, Ross would often help load ships or railroad ice boxcars. Ross considered his coworkers his friends.

They'd helped him build his home, and they helped each other at work.

A loud popping sound precluded a block breaking loose. The workers looked up and saw the block falling toward the lubber-board. There wasn't enough time to scatter. Two men were bounced off the board and into the water. One man could swim the short distance to the wharf, where he was helped out of the river. The other worker was in trouble.

Early morning August sunshine promised a warm day in Rochester. Ice workers still wore wool jackets and smoke-dried gloves for protection from the cold ice. The worker was trying to hold on to a two-foot square block of ice to no avail. He did not know how to swim. His wet jacket was heavy and pulled him underwater. Ross was quick to remove his boots and jacket. He was glad his father had taught him and his brothers how to swim when they were young children.

Ross ran to the edge of the wharf, leaped into the air, and entered the water headfirst, swimming to the spot where he'd seen the worker go down. He remembered his experience under the ice and kept himself calm so that he would not feel the need to breathe. His ears started to hurt. He saw the worker's jacket on the bottom of the river. He realized the worker must have taken it off underwater. He was trying to survive.

Ross felt the urge to breathe but followed the bottom anyway. The visibility under the water got better. Ross figured they were away from the ship's shadow. Ross could not stay down any longer. He decided to come up for air. As he rose from the bottom, he saw his coworker lying lifelessly a few feet from him. Ross grabbed his coworker's arm and struggled to the surface.

Ross was winded and could barely swim when he reached the surface and the much-needed air. From deep inside him came the strength to pull his victim to shore. Men grabbed the drowned man and pulled him to the wharf. Ross was hanging on to a board, when he heard the man choking up water from above him. His friend was alive.

A moment later, Ross regained his breathing and his strength. He climbed up the side of the wharf with discernible strength. His coworker looked at him and said, "Where is my jacket?" Ross turned around and dove back into the water. This time, he was only underwater for seconds. Ross rose to the surface and raised the jacket into the air. Cheers filled the wharf. Ross brought the jacket to his coworker. It seemed as if getting the jacket was more of a feat to the other workers. Ross believed it was certainly a happier task.

John Boyd, Ross's boss, called him into the office. Mr. Boyd thanked Ross for his ability and his bravery and told Ross he had an assignment for him. John Boyd knew about Ross's dedication to teaching his coworkers how to survive when they fell under the ice. He asked Ross to write everything he knew about ice and water rescue so that the company could put it in a safety pamphlet. Ross had hated writing essays in school. His spelling was poor. However, he could not say no to his boss. Ross agreed to write a rescue and safety guide. Ross would work on it at home, and he thought maybe Lydia would help him, as she had in school.

Ross was still damp when he led his pony cart away from the icehouse for his deliveries. When he'd finished for the day, he went back to the icehouse to stable his pony. A newspaper writer was waiting for him. Ross was too shy to answer the newsman's questions, but his coworkers were glad to answer questions and provide a description of the morning rescue.

Ross cleaned up and walked to Trina's that night. He saw Trina every night now that they were engaged and soon to be married. Ross wanted to talk about the safety pamphlet, but Trina was engulfed with wedding plans. Ross went home.

Lydia was happy when Ross asked her to help him write the pamphlet. They talked about it for an hour. Lydia organized the parts, and Ross would write up each part one at a time. The task did not seem as daunting with Lydia's help. Ross started writing. He said nothing about the day's activities.

The next day, work went as usual for Ross. He thought about what to write when he got home. Ross's father was home when Ross arrived.

"Is there something you've forgotten to tell me?"

Ross did not know what to say or what his father was talking about. Ross's father threw a copy of the newspaper onto the table in front of Ross. Ross looked at the headline: "Ross Donahee Risks Life to Save Another."

"Oh, that's nothing," Ross said.

Ross's father was smiling, when Ross's mother spoke. "You could have drowned yourself or gotten hurt."

"Mother, I was in no danger at all."

Ross tried to read the article while his mother continued reprimanding him. Ross's father finally took the paper and proudly read the article out loud. When he'd finished, Ross's mother had to get the last word in.

"I just want my son to be safe, not a hero like his reckless father."

Ross thought of his coworkers, and for a moment, he thought of their mothers and families. They all would want their ice workers to be safe. Ross was more determined to work on his pamphlet. He hugged his mother and assured her that he would be safe. Ross's mother held on for a long time but said nothing.

Ross, with much help from Lydia, finished the four-page pamphlet, titled *Work Safe*, just before the wedding. Ross gave the work to his boss with pride. John Boyd read it in front of Ross and told him it was excellent work and was sure to save lives.

Ross used some of the money left from his saving to build the house to take Trina out to buy furniture. Trina wanted everything in the store. Ross had to limit her to a bed and a kitchen table and chairs. Other items would have to wait. The house was ready to move into. A wedding was all that was needed.

Ross's wedding was small, with just family in attendance. There was no alcohol. Ross could not wait for the gusts to leave. He had a desire that needed satisfaction. Lydia warned Ross not to hurt Trina. Ross did not understand, because he had no intention of ever hurting his wife. Still, Ross had been a gentleman for too long.

The wedding guests were hardly off the front yard when Ross grabbed Trina and carried her upstairs. Trina suggested they wait because she was scared. Ross tried kissing Trina, and she complained that he needed a shave. Ross tossed her onto the bed and pulled at her dress. Trina cried and demanded that Ross go back to his parents' house and leave her alone. Ross was frustrated, angry, and ready.

Ross went to the front porch, where he smelled his father's cigar coming from far across the field between them. He thought of the times he'd heard the commotion coming from his parents' room, which had seemed to last all night. He wondered how Lydia knew that loving could hurt. Right now, Ross was hurting. His testicles felt as if they were going to explode. Trina appeared at the door and apologized for turning him away.

Ross had not heard Trina come downstairs. She was wearing a nightgown. Ross was at a loss for words. Trina suggested they go to bed and try tomorrow. Ross went to bed. He did not touch or look at Trina. After a few minutes, Trina told Ross not to move. She reached over and touched him. Trina was an only child with no brothers. She told Ross that she had never seen a man down there. Trina reiterated that Ross not move, especially his hands, which had groped her fervently earlier. Trina ran her hand down Ross's stomach and slid her hand into his pants.

"You're ready."

"I've been ready since the first time I saw you."

"Don't move!"

Trina pulled her nightgown up and got on top of Ross. Ross was trembling with anticipation. Trina held him in her hand and eased him inside her. She started moving slowly. Ross tried not to move. Trina was starting to like the way it felt.

"Why is it so soft?" she asked suddenly.

Ross was sound asleep. Trina got off and wondered what was so wet. Trina could not fall asleep, so she dressed and went for a walk. Karl and his wife, Gwen, were out for a walk and saw Trina before Trina could hide. Gwen sent Karl home and asked Trina to walk with her. Trina was too embarrassed to deliberate on her wedding night, but Gwen understood and started asking questions that showed great insight.

Gwen told Trina that a man needed instructions, or lovemaking would be a painful chore for a woman. Trina revealed how she'd gotten on top and what had happened. Gwen seemed stunned at the thought of the woman on top. Gwen suggested Trina try it again but not be angry if Ross lost control and took over. Trina went home.

After Sunday Mass at Saint Patrick's Church, Trina and Gwen talked as if they were best friends. They seemed happy. Karl told Ross that he hoped his first night with Trina had been good. Karl mentioned that last night had been unusually great for him. Sunday dinner at the Donahee house was hurried. It seemed all the boys had things to do. Ross's parents, Matt and Jade, wanted to take a nap. Love was copious.

Ross's younger sister was alone. Lydia decided to take the horse and carriage out, something she never did alone. Most of her family outings were near Lake Ontario. She remembered how her father had taken her brothers to the beach and taught them how to swim. Lydia found herself at Lakeside Beach. Lakeside Beach was different. The railroad had bought the land around the beach two years ago and constructed a boardwalk and an amusement park. Lydia decided to walk the boardwalk. She spent some time at a sideshow called Japanese Village. The show made her think about parts of the world she would never see. Lakeside Beach was becoming a wild and rowdy place.

Ross saw Lydia come home with the carriage. He met her at the stable and helped put the horse up. They talked about how the world was changing and how she was never allowed to swim at the beach because she was a girl. Ross would have done anything for his sister, but he had no idea how to deal with those types of social unfairness. He brought Lydia to his home, thinking that maybe a visit with Trina would cheer her up.

Lydia noticed that Trina was walking strangely. She jumped to the conclusion that Ross had hurt her. Trina assured Lydia that she was fine and that Ross was the one who was hurting. Trina and Lydia talked for hours. Lydia was smart, but her sex education had consisted of bits and pieces of conversations. Lydia knew much more when she left. She ascertained that she would never get married.

Ross was outside raking leaves and preparing the house for winter.

Lydia finally left the house. She could not look at Ross, knowing what he was doing to her friend, even though Trina liked it. Ross hollered goodbye to Lydia. She kept walking, and Ross thought he heard pig sounds coming from his little sister. Ross went inside. Trina was nowhere in sight. He called her name, and there was no answer. Ross went upstairs and found Trina in bed.

"You need more practice." Trina was provocative.

Ross responded.

Lydia was with Trina almost every evening. Trina was a good wife and a good cook. Ross came home from work and found Trina serving coffee to Lydia, Gwen, and Ross's mother. No one seemed to hear Ross state that he was going outside to shovel snow. Of course, it wasn't snowing yet, but the nights were getting cold. Ross's father and brother were probably on the porch, smoking cigars. Ross wanted to avoid the smell of cigar smoke.

Ross walked north on Lake Avenue. He had his health, a good job that he enjoyed, and a wife he adored. Ross thought about Lydia. She was smart and had a job but had no interest in finding a husband. Ross knew several good men, but none was good enough for his sister.

Ross watched his shadow get longer and then shorter as he walked by the gaslit areas. On the other side of the Genesee River, the streetlights were powered by the Rochester Electric Light Company. Ross's house was lit by oil lamps. Ross enjoyed the smell of the oil and thought gas was dangerous. One of the downtown buildings had caught fire because an employee blew out the fire instead of turning the gas off. Ross rounded the corner and saw his home with the nice yellow light from the oil lamp glowing in the window. His home was safe.

Fall came and went quickly. Ross was living a good life. He wanted to get Trina a dress she'd seen in the window of Sarah Bacon's dress shop on St. Paul Street. Christmas was coming soon. Ross asked Lydia to help him at the dress shop to get the right dress and size. Lydia was happy to help.

Lydia brought a friend from work who was the same size as

Trina. Sarah Bacon fit a dress on Lydia's friend as Ross and Lydia watched. Mrs. Kelly, Trina's mother, happened by the dress shop. She saw Ross and Lydia's friend. Lydia was out of view. Word got to Trina before Ross made it home.

Ross was hungry when he got home and did not smell his dinner cooking. Trina tried to coax information from Ross as to why he was late from work. Ross planned on surprising Trina for Christmas, so he made up a story about working late at the icehouse. Trina was obviously upset and told Ross to cook his own dinner. She was going to her mother's. Trina left with a slam of the door.

Ross was hungry and did not know how to cook. He meandered next door to his father's house. His mother was serving dinner. Ross joined the family for dinner. No one asked why he was there. After dinner, Ross's father asked him why he was not home with Trina. Ross told his father that Trina was mad at him and that he did not understand why. Ross told his father that Trina had gone to her mother's house.

"You'd better go over there and fix things," Matt said.

Ross agreed, and he went to the Kellys' house. Lydia snuck out of the house without Ross seeing her. Mr. Kelly, Trina's father, made Ross sit on the front porch in the cold. Mr. Kelly joined him. Lydia came out, which surprised Ross because he'd just seen her at his father's house. Lydia bid them a good night and walked home alone. Trina came out and hugged Ross, suggesting they go home. Mr. Kelly shrugged and went back inside. Trina was excited. Trina asked Ross if he'd bought her the dress she'd been looking at. She explained, "Lydia only told Mother and me that she was with you and assured us that nothing bad was going on." Ross still wanted to surprise Trina on Christmas but did not know how to respond. Trina persisted. "Is it the pink one?"

"Maybe."

Trina held Ross's arm as they walked home. Trina had eaten dinner with her parents. She was worried that she had not fixed Ross dinner. Trina was happy that they lived so close to their families. So was Ross. The next morning, Trina was sick to her stomach. She vomited twice. Ross was worried about her when he left for work. Ross never missed work. He was anxious when he got home.

On Christmas morning, Ross gave Trina the new dress, the pink one she liked. She put it on, and it was tight in the middle. Ross said he could take it back and get it fixed. He did not know the proper term. Trina gave Ross his present. She told him she was pregnant. Ross was excited, even though he was not surprised.

Ross's wife wore the dress anyway when her parents came over for Christmas breakfast. Later that day, Ross and Trina went to Ross's parents' for Christmas dinner. Ross gave Lydia a copy of the ice-safety pamphlet his boss had professionally printed and distributed to the workers at the icehouse. The cover of the four-page pamphlet was printed on tan stock with red lettering. On the front cover was the title *Work Safe Techniques for Self and Team Rescue on the Ice and Water.* "Written by Ross and Lydia Donahee" appeared below.

Lydia was shocked at the credit Ross had given her for the pamphlet. She loved seeing her name on the cover. Lydia admitted to Ross that she'd really enjoyed transferring his ideas to words. Lydia hugged the pamphlet and then Ross. Ross's first Christmas with Trina was a magnificent day.

That winter of 1886, Ross and Lydia's safety pamphlet was credited for saving two lives in the Finger Lakes region. John Boyd sent copies of Ross's pamphlet to other ice businesses. The confidence Ross had given Lydia allowed her to volunteer to edit the church bulletin. Lydia continued the women's rights meetings and wrote some articles on women's right to vote. Trina grew.

Trina and Ross were excited about having a baby. However, they were both worried about the process. Trina was big, uncomfortable, and exhausted from walking to and from the outhouse. Ross was working longer hours now that the summer season had brought a large demand for ice. Trina's mother checked in on Trina during the day, and Lydia stopped by on her way home in the evenings.

Lydia and her mother, Jade, went to a Sunday women's meeting while Ross stayed home with Trina. Mary Dickinson had been a member of the first class of Rochester General Hospital's School of Nursing in 1883, just three years ago. Hearing that Ross's wife, Trina, was past her due time, Miss Dickinson suggested she look into the program the Sisters of Charity had organized at Saint Mary's Hospital on West Main Street.

Lydia and her mother stopped at Ross's house after the meeting. Ross was beside himself. He'd brought over his sister-in-law Gwen, who was also pregnant. Gwen was cleaning Trina's blood when Lydia and her mother got to the house. Trina was bleeding but was not ready to give birth. The women sent Ross to get his father's carriage.

Ross, Karl, and their father came with the carriage. Trina was able to get up and walk. Ross drove the carriage with his mother holding Trina in the back and Lydia up front with Ross. Ross's brother and father walked down Lake Avenue and rode the omnibus to Main Street. The hospital had a large waiting area, where the Donahee family waited while Trina was being cared for.

Saint Mary's Hospital was one of the oldest hospitals in the area. The hospital had opened in 1856 and earned a grand reputation. Wounded Civil War soldiers, including Ross's boss, had been sent by railroad to Saint Mary's Hospital. The excellent staff had been able to nurse many of those soldiers back to good health. Many of those grateful men contributed monies regularly to the hospital.

Around Rochester, many of those Civil War veterans had jobs and were starting families and businesses. Rochester enjoyed a booming economy. The city and surrounding area were growing in wealth and population. That night, the Donahee family hoped the population would grow by one more.

Fortunately, Sunday night was a slow night at the hospital. There were no work-related accidents coming into the hospital. The hospital staff took Trina to a room. Ross and his family had to wait. For Ross, waiting was a hard job.

Ross paced the floor and could not relax. Karl was sitting with Gwen, holding her hand and becoming more frightened the longer they waited. Matt fell asleep while Jade and Lydia gabbed on. The nurse came out and asked for Mr. Donahee.

All three Mr. Donahees jumped up and stared at the nurse. The women stood right there with them.

"Which one of you is the father?"

Ross and his father, Matt, both answered, "I am."

The nurse looked at them intensely before looking at Ross and saying, "You have a healthy daughter."

"How is my wife?"

The nurse turned, telling Ross and his family that she would let them know shortly. An hour passed before the nurse came with any more news about Trina. She told the family that they'd been smart to bring Trina to the hospital and that Trina had some problems but would be fine. Ross was confused when the nurse asked for Lydia. Trina wanted to see Lydia. Ross and everyone else had to continue waiting.

A short time passed before Lydia came out with the nurse.

Lydia was holding a baby girl. The family checked the girl over, but before Ross could hold her, the nurse made Lydia take her back. The nurse told the new grandparents, aunts, and uncles that there was nothing they could do, and Trina needed to spend the night at the hospital.

Karl and Gwen left with Matt for home, while Jade stayed with Ross and Lydia. Lydia stayed with Trina while she slept. Ross sat with his mother. They talked about a variety of subjects until Ross's mother fell asleep. Ross was amazed at how intelligent his mother really was. He was wondering what kind of father he would be, when Lydia came out holding the baby again. Lydia, talking to the baby, said, "Odessa Donahee, this is your father."

Ross held his tiny little girl in his arms. He was terrified that he might break her, because she was such a tiny person. The nurse came out and made Lydia take the baby back to Trina. Ross asked the nurse how his wife was doing. The nurse explained that she was resting.

Ross had not been asleep long, when the nurse woke him to tell him that Trina was asking for him. Ross and his mother were escorted to a room where Trina was lying in a bed and holding Odessa. Lydia was sitting in a chair. Ross thought Trina and Odessa were beautiful together. Ross's mother held the baby. Lydia stood next to them. Ross thought about the three generations of Donahee women and how different from each other they were.

A window in the waiting area revealed that the sun was going to rise on the horizon. Ross and Lydia left their mother with Trina while they found an omnibus that would take them home. They would go to work. Ross's father was hitching the horse to the carriage. Lydia made Ross get some items for Trina so his father could leave them at the hospital. Ross's father got some items for his wife, Odessa's grandmother.

Ross got home late on Monday. Lydia was barking orders to Karl and her father. She had been to the hospital, and Trina and Odessa were ready to come home. The carriage was ready. Ross left for the hospital with Lydia. Trina was weak and needed Ross's help to climb into the carriage. Ross's mother handed Odessa to Trina. Lydia rode up front with Ross. They drove home carefully. Ross was transporting precious cargo: his family.

Ross helped Trina upstairs, and Lydia carried Odessa. Karl made a crib for Odessa in the bedroom. Lydia had her father and brother bring her bed into the other bedroom. Ross thought it was nice that his sister moved in to help, until Lydia told Ross he had to sleep in the other room. Ross came downstairs for the dinner that Trina's mother had fixed for them. Ross gave his mother a hug and walked her home. Trina needed time to fully recover. Ross's and Trina's mothers would take care of Trina and Odessa during the day while Ross worked. Lydia would be there at night.

The nurse at Saint Mary's Hospital told Ross that Trina should not have any more children. Ross loved his wife and was beside himself. A week after the birth of Odessa, Trina was feeling good. She missed sleeping with Ross. One morning, a fussing Odessa woke Lydia, who shared a bed with Trina. Trina was not in bed.

Lydia picked up Odessa and headed downstairs to find Trina. Trina was nowhere to be found. Lydia finally found Trina asleep with her with her arms entwined with Ross.

"You animal."

Lydia's voice woke Ross and Trina. Lydia placed Odessa in Trina's arms. Odessa and Trina fell back asleep. Lydia went to the other bedroom and tossed restlessly in bed. No one heard Ross leave for work that morning.

Trina's mother arrived just as Lydia was leaving for work.

Lydia was shaking her hands at the thought of work. She'd been assigned a new machine made by the gun company Remington. The machine was used to create invoices for large customer orders, but it left Lydia's hands sore. Trina and Odessa were still asleep.

A loud knock on the front door woke Trina. She came downstairs to find two deliverymen carrying a strange piece of furniture into the house. Trina's mother directed them to put it in the kitchen.

"What's this?" Trina asked.

"A gift from Ross Donahee."

The women knew what an icebox was from listening to Ross describe them, but they'd never seen one before. The icebox was a beautifully ornate piece of oak furniture that did not match the kitchen's white cupboards. Trina loved it, and her mother was jealous. Ross delivered a block of ice, which he put in the top section of the icebox.

Ross's mother saw him come home in the ice cart and hurried over to see what was wrong. Happy to see that all was well, she considered the usefulness of the icebox. Ross had to hurry on his route. Ross's mother insisted on a trip to the market. Trina readied Odessa for her first shopping trip. They bought vegetables and some lemons to make lemonade.

Lydia came home to find Trina's mother still there with her mother and Trina. They were sitting on the front porch, drinking from glasses. Lydia was tired from work but gladly accepted Odessa when Trina handed the baby to her. Trina walked into the house and came out with a glass of something to drink. Trina traded with Lydia—the baby for the drink. Lydia was stunned at the cold glass. She tasted the cold lemonade. Lydia was both relaxed and rejuvenated. She sat down, holding the lemonade and looking at it. She half finished the glass, savoring small sips, before she proclaimed, "How'd you get it so cold?"

The women simply got up and told Lydia to follow them. When they showed Lydia the gift from Ross, she thought he must have felt guilty for sleeping with Trina. Ross got a warm welcome from the women when he came home from work. He told them he'd ordered the icebox when Odessa was born so she could have fresh milk every day. Of course, Ross did not realize it would be a long time before Odessa would be weaned from her mother's milk. Still, the icebox was a welcome modern convenience. Lydia exclaimed, "Times are changing!"

Ross and Trina slept together that night with Odessa's crib next to them. They were in love. But they had to be careful. Ross did not want to lose Trina by getting her pregnant. Lydia constantly reminded her brother about what could happen if he did. Lydia continued to stay with her brother and Trina. She liked being referred to as Aunt Lydia and became close to Odessa. Trina was happy to have the help.

Trina adjusted well to her family and continued her duty as a good wife. Trina's and Ross's mothers stopped coming over so often. Trina had dinner ready for Ross and Lydia every night. Odessa was well cared for. Ross began working longer hours and even some Sundays when large conference places had special occasions.

The Rochester area grew to more than sixty-two thousand people in the 1880s. Ross had trouble guiding his pony cart through the busy streets. John Boyd hired more workers to deliver ice. As the weather cooled off that fall, many of those workers began laying stone block in fields near the icehouse.

Winter came, and workers poured water onto the blocks. The water froze fast. The workers would shovel off the snow and harvest the ice for shipment or storage. Ross was still cutting ice from lakes and rivers. Using the railroad, Ross was working farther from home and coming home later. One area was west of Carlton on Oak Orchard River. Ross would have to spend the night at the site. He missed his family when he was away, but he did not mind spending time with his coworkers and friends.

One day Ross was breaking the path cut in the ice the day before. The ice team would cut a path to the center of the river so they could cut the thicker ice from the center and float it to the shore, where a mechanical lift could pull the ice out of the water and load it onto a horse cart. Ross heard a soft snorting sound coming from behind him. An image of his father with clenched fists facing a bear entered his mind.

Ross clenched his gloved hands, jumped up, and turned to face his foe. He heard laughter from the shore as he looked down at the tiny little beaver. The furry beaver ran past Ross and disappeared in the water that Ross had just cleared.

"Ya need a gun?"

"Was that your pet?"

"Don't pee on the good ice."

Ross enjoyed the distraction while it lasted. He was reminded that the ice ponds and streams were sometimes desolate and isolated places. Ice seemed to be alive when one was working on it. Ice moved and made its own moans and other unnerving sounds as it froze or melted. The ice was moving now. Ross could tell by the water oozing up like cataracts. Violent movement of water under the ice preceded a sound much like a railroad train moving fast but with a clattering sound. No horse would have ventured onto the ice.

Ross turned his head and saw the mammoth creature charging from the opposite shore. There was no clenching of fists or time to think about a fight. The massive creature shook the ice so much that Ross bounced off the ice and onto his backside as the creature ran past him. The creature was as large as a locomotive, with giant black eyes and antlers that eight men could have hung from. The creature left indentations in the frozen ice where its hooves pounded down. Steam lifted away from the tan hide of the creature.

Ross barely had time to turn his head to see the creature run away from him toward the spot where his crew was readying the lift system. He only saw the back end of the monstrous creature disappear into the woods. As fast as the commotion had come, it was gone. So was Ross's team of ice workers.

Ross looked around the shore and hollered, "Where'd everyone go?"

Ross noticed scared workers appearing from behind trees and bushes. Bravely, Ross shouted out, "Now, that was my pet."

Ross was the only one laughing this time. He had never seen a moose before but figured that was what the creature was. Ross had not had time to be scared, but his coworkers had. No one was injured, and the creature was gone. Moose were not indigenous to the area but sometimes came onto the ice along the shore of Lake Ontario from the Adirondack Mountains. Work continued.

Ross was growing bigger and stronger. Ever since his ox roast—or cow roast, as he called it—Ross had craved beef. Unfortunately, meat, especially beef, was expensive. That night was Thursday, and Thursdays were the one night of the week when Trina cooked beef. Ross did not talk much on beef night. As he was enjoying his dinner, he wondered how moose would taste.

Several people had donated land back to the city behind Ross's house. Although that had happened years ago, Ross noticed more people clearing the land. Ross got much of his firewood from the area and often enjoyed a peaceful walk after dinner. Sometimes

Ross walked with Trina, but that cold February night, he was alone with his thoughts. The city was developing a family park in back of his house that would be called Maplewood Park. Ross figured it would be a good place for children to play.

AUNT LYDIA

R oss lived in a house with all women. Even though Odessa had just turned five years old, she was like a tiny woman. Lydia encouraged her to think freely, while Trina had her help with the household chores. Ross had been careful not to get Trina pregnant since her hard birth when Odessa was born. Ross was no longer the young man at work, and he felt weak and tired on that warm summer night.

He walked into the house after work. Lydia was reading to Odessa while Trina was fixing dinner. Ross said hello to Lydia and picked up Odessa to hug her. He put her down so Lydia could finish reading the book to her. Ross walked into the kitchen. Trina had her now old pink dress on and smiled at Ross. She looked good, and for the first time, Ross lost control.

Ross picked Trina up and threw her over his shoulder. They headed for the stairs.

"Dinner will burn," Trina said.

"This won't take long."

As Ross turned to go up the stairs, Odessa thought he was playing a game with her mother. Playfully, Ross's wife told him it had better take a while. Trina was smiling and waving bye-bye to Odessa. Lydia was on her feet, protesting to her brother. Ross did not care, because he felt he could do what he wanted as long as his wife wanted the same.

The lovemaking was quick. Ross apologized for his lack of control and told Trina he could not avoid her, because she was too beautiful. Trina put her hands on his face and kissed him passionately. Two hours later, they came down just in time to put Odessa to bed. Lydia left dinner on the table and went to bed. Ross and Trina ate cold chicken stew and soggy bread pudding. They enjoyed the cold dinner and each other.

Lydia still attended meetings for the newly formed National American Woman Suffrage Association. She met a young lawyer at one of the meetings. Zachariah Smith represented and helped write correspondence for the organization. Lydia did not agree with Trina that men needed big arms. Zachariah had a big heart and bright mind.

Zachariah started courting Lydia. Ross was insistent that he was not good enough for his sister. The courtship was slow. Zachariah worked for organizations that often required Saturday night meetings that he had to attend. Lydia said little about him to Ross. Trina told Ross to be kinder to his sister and reminded him that this was Lydia's first courtship. Ross reminded Trina that she was his first courtship. Trina yelped and ran upstairs, yelling, "No! No! Don't take me now."

Ross chased her upstairs. They were connected on their bed when they heard, "Wee! Wee! This is fun! Wee!"

Odessa had followed them upstairs. He hadn't noticed her climb onto the bed with them. When Ross and Trina heard Odessa, they stopped what they were doing and played bounce on the bed with their daughter. It was harmless fun. Lydia came home for dinner and asked Odessa what she'd done that day. Odessa told Lydia that she'd played bounce on the bed with her mommy and dad. Ross got Lydia's stern look of disapproval. Ross, Trina, and Odessa were all so happy that Lydia decided to accept the fact that she lived in a loving family. Ross believed it was okay to break the rules of society once in a while.

Later that night, Trina told Lydia that she was pregnant, so she and Ross could go wild. Lydia was shocked and asked what Ross thought of her pregnancy. Trina told Lydia that she hadn't told him. Trina was afraid he wouldn't want her anymore if she told him. Lydia made Trina promise to tell Ross about the pregnancy. She did, and Ross wanted her more.

Ross felt he was living a normal life—even better than normal. He refused to think of the possible consequences of Trina having another baby. Ross couldn't bear the thought of losing Trina, but she was already pregnant, and there was nothing he could do about it. Ross became more nervous the closer Trina got to her due date.

Arrangements were made to take Trina to the hospital before the due date. Lydia planned on taking time off from work to take care of Odessa. Ross figured they had two weeks to go until the birth, and Trina was fine. Ross left for work on a Wednesday morning. About an hour later, Trina felt labor pains starting. Trina walked with Odessa next door to her in-laws' house. Gwen was home with her four children. Trina went into labor right away. Gwen had been helping a midwife deliver babies. Trina's mother-in-law, Jade Donahee, went to Trina's mother for help. She wasn't home.

Gwen prepared the living room couch. There was no time to get Trina to a bed, let alone a hospital. Trina let out a soft cry. The front door opened, and Jade Donahee walked in just in time to see her new grandson born. Trina could not remember the birth of Odessa, but this time, it was easy. Hunter Donahee entered the world with a smile.

Lydia came home and found the house empty. She looked at her parents' house, and all looked normal. The carriage was missing, but that was usual because her father often got home later than she did. Lydia figured Trina and Odessa were next door, but that was unusual because Trina always had dinner going when Lydia got home.

Lydia knocked on the front door of her in-laws' house. Her

mother answered the door. Odessa was sitting in a chair, holding Hunter. Trina was sitting on the couch, smiling. Odessa said, "I've got a new baby brother."

Lydia looked at her and the baby. "Whose baby is it?"

Trina was grinning. She stood up and ran her hand over her stomach.

"Lord's mercy! Are you all right?" Lydia said.

Trina felt fine. She asked Lydia to go home and wait for Ross so he wouldn't be scared. Ross's mother told her she could bring Ross back for dinner. Lydia took Odessa back home to wait for Ross. Ross was late that night, and Trina was anxious to be home when he got there. Lydia's father came home and brought Trina over in the carriage. He helped her up to bed and left her in Lydia's care. Ross came home to find Lydia in the living room, reading to Odessa.

"Where is Trina?"

"Upstairs in bed."

That was all Lydia said with a smirk that she tried unsuccessfully to hide. Ross had been abstaining from his wife so he didn't hurt her before the delivery. Still, something was different. Ross did not smell dinner. He ran upstairs and opened the bedroom door. Ross's wife was holding their new baby. The baby waved his healthy little arms as if to say hello to his father.

It took awhile for Ross to understand that Trina had had an easy birth. Trina held Hunter Donahee up so his father could hold him. Ross glowed with pride that he had a son. Hunter fell asleep contentedly in Ross's loving arms. Ross sat with Trina until she fell asleep. He carefully put Hunter in Odessa's old crib and went downstairs. His mother was there with some dinner for him.

Ross was a happy man. He liked his job, his family was safe, and he was financially secure. The next night, Zachariah Smith came for dinner. One of his clients had given him a Kodak black box camera that used a new kind of film. He took photographs of Ross's family: one with Odessa holding Hunter, some with the whole family, and several of Lydia. Ross noticed that Lydia seemed to enjoy having her picture taken.

Ross appreciated Zachariah for taking the pictures, and he was eager to see them when they were developed. Lydia took Zachariah next door to take more pictures of Karl and Gwen and their children. Having a portrait painted was an expensive ordeal and well above Ross's resources. Ross was starting to accept the attorney, not just for his kindness but also because he seemed to make Lydia happy.

Zachariah had to take a hundred pictures before he could take the camera to Kodak for development. When Kodak developed the hundred pictures, they would load the camera with film for another hundred pictures to take. Ross knew George Eastman, who'd started the Kodak Company, kept Zachariah busy with legal matters.

Odessa treated Hunter much the same way Aunt Lydia treated her. When Hunter was a year old, Zachariah proposed marriage to Lydia. Lydia wanted to marry the kind and successful lawyer, but she did not want to leave Ross, and she did not wish to leave Odessa, because she felt like a second mother to her.

Ross told Lydia that she had to consider what she wanted. Ross and Trina would be forever grateful for Lydia's role in the family. She was much more than an aunt. Ross had to agree to let Lydia take Odessa once in a while before she would agree to marry Zachariah Smith.

Zachariah and Lydia had a grand wedding at Saint Patrick's Roman Catholic Church, followed by a reception at the Rochester Club Ballroom. The reception was an elegant soiree. Ross met many of Zachariah's business contacts who were in attendance, including George Eastman; John Jacob Bausch; Henry Lomb, who employed many specialized workers in the vision lens industry; and several other industrious businessmen in the Rochester area.

Lydia moved into a house in the Charlotte area, north of Rochester. It was close to Ross's home, but she felt not close enough. Lydia came to Ross's house often and would take Odessa to Ontario Beach to ride the new merry-go-round. Ross's father left the railroad because he was getting too old to negotiate deals effectively. Karl was working hard at William Kid and Company and enjoying making steam engines for drilling and farm use.

Hunter turned five years old in 1897. While Odessa loved the rides and sideshows at Ontario Beach, Hunter loved the water. Hunter made Lydia nervous when they took Hunter to the beach. Hunter had no fear of the water, even on days when the waves turned muddy and rolled along the shore, sweeping anything and anyone out into the water. On such days, Lydia would hold Hunter's hand firmly.

After four years of marriage to Zachariah, Lydia had no children of her own. She had become close to Odessa and Hunter. On one of their outings to the beach, while the water was calm and cold, Hunter and Odessa were walking on the sandy beach. Hunter saw a large fish swim along the shore. He tried to catch it.

Hunter seemed surprised when he tried to stand up and there was nothing under his feet. Zachariah, always diligent, was in the water immediately. Hunter's dark eyes looked up at Zachariah from under the surface. Hunter was smiling. Zachariah picked him up.

"It's time you learned to swim."

Lydia protested that Hunter was not old enough to learn to swim. Zachariah took Hunter out to where the water was up to his chest. With his hands firmly on Hunter, Zachariah put him in the water and told him to swim.

Hunter kept his head above water and moved his feet and hands. Zachariah let go of him, and Hunter was swimming. Zachariah told Hunter to swim toward shore. Hunter swam to the shore. He walked out of the water and ran to Odessa and bellowed out that he could swim. Hunter turned around and ran back into the water. Odessa wanted to go swimming too. Lydia was afraid to leave Hunter with Zachariah, who was freezing in the cold water with his clothes on. He seemed to enjoy watching Hunter take to the water and was vigilant in watching him.

Lydia had packed her bathing suit and Odessa's. They went to the changing room. Women had to swim with a bathing suit that covered them completely, including their ankles, feet, and arms. Lydia and Odessa emerged from the dressing room with their matching swimming suits, including hats. Lydia was envious of the fact that men had fewer restrictions. She'd learned to swim with her brothers when they were young, and they wore their undergarments.

Lydia walked ankle deep in the water with Odessa. The water was freezing. Lydia looked at Zachariah. He was pure white from the cold. Hunter was sliding through the water with ease. He swam up to Aunt Lydia and Odessa and splashed them. Odessa took off after him. They were in water too deep to stand in, with Zachariah an arm's reach away. Odessa started splashing Hunter back. Hunter dipped under the surface. Zachariah was not fast enough to catch him. Lydia came into the cold water.

Odessa let out a shriek. A moment later, Hunter emerged, laughing. Odessa swam away from Hunter, using her arms above water. Hunter watched for a moment before he put his face in the water and took off after her. Hunter was swimming like a puppy dog, but now his little arms were reaching above water and pulling him through the water quickly. Zachariah could no longer keep up by walking on the sandy bottom. He broke into a swim.

Hunter couldn't catch his sister. Odessa was too fast. They quit splashing and just swam. Zachariah was happy swimming with them, because he was warming up. Lydia was shivering uncontrollably and got out of the water. She walked along the shore, ready to jump in if needed.

Lydia wanted to go put her warm clothes on, but she was afraid to leave the children and Zachariah. The sun was out, and Lydia found herself warming. She sat on the beach and watched her husband play with his nephew and niece. She wondered whether she would ever get pregnant and give Zachariah a son.

Odessa was first to leave the water. Zachariah figured Hunter would stay in the water all day if he let him. Hunter reluctantly left the water when encouraged by Zachariah. Lydia and Odessa went to the changing room and dressed. They hung their wet bathing suits on a line outside the changing room. Zachariah got the dry clothes they'd brought for Hunter and changed him. Zachariah would have to let the sun dry his clothes while he wore them. The sun was out, and it did not take long.

Odessa and Hunter spent that night at Aunt Lydia and Uncle Zachariah's house. Zachariah fell asleep in is chair while Lydia read to Odessa and Hunter. The children were asleep soon. Lydia put them to bed and went back downstairs to get her husband. Zachariah was too tired to go up to bed. Lydia fell asleep on the couch.

The next morning, Lydia dressed the children for church and packed their weekend items. Ross and Trina were waiting outside the church when Zachariah pulled his carriage up to the parking area. The children were excited to tell their parents about their weekend with Uncle Zachariah and Aunt Lydia.

Hunter bragged about learning how to swim, while Odessa proclaimed that she could swim faster. Lydia asked Trina about her Saturday without the children. Trina just smiled.

"Where'd my brother take you on your night off?"

Trina just kept smiling.

Lydia looked at her brother. "You had a day with no children, and you did not take your wife anyplace?"

Ross just smiled. He looked at Trina, who smiled more and shrugged. Lydia thought about what a gentleman her husband was as they walked into church. Lydia and Zachariah sat with Ross and Trina, with Odessa and Hunter between them. Karl and Gwen sat with their children in front of them. Jack and Felicia sat with Lydia's parents in the front pew. Matt and Jade Donahee were proud parents and grandparents.

ODESSA AND HUNTER

O dessa would often take Hunter to the park behind their home to play. Hunter always seemed to find or attract other children to play with them. They were playing hide-and-seek one day, when Odessa let out a bloodcurdling scream. Hunter went running. Odessa was clinging to a tree branch with her feet dangling just inches above a nest of brown snakes. Other children had gathered but kept a firm distance. Hunter did not.

Hunter had seen rattlesnakes before, and at five years old, he knew the differences among several snakes. These were harmless garter snakes.

"They are harmless."

Hunter realized his words meant nothing because his sister was too scared to listen. Hunter calmly stepped into the indentation on the ground under his sister's feet. Most other children just turned and ran, but some watched as little Hunter picked up the snakes one at a time and tossed them away from his sister.

"You can come down now."

Odessa managed to pull herself up on the branch while Hunter rid the area of snakes. Hunter wished he was older so he could reach his sister and pull her down to safety. Odessa did not come down until Hunter told her that he was leaving and that when he left, the snakes would surely come back. Hunter turned and took one step, when his sister passed him, running.

Odessa was babbling about the nest of snakes. With tears running down her face, Trina, her mother, asked, "Where is Hunter?"

"Back there playing with the snakes."

Trina took off running and calling for Hunter. She saw some older children and asked whether they had seen a little five-year-old boy with a blue shirt.

"Ya mean Hunter?"

"Yes, that's his name."

"He's back by the pond with some other children."

Surprised at the children's calmness and knowledge of who Hunter was, Trina calmed a bit and headed in the direction of the pond. A larger child, probably a twelve-year-old, was running away from a group of laughing children. Hunter was standing in the middle, holding something that the others seemed interested in. When Trina was close enough, she realized Hunter was holding a snake.

Trina was a good mother. She was protective of her children. She was terrified of snakes. She told Hunter to get rid of that thing and get home right now. Hunter looked up and saw his mother backing toward the house. Hunter offered the snake to his friends, but there were no takers. He let the snake go on the ground. While the other children watched the snake slither away, Hunter turned around and walked backward like his mother. Hunter knew his mother wanted to spank him, but she was afraid to touch him, because he'd touched a snake.

When Hunter and his mother got to the house, Trina made Hunter stay outside and scrub his hands with soap and lye. Hunter and Odessa had never seen their mother so mad. Odessa tried to calm her mother down to no avail. Odessa went outside and told Hunter she was sorry she'd gotten him in trouble. She thanked Hunter for saving her from the snakes. Hunter just grinned.

When Hunter's father got home, his mother demanded Ross take Hunter upstairs for a spanking. Hunter hid when his mother met Ross at the door. Odessa was crying and begging her father not to hurt Hunter. He was a hero! Odessa gave her side of the story as Ross led his son upstairs. Ross and Trina supported each other when it came to disciplining the children. Hunter's father did not like coming home to such duress. Hunter explained what had happened. Ross told Hunter that he was proud of him and that Hunter had done the right thing. Hunter was shocked when he got the spanking anyway. Ross told Hunter that the spanking was for upsetting his mother.

Trina babied Hunter for the rest of the night. Ross let her because he was proud of his son. Odessa was angry with her father for spanking Hunter for saving her. Dinner was quiet that night. Hunter was not satisfied and was thinking of a way to get revenge on his mother.

The next morning, while Trina was cleaning up after breakfast after Hunter's father had left for work, Hunter put his plan in motion. He snuck out to the park and caught a snake. Hunter hid the slimy creature in his trouser pocket and brought it home. When he was sure his mother wasn't looking, he put the snake in her garden box, where she kept her gardening tools. Hunter waited all morning for his mother to go work in the garden.

Hunter had not shared his plan with Odessa, and she was at school. Hunter had no one to stick up for him or protect him. The whole world must have heard his mother call his name, and she looked right at the window where Hunter was peeking out at his mother. His mother never spanked him, but he knew he would have to spend the day in his room, waiting for the beating that was sure to happen when his father got home. Hunter went out the back door. His mother was right there. She pointed to her garden toolbox and asked Hunter to look inside and tell her if that snake was the poisonous kind.

Hunter did not have to look in the toolbox, because it was the garter snake he'd put there. Acting innocent, Hunter carefully walked over to the toolbox and looked inside. His little friend looked back at him.

"Nope. He's the friendly kind."

"Can you get rid of it? Take it far, far away. Please."

"Sure, Mother."

Hunter heard the back door slam as he picked up the snake. He thought he saw his mother peering out the same window he'd been watching from. Hunter carried the snake back to his playground.

Hunter did not even tell Odessa about the snake when she came home from school. He was sure his father would beat him to death when he came home from work. Hunter did not eat much for dinner. Odessa read him a story after dinner, and they went to bed. Not a word was said about the snake in the box.

The next day, after Odessa went to school, Grandpa Matt Donahee came over. He asked if he could take Hunter to the park. Hunter's mother was happy to let him go. When they were far from the house and from Trina's ears, Grandpa Donahee said, "So you put a snake in your mother's garden box."

Hunter was not going to lie and admitted his guilt to his grandfather. Grandpa Donahee laughed. They talked about the prank, and Grandpa Donahee made Hunter promise not to do it again. Hunter promised and told his grandpa that he wished he'd gotten a beating, because not talking about the prank made it worse. Grandpa explained that Hunter's parents loved him very much, and his mother was afraid that his father would beat him too severely if she told him what Hunter had done.

Hunter enjoyed his time with his grandpa. They identified different birds by their colors, shapes, and sounds. Hunter's grandpa took him out to explore nature and talk about political events around the Rochester area often. Hunter liked listening to his grandpa.

Hunter asked his grandpa about the story he'd heard about his grandpa killing a bear with a knife. Grandpa Donahee explained that killing the bear had been sad because the bear had just been protecting its territory. Hunter understood.

As the weather got colder, Grandpa took Hunter out less often. Hunter noticed that Grandpa was having trouble breathing.

Jade Donahee walked into Matt's den. Matt took out the knife that he'd hidden in his drawer for the past forty-two years. A friend had given the knife to him, and Matt had used it to kill the bear that was surely going to kill him. Matt had not thought of Stony in many years. The rest of the story was one that Matt did not want to tell his grandson. Stony had been a friend until he'd become a slave catcher before the war. Matt had shot Stony to protect his family.

Matt wrapped the knife in some brown packing paper and told Jade he wanted Hunter to have it. Matt took Jade to bed. It was the last time. Matt died peacefully in his sleep that night. He was seventy-three years old.

News of Mathew Donahue's wake was in the newspaper. Jack, Karl, Ross, and Lydia were there with their spouses and children. Hunter sat with his grandmother, who fought back tears as old friends and prominent people from the area around Rochester paid their respects to her husband. Mathew Donahee was buried at Holy Sepulchre Cemetery on Dewey Avenue in Rochester, New York.

Hunter received his grandpa's knife for Christmas. Grandma Jade told Hunter that it was the same knife his grandfather had killed the bear with. Ross made Hunter put the knife away until he was old enough to use it. Ross hoped Hunter would never actually need the knife. Jade kept busy with Gwen and all her children.

Hunter told the story about his grandpa killing the bear to all his friends and said he had the knife that had killed the bear. While the knife was safely stored in his house, Hunter often imagined running into a bear in Maplewood Park. Hunter became a popular child among children in the neighborhood. He could tell a story and make it believable—maybe because everyone had heard about the snake story and knew Hunter had no fear.

The following fall, Odessa was entering the sixth grade, and Hunter started school in the first grade. Odessa worked hard for her grades, while Hunter learned math easily. Hunter's reading was advanced because of all the time his sister, his mother, and Aunt Lydia had spent reading to him. Hunter became a good student. He was not shy. He talked to anyone from any grade, and he listened to what they would tell him.

Hunter's teacher, Sister Mary Alleluias, heard the snake story and was afraid Hunter might bring a snake to school if she was mean to him. She was not afraid of snakes but was afraid for the rest of the students if Hunter played such a prank. One day she announced that she'd brought a friend with her to school. She told the students that her friend looked scary but was really harmless and would not bite them as long as they did not scare him.

The students tried to guess what was in the box. They guessed a puppy, a cat, and even a skunk, but no one guessed right. Finally, the teacher reached into the box and slowly lifted out a beautiful four-foot-long tan milk snake with symmetrical brown markings. Students kept their distance. The teacher talked about the snake and invited the students to come pet the snake. No one volunteered.

Hunter's grandpa had showed him a milk snake when they were at a farm. The snakes were welcome at the farm because they ate rodents and small animals that could ruin the farmer's produce. Hunter asked if he could hold it. The class cheered. Sister Mary Alleluias knew the snake could bite, even though it was not poisonous. Hunter went to the snake while Sister was holding it. He held out his fist slowly in front of the snake. The snake's long forked tongue tasted his hand, but it did not bite. He carefully took the snake from Sister Mary Alleluias's hands. The snake was heavy. Hunter proved his courage and put the snake back in the box. Sister Mary Alleluias sighed in relief.

Hunter decided that nuns were special and were afraid of nothing. Hunter was not afraid of many things, but nuns were certainly one of the things he feared. Maybe that was why Hunter did so well in school. However, Hunter wanted to know more about those kind and fearless women who dressed in black.

When Hunter's teacher asked for a volunteer to help with a project, Hunter was the first to volunteer. Often, Odessa would end up helping Hunter as well. Hunter and Odessa both found joy when they were helping other people. Perhaps that was why a year after Odessa graduated from sixth grade, she began volunteering for the newly published *Catholic Journal* with her aunt Lydia. In 1898, Hunter was in second grade and saw less of Odessa. He missed her.

Because Hunter listened to people, they in turn listened to him. Hunter was developing leadership skills that helped him organize students to do good things and bad. Hunter approached all the students in the school and got them to play a practical joke on the nuns one day. The school had two classrooms, one for grades one to three and the other for grades four to six. Hunter arranged for the students to all go to the wrong classroom one morning. The plan was perfect, and everyone participated.

The nuns had heard about the prank and were ready. In the first classroom, the nun announced that they were going to the church to scrub the floors, while the other classroom got to have a picnic. The other nun announced that the other class was going on a field trip while her class stayed and scrubbed the schoolrooms. All the students were mad at Hunter. At recess, both groups merged in the schoolyard to find that the whole school was having a picnic. The cancellation of afternoon classes made Hunter a hero again.

Hunter had to stay after school and clean up the schoolyard. The nuns got him back. Hunter did not mind. He was satisfied that his prank had been a social success, and a little extra work did not bother him, especially when the nuns came out of the school and helped clean up, making the task fun.

The nuns asked Hunter what he'd learned. Hunter could not answer. He had to write his first essay on the outcome of the prank. Hunter stayed up late that night and wrote the essay. He let his mother read it. She was horrified at what Hunter had done and vowed to speak with his teacher. Hunter's essay was optimistic, because he only wrote of the good things that had happened. He even wrote that he was happy to have the opportunity to write the essay. He figured his teacher would not make him write again. He was right.

In school the next day, Hunter had to read the essay to both classrooms. The students cheered. Still, it was hard to pull a prank on the nuns. They anticipated his actions and reprimanded him after school. He received an A on his essay.

Hunter's father bought a new transportation device that interested Hunter greatly. It was a Peerless bicycle made by the Rochester Cycle Manufacturing Company. Hunter watched his father ride the bicycle to work every day. On weekends, Ross would give Hunter a ride, letting him sit on the handlebars.

Hunter loved the feeling of wind in his face. Hunter had seen bicycles before but never one with wheels the size of the ones on his father's bike. Hunter's father promised to take him to Driving Park to see bicycle races.

Hunter's grandpa had taken him to see horse races when he was little, and Lydia had taken Hunter and Odessa to see Buffalo Bill's Wild West Show when it came to Driving Park. There was talk about closing Driving Park to create a faster road into downtown Rochester, so Hunter and his father had to go soon.

A month later, a bicycle race was scheduled for Saturday. Ross made arrangements to leave work early. Hunter's mother wanted to go, and so did Lydia. The Donahee family went to the race together. Lydia drove Hunter and the rest of his family in her carriage. Hunter's father rode the bicycle.

Hunter watched several bicycle racers and spectators at the race. Ross found good seats for his family, and they waited for the race to begin. Ross excused himself for a moment and left Trina and the children with Lydia. The race was about to start, and Ross had not returned. Trina was worried and looking for him. The race began, and Hunter yelled with excitement and pointed. "There's father!"

Sure enough, Ross Donahee was in the race. Hunter counted twelve bicycles, which were racing in the first of three races. On the first curve, one of the bicycles went down. The rider violently rolled on the racetrack. Another bicycle hit the rolling rider, and his bicycle flipped over in the air. They made their way off the track with their bent and mangled bicycles. One of the riders was bent over in obvious pain, but Hunter quickly turned his eyes to his father.

The other ten bicycles slowed down until they were past the accident. Hunter's father was in third place. The race was four laps around the track. Ross passed by on the second lap and moved back to fourth place. On the curve in front of Hunter and his family, Ross seemed to outpower the other riders. He passed one rider and then another.

On the third lap, it looked as if Ross would move into first place. Ross was bigger than the other riders, and he was a powerfully strong man. On the last lap, Ross moved back into third place, and he finished the race in fourth place. Hunter was proud of his father. A second group of riders started the next race before Ross got back to his seat. Hunter was proud and did not understand why his mother was furious.

Ross was thirty years old but felt fifty after the race. Younger and smaller men were winning the races. There were three races, with twelve riders in two and eleven in the last race. A fourth race consisted of the top three winners from each race. Ross did not make it to the final race but was happy. The fourth race was intensely exciting. The bicycles were so close they looked as if they were connected. On the final lap, the second-place rider hit the first-place rider.

There was a loud sound of metal grinding as the bicycles became entwined, and the riders spewed over the track. The race continued, but the spectators were watching men bring stretchers out to the fallen riders. One was rider able to walk with some help. The other rider was not moving when they put him on the stretcher.

Ross told his family that the race was fun, but it was his first and last. Trina bellowed that it should not even have been his first. After the race, Ross went over to get his bicycle and checked on the injured rider. Several spectators looked his bicycle over and complimented him on a good race. The injured rider had a broken leg and a huge gash in his forehead. Ross knew he would not have been able to work if that had happened to him. Trina reminded him of that fact.

The Donahees loaded into Lydia's carriage, with Ross next to them on his bicycle. Ross pulled ahead of them on the way home. Hunter encouraged Lydia to drive faster. Hunter's mother looked at him and demanded that there would be no more racing for their family. Lydia drove slowly, and Hunter was quiet.

Odessa talked about her new job at Hennery Likly's Brass Company. Lydia had helped her get a job on the third floor using a Remington sewing machine to make trunks. Likly's was a big business in Rochester and employed fifty people. Lydia worked as a bookkeeper. Likly's was a good place for Hunter's aunt and sister to work.

Ross did not ride as fast as he had in the race, but he was home well before the horse carriage. Ross was cleaning and oiling his bicycle when the carriage pulled up to the house.

Hunter jumped off the carriage and ran over to his father. "Can I help?"

"Sure! Help turn it upside down, and you can oil the chain."

Hunter helped his father turn the bicycle upside down, resting it on the seat and handlebars. Hunter poured drips of oil onto the chain as his father turned the pedals and wiped the chain clean. Trina invited the women inside to make some fresh lemonade. Lydia squeezed the lemons while Odessa got out the glasses. Trina used an ice pick to break slivers of ice from the top compartment.

They brought a tray of lemonades to the front porch. Trina was horrified. Ross had put Hunter on the bicycle and was pushing him along while Hunter steered.

"He's too little for that contraption! His feet barely reach the pedals."

Ross hated to crush his son's dreams. As he helped Hunter from the bicycle, he whispered, "We won't tell the women when you do ride."

Hunter learned that some secrets were okay as long as they put people's minds at ease. Trina and Odessa chastised Ross and Hunter. Aunt Lydia said she wanted to learn how to ride a bicycle. Laughter rang out at the thought of a woman riding a bicycle. All but Ross laughed, because Ross knew his sister was serious.

"How about now?" Ross said.

Lydia looked at the bicycle for half a minute before she stood and opened the front door. She looked at Ross and asked, "Are you coming?"

Ross simply got up and followed Lydia inside. Ross came back out to the front porch to be further chastised for thinking his sister could ride a bicycle. Trina led the argument. Odessa stared at the bicycle while Hunter got up and looked over the bicycle closely. Lydia stepped out the front door wearing a pair of Ross's trousers bound at the ankles and knees. She was serious.

Trina put her hand to her mouth and gawked at Lydia's lack of propriety. Trina called her son to her side and held her hands over his eyes. Hunter struggled to free himself and was excited that his aunt Lydia was going to ride a bicycle. Ross led Lydia to the bicycle and showed her how to get on and off. Lydia held the handlebars, swung her leg high in the air, and sat on the seat.

Trina said, "How disgraceful," and she ran into the house.

Ross told Hunter and Odessa to watch from the front porch. Ross had protected Lydia all her life. He was her big brother. Ross held the handlebar and back of the bicycle while Lydia moved the pedals and tried to balance.

Ross was exhausted running beside his sister, but he would not let go of the bicycle. Lydia was steering smoothly down the driveway but had trouble turning in the grass. Lydia begged Ross to let go, but Ross was too protective. Lydia stopped begging and ordered Ross to let go. He did. Ross bent over to catch his breath and watched his sister ride away on the driveway. When Lydia got to the end of the driveway, she started to turn on the grass. The bicycle went over, spilling Lydia onto the ground.

Trina came running out of the house and ran behind Ross toward Lydia. Hunter and Odessa followed closely. Lydia had gotten up and tipped the bicycle upright. With tears in her eyes and mud on her clothes, she saw Ross running for her. She screamed, "Get away!"

Ross stopped in his tracks. He knew his sister's determination. Trina, Hunter, and Odessa caught up to Ross. Lydia indignantly got back on the bicycle and rode past them. Lydia made several successful turns on the grass. She stopped in front of Ross and told him she had to go down the paved street. Ross said, "Not dressed like that."

Trina smiled, but her smile disappeared when Ross took off his hat and told Lydia to tuck her hair up. Ross helped put the oversized hat on his sister and asked her to stay in his sight. Odessa looked at her aunt and said, "I'm going to learn to ride the bicycle next."

Lydia smiled at her niece and rode off. Trina grabbed Odessa's hand and lectured her while walking back to the house. Ross, followed by Hunter, walked to the road to make sure Lydia was safe. Lydia rode down the road and turned around with a giant smile on her face. Hunter told his father that he had the best family in the world. Ross agreed. Aunt Lydia turned into the driveway and rode the bicycle to the front porch. She sat there immersed in her victory over the machine.

Ross and Hunter got there as Lydia finally threw her leg up in the air and stood next to the bicycle. Lydia hugged her brother and thanked him. Odessa went inside with Aunt Lydia to help her change and clean the mud off her. Hunter begged his father to let him try the bicycle again. Trina told Ross that it was time to put the bicycle away. Hunter helped him.

Lydia came downstairs looking presentable. She thanked everyone for a wonderful day and told her brother and his family that she had to get home. They bid her goodbye as she gracefully got on her carriage. Lydia was the only woman Trina knew who drove a carriage alone. Hunter and Odessa watched their aunt Lydia drive away.

Trina told Odessa to take Hunter to the park while she talked to their father. Ross knew he was in trouble but was not sure whether it was for racing or letting his sister learn to ride the bicycle. Trina grabbed Ross by the arm and started telling him how disgraceful his sister was for wearing men's clothing and throwing her leg in the air like a dance-hall girl. She led Ross upstairs, babbling on about Lydia's women's rights ideas. When she got Ross into the bedroom, she told him that just watching Lydia on the bicycle excited her sexuality.

Lydia was spending more time at her mother's house next door to Ross and Trina's home. Odessa would often go visit when Aunt Lydia was there. Trina got tired of Hunter's begging to ride the bicycle. Ross taught him how to ride by leaning forward, because Hunter could not reach the pedals when sitting on the seat. Hunter could ride okay, but he had trouble getting on and off. Ross simply told him he might be big enough the next year.

Trina had calmed down about Lydia's bicycle adventure. Bicycling was becoming a popular exercise and transportation activity. Lydia was Trina's best friend and sister-in-law. Jade invited Trina and Odessa over when Ross got home. Ross was working with Hunter on his bicycling when Trina and Odessa left to go to his mother's house.

Jade, Lydia, and now Odessa were interested in the women's rights movement. Trina was more into propriety, tradition, and family. When Lydia came downstairs wearing her bicycling garb, Trina looked at the bloomer-type bottoms and lacy collar and sleeves. No one knew what Trina would say about the outfit. Trina walked over to Lydia and hugged her. Trina told Lydia that her strange outfit looked mighty comfortable and that she wished she were brazen enough to wear such clothing. "It seems more appropriate than your brother's baggy trousers."

"I'm glad you like it, Mother," Odessa said.

Trina looked up and saw her daughter coming downstairs with a similar outfit on. Trina proclaimed that she needed to sit. Lydia said she'd told her husband she was going to ride a bicycle. "After a small argument, he not only agreed to let me ride but also said he would buy me a bicycle if I had someone to ride with. I suggested Odessa, and Zachariah offered to buy her a bicycle too."

"Is it all right, Mother?" Odessa asked in an excited voice.

"It's up to your father."

Trina realized that in order to keep her family happy, she would have to accept the changing world. Odessa left to walk home to ask her father. Lydia went with her. Trina was grateful that it was getting dark outside. Trina looked at her mother-in-law and proclaimed that at least they weren't dancing at the theater. Jade was a strong seventy-two-year-old woman who believed women should have the same freedoms men had. The bicycling outfit gave the girls some of that freedom, but Jade agreed that the outfits were racy.

Zachariah was sitting on the porch with Ross, watching Hunter ride the bicycle, when the women's cackling across the lawn interrupted their conversation. The men stood politely and were shocked at what they saw. Zachariah had told Ross that Lydia was making riding clothing and that he'd promised to buy Odessa a bicycle to ride with Lydia.

Nothing could have prepared the men to see the two women in feminine men's clothing. Smiling, the women turned and asked the men how they liked their riding outfits. Ross was speechless. Zachariah looked at Ross and told him he loved his sister dearly and was sorry for her influence on Odessa. Ross just told the girls he would teach Odessa how to ride, and they could not go anywhere until he was satisfied they could ride safely.

A month later, an early snowfall marked the end of the bicycle season. Although some were out riding in the snow, Ross felt it was hard on the machine and dangerous for the rider. The bicycles were put away. Hunter shoveled snow, carried firewood, and did odd jobs for people in the neighborhood. He was determined to get his own bicycle.

Ross had been expected to work as a child and give his money to the family. Ross and Trina agreed that their children would finish school. Any money they earned would go to the children's savings. Hunter saved his money and still did volunteer work at the school and at church. Hunter figured that if he got a job for the summer, he could buy a bicycle the following summer.

Hunter had to take care of his own yard and help his mother in her garden before he could work for anyone else. He made many acquaintances at school and at church. Most of his school chums were looking for summer work too. Hunter's ability to talk to anyone provided the advantage of meeting people at church who might pay him to work. Hunter was only seven years old and could not work in a factory until he turned eight.

Members of Saint Patrick's Church knew Hunter from his volunteering for the church, including the fine job he did with yard work. An elderly couple, Mr. and Mrs. Barns, heard that Hunter was looking to earn some money. They asked him to come to their house on Monday morning. Hunter showed up and was introduced to Cleopatra, or Cleo, as she was called.

Cleo was a large German shepherd that was ferocious looking and had a bark that echoed when Hunter knocked on the Barnses' door. Hunter soon discovered that the dog was very friendly and only barked when she heard a knock on the door. Mr. Barns asked Hunter to play with the dog for a few minutes. Hunter did, and he liked the dog. More importantly, Cleo liked Hunter.

Mr. Barns attached a leash to Cleo's collar. He handed the other end of the leash to Hunter and told him they were going to take Cleo for a walk. Cleo could pull hard, but Hunter kept a good hold on the leash. Mr. Barns walked slowly and used a cane for balance. The dog peed often, and finally, Cleo excreted a huge turd. Mr. Barns pulled a paper sack from his pocket and handed it to Hunter. Hunter had to turn the bag inside out and pick up the turd. They walked slowly back to the house. Cleo wanted to walk faster.

Mr. Barns told Hunter he would pay him ten cents to walk Cleo every morning and evening. Hunter agreed with excitement. Ten cents a day was more than he made doing a full day's worth of yard work. Other people saw Hunter walking Cleo and asked him to walk their dogs as well. Hunter's first business was Hunter's Dog-Walking Service.

Hunter almost had enough money to buy the bicycle when school started. He did not want to go back to school, but it was important to his parents. Hunter continued to walk dogs before and after school. He got some of his school chums to walk the dogs he didn't have time for. Hunter paid his chums five cents and kept a nickel for organizing the schedules.

One Saturday, Hunter was walking Cleo, when his aunt Lydia and his sister, Odessa, came down the street on their bicycles. Cleo wanted to chase the bicycles, but Hunter held tight. He commanded Cleo to sit. Cleo sat while Lydia and Odessa stopped to say hello. Hunter introduced them to Cleo. Cleo was friendly. When the women rode away, Hunter had to hold her from chasing them.

Hunter watched them ride away with envy. But he had something he enjoyed more than riding a bicycle. He had his own business, and he had happy customers and employees. Hunter got home just as the sun was setting to find out that he was going to have something else. His parents told him he was going to have a baby brother or sister. Odessa was grown up at fourteen years old. She worked all week except for Saturday afternoons and Sundays, when she had fun with her aunt Lydia or her friends. Hunter thought a new brother would be fun.

Hunter was walking Cleo before school one day, when Cleo heard something that made her bark and pull hard on the leash. Hunter heard a high-pitched sound coming down the road long after Cleo heard it. Horseless carriages were a new invention that Hunter had heard about. As the noisy machine got closer, Hunter had to wrap the leash around a tree to prevent Cleo from chasing the fast-moving horseless carriage.

The carriage looked strange without a horse in front of it. It was painted a shiny black color and had steam pouring out of it. People came out of their homes to see what the noise was. The horseless carriage was gone, but Cleo was still barking. Residents along the street started yelling at Hunter to quiet the dog. Hunter finally got Cleo under control and continued his walk. After seeing the automobile, Hunter forgot about getting a bicycle for just a moment.

Hunter walked all the dogs on weekends, and that was when he collected his payments for walking the dogs. On a cold winter morning, Hunter was out doing his dog walking. He went to the Barnses' house to get Cleo. A younger woman answered the door.

"Who are you?" the woman asked.

"I'm Hunter, and I'm here to walk Mr. Barns's dog, Cleo."

"Mr. Barns died last night. I'm his daughter."

Hunter hid his sadness. Mrs. Barns came to the door with Cleo and her leash. Hunter told Mrs. Barns that he was sorry to hear about Mr. Barns and that Mr. Barns had been a good man. Cleo walked slowly that morning. She did not bark at birds or watch the carriages go by. Hunter knew Cleo was sad. Cleo urinated but did not defecate that morning. She did not go far before she turned back toward home.

Hunter took Cleo back home. She usually eagerly leaped to the top of the stairs, but he had to coax her up the front stairs that day. Mrs. Barns asked Hunter to come inside. She showed Hunter how to feed Cleo and fill her water pail. She gave Hunter some cookies and asked him to sit at the table with her. Hunter sat while Mrs. Barns, with tears in her eyes, explained that she was going to move to her daughter's house. Cleo could not come with her.

"I need you to find Cleo a good home where she will be loved."

"I will do that for you."

"I leave today, so Cleo must go now."

Hunter got up and went to Mrs. Barns. He stood next to her while she sat with tears flowing. Hunter hugged her and looked at Cleo. When he told Mrs. Barns he would take Cleo, Cleo's ears perked up just a little. Cleo got up and ate her food. Hunter said his goodbye to Mrs. Barns, who hugged Cleo and Hunter. Mrs. Barns gave Hunter Cleo's food dish and water bucket. Hunter left before his own tears showed.

Cleo was calm while Hunter walked his other dogs. At the end of the day, Hunter headed home with Cleo. He wondered if his parents would let him keep Cleo. He got home and walked inside with the dog.

"You can't bring that monster in here," Trina said.

Hunter introduced Cleo to his mother and explained, "Cleo's owner died, and she has no place to go." Hunter's father was sitting in his favorite chair, and Odessa was in her chair. Hunter's mother stood up with her hands on her round stomach. Hunter told his mother that Cleo was his best-behaved dog.

"He'll eat the new baby," she said.

Hunter argued, "Cleo is short for Cleopatra, and he's a she who doesn't eat children."

Hunter's mother was tired as she sat down. Cleo walked over to her and lay by her feet, looking up at her with her big brown eyes. Odessa said that she knew Cleo and that Cleo was a good dog. Cleo looked at Odessa, walked over to her, and put her head on her lap. Odessa immediately fell in love with Cleo. Hunter's father called Cleo's name, and she went right to him. He scratched her neck. Hunter's father suggested that because it was too late to do anything with her that night, they should let Cleo stay at least for the night. Hunter thanked his father as he looked at his mother for her answer.

"Just for tonight," she said.

Ross Donahee laid down the rules and let Hunter know that he was responsible for any problems Cleo caused. Hunter had been carrying Cleo's food, food dish, and water bucket all day. He finally went to the kitchen and set them down. Cleo stayed in the living room and lay by Trina's feet.

Hunter filled Cleo's water dish and put some food in her food dish. He called Cleo. She came to the kitchen and ate her food. She seemed less sad than she'd been earlier. After Cleo ate, she went to the front door and sat looking at the door handle. Hunter said, "She needs to go outside after dinner," and he grabbed her leash. Hunter's father stood up and told Hunter that he had been walking dogs all day and hadn't even had time to take his coat off. Hunter's father walked Cleo that night.

Cleo slept on the floor in Hunter's room that night. She nudged her nose up to the bed. Trina had warned Hunter not to let Cleo sleep in the bed. Hunter put a blanket on the floor for Cleo, and she seemed content. When Hunter woke, Cleo was gone. He came downstairs and found Cleo lying next to his mother on the couch. Cleo got up when she saw Hunter.

Hunter got dressed and went outside to shovel snow and walk Cleo. He took the leash off Cleo while he shoveled snow. She stayed with him and played in the snow he was shoveling. When Hunter had finished shoveling snow, he took Cleo back inside. Cleo went to the woodstove and snuggled in front of it.

Hunter's father and Odessa were dressed for church. Hunter's mother did not want to venture out in the snow in her delicate condition. She stayed home with Cleo while the rest of her family went to Sunday Mass. Hunter had to get there early to shovel snow at the church. His father and some other parishioners helped.

Hunter left church to walk his dogs and shovel more snow. When he got home, Cleo was cuddled on the floor next to his mother.

"I guess we will keep her," Trina said.

Hunter was overjoyed at his mother's proclamation. Cleo became part of the family. Hunter's father was especially attached to Cleo, but when he was at work, Hunter's mother was Cleo's best friend. Cleo was loveable—and Cleo seemed to know it.

Hunter didn't understand what was so special about the start of the twentieth century, but it was happening.

Early in the year, Hunter got his baby sister. Her name was Helen Raeleen Donahee. Hunter had earned enough money to buy his bicycle but figured he was too busy with dog walking and school, so he decided to wait to buy one. Cleo stayed near Helen as her protector. Nobody could raise his or her voice around Helen when Cleo was present. No one had to.

Hunter turned eight years old in the summer of 1900 and started third grade in the fall. Odessa worked all week and on Saturday mornings. She was a big help with Helen while at home. Trina was home with Helen and Cleo during the days. Hunter had a bunch of cousins living next door with Grandma Jade, Aunt Gwen, and Uncle Karl. Hunter's cousins did not stay in school long, because there were many jobs in Rochester.

People came from all over the world to work in the Rochester area. The population rose to more than 160,000 people in 1900. The best jobs were the technical jobs that involved developing film or grinding glass and selling men's clothes. New houses were being built, and more farm wagons came to and from the city. Horseless carriages were seen more often.

Hunter completed sixth grade in 1904. He maintained good grades throughout school and built many relationships. Hunter wanted more education, and with his parents' blessing, he enrolled in public grammar school for grades seven and eight. Hunter enhanced his knowledge and his personality.

That year, Hunter sold his dog-walking business to a former classmate at Saint Patrick's Cathedral. Hunter advised the new owner to use younger boys to walk the dogs, because younger boys were easier to manage. Hunter received a whopping eighty dollars for the business. With his free time, Hunter took Red Cross first-aid classes from Major Charles Lynch.

Clara Barton had started the Red Cross in Dansville, just south of Rochester. The organization had received a congressional charter in 1900 and was considered a worthwhile charitable organization. Hunter was interested in raising money for the organization, but many of Hunter's contacts were too poor to donate money.

On a family outing at Ontario Beach one day, Hunter heard shouts down the beach. A swimmer who'd gone out too far was in trouble. Hunter jumped into the water, and using his powerful swimming skills, he reached the drowning man and pulled him to the beach. Hunter was breathing hard but did not hesitate to evaluate the man. The man wasn't breathing. The man's family was horrified when Hunter tilted the drowning victim's head back, pinched his nose, and started breathing into the man's mouth.

Horrified people were screaming at Hunter to stop. Hunter kept doing what he'd been taught in first-aid class. After a minute or two, the victim coughed. Hunter pulled him onto his side to let him cough out the water. The man was breathing. A big man helped the victim to his feet. He looked at Hunter and asked, "How did you know to do that?"

Looking around at the many gawkers standing around, Hunter replied in a loud voice, "The Red Cross teaches how to use mouth-to-mouth resuscitation in their first-aid classes."

Hunter turned and walked back to his father, feeling proud that he'd performed his first aid properly. Ross was proud of his son and told him so. Hunter took his four-year-old sister Helen back into the water. A news writer heard about the rescue and remembered that a Ross Donahee had saved a drowning man in the Genesee River. The headline in the next newspaper read, "Another Donahee Saves Life Thanks to Red Cross Training." The news got to the Red Cross, and Hunter was rewarded with a letter of achievement and bravery. Hunter was becoming as well known as his grandfather was in Rochester.

Hunter's schooling was not going well. The public school system was teaching the same things in seventh grade that

Hunter had learned in fifth grade at the Catholic school. Hunter spent less time doing the repeat work and more time socializing. He found a new pastime: girls. Hunter had always liked everyone, including girls. Girls in the public school were different. They liked Hunter not as the friendly boy he was but as a young man. Margaret O'Reilly was taller than Hunter and wore her copper-colored hair in a ponytail. Other boys teased her for having freckles. Hunter noticed how sad she was when they teased her. While some girls were teasing Margaret about her freckles one day, Hunter spoke out.

"You're jealous because deep down inside, you wish you had red hair and freckles. Freckles signify rare beauty."

One of the girls agreed. "I see the way the boys pay attention to Margaret, and I think Hunter is right."

Margaret kissed Hunter on the cheek. Hunter enjoyed the kiss and being so close; he liked the way she smelled. Hunter kissed her on the cheek. Smiling, he looked at the girls and said, "Margaret tastes like strawberries."

The other girls started laughing and wanted Hunter to tell them what they tasted like. Hunter wanted to taste them all but simply told the other girls, "I only kiss the prettiest girl in school."

The girls and boys no longer teased Margaret. Hunter developed a desire for strawberries. His mother made strawberry jam in the spring, when strawberries were in season. That night at dinner, Hunter asked his mother for some of her strawberry jam to put on her fresh bread. Margaret tasted better than strawberries.

Hunter talked to his grandmother often. During one of their talks, Hunter's grandmother brought up the subject of man-and-woman relationships. Hunter had to promise to always treat women with respect and to never think that if he married a woman, she was to wait on him like a slave. Hunter promised to never have a slave wife. He vowed to keep his promise.

Hunter left school after the first month. He was not learning anything new and figured it was time to get a full-time job. Hunter considered the many technical jobs in Rochester, but he would need to finish school and go to a technical school to work in such a field. A friend of Hunter's told him that the mill he worked at was hiring and that Hunter could get a job at the mill.

Robert Timothy French hired Hunter to work at the mill. The mill turned wheat into flour, but Hunter was given a new task working for French's sons: grinding mustard seed and mixing it with turmeric from India. Hunter's mustard flour made a bright yellow spread. A few months earlier, the Frenches had sent their mustard to the Saint Lewis Fair, where it was used with a new American food item called the hot dog, made by Tobin. French's couldn't make enough of the spread.

Hunter enjoyed working for French's and was quick to volunteer to play on the company baseball team. On Sunday afternoons, French's Flour Mill would play baseball against other businesses with teams. Hunter enjoyed the hard work because he was building up muscles like his father's and meeting new people. A flour mill was hard and dangerous work.

French's did not hire children, because children were likely to get hurt with all the open machinery. Hunter had much respect for the machinery and was always careful when working around moving machine parts. Hunter wore a loose-fitting shirt one morning. The shirt got caught in a gear that wrapped the shirt around its shaft. Hunter was about to be sucked into the machine pulling his shirt.

Hunter's eyes barely saw his shirt get caught, but his body felt the quickness of the force that was about to suck him into the gears. Hunter did not have time to think; he reached above his head and braced himself to a rafter. He planted his knees on the side of the machine. With a quick jerk, it was over. The machine whined for a moment, turning Hunter's shirt into shreds that fell onto the floor. Hunter stood shirtless but continued his work, preventing a buildup of processed mustard seeds.

Hunter learned every aspect of the millwork and became a valued employee. Mr. French recognized Hunter's interactions with the other employees. Hunter was interested in any part of the process that added quality to the finished spread or flour. He learned that quality food was socially enticing because people were happy when the food they ate or were served was of good quality.

An expeditious meal consisted of a hot dog in a bun with mustard on it. As hot dog restaurants became popular for their expeditious meals, the need for mustard grew. Hunter was well aware that in the growing city of Rochester, such expeditious meals were becoming popular for people who were often in a hurry. Hunter mentioned to Mr. French that in the summer months, there were five thousand people visiting the park and shops at Ontario Beach. He said they should serve hot dogs with mustard. French offered Hunter a job in sales. Hunter figured it would be fun to sell the mustard and other products French's made, because he knew they were high-quality products and sold at reasonable prices.

Hunter used his personality and skills to sell products. He was good at it. The company let him use their horse-drawn buggy to sell and make deliveries. Hunter met many women while selling, but none were dedicated like his mother. Hunter worked many hours and had to stop volunteering for organizations, such as the Red Cross. He enjoyed time at home with his sister Helen and ever-faithful dog, Cleo.

In the spring of 1909, Cleo stopped eating. She was ill.

Hunter's mother spent her days with Cleo because Helen was at school. Cleo slept in Hunter's room, but she had trouble getting up and down the stairs, so Hunter carried her.

Hunter did not see his mother cry often, but when Cleo died, the tears rained out. Hunter's father had Hunter bury Cleo way out in the backyard. Hunter was thankful he was alone. He could not hold back his tears as he lowered Cleo into her grave. Hunter noticed his father go outside to fight back the tears. Ross had been very attached to Cleo.

A week later, one of Hunter's cousins from next door came running up the porch steps. She went to Ross and told him that something was wrong with Grandma. Ross took Hunter with him next door. Jade Donahee had taught her children to be fair and kind to others. Gwen was hysterical, and her husband wasn't home from work.

Ross looked at his mother, who was sitting in a living room chair. He walked over and felt her arm and her forehead. Ross moved his hand over her face and closed her eyes. Jade Donahee died in the house Matt built for her. Ross picked her up in his massive arms to carry her to her downstairs bedroom. He asked Hunter to take his bicycle to go get Uncle Jack. Hunter saw his father's tears before Ross could set her down on her bed and close the door behind him.

Hunter got to his uncle Jack's house and knocked on the door. Aunt Felicity answered the door.

"I need to see Uncle Jack."

"I can tell by looking at you that something is wrong. What is it?"

"Grandma is dead."

Felicity told Hunter that his uncle Jack was not due back for a few hours. He was engineering the train from Niagara Falls. She would tell him, and they would be over as soon as he got back.

Hunter had ridden like the wind to get to his aunt Felicity, but he rode much slower on the way back. Hunter thought of how his grandmother had taught him to always be kind to other people.

Hunter's grandmother had taught Hunter much more than to be kind. Hunter's kindness had led to his success at school, in society, and at work. Hunter was seventeen years old and made more money than his father. Hunter still had not bought a bicycle for himself. Between contributing to his family, his church, and the Red Cross, Hunter never felt he could justify the expense of a bicycle.

Uncle Karl was home when Hunter got back to his grandmother's house. Hunter's father's eyes were red, but there were no tears. Hunter's mother, Trina, and his sisters, Odessa and Helen, were there. Hunter's father asked him to take his sisters home. Odessa was now twenty-two years old, and Helen was nine. They both had tears streaming down their faces and were whimpering. Hunter held his tears back like a man.

The girls went into the house and sat at the kitchen table. Hunter went to his room and got out his grandpa's knife that his grandma had given him after Matt Donahee died. Hunter's grandfather had been a strong man who'd killed a bear with that knife. Hunter wanted to be like his grandfather. His grandmother's words made him go downstairs to console his sisters. Hunter was good at consoling his sisters, and in doing so, he consoled himself.

A Cunningham hearse pulled up to the front of Jade Donahee's house. Ross and Trina came home shortly after the hearse left. The family met at the Macken Funeral Home the next evening. Jade's children, Jack, Karl, Ross, and Lydia greeted guests. Emma Webster came with her son. Emma was Jade's best friend and had been active in the women's suffrage movement and, years ago, the abolitionist movement.

Hunter greeted several coworkers, customers, and people from the Red Cross. He introduced them to his family. Hunter seemed to know everyone in the city. He kept Helen by his side, while Odessa stayed with their mother and Aunt Lydia.

Hunter listened while everyone told old stories. Emma Webster told the best stories that made it sound as if Grandma Donahee had lived an exciting life. Hunter listened to guests with one ear and the stories with the other ear. Emma Webster could not stay long. She was seventy-eight years old. Even though they'd been the same age, Mrs. Webster seemed much older than Grandma Donahee had. Hunter helped her outside while her son got their coach. Mrs. Webster told Hunter that he reminded her of his grandfather. Hunter was pleased.

HELEN

A sun-brightened sky broke way to daylight on a warm August Friday in 1910. Ross took off on his bicycle to get the pony cart and start his busy ice delivery day. Odessa met her aunt Lydia, and they walked to Likly's Brass Company to start work. Hunter wore his fedora low in the front to shield his eyes from the rising sun when he turned to look for other travelers. Hunter was traveling west to Spencerport and Brockport before turning south to Chili and Churchville. He was delivering French's products and then selling mustard.

Trina said her goodbyes as her family went out to work. She would be home alone once Helen left for school. Helen walked to school. Trina and Ross had agreed to let Helen join some friends after school to go to the new Sea Breeze Park for the afternoon. After school, Helen worked for Kodak, packing film cartridges in boxes. She did not have to go to work that day.

Helen and three of her friends walked with excitement to catch the electric car to Sea Breeze. The girls talked about all the fun things they planned on doing. Sea Breeze used to be just a picnic park located where the west side of Irondequoit Bay met Lake Ontario. A restaurant that served Helen's favorite food, hot dogs, had opened at the park. A carousel and the figure-eight roller coaster sounded exciting.

The electric trolley car was just loading when Helen and her friends arrived. They felt lucky to be able to sit together, because the open car was full of passengers. The northwest side of Rochester was generally flat compared to the south and east sides. The electric trolley car provided a fun ride, letting in a cool breeze through the open doorways as it moved along outside the city. Helen and her friends could smell the fresh air from the lake as the temperature dropped to a comfortable eighty degrees. The girls and the other excited passengers arrived at Sea Breeze.

Helen heard people laughing and talking in fast and excited voices. The smell of hot dogs, fried bread, and other strange foods filled the air. Helen felt like running but remembered to be a lady and walked with dignity to the park entrance. A bubbling hunger emerged in Helen's stomach when she saw the colorful carousel and other unique rides. Helen's eyes sparkled when she sat on a bench on the carousel, and it started to move.

The girls rode many rides more than once. They ate hot dogs with mustard. Helen proudly told her friends that her brother, Hunter, worked at the mustard factory. They drank Richardson's root beer and liked the bubbles that tickled their noses. Helen thought about how her sister, Odessa, and her aunt Lydia traveled on bicycles to exciting, fun places. She could not wait to get home and tell of her adventure.

After a day of fun, Helen and her friends boarded the electric trolley car for home. The sun was getting ready to set. Helen sat back on her bench seat and thought about her day and memories that would always be close and easy to compare future events to. Helen closed her eyes. The electric car bounced a bit and made plenty of noise. Helen must have been tired and fallen asleep.

"Helen!"

Hearing her name woke Helen from a sound sleep just as she fell from the seat and rolled off the electric car. She reached for a railing, but it was too late. The car stopped. Men went back to find Helen. She was dead.

The Donahee family was home waiting for Helen when the news arrived about the accident. Screaming, crying, guilt, and rage filled the house as the family received the news. Some emotions settled by the time ten-year-old Helen was buried next to her grandparents. A quiet sadness filled the cemetery. Hunter believed all the prayers were sure to send Helen straight to heaven. Hunter would never forget his little sister.

HUNTER BECOMES A MAN

A year later, Hunter's mother, Trina, died at forty years old. Hunter turned nineteen, while Odessa was twenty-four and not married. Six months later, Ross became ill and could not work. Hunter became the man of the house, with Odessa working and taking care of their father. Ross Donahee died a month later. Hunter's parents were buried next to his grandparents and his sister.

Hunter's father never drank alcohol or smoked, but Hunter developed a taste for alcohol and cigars, as his grandfather had. Hunter traveled a larger area while selling French's products, which forced him to spend days away from home. Hunter enjoyed having a drink with other business travelers and sharing business information.

Hunter met a salesman from Fee Brothers who introduced him to bar mixes. Hunter liked the Fee Brothers people and left French's to work for them. Hunter was able to learn more about world events while talking to Fee Brothers customers. The assassination of Franz Ferdinand and his wife in June 1914 caught Hunter's interest.

This Austrian-Serbian conflict eventually involved Germany, Russia, and France. As war escalated over the next few years, farmers in the Rochester area were producing more food to send to Europe. Hunter's sales and income increased as Rochester's economy benefited from the war. Russia, France, and Great Britten made up the group of nations called the Allies. Hunter waited for the United States to join the Allies. They were at war with the central powers of Germany and Austria-Hungary.

In May of 1915, a German submarine sank a British ocean liner, the *Lusitania*. The *Lusitania* carried war supplies from the United States, as well as American civilians. Hunter took the death of his fellow Americans personally. The United States remained neutral even after Germans sank more ships from the United States. Hunter read that President Woodrow Wilson sent a representative to mediate peace talks to end the war.

Germany tried to enlist Mexico in the war with a promise that Mexico could regain some areas of the United States. This angered Hunter and other Americans. Hunter tried to talk to his friends about the global events. People felt that the United States should stay out of the war because it was not their business. Hunter disagreed but kept talking with customers to gain a better perspective.

Hunter spent more time away from home, working at Fee Brothers and the Red Cross again. Hunter raised much money for the Red Cross to use to help the war soldiers. When the United States entered the war in 1917, the Red Cross begged Hunter to stay in Rochester because his fund-raising skills were needed more than his soldiering. Hunter agreed. He did not miss Sunday Mass during the war. He fervently prayed for the soldiers.

Hunter knew several families who lost fathers or sons in the war. His older cousin who'd grown up next door to him was buried in France. Hunter's uncle-in-law, Zachariah Smith, was killed in London while negotiating war supply deliveries for the United States. Hunter's aunt Lydia was alone. With only Hunter to care for her, Odessa moved in with her aunt Lydia. The family house was sold, and Hunter moved into a small apartment near Saint Patrick's Church. The war ended in 1918.

LOVE AND LIFE

Hunter had seen Margaret O'Reilly in church several times. Margaret was a red-haired, freckle-faced girl Hunter had gone to school with. She was prettier than any girl Hunter had met while on the road. Hunter wanted to court Margaret at her home. She lived with her father, Michael O'Reilly. The first time Hunter met Big Mike, as Margaret's father was called, was an occasion.

"Hello, Mr. O'Reilly. I came to ask your permission to court your daughter."

"So you want to court my daughter, do ya?"

"Yes, sir."

"We'll see whether you're good enough. Step off the porch, boy, and put 'em up."

Hunter was no match for the big Irishman. Big Mike would punch Hunter and laugh as he hit the ground. Hunter would get back up and get knocked down again. Hunter was a good fighter and got a few good punches in, but Big Mike just knocked him down again. Hunter was determined and would not give up. Finally, Big Mike extended his hand to help Hunter off the ground. Hunter took Big Mike's hand.

"So you are not such a bad fighter! Now let's see whether you can hold a drink."

Margaret got home and found her father and Hunter sitting on the front porch, passing a bottle back and forth and singing Irish folk songs. She was furious. Hunter wasn't sure whether Margaret was mad at him or her father. Hunter left for his small home, singing all the way there. Hunter gained permission to court Margaret from her father. Now he had to find out whom Margaret's obvious anger was directed at.

Hunter was twenty-eight years old, the same age as Margaret. He found it hard to believe that Margaret was unmarried, but he had an idea that her father had something to do with her lack of suitable courters. Hunter, as decided by Margaret's father, was going to court her on Saturday evening. Hunter brought flowers. A bottle of whiskey might have been a better choice.

Hunter knocked on the O'Reillys' front door, hoping Margaret would answer. Big Mike answered the door and made fun of the flowers and of Hunter's good suit. Big Mike took the flowers, bit one, and chewed it before spitting and throwing them onto the porch.

"They're not for you. They're for Mrs. O'Reilly," Hunter said.

Hunter bent down and picked up the flowers. He was expecting another fight, but it did not come. Big Mike took the flowers and called Margaret to the door. He handed the flowers to Margaret and told her to stay inside. Hunter got a glimpse of Margaret as she took the flowers. She was beautiful, wearing a green dress that emphasized her red hair. Big Mike closed the door and sat on the porch step. He told Hunter to sit with him and pulled a bottle out of his pocket.

A melancholy Big Mike took a swig from the bottle and offered Hunter a drink. Hunter accepted the bottle but drank only a taste. Big Mike explained that Mrs. O'Reilly had been a fine woman and would have liked the flowers. She'd passed away young. Hunted told Mr. O'Reilly he was sorry. Hunter listened to Mr. O'Reilly declare that Margaret was special. She was all he had.

"If you hurt her, I will hurt you."

Hunter saw the sincerity in Big Mike's eyes. He had to choose his next words carefully. "Margaret is special, and I too want to keep her safe."

"Come back next week."

Hunter felt disappointed as he got up to leave. He saw Margaret wave from the window. She lifted his spirits as he walked away. As Hunter walked the three miles back to his apartment, he thought of Margaret and how good she'd looked, even though he'd only seen part of her through the door. Hunter thought about his own sisters and how Odessa had never married and how no man would have been good enough for his little sister, Helen.

Time seemed to slow down that week. By Saturday, Hunter felt as if a month had passed rather than a week. He was determined to see Margaret Saturday evening. He dressed in his best sales suit, but instead of flowers, he brought a pint of Irish whiskey.

Big Mike answered the door again. Hunter handed him the bottle. He looked at it for a long moment before he commented.

"If you're still here when I finish this, we'll have another fight."

Big Mike opened the bottle as he called Margaret to come. He walked inside after she came out. Hunter wanted to know for sure how Margaret felt about him. Hunter's grandmother had made him promise to only marry a girl who loved him and whom he loved back and to never marry what she termed a "slave wife." Hunter planned on keeping his promise to his grandma.

Margaret sat on the front porch bench with Hunter. They whispered softly as they discovered each other's intentions. Margaret made it clear that she'd respected Hunter ever since her school days, when Hunter had made her comfortable in school. No one had ever tormented her again. Boys had taken favorable notice of her, but she was not interested in other boys. She had not realized it back then, but she understood now that she was in love with Hunter Donahee.

Hunter trusted Margaret. The sound of glass rolling across the floor signaled that Big Mike had finished his bottle. Big Mike had promised Hunter a beating if he was still there when the bottle was empty. Hunter wasn't worried about the beating. He was worried about any repercussions toward Margaret. The front door opened, and Big Mike swayed drunkenly in the doorway.

Hunter moved quickly to the front yard and readied his fists, hoping Big Mike couldn't fight as well drunk. Big Mike had an uncanny way of smiling when he fought. Hunter recognized the smile as the large drunken man came down the steps with the agility of a younger man. Big Mike put his fists up and said, "You're a brave man."

Hunter was ready and dodged the first swing, but a second fist caught Hunter in the jaw. Hunter stayed on his feet but did not swing back. He relaxed his hands and tried to dodge another hit. Hunter was on his back but only for a moment before he was back on his feet. Big Mike's smile was gone. With much difficulty, Hunter said, "I will not hit the father of the woman I love."

"I promised you a beating, and me word is good."

The next punch was so quick that Hunter could not dodge the massive fist. Margaret's soft voice was the next thing Hunter heard. She was wiping Hunter's swollen face with a warm, wet towel. Hunter was enjoying her touch. Hunter regained his wits and realized he was inside Margaret's house. Big Mike was snoring in a chair on the other side of the room.

"How'd I get here?"

"Daddy carried you in."

Hunter looked around the house and noticed there were

few furnishings and no pictures. It was the home of a poor man. When Hunter was able to stand steadily, he and Margaret went to the kitchen table. They could not talk in the living room, because Big Mike's snoring was too savage. Margaret gave Hunter a cool drink from a modern icebox. The house seemed poor, but there were quality foods in the kitchen.

Hunter was afraid Big Mike would wake up, so when he felt strong enough, he bid farewell to Margaret. Margaret's voice was quiet, but her eyes and actions told Hunter how she felt. Margaret's soft, gentle hands cupped Hunter's face. With a power stronger than Big Mike's fist, Margaret brought Hunter to her lips. She held him there. The couple exchanged more feelings and thoughts than words could have provided in years of courting.

Margaret slowly let go of Hunter. Hunter was speechless as he headed for the front door. All he said was that he would see her next Saturday. Hunter walked away feeling Margaret's eyes watching him from her front porch. For a moment, Hunter was thankful for Big Mike's threat to harm him if he hurt his daughter. He wanted Margaret in a bad way.

Hunter followed his sales route that week without enjoying the women he used to flirt with. He had been with women before, but he'd never wanted one as much as he wanted Margaret. Hunter was deeply in love with Margaret. He had more questions for Margaret. They did not seem as important anymore, but they needed answers.

Big Mike was sitting on his front porch with a pint of whiskey when Hunter came calling on Saturday evening. Hunter's mind was not on getting a beating from Big Mike. They greeted each other, and to Hunter's dismay, Big Mike asked for a conversation.

"You came for more?"

"I came to see Margaret."

"It's no fun fighting a man who won't fight back."

"It is troublesome to Margaret when we fight."

"That it is. She gave me an earful last Sunday. You won't have to worry about fighting no more. Unless, like I said, you do anything to hurt her."

Big Mike offered Hunter a sip from his whiskey. Hunter accepted. Margaret opened the front door. With a "Humph," Big Mike went inside. Hunter sat beside Margaret on the porch bench. He brought up his promise to his grandmother about not having a slave wife. He assured Margaret that if he took her away from her father, she would no longer have to serve another man as if she were a slave. Margaret's mood changed. Hunter watched tears form as Margaret exclaimed that she would not abandon her daddy, because he needed her. Hunter saw the tears and felt bad.

"How can you want to stay with such an abusive man?"

Margaret protested that her daddy wasn't like that. "He is sweet and kind and has never hurt me."

"So if I marry you, I get your father too."

Margaret's tears stopped. She stared at Hunter. She smiled and reached for Hunter's hand. Hunter was confused, although all his questions had been answered. He looked into Margaret's eyes and asked what had made her change.

"Married. You said if you marry me, you get my father too. Hunter, do you really want to marry me?"

There was only one answer to Margret's question, and Hunter did not hesitate to answer her. A lot had just happened in a few seconds, and Hunter needed to think for a moment. He liked and respected Big Mike but knew that Big Mike would always create problems. Margaret was worth the trouble. Margaret was a slave to her father, and it would be up to Hunter to make sure even her father treated her with the love and respect Hunter's wife deserved. Hunter told Margaret that she was the only girl for him and that of course he wanted to marry her. This time, Hunter put his hand on the back of Margaret's head and drew her in for a long kiss.

Hunter wanted Margaret to meet his sister Odessa and Aunt Lydia, and he knew the women would like each other. New questions filled Hunter's mind: Where would they live? How would the bills get paid? Hunter figured these problems could be worked out.

Hunter always had a plan for business and life. He'd imagined getting on a knee and asking Margaret to marry him. In his mind, he'd felt the elation when she said yes. Now Hunter didn't even remember asking Margaret to marry him. As he thought about it, he decided that Margaret had asked him to marry her. It didn't matter, because Hunter and Margaret had agreed to get married. Now Hunter had to ask Big Mike's permission, and he told Margaret that he needed to ask her father's permission to marry her. A baritone voice from behind the door said, "You've got it."

Margaret stood and hugged her daddy before telling him to go back inside. He went. Margaret's arms found their way around Hunter's neck. Her lips met Hunter's, and they swayed in the cool fall breeze that swept over the front porch. Hunter, Margaret, and Big Mike went to church together on Sunday. They sat behind Karl and Gwen, who moved to the front two pews with their children and grandchildren. Aunt Felicity came alone because her daughter had moved away, her son had died in the war, and Hunter's favorite uncle, Jack, had died of consumption.

Odessa and Aunt Lydia saw Margaret with Hunter at church. They grabbed her and took her outside, leaving Hunter with Big Mike. Mass was starting when the women hurried back inside and to their seats. Gwen looked as if she might break her neck trying to turn around to see Margaret. After Mass, all the women in Hunter's family reprimanded him. Hunter and the O'Reillys were invited to Sunday supper at Karl's house.

Odessa and Aunt Lydia acted angry toward Hunter for his secret engagement to Margaret. Hunter had not thought it was a secret; it had just happened fast. Nonetheless, they seemed to like Margaret, and that was important for Hunter. Hunter's sister and aunt were lively women. Hunter listened to them complain that the 1917 election was boring because there was no opposition for the attorney general and two judges who were elected. Hunter promised them that next year's presidential election would prove more interesting.

Hunter stayed close to Big Mike during supper because he was afraid Big Mike might start or finish a fight. Big Mike limited his drink and was quite friendly. Hunter enjoyed giving Odessa and Lydia the limelight as they passed photographs of a trip to the Shadigee Hotel and Point Breeze and talked about a fall trip they were planning with two of the nuns at church. They were going to Watkins Glen to see the fall tree colors. They told Hunter they were going in the priest's automobile.

Karl, Hunter, and Big Mike talked about work and the fall harvest, which kept Big Mike busy until winter. Lydia politely interrupted and asked how October 20 sounded. No one was sure why the date was important, so they just told Lydia it was fine. When Hunter finally got to talk with Margaret, she was excited. The women had Hunter and Margaret's wedding all planned. On October 20, 1918, Hunter and Margaret were to be married at Saint Patrick's Church.

Hunter found Margaret and escaped out the back door. He showed Margaret the house next door that his father had built. Ross and Trina Donahee had gotten the land from Hunter's grandfather Mathew, who'd built the house Karl and Gwen lived in. Margaret asked several questions about Hunter's grandmother

Jade Donahee, the one who'd made him promise not to have a slave wife. Hunter was proud of his ancestors and rightfully so. At the horse stable, Hunter stopped and stared at his father's old bicycle. He told Margaret how hard he'd worked to buy a bicycle for himself. By the time he had saved enough money, there had been other things more important than the bicycle.

Margaret found the fact that Aunt Lydia and Odessa rode ladies' bicycles and wore special clothing to ride fascinating. Margaret seemed obsessed with the adventurous lives that Lydia and Odessa lived. Hunter felt a little inept that he might not give Margaret such an exciting life. Margaret hugged Hunter and told him they didn't have what she had: she had Hunter's love. She kissed him long and felt his body change. Hunter refused to let her go.

Lydia came looking for Margaret. She saw Hunter holding her and told him he was worse than his father and said to let her go. Hunter did not know why she compared him to his father, but the thought made him proud. They went back inside to end the Sunday afternoon. People said their goodbyes and left for their respective homes.

Hunter walked to his apartment, and for the first time, he realized how small and lonesome the place was. He got out the knife his grandfather had killed the bear with and held it in his hand. Hunter wondered what stories he would tell his grandchildren one day. Hunter's grandfather had taken risks and been successful. His father had been dependable and steady. Hunter considered himself dependable and sociable, but he wanted more excitement and more success in his life. He wanted to be like his grandpa.

Hunter only saw Margaret on Saturday evenings and Sundays. His apartment was lonesome. Big Mike told Hunter that he was to move in with Margaret and him after the wedding, but he would have to pay his share of the rent. Hunter agreed. Saturdays came too slowly.

Hunter arrived at Margaret's in a cheery mood. Margaret met Hunter on the porch and told him that her father had not come home from the farm. Hunter offered to go look for Big Mike. Margaret explained that he often stopped at the tavern on payday, and he would eventually stagger home. She told Hunter to stay. Then she told him that he needed to leave. Hunter knew he should leave, because it was hard to control his desire for her.

Hunter was about to leave, when Margaret asked him to help her with something in the kitchen. Hunter followed Margaret into the kitchen and asked her what she needed help with.

"Unbuttoning these buttons."

Hunter watched Margaret unbutton and began to help. Several hours later, a knock on the door interrupted their lovemaking. Hunter threw his trousers and a shirt on to answer the door. He saw the police car in the driveway before he opened the door. Police officer Odes Toad asked for Margaret. Hunter told the officer that Margaret was busy and asked how he could help. The policeman said he needed to see Margaret. Margaret showed up at the door with a towel wrapped around her.

"Hello, Officer Toad."

"Hello, Margaret. I have your father again. We'll release him in the morning when he sobers up."

Office Toad gave Hunter a stern look before he left. Hunter knew he had all night with Margaret. He enjoyed the night, even though it was two weeks before the wedding. Morning came, and Hunter wore the same clothes he'd worn Saturday night. They were his church clothes anyway. Big Mike came home and found Hunter and Margaret waiting on the cold front porch. They were ready for church. Big Mike went inside to get ready for church. He was not wise to what had gone on in his house all night.

Hunter had trouble staying awake in church, and Big Mike noticed Margaret elbow him more than once. After church, Odessa and Lydia invited Hunter, Margaret, and Big Mike for supper. After supper, Big Mike was disappointed that the only thing to drink was sherry. He drank enough to fall asleep in a chair. Hunter was asleep in the chair next to him. Margaret was full of energy and conversed eagerly with Odessa and Lydia about the wedding.

Big Mike gave his daughter to Hunter at the wedding. At the altar, he asked Hunter in a whisper whether it was too late to give her away. Hunter simply stated that it was too late not to give her away. Hunter and Margaret had thought they'd gotten away with deceiving Big Mike. Big Mike smiled at his daughter's glowing face, and all was right.

The Rochester Club Ballroom was used for the reception. Friends of Lydia and Odessa from the *Catholic Courier* newspaper had helped decorate the reception area. Hunter's customers and coworkers from Fee Brothers attended. Many prominent people Hunter had met while doing Red Cross work came to the wedding reception. George Eastman, a friend of Lydia's, had donated a photographer to take photographs of the wedding and reception.

Margaret felt like a queen and looked beautiful in the dress Odessa had sewn for her. Hunter insisted on a fully stocked bar, at which Fee introduced new drinks for attendees. Big Mike was in his glory at the bar. Hunter had used most of his savings to pay for the extravagant wedding. He'd bought matching gold rings that he and Margaret gave to each other in the church. An orchestra played music, and guests danced. Hunter believed the event was truly an exuberant celebration.

Big Mike had too much to drink. He was ready for a fight. Officer Toad was ready with ten off-duty police officers. He should have brought more. Margaret pleaded with her father to stop his behavior before her wedding day was ruined. Big Mike took a bottle of whiskey from the bar and left. The festivities continued.

Margaret noticed that many—too many—young women were congratulating Hunter on his marriage. Margaret confronted Hunter. She confided to Hunter that he seemed to be flirting with the women.

"I appreciate beautiful women, and that is why I love you so much."

"I'll be keeping a close eye on you."

Hunter assured Margaret that there was no need, because she was the only woman for him. Margaret seemed satisfied and even happy with Hunter's statements. Still, Hunter was careful not to pay too much attention to any other woman for the rest of the day. The guests were expected to leave at five in the afternoon, when the orchestra finished. People stayed and enjoyed conversing with each other. At seven in the evening, Hunter sat with a friend from work and enjoyed a drink.

Odessa and Lydia got a bottle of sherry and shared it with Margaret. Margaret told Lydia she missed her mother and was glad Aunt Lydia made her feel so good. Odessa had arranged a car to drive the couple home after the reception ended. Hunter and Margaret left with sincere thanks to Aunt Lydia and Odessa for all they'd done.

The newlywed couple had trouble staying awake in the car. If not for the bumps in the road, they would have slept. Big Mike was not home when they got there. As exhausted as they were, a new energy filled their bodies. Hunter did not know how late it was when they fell asleep.

The smell of coffee brewing woke them after the sun rose. They came downstairs to find a sober Big Mike brewing them coffee and reminding them that they had to hurry, or they would be late for church. Their first day as husband and wife was a good day.

Work was busy because the wedding had brought new customers wanting Fee Brothers drink mixers. Travel was becoming congested, with roaring cars and trucks replacing horse carriages and omnibuses. The telephone almost eliminated the role of the salesman in Rochester, but the phone was a convenience and did not help distribute new items. Hunter was reduced to a deliveryman and was unhappy.

Many people lost jobs to modern machinery that negated manual labor. Hunter kept working to support his wife and father-in-law. Winter brought cold weather and no farm work for Big Mike. Hunter was the sole support for his family. Hunter hurried home at night to Margaret, which caused his sales to drop. There was talk of an Eighteenth Amendment that would prohibit the sale or transportation of alcohol, which was a factor that could further hurt Hunter's sales.

Hunter had much on his mind as he drove in a snowstorm in Pittsford, on the southeast side of Rochester. Hunter was driving a Cunningham four-cylinder car that had been converted into a truck with a wooden back to carry goods. The truck broke traction while negotiating a steep hill and started sliding backward.

Hunter applied the brakes, which made the truck slide faster. Hunter's hands were frozen from the cold, which made it difficult to steer the truck. The truck came to a rapid stop when it went off the road and backed into a maple tree. The impact sent heavy snow from the tree's boughs onto the truck. Hunter could not get out of the snow-covered truck.

Hunter sat there for a while before he tried driving the truck. He could not see anything through the snow covering, but he could feel the truck move just a little. He played the clutch in and out. The truck moved about an inch before the tires started spinning in the snow. Hunter gave up trying to drive out and started digging up through the snow. He had to pull the snow into the truck, leaving less room for his body to move.

He was about ready to give up, when a dark spot in the snow showed. Hunter felt a tree limb in the dark spot. He pulled himself up, and snow filled the truck. Hunter's head was out of the snow.

"Someone left a head in the snow."

Hunter looked down to see the source of the voice, but no one was there. He pushed the branch down, and he came up higher. There was a man with a plow horse in front of the pile of snow.

"Ya all right up there?"

"Fine now."

"Whacha doin' in a tree?"

"Trying to get out of my truck."

The man started to laugh when he made eye contact with Hunter. Looking down from the tree branch, Hunter saw the humor in the situation. Hunter climbed out a bit and slid down the snow on top of his truck. He landed on his backside next to the man. The man reached out to help Hunter to his feet. Hunter stood and looked at the snow pile with his truck inside. He could see the back of the truck. All the snow had fallen at the driver's seat. The man with the plow horse had seen the truck back down the hill and hit the tree. He'd seen automobiles slide down the hill before. He'd gotten his horse and come to help. Hunter pushed enough snow from the front of the truck to tie a line to the bumper. The plow horse did the rest.

The farmer told Hunter that he would have better luck in the morning negotiating the hill. He said that his horse stable had heat and that Hunter could spend the night there. When Hunter heard the word *heat*, he took the man up on the offer. After scooping snow away from the driver's seat, Hunter tried to start the engine. It started, and he followed the plow horse to the barn.

Above the entrance door on the barn was a sign: Slippery Hill Inn. Hunter parked his truck next to a snow-covered Ford model T. Inside the barn was a shivering man who introduced himself as Abraham Calderon. He was wrapped in a horse blanket, with his clothes drying on a line by the woodstove. The farmer pointed to a second cot in the room and told Hunter he could stay there. Hunter said thank you and joined Abraham by the stove.

Hunter stripped down and hung his clothes on the line near the stove. Abraham sold cigars and sundries to shops in the area. Hunter gave him his sales pitch on Fee Brothers products. The next morning, Abraham added Fee Brothers to his complement of products. The two salesmen left goods to pay the farmer for his help. The snow was deep, but the improved visibility helped the travelers up the hill and on their separate ways.

Hunter went to Fee Brothers and cleaned out the truck. He loaded more products to take to Webster, Williamson, and back along the lakeshore. Hunter knew Margaret would be worried about him, so he stopped at home before venturing out into the countryside. She was happy to see that he was okay. She'd missed having him home and been extremely worried. Big Mike was out shoveling snow.

Traveling around the Rochester area alone, Hunter often thought about his grandfather surveying for the railroad many years ago in the mid-1800s. Hunter realized how lucky he was to travel in a truck rather than walk through the woods. The south side of Rochester was still wilderness, but he encountered many other travelers on the way.

In springtime, on an overnight trip to Dansville, Nunda, and Mount Morris, the snow was melting, and a cool rain fell. Hunter was leaving Dansville to drive over the mountain to Nunda. At the bottom of the mountain, the rain and fog were so thick that Hunter had to hang out the side of the truck to see the road underneath him. He got to the area where he remembered an old wooden bridge that went over Keshequa Creek on Coopersville Road. Hunter could hear water rushing in front of the truck. He could not see the source of the water in the heavy fog. He decided to get out of the truck to make sure the wooden bridge was in good shape before driving the truck across.

The bridge was in front of the truck when Hunter got out to look. Hunter could hear the water flowing in the creek but could not see it. He moved between the sounds of the creek and his engine chugging slowly. Looking down at the road around his feet, Hunter inched his way to the bridge. The bridge was maybe ten feet in front of the truck but seemed like a mile.

Hunter noticed that the rain and melting snow had washed away two inches of road along the edge of the bridge. He stepped onto the bridge and found it was sturdy. Still, Hunter was afraid to drive over the eroded edge. He thought about the time it would take to go back and find a new route to Nunda. Hunter started making his way to the truck, when he heard a deep growl. The sound was coming from the direction of his truck. Hunter, with one hand on the side of the bridge, looked down through the eroded crack between the bridge and the road. The sound of roaring water was below, but fog negated a visualization of the creek.

The growling sound got closer. Hunter thought the sound came from coyotes or wild dogs. He let go of the bridge, clenched his fists, and stepped over the missing piece of road. When he got one step closer to the truck, the growl got louder and was accompanied by the sound of the truck rattling, as if a giant creature had picked up the truck and was shaking it. Hunter stepped faster toward the truck. It came into view a few feet in front of Hunter. No creature was in sight. Hunter climbed into the truck, bent his head out, and looked toward the back of the truck.

A giant head with huge white teeth and big black eyes seemed to see Hunter at the same time. The head moved from the top of the truck to the side. It was connected to a massive black body. The bear was coming for Hunter. Hunter couldn't find the clutch but somehow got the truck moving. He sped over the gaping crack and onto the bridge. He kept going, not knowing whether the bridge was safe. It was.

Hunter drove with his head out the window, peering through the fog at the road beneath him. He did not look back for the bear. He was too scared. Hunter got to higher ground, and the fog left the road. Hunter parked the truck and walked around to see what damage the bear had done when shaking the truck. The top hinge on the back door had been nearly ripped off the truck, and there were giant muddy bear prints all over the back of the truck.

Hunter continued his trip to Nunda, thinking about his own fear and wondering how a man could possibly kill a bear with a gun, let alone a knife, as his grandfather had. Hunter parked his truck in front of the Nunda Hotel. As he got out of the truck, he noticed men laughing at his truck.

"What! A bear tried to eat your truck?"

"On Coopersville Road, coming from Dansville."

"Hey! Those really are bear prints."

People came from the hotel and the lumberyard across the

street to see the bear prints and damage to the truck. Hunter tried to tell how scared he'd been, but people were simply interested in the story of a bear attacking a truck. By the time Hunter brought his delivery into the Nunda Hotel, he was ready to tell the story. Hunter was a grand storyteller, and people listened to him with interest. Hunter had learned that storytelling was a beneficial part of selling.

When Hunter got home to Margaret, his story was about the customer's response to the bear story more than the bear story itself. Margaret was concerned anyway. Big Mike was working long days at a farm in Hilton and had to take the train early in the morning and late at night. Often, he would stay at the farm to avoid the travel time. Margaret had gotten pregnant as soon as she married Hunter and was due to have their baby soon.

Hunter asked to work close to home as she got close to her delivery time. Odessa and Aunt Lydia took turns stopping in to check on Margaret. Hunter started working inside the factory, installing new machinery that would greatly increase Fee Brothers' production. He took the electric trolley car to and from work. More people were moving to the city of Rochester for factory jobs as the nation became a country of consumers. Hunter liked the country and the small towns surrounding Rochester because the people seemed friendlier and lived at a slower pace than did city people.

Lydia found a midwife who lived near Margaret. The midwife stopped by every morning to check on Margaret. Margaret learned that when she needed something, her sister-in-law, Odessa, and Aunt Lydia were adept at finding the best and friendliest people. Margaret felt close to having her baby but said nothing to her father or Hunter. She was home alone when the labor pains started.

Fortunately, the midwife stopped by to check on Margaret

early that morning. Her knock on the door was answered with a scream from inside the house. She ran inside and found Margaret bent over the kitchen table, holding her stomach. She timed the contractions and told Margaret to take it easy and get off her feet. They sat in the living room for hours. The contractions seemed to stop. Margaret was scared and begged the midwife to stay. She did.

At dinnertime, Odessa and Aunt Lydia came over to Margaret's house. They asked Margaret how she was doing. Margaret said she was fine, but when Lydia saw the midwife and asked whether Margaret was having labor pains, Margret answered with a scream. The women put Margaret to bed and readied for a new birth. Big Mike came home early because he was concerned for his daughter. He saw she was in good hands, and the women told him to go outside. He took a bottle of whiskey out to the front porch. Every time he heard a scream, he took a drink and wondered where Hunter was.

By the time Hunter got home, Big Mike had finished half the bottle of whiskey. Big Mike stood to greet Hunter by saying, "My daughter is in pain."

Hunter was worried for Margaret and asked Big Mike how she was. Big Mike did not know, because the women had made him go outside. Hunter opened the door and walked in to meet Odessa, who quickly escorted him back outside, telling him to wait. She said it wouldn't be long. A scream came from inside, and Big Mike took a swig from his bottle. He offered Hunter the bottle, and Hunter accepted it and took a swig of the whiskey.

This went on for an hour before the longest scream made Hunter cringe. Then it was quiet. A moment later, Hunter and Big Mike heard a baby crying. Odessa opened the door and said, "It's a girl."

She closed the door and left Hunter and Big Mike on the front porch. They finished the bottle of whiskey. Hunter snuck around the back door and got some cigars. The two men sat quietly smoking the cigars on the front porch, waiting for more news. Odessa opened the door and told the men to rid themselves of the cigars so they could come in and see the baby.

Aunt Lydia was holding the baby when the men came in. Hunter asked how Margaret was. Lydia told him she was in with the midwife and would be resting soon. Hunter looked at his little girl and fell in love in a new way. Big Mike looked at her and, with the only tear he had ever shed, declared, "She looks just like my Margaret."

In July 1919, Megan Jade Donahee had thin red hair and freckles. She had loving parents and aunts and a grandpa who would make sure no harm ever came to her. Margaret called Lydia's name, and Lydia took the baby back to her. A moment later, Hunter went to see his Margaret. Hunter wanted his wife and little girl to have many of the new things being manufactured that made life easier.

Hunter noticed electricity lines being hung along poles and coming closer to the house. Sewer pipes helped take the smell of the outhouses away. Stop signs were being erected at street intersections. A new traffic-light system was installed downtown, with red lights that signaled to stop and green lights that signaled to go, while yellow lights signaled to get ready to stop. Loud bells and whistles were at the waterfront and factories. Hunter's daughter, Megan Jade Donahee, entered the world at a wonderful time.

THE FARM

The post–World War I era boosted the economy in the United States. Companies, including Fee Brothers, were exporting more goods to other countries. The center for farm goods was moving from western New York to the midwestern states. Hunter was making good money but wanted more. Like his grandfather, Hunter was willing to take a risk.

The United States had increased its food exports during the war. Postwar stockpiles of food, such as corn, wheat, milk, and pigs, drove the prices back down. The population of Rochester had doubled since Hunter had first started reading newspapers a decade ago. The population of the country was increasing. Hunter saw opportunity in farming in the Midwest.

Hunter was enjoying his job less as he became restless for a new economic opportunity. The city was getting crowded, and Hunter and Margaret agreed that the country was the best place to raise Megan. Big Mike agreed. Hunter began looking at farms for sale. There were many, because the growing economy did not include farming. Hunter figured that farming would catch up and was the economic future.

Hunter went back to selling and traveling. He wasn't looking forward to the snowy, cold months ahead. Big Mike would soon be out of work. Hunter heard of a farm for sale in Kansas. Hunter packed up Margaret, Megan, and Big Mike; used his savings to buy the farm; and boarded a train west.

Megan was a few months old, and the motion of the train seemed to relax her. Margaret had never ventured far from Rochester, and Big Mike simply said, "If you've seen one farm, you have seen them all." Hunter was looking forward to harvesting the crops that were left in the fields. Kansas had a longer growing season than western New York, which meant more and larger crops. Hunter figured he could survive the season with what was left in the fields at the farm he'd bought.

Hunter paid thirty-five dollars an acre for the land, which usually went for sixty-two dollars per acre. The farm had a stable for horses, cows, and pigs. A three-bedroom house sat on the farm, which Hunter figured would be large enough. The scenery was beautiful as they went through Ohio and Illinois. Margaret wanted to spend more time seeing all the places the train passed. The loud whistle of the train made Megan cry, but she was quick to settle down.

On the third day, Hunter broke down and paid for a sleeper berth that Margaret could sleep in. The next morning, the train pulled into Lawrence, Kansas, where Hunter unloaded his family and met with the agent who'd sold him the farm. Papers were signed, and the agent turned over an old farm truck that came with the farm and directions to the farm.

Hunter had to buy four gallons of gas before heading down the dirt road to the farm. The farm came into view a half mile before they got there. The farm was nestled on the side of a hill with a hundred acres of wheat and corn that shone golden in the sunshine. The lower fifty acres were down by a small river surrounded by apple and cherry trees. The farm was beautiful.

The house obviously needed work. Some storm shutters were crooked, while others were lying on the ground. The roof had wood shingles that looked to be in good shape. Weeds around the house looked like thick woods. There was no paint on the sideboards of the house. They pulled in front of the house and all got out and went inside. Margaret did not want to set Megan down because of the dirt. Big Mike instantly started cleaning.

Hunter had to go to the well outside to get water. He started a fire in the kitchen stove to heat the cleaning water.

The house filled with smoke. Big Mike told Hunter he could fix the issue. He found a long rope and tied a brick to the rope. Mike went up onto the roof and bounced the rope and brick down while Hunter brought a bird's nest through the flue. Margaret took Megan for a walk to the barn. She thought the barn was cleaner than the house. A loud noise scared Margaret. She grasped Megan tightly and went for the door. The clamoring of horse hooves sounded as a horse ran in a back door, through the barn, and out the front door. The horse stopped at the well. Margaret carefully walked to the horse and saw that the well filled a trough. Margaret pumped water into the trough, and the horse drank thirstily.

Big Mike came down from the roof and was surprised to see the horse. No one had said the farm came with a horse. Hunter talked about buying a tractor if he could sell enough crops to pay for one. Big Mike had used horses before and would be content with the big plow horse. Hunter realized he was lucky to have Big Mike with them. Big Mike tended to the horse while Margaret explored the grounds. Behind the house was a large garden that had many vegetables that were rotting.

However, squash, cabbage, lettuce, and others were still good. Margaret laid Megan down on her blanket and picked some carrots, potatoes, and sweet potatoes to make some vegetable stew for dinner. Margaret's father saw her in the garden and came to help. He carried Megan in his big hands while Margaret put the vegetables in her pink skirt to carry inside.

The smoke had cleared, but Hunter was black from the smoke and cleaning the stove and kitchen. Margaret put the vegetables on the counter and found a cooking pot. She went out to the well and got water to put on the stove to start the stew.

Hunter found canning jars in a fruit cellar in the basement. The Donahees' house was going to be their home, and the potential of that happening became more evident as they cleaned.

The vegetable stew was their first meal in the house, and it was good. Hunter wanted to go outside to devise a plan to harvest the crops. Big Mike told Hunter they would start by picking food that was still good in the garden. Margaret would have to boil, pickle, or preserve the food for the winter. While Hunter planned, Big Mike just did what needed to be done.

Wednesday morning ended the first night at the farm. All slept well after cleaning the house. Hunter and Margaret slept upstairs with Megan, while Big Mike slept in the downstairs room that would have been the dining room. An awful noise woke them all an hour before sunrise. It sounded as if an animal were being brutally murdered. Hunter and Margaret came downstairs to find Big Mike stretching his arms up to the ceiling.

"What's that awful noise?" Margaret asked.

"Rooster," Big Mike replied with a smile. "It's time to get to work."

Big Mike looked at the drowsy Hunter and told him to get dressed. Hunter went upstairs and put his old clothes on. After a visit to the outhouse, they headed to the apple orchard in the truck. There would be a good apple harvest, but the cherries were done until spring. Next, they drove to the corn and found ants eating the roots. Big Mike told Hunter that the entire cornfield would need to be plowed and reseeded. The wheat field was good but would have to be harvested in the next two weeks.

They drove back to the barn as the sun was rising. Big Mike knew a lot about the farming process, while Hunter knew nothing. They were getting the tools they would need ready, when the familiar smell of coffee came from the house. They went inside for breakfast but were sent outside with soap to wash before eating. Margaret had made sweet potatoes and coffee. It was a good breakfast.

Using some wood crates, Hunter and his father-in-law went to work in the vegetable garden. Hunter learned how to tell ripe vegetables from those not ready and rotten while picking. Hunter tried to match the work his father-in-law did, but Big Mike was a strong man who worked hard. Margaret finished her household chores and joined the men in the field. She worked like her father, making Hunter feel guilty that he could not afford to hire people to harvest the crops. Hunter remembered his promise to his grandma not to have a slave wife. Margaret was his partner in several ways but worked like a slave.

By Saturday, the farm showed that the family might survive the winter. They filled the pickup truck with wheat and drove into town for supplies and to sell the wheat. Margaret sat between Hunter and her father, holding Megan, in the front seat of the old truck. Their farm was between Spring Creek and old Wakarusa Creek Road. It was a dusty dirt road with tall trees and tall grass on each side. The six-mile ride to Pudora took an hour in the old truck.

Pudora was a small town on the southern shore of the Wakarusa River, a tributary of the Kansas River. They parked the truck at the mill, with two other trucks in front of them. Margaret and her father took Megan up the street to the general store to buy coffee, bullion, and other supplies. Hunter went to the mill office to make arrangements to sell his wheat. Wheat prices were high at $2.45 per bushel. Hunter was happy with his ten bushels for his first week.

Hunter went to the hardware store and bought oil and a wire brush to clean some old equipment at the farm. Big Mike was nowhere to be found. Margaret and little Megan were waiting at the truck. Hunter looked for Big Mike. He checked the general store, the hardware store, and the churches. Pudora had a Baptist church on the west side of the street and a Catholic church on the street that ran behind Main Street. They were the only two streets in the small town.

Hunter was making his way back to the truck, when another farm truck stopped next to his truck. Big Mike got out and put something in the back of Hunter's truck. The stores did not sell liquor in Pudora. Big Mike had found a place to buy a brown jug of corn whiskey. The ride home was pleasant.

Big Mike rode in the back of the truck with the supplies. Hunter enjoyed Margaret's company in the front seat. He drove slowly because the ruts in the road were hard and shook the truck so badly that they thought it might fall apart. They passed the Adams farm, which had a modern tractor and wheat thrasher. There were ten workers around the equipment, and Hunter estimated they were loading a bushel of wheat a minute onto the big carts that horses pulled beside the thrasher. The calculator in Hunter's mind was working. He would need a big loan to modernize his farm.

Leaves were falling from the colorful trees. Margaret commented on their beauty. A family of deer was drinking at the creek. When they got to their cornfield, Big Mike yelled, "Stop!" He got out of the truck and pointed out that there were chickens in the cornfield. That explained why the rooster was hanging around.

Hunter took Big Mike's advice and decided to go to the barn to fix the dilapidated henhouse by the barn and round up the hens. Margaret was excited to have fresh eggs. Hunter and Mike went to work on the henhouse and repaired a fence around it. Margaret put the supplies away. It was time to gather the hens.

They got to the cornfield in the truck. Hunter and Margaret saw a hen and chased it. Big Mike snuck into the field and emerged with two hens. Margaret fell in some mud while chasing a hen. Hunter helped her up. They had no hen, and that made Big Mike laugh. Mike took his hens to the henhouse and walked back. Hunter and Margaret had no hens. Mike walked into the cornfield and emerged with two more hens and no mud on his clothes.

Hunter was determined to catch a hen. He had one when Mike got back. Hunter was proud. After a couple of hours, they had eight hens, and the rooster showed up at the henhouse. Big Mike had Hunter and Margaret pick some corn that was dry and not rotten so they would have feed for the hens. Hunter and Margaret went to the well to pour pails of water over each other to wash the mud off each other. Big Mike sat on a tree stump in the front yard with his brown jug.

Margaret wanted to fix a good meal with the supplies they'd gotten in town. She was exhausted. Hunter felt guilty for all the work Margaret had to do, so he helped her make another vegetable stew. Hunter remembered when his father had demanded beef on Thursdays. Megan was worn out from all the fresh air and fell asleep early. Margaret was asleep soon after. Hunter took the truck to the apple orchard and picked a bushel of apples for Sunday.

Megan woke up early, before the rooster, and Hunter got up with her. He put her carefully to her mother's breast. Megan was three months old. Hunter put her in a chair when she fell back asleep. He made coffee and dressed for work. He forgot it was Sunday. Big Mike woke from the smell of the coffee and got dressed for work.

Megan snuggled in her grandpa's arms while Hunter cut wheat. Hunter had only been on the farm for six days, and he felt his strength building. He cut more wheat per hour than he'd previously cut in two hours. He didn't want to stop, but Margaret was calling out, "Where is Megan?"

Big Mike held her up above his head. Margaret's whole body relaxed, which was obvious even from a hundred yards away in the field. Fifteen minutes later, Margaret was walking toward them, dressed in her church dress. It was time for church. Hunter wore his best salesman suit, while Big Mike put on a clean shirt and his jacket. Margaret fixed Megan's hair, and they got in the truck, with Big Mike in the back. They took the wooden crate of apples Hunter had picked the night before.

The trip to Pudora was fast, and Hunter parked at the church with other farm trucks and horse wagons. The small church was full, and the people welcomed the Donahee family to the congregation. The sermon talked about Matthew 5:1–12, including the verse "Blessed are the poor, for theirs is the kingdom of heaven." Hunter realized that the church was full of poor farmers. Hunter had no intention of becoming a poor farmer.

After church, Margaret sent Hunter to fetch the apples. They were a treat for the children who came to church, but everyone enjoyed an apple. The priest told Margaret he knew some families who would really enjoy some apples, so she left what was left in the crate with the priest. They stayed and talked to people for some time after church. Hunter was in his glory, listening and talking to other farmers. It was Big Mike who insisted they get back to the farm. They had work to do.

The Adams family was at church with their nine children. The children were the workers they'd seen working in the field next to their farm. Mr. Adams explained to Hunter that he had a successful farm. He'd borrowed money to buy more land and good machinery to grow more produce. The interest and payments on the loan had made his farm less profitable than before, when he'd done less work and done it the old-fashioned way.

By December, the crops were harvested, and the garden was emptied. Hunter calculated the cost of a tractor and a thrasher for the following year. Despite the problems other farmers had when they borrowed money, Hunter was sure his farm could make the payments. He decided to wait. They had enough food and money to get through winter and buy seeds for the spring planting. Hunter was looking forward to less work during the winter months. He was mistaken.

After taking the last of the crops to market on the Saturday before Christmas, Hunter drove the truck home. Big Mike said, "We're wasting daylight."

They hitched the horse to a plow, and Big Mike showed Hunter how to plow the corn under. Snow was falling, the ground was getting wet and muddy, and it was getting dark. Big Mike picked out corn that was good enough for chicken feed while Hunter sweated away happily with the plow. Darkness fell across the farm, but the snow made it easy to see.

Big Mike told Hunter they needed to keep going and get as much done as possible before the ground froze solid. Hunter did not like plowing, not because of the work but because there would be no crops to sell for money until next summer. Hunter thought of money, or lack of it, while Big Mike thought about getting the work done. They made a good team.

The snow was coming down harder, and the temperature dropped. They plowed until they could no longer see the rows of corn in front of the horse. They left the plow in the field and walked the horse back to the barn. They could not see the house by the time they had the horse in the barn.

Margaret and Megan were asleep when Hunter and Big Mike came in the back door. They took their frozen boots and jackets off in the back mudroom. Margaret had left a kettle of hot beans with pork on the stove. Dinner was good. Hunter added wood to the fire before the rest of the working farm family went to bed. Snow fell all night.

By morning, a full-out blizzard had struck the area. Hunter did not want to go to church, but Margaret insisted. Hunter carried firewood inside to dry. Big Mike swept off the truck and shoveled a path for Margaret to carry Megan to the truck. Megan was bundled warmly. They crammed into the truck. Big Mike had to get out to push at the end of the driveway to get on the road. It was hard to find the road as Hunter clenched his jaw and drove on. They got as far as the Adams farm before Big Mike got out of the truck and walked in front to help Hunter find the road.

They got stuck in the snow again about a mile from the farm. Margaret said, "The good Lord will forgive us for not going to church today."

Hunter was relieved. Big Mike could not push the truck out of the snow. It was time Margaret learned to drive. She put Megan on the seat and slid over to the driver's side of the truck. Hunter showed her how to work the clutch and put the truck in gear. Hunter and Big Mike pushed while Margaret operated the clutch and steering wheel.

With the truck turned around, they made their way back to the farm. Big Mike and Hunter walked next to the truck, telling Margaret which way to steer. Hunter and Mike followed the truck when they got to the driveway.

"How do I stop?"

Margaret's frantic voice was far ahead of the men. The truck was going downhill in the driveway and gaining speed. Hunter ran faster than Big Mike. By the time Hunter got to the truck, Margaret had turned to miss the house and run into a snowdrift. The truck came to a stop. Hunter made sure Margaret and

Megan were okay, when Big Mike got there and said, "Running into a snowdrift works fine to stop the truck, but the brakes work as well."

They went inside. Hunter added wood to the kitchen stove and started a fire in the living room stove. Hunter gave a sermon that he remembered from his childhood. The house was getting toasty warm, when Big Mike told Hunter it was time to go outside to work. Hunter protested that there was too much snow to plow.

"We're not gonna plow. We're gonna prune the cherry trees."

Reluctantly, Hunter agreed. They got out of their church clothes and dressed for the cold. Margaret stayed inside and reminded them that she would have a good supper ready for midday. The snow and wind made it bitterly cold outside as Big Mike and Hunter carried saws and ladders to the far end of the farm, where neat rows of cherry trees were resting for the winter. Mike showed Hunter how to prune the trees so that the spring crop would grow fully.

The snow stopped falling, and the sky turned a beautiful shade of blue. The winds continued, and it seemed colder than when it was snowing. Hunter kept up with Big Mike as they each started in separate rows of trees.

Big Mike looked at the sky and the bright, cold sun. "Time for dinner."

Hunter had forgotten about the time but was ready to go to the warm house. They left the ladders in the orchard and carried the saws to the barn. Mike wiped the saws clean with an oily rag. Margaret had made beef stew with sweet potatoes. She'd baked an apple pie for dessert. Dinner was excellent but ended too soon for Hunter. They were back to the orchard till dark.

Monday morning, a cold rain was falling on the snow. They got out the horse and went back to the cornfield to plow. The snow created an insulated blanket over the ground, making the plow go through the soil easier than before. By the end of the day, the snow had melted, the field was muddy, and the sun was warm. Hunter had one more task that needed to be done.

That night, Hunter wrote a letter to his sister Odessa and his aunt Lydia. He told them how much work the farm was and how Margaret worked in the field with Megan, her father, and her husband. Hunter described his economic outlook as good. He missed his sister and aunt but not as much as Margaret missed their company.

Christmas passed, and the new year, 1920, promised to be a good year for the farm. Throughout the winter, there was never a day when Big Mike and Hunter did not spend time working on the farm. Megan grew bigger and was crawling all around the house. Hunter and his family met other farmers in the area, but Hunter missed Rochester and the small towns around the city.

Spring came, and the farm was ready. Hunter bought seeds and planted their vegetable garden and corn. He liked to see the wheat growing. Wheat was his largest crop for cash, and he was getting low on money. By June, the cherries were getting ripe. The well-pruned cherry trees produced an abundance of cherries. Mike explained that they had to be picked before the blackbirds ate them.

The cherry crop brought in enough money to last the summer. It was mid-June when the cherries were finished, and the corn was ready. Hunter wanted to hire some farm workers to harvest the corn but couldn't find any. Megan was walking and talking some, so Margaret brought her to the fields and helped with the harvest.

Margaret went back to the house to fix meals and brought the noon meal to the field for the men. She was getting good at driving the truck. They had fresh asparagus, peas, corn, and salted pork. The vegetable garden was grand. Hunter figured that with the corn crop, he would have enough money to buy a tractor and some land next to his farm. Things changed.

The first load of corn that Hunter took to the mill was full and of high quality. The mill paid half of what corn had gone for the previous year. Hunter's dream of a bigger farm with a tractor vanished. The price of wheat was dropping even lower than corn. Hunter would have a hard time surviving the winter.

They continued to work hard to harvest their crops all summer and received less money for their crops. Margaret felt fortunate because she had everything she and Megan needed. The Adams family stopped coming to church on Sundays. Margaret noticed that the children worked in the field without shoes. The low price of crops hurt the large farmers with loans more than the smaller farms.

Megan played near the creek while the wheat was being harvested. Margaret heard Megan call out, "Pretty!" When Margaret looked at Megan, she saw Megan chasing a six-foot-long brightly colored orange-and-red snake. Margaret scared Megan when she jumped to her side and scooped her up in her arms.

"Kill it! Kill it!" Margaret screamed.

Big Mike walked up to the snake and picked it up. He told Margaret it was a harmless corn snake, and corn snakes kept rodents out of the crops. Margaret decided it was time to go start dinner and left with Megan. Margaret kept a close watch on Megan after that.

Margaret was busy canning foods in the fall. She had cherries and strawberry jam from the spring. She canned peas, beans, and tomatoes for the winter months. Hunter and her father were picking apples. Hunter and Big Mike took a load of apples to

Pudora and stopped at the general store for some brown sugar and salt for Margaret.

Winter came late in Kansas in 1920. The Donahee farm was plowed, and the small crew of two worked hard to ready for the spring season. Margaret was with child again and was happy about her life. Hunter did not have his tractor. He thought about the bicycle he'd worked hard for and never gotten. The tractor was different because he considered it a necessary tool.

Winter came hard, and Hunter was chopping wood for the stove. Margaret wrote letters to Rochester more often, but they were not as optimistic as they used to be. Big Mike stopped getting his weekly brown jug, because money was tight. The farm work never ended. Dark night came with frigid wind whistling around the house, threatening to blow away anyone who ventured outside. A faint knock was heard on the front door.

Margaret recognized the young Adams boy. He had a ripped jacket with no buttons to hold the cold air out. His feet were wrapped in rags, and he looked white, as if his blood were frozen. Margaret wondered if the eyes got smaller as a child froze to death.

"Mama's in a bad way. Can ya come help her?"

"Come in, boy, and get warm."

"Can't. Papa would kill me if he knew I waz here."

"I'll take you back."

The boy turned and hurried away before he could hear Margaret's words. Margaret and Hunter bundled up to go outside. Big Mike stayed with Megan. They drove the truck, following the boy's disappearing foot tracks in the snow. Margaret was hoping to catch up with the boy, but they followed his little footprints to the Adams house.

Mr. Adams was like most farmers in the area: he was always

willing to help others, but his pride prevented him from asking for help. Mr. Adams stood on the front porch and asked Margaret how he could help her. Margaret simply told the big farmer that she'd come to visit Mrs. Adams, and she pushed the big man aside and walked into the house. Hunter shrugged and said hello to Mr. Adams.

Hunter heard the Adams children in the barn. He noticed a small fire through the cracks in the barn. The children were keeping warm but in a dangerous way. Hunter figured that equipment with petrol was kept in the barn. A single ember from the fire could cause a dangerous explosion.

Mr. Adams opened the front door, but Mrs. Donahee told him to stay outside. He came down the steps with Hunter.

"Wife's havin' another baby. Me oldest girl is in there to deliver. Spose we could use yur wife."

Hunter paced back and forth with Mr. Adams, occasionally checking the children in the barn. The two farmers talked about crop prices and farming techniques. It was obvious that the Adams family, with their larger farm, were worse off than Hunter. Mr. Adams would need to borrow even more money for seeds in the spring. Mr. Adams was worried about another mouth to feed. He was hoping for a son to help in the fields.

Hunter noticed a lack of screams from Mrs. Adams. He felt the quiet was not good. The young Adams girl scurried from the kitchen stove to the bedroom. Hunter wanted to see Margaret to make sure she was all right. Hunter and Mr. Adams took turns going to the barn to get warm. The young Adams girl came to the door and asked for Mr. Donahee. She gave him a list of things to get from their house. Hunter excused himself from Mr. Adams and left to fill the list.

Hunter got home and found Megan asleep in Big Mike's downstairs bedroom. Mike was awake and waiting for news.

Hunter quietly crept to the fruit cellar and grabbed some potatoes, a slab of pork, and various canned goods. Upstairs, he added a loaf of bread that Margaret had made to have for breakfast. The list said to put everything in a small sack and bring it back with another sack of apples. Hunter returned to the Adams house with the food.

Mr. Adams looked at the sack and told Hunter he did not take charity. The front door opened, and Margaret stepped out.

"It's not charity. I'm hungry."

The men carried the food inside. Margaret took three apples and told Hunter to take the rest to the barn because the children had had no supper that night. Margaret hurried the men back out into the cold. The children devoured the apples, and Hunter's heart went out to them. They were thin and hungry.

The men stayed in the barn while Mr. Adams carefully added a log to the small fire. The wind whistled through the cracks in the barn walls, reminding them of the storm outside. Mr. Adams and Hunter headed to the front porch to wait for news. The children watched from the barn door before they closed it tightly.

About midnight, the faint cry of a baby sounded cheerfully inside. The baby stopped crying, leaving an eerie wind singing through the air. The Adams daughter came to the door and asked, "Daddy, can you bring more wood for the fire?"

"How is Mother?"

"Fine. She had a hard time. Oh! It's a boy."

Hunter helped with an armful of firewood. They wanted to stay to see their wives, but they were shooed away out into the cold again. Finally, Margaret came outside. She complimented Mr. Adams for having such a smart daughter and told him how well she'd helped with the birth. She explained that Mrs. Adams had lost a lot of blood and was very weak and tired. Mrs. Adams was ready to see her husband but only for a moment. Hunter was left out in the cold as Margaret followed Mr. Adams to his wife.

Mr. Adams looked at his wife holding their new son. He smiled. A few minutes went by slowly before Mr. Adams came out. He told Hunter that his wife would be out soon, and he was going to get his other children to quietly go inside to bed. He thanked Hunter and shook his hand. Margaret came out after the children were settled.

In the truck going home, Margaret told her husband that Mrs. Adams was half starved, as were the children. She would go back in the morning. "No neighbor of mine is going to go hungry as long as we have food in the pantry."

Hunter was proud of his wife. He thought of his father, who'd always worked delivering or cutting ice, and his mother, who'd been comfortable at home, cooking and taking care of the house. Then he thought about his grandma Jade and the promise he'd made to her. "Never make a slave of your wife," she'd said. Hunter felt guilty and missed Rochester's wealthy workers.

March came as the winter was warming, and it was Margaret's turn to give birth. Mrs. Adams and her daughter came to help when the time came. Margaret had an easy time. Luke Donahee was a healthy baby born in March 1921. Luke had red hair and freckles. Hunter was happy to have a son who one day would be a big part of the farm.

In spring, Mrs. Adams and the new baby were fine. During the rest of the winter, Margaret had taken food over twice a week and asked Mrs. Adams to try her cherries or asparagus. Mr. Adams accepted the food that way, considering that it was not charity. Mr. Adams asked Hunter to take him to the railroad station on his way to town. He was going to Chicago because he'd heard there were jobs there. He planned on making enough to keep the farm going, or he was going to send for his family when he got work and saved enough to rent a home and pay for their trip to join him. The bank foreclosed on his farm a week after he left. Mrs. Adams and the children were still living in the house.

Hunter bid on the Adams family's farm and equipment. Their farm was twice the size of his, but Hunter figured that with the tractor and thresher, he and Big Mike could handle the work on both farms. Hunter had the high bid, the only bid, but the bank would not grant him a loan. Hunter was busy getting ready to plant for the season. The snow was melting fast.

The spring rain, mixed with the melting snow, made the Wakarusa River and Spring Creek overflow their banks. Spring Creek rose high enough to fill the lower orchards with water. The Adams farm had water up to the house and in most of the fields. Tuesday evening, the sky opened, and rain fell as if the farm were under a waterfall. By morning, the creek had risen to the edge of Hunter's wheat and cornfields.

Margaret could not get the truck out of the driveway to check on the Adams family. Big Mike and Hunter were busy digging a trench in case the waters of Spring Creek reached the fields. Margaret could barely see them in the field when she started walking to the Adams farm. She left two-year-old Megan with Luke. Margaret got a hundred yards down the road before she saw the water flowing violently over the road. One of the Adams children was floating in the water.

Margaret raced to the water and started walking in the fast-moving water up to her thighs. She got to the child. It was the same boy who'd come the night the baby was born. Margaret fell in the water next to the boy but caught ground with her feet and managed to get up and bring the boy to safety. She sent the boy to get Hunter and her father.

Margaret climbed up the side of the road, where the water

was ankle deep but moving fast. She made her way another fifty yards, where the water was deeper and slower. With easier walking, Margaret gained confidence. However, she slipped, and the water moved her across the road and into a tree. Margaret tried to pull herself up with the tree, but the ground was too slippery. She was hanging on to the tree, worrying about the Adams children, when she heard splashing coming toward her.

Hunter took his boots and coat off and walked through the water with ease. Margaret noticed his shirtsleeves rolled up and the massive arms he'd developed by working on the farm. She knew she would be safe in those arms. Hunter picked her upright, and they headed for the Adams farm together. Margaret was shocked at what she saw when the farm came in sight.

The house was completely gone. Next to the barn were the children, Mrs. Adams, and her baby. They were sitting on the farm wagon, with water rising around them. The water was deep, up to Margaret's shoulders. Hunter left Margaret holding on to a tree while he went to the family. Hunter wondered where Big Mike had gone and wished he were there to help carry the children to higher ground. Hunter grabbed one of the smallest children and told her to hold on tight around his neck. He took her to where Margaret was and helped Margaret to high ground with the child. Hunter turned back to get the next child, when the sound of water splashing got his attention. Big Mike had arrived with the farm horse.

The horse was afraid of the moving water, so Mike left the horse with Margaret and the child. Big Mike headed for the other children right behind Hunter. Hunter had another child and was making his way back. Big Mike had two children. Some of the older children walked alongside Hunter and Big Mike. Mrs. Adams and the baby were the last to get through the water.

The two men had to help ten children and two women get

through the water. The high ground was too slippery, so they worked their way up the road with three of the youngest sitting on the plow horse. They made it back to the Donahee farmhouse, which sat on higher ground. The Adams boy Margaret had rescued from the flooded road was holding Luke and playing with Megan.

Hunter and Big Mike went back to work on their digging. The rain subsided, but the creek was still rising. It would be another day before the creek slowly began to regress. Hunter's farm survived the flood with minimal damage. The Adams family lost their home, and much of their farmland was destroyed and eroded away. Margaret, Megan, and Luke moved into Big Mike's downstairs bedroom with Mrs. Adams and her baby. The girls and six of the young boys slept upstairs. Hunter, Big Mike, and two of the older Adams boys moved into the barn.

The boys were a big help in getting the farm back in good order. They spent the summer helping the Donahees plant and harvest crops and the garden. In the fall, Mrs. Adams got a letter from her husband. He told her he was making enough money to come home and make the payments on the farm to keep the bank from foreclosing. She had Margaret help her write a letter back to explain that the farm was gone.

A week later, Mr. Adams sent enough money for his family to take the train to Chicago. Margaret packed enough food for the journey, and Hunter filled the truck with the Adams family and took them to the train station. Margaret missed the companionship. Hunter and Big Mike missed the help. The two families had eaten most of the food from the garden while the Adams family were living there. Margaret canned what she had left.

Wheat prices dropped again, and the farm was economically less secure than it had been a year before. The fall was mild, and snow came late. By January of 1922, the Donahees were rationing food, and money was short. Margaret missed western New York and wrote to Odessa and Lydia often. The prices of wheat and corn were so low Hunter did not have enough money for seeds. Hunter's farm days were finished.

Hunter put the farm up for sale. He was lucky he did not owe a mortgage on the farm. There were no buyers. The farmers' association suggested Hunter auction the farm. Only one bid came in, and it would not even pay for passage back to Rochester. Hunter told Margaret he was thinking of going to Chicago to find work. Margaret told him to take the low offer on the farm because they were going to Rochester. Hunter was shocked.

"How're we going to pay to get there? Where'll I work? And where will we live?" he asked.

Margaret replied, "With God's blessings. And your sister and aunt will send us the train fare home. The rest will be up to you."

Margaret did not wait for Hunter's response. She got out her letter paper and wrote to Hunter's family. The money was sent by Western Union a week later. Hunter loaded the family and what few belongings they had and drove to the train station. He sold the truck for ten dollars and boarded the train with Margaret; their children, Megan and Luke; and Big Mike.

Three days later, Big Mike was working on a farm in Hamlin, New York. Margaret and her children were with Odessa and Lydia. Hunter was out looking for a job. They all were happy to be back in Rochester. Rochester and the towns surrounding were live with activity. Hunter had to prove himself an adequate provider and, thus, a real man.

THE SALESMAN

Hunter's best suit was tattered and old. He wore it anyway. Michaels-Stern and Company had made it when he worked for Fee Brothers. Hunter was too embarrassed to go back to Fee Brothers, because he felt like a failure on the farm. He was walking toward downtown Rochester from his sister's home, when he realized he was near the clothing company. Hunter went to Michaels-Stern and Company just to look at a new suit.

A salesclerk wanted Hunter to try on a new style of suit, but Hunter told the clerk he'd just gotten back from Kansas and had no money, but when he found work, he would be back. An older gentleman heard the conversation and approached Hunter. He introduced himself as Mr. Michaels and told Hunter he'd overheard his conversation. Hunter recognized the business approach. It reminded him of his days as a salesman.

"I am Hunter Donahee." Hunter held out his hand.

Mr. Michaels shook Hunter's hand and asked him to please try the suit on anyway. Mr. Michaels said he would like to see how one of their new suits looked on him.

Reluctantly, Hunter tried on the suit. He looked in a full-length mirror and liked what he saw. Hunter had a small waist, powerful legs, and big arms. He had not seen himself in a mirror since before the farm. Mr. Michaels and the clerk walked around Hunter and looked at how the suit fit. They made him try a different new suit.

The second suit was chocolate brown. They had him put on a white shirt with a red tie and a tan vest. The vest emphasized his massive chest and tapered down to his small, muscular waist.

The brown suit matched his dark farmer's suntan. Hunter looked in the mirror, and his confidence was back. Hunter had not expected to look so good. He spoke with enthusiasm. "I could sell these suits all day long."

Mr. Michaels was glad to hear Hunter say that. Hunter was still basking in his confidence. Mr. Michaels told him, "Of course, you would have to wear such a new suit while working here."

Mr. Michaels offered Hunter a job selling men's clothing for what seemed a huge salary, plus commission. The pay was more than Hunter had imagined.

"When can you start work?"

"Now, sir, and thank you."

"Mr. Kennedy here will show you the ropes."

Hunter used his professionally firm handshake with Mr. Michaels and then with Mr. Kennedy. Mr. Kennedy walked back to an office with Mr. Michaels. While they were talking, a customer came in. He was a farmer from Holly, west of Rochester. Hunter did not waste time. He introduced himself to the customer and discovered the customer was a farmer who could not manage his farm's business anymore. He needed a suit to find a job.

Hunter showed him the blue suit he'd tried on first. The customer bought the suit, a French-cut shirt, cuff links, two neckties, a hat, and a pair of shoes. Mr. Kennedy watched in amazement as Hunter used his sales skills and talked about going from farming to work in the city. It was as if Hunter and the poor farmer were the best of friends. Mr. Kennedy helped Hunter write up the invoice. After the happy customer left wearing his new ready-made suit, Mr. Kennedy showed Hunter where the more expensive suits were and suggested Hunter push the higher-priced clothing.

Hunter said, "I will when they can afford a high-priced item."

Hunter felt dashing in his new brown suit with the straight pants and narrow lapels. His confidence grew with every customer he served. Hunter proved to Michaels and himself that he was meant to sell. Hunter took to walking rather than taking the trolley or omnibus home and to work. He wanted to keep in good physical condition. That first day, Hunter walked home in his new suit with brown shoes and a bowler hat.

Margaret liked Hunter in his fancy clothes and thought her two dresses were old. The children needed new clothes as well, but now that Hunter and Big Mike were working for regular pay, he assured her those things would come. Odessa and Lydia were wonderful hosts and made Margaret feel more than at home, but Margaret was looking forward to a house of her own.

Big Mike came home for Saturday evenings and Sundays. The rest of the week, he slept in a bunkhouse in Hamlin near the farm. Hunter worked six days a week and made good commissions. He left at six in the morning and did not return home until ten at night. Odessa and Lydia went to work together, leaving Margaret at home with the children. Hunter started saving money.

Margaret enjoyed the new toilet and bathtub with running hot and cold water. She did not miss going outside to the well and heating water on the woodstove or using the outhouse. Megan had learned to use the toilet, but Luke was still in cloth diapers. Margaret insisted that when Hunter found a home for them, it must have indoor plumbing.

Hunter was making money, but based on his experiences on the farm, he was afraid to buy a house with a big mortgage. The cost of a house had gone up dramatically in the three years he'd been away from the Rochester area. Hunter looked at houses when he had time, but he did not have his heart set on buying a house in the city. The Rochester, Lockport, and Buffalo Railway was an electric interurban trolley system. For twenty-six cents, he could commute to and from Brockport. The monthly pass was only $1.40.

Hunter figured it would be cheaper to buy a home in Brockport and commute to work. Odessa and Lydia offered to watch Megan and Luke while Hunter took Margaret to Brockport to look for a home. Hunter had been working for three months, and he offered to buy Margaret a new dress for the trip. She claimed it was too expensive but let him buy her the material to make a dress. Odessa had a sewing machine and was eager to help. They boarded the trolley on a Saturday afternoon in their fine attire and planned to come back on Sunday night.

Margaret's new dress was modern, and it showed her ankles. The couple got off the trolley in downtown Brockport. They checked in at the Towpath Hotel. They had an upstairs room with a view of the newly widened Erie Canal. Hunter had developed a vivacious hunger for Margaret since he'd started working for Michaels. They spent the afternoon in their hotel room. With no children, father-in-law, or sister and aunt, they enjoyed each other. By the time they left the hotel, other people looked at them as if they were special people. They felt special.

Hunter was right that housing was cheaper in Brockport, but many others had figured that out. There were no homes in Brockport for rent, and the ones for sale were too big and expensive. Hunter made Margaret feel beautiful, which was easy because it was true. He took her to dinner at a fine restaurant in Brockport. Then they went back to the hotel to satisfy their physical desire for each other.

Sunday morning, Hunter and Margaret went to the Nativity of the Blessed Virgin Roman Catholic Church on Main Street in Brockport. The church was similar to their church in Rochester, but the parishioners reminded them more of the Kansas church they'd attended. Brockport would be a nice place to live.

After church, they walked to the shops on Main Street and back to the canal. Before they'd left for Kansas, horse- or mule-drawn barges had used the canal. Steam- and diesel-engine-powered boats now pulled the barges along the canal. The trees along Main Street were gorgeous hues of orange, yellow, and red. They ate lunch at a small café near the trolley.

The restaurant had tables outside, from which they could see all the activity around the canal area. No one wore the uncomfortable Victorian outfits that had been customary a few years ago. Women wore dresses that were short enough that they didn't drag on the ground. Most men wore more comfortable suits, while others wore the black suits and homburg hats that signified an upper economic class. There were automobiles made from all parts of the country rather than the local Cunningham Company's automobiles. Farmers came to town wearing their coveralls and driving trucks. Times were changing.

Boarding the trolley back to Rochester, Hunter opened the door and helped Margaret up the steps. He looked at the door for a moment and thought of his sister Helen and her tragic death, when the trolley had been open and had no doors. The air was cool, flowing through the trolley windows as it moved along. Winter would be there soon, and they still lived with Hunter's sister Odessa and his aunt Lydia.

Michaels-Stern and Company's men's clothing factories were doing well. Michaels opened a new factory and outlet in Penn Yan, New York. Mr. Michaels asked Hunter to go to Penn Yan to train the retail staff in procedures and sales skills. Hunter agreed to go. He missed the adventure of the road and was getting tired of working in the confines of a storefront, even though he enjoyed his customers.

In April 1923, Hunter made it to Penn Yan to hire and train men to work in the clothing store. Penn Yan was about fifty miles southeast of Rochester and was nestled on the north side of Keuka Lake. The countryside consisted of hills, rivers, and lakes. Hunter loved the area, but he had little time to enjoy the geography. He was busy working and making money.

A salesclerk Hunter was training, Charlie Pike, thought he knew the name Donahee from someplace. He and Hunter exchanged information, but no explanation of the familiarity of the name Donahee came to Charlie. Charlie was a volunteer fireman who knew everyone in Penn Yan. The day Hunter was to leave, Charlie brought in a training pamphlet firemen used in the Keuka Lake area. It was titled *Work Safe* and had been written by Ross and Lydia Donahee in 1886. The four-page pamphlet had been written before Hunter was born, and Hunter had never heard of the pamphlet. Charlie gave Hunter his copy.

Riding the train home, Hunter thought about his father. He'd been a tough man who delivered heavy ice blocks to customers. Hunter remembered his father as a kind and fair man who was fearless. Ross Donahee had raced his bicycle, but Hunter had never thought of him as a literary man. Hunter read the pamphlet several times and was amazed at the contents' organization and succinctness. Hunter could not wait to ask his aunt Lydia about the pamphlet and his father.

Hunter always put work first because without work, his family would suffer. Hunter got back to Rochester and went right to Michaels-Stern. Mr. Michaels listened intently to Hunter's report, especially his request that fewer high-end suits be displayed at the outlet in Penn Yan, not because there was a lack of wealthy people but because the people did not display their wealth as people from the city did.

Hunter went home to find a surprise: power lines were

strung along Lydia's street. Lydia had hired an electrician to install electric lights and plugs. Hunter's family was staring at a big wooden box with voices telling a story. Hunter had gone from a Kansas farmer to a city salesman, and he missed the country. Margaret was happy to see him.

Margaret was due to have their third baby in June 1923. Lydia and Odessa insisted she have her baby in the hospital for safety reasons. Margaret agreed, and plans were made. Lydia sold her horse and carriage because a neighbor told her that if she got rid of the smelly horse, he would drive her wherever she wanted to go. Hunter figured that the neighbor was a widower and liked Lydia's company. Lydia would have her neighbor and his car ready when the time for the birth got near.

William Robert Donahee had different ideas. Lydia and Odessa took turns taking time off from work to be with Margaret and the children. Margaret started labor at noon on a Wednesday. Lydia told the neighbor to go get Odessa from work and come back to take Margaret to the hospital. When they got back to Lydia's house and headed up the porch, they heard a baby cry. It did not sound like Luke. Odessa opened the door to find Margaret holding a new baby. Lydia said, "Little William just couldn't wait."

Odessa took to William while Lydia tended to Margaret. The neighbor went home with his automobile. William was different from Megan or Luke. He had dark hair and looked more like his father. When Hunter got home from work, he saw four-year-old Megan sitting the living room, holding a baby. He did not understand.

"Daddy, do you like my new baby brother?"

It took a moment for Hunter to assimilate the information and conclude that Margaret had had the baby. Odessa just sat there smiling. He told Megan that he liked her baby brother just fine. Hunter asked if he could hold him for a minute. Hunter held William and thought he would grow to be a fine man. Finally, he asked Odessa about Margaret.

"I'm right here."

Hunter turned around and saw his wife standing in the doorway. Her stomach was gone, and she was glowing. Lydia was right behind her. Lydia told her that was enough and said it was time to go upstairs to bed for rest. Hunter handed William to Odessa and went to Margaret. She put her arms around his neck.

"Isn't he gorgeous?" she said.

She kissed Hunter before he could answer. Hunter gently lifted her up and carried her up the narrow staircase. Lydia followed. Hunter lovingly put her on the bed. He wanted to lie next to her, but Lydia said Hunter was to sleep in the living room for the next few days. She confirmed that Margaret had had an easy birth. Hunter had learned a long time ago not to argue with Aunt Lydia. He said good night to Margaret and headed downstairs.

Hunter continued working and traveling to different stores to train sales personnel. He enjoyed the people but felt discontented when he did not travel to other stores. The confines of the retail outlet store made Hunter's mind wander to the farm and more so to the small communities, such as Clyde and Penn Yan, where he taught sales techniques.

At home, Hunter finally asked Lydia about the pamphlet she and his father had written. Unlike most people, who got sad when talking about deceased loved ones, Lydia got excited to talk about her brother. She told Hunter that Ross had been the grandest big brother a girl could have. Hunter sat for hours listening to his aunt describe his father at a time before Hunter was born—a father he felt he'd never known that well.

Hunter had heard the story of the bear his grandfather had killed, but he'd never heard about the one in Yates, where his father, Ross, had fallen off the buckboard after a bear spooked the horse. Matt Donahee had faced the bear with his fists, ready to fight the giant animal. Little Ross had been right behind his father with his tiny fists up and ready. Hunter learned that his father had been more than a kind and fair man who happened to be a hardworking provider for his family. He wished he could talk to his father again, not so much as father to son but as man to man to find out how astonishing his father really was.

Hunter thought it would be fun to take a trip to the Shadigee Hotel. Lydia agreed that it would be fun. Megan interrupted. Odessa needed Lydia to help with Luke. It would be two years before Hunter and Lydia talked about a trip to the Shadigee Hotel again.

Hunter noticed that the trolley was getting overcrowded, as were the streets of Rochester. Rochester's population was almost three hundred thousand people. Hunter had to wait in a line to buy his cigars at the newsroom. He wanted to get out of the city for a few days. He talked to Aunt Lydia, and she was excited to arrange the Shadigee trip.

In the spring of 1925, Hunter, Lydia, Odessa, Margaret, and the children—Megan, Luke, and two-year-old William—started their vacation. They loaded into a steam train that left from Rochester toward Yates a mile or so south of the Shadigee Hotel.

Lydia had made the trip by train with her family when her brother Jack was the engineer. She had been twelve years old, and now she was fifty-four years young. This time, the train was older and more rickety. Lydia's younger brother, Ross, and her two older brothers, Jack and Karl, had passed away. Lydia remembered the good time she'd had, and she shared her experience with her great-niece and great-nephews.

The train made fewer stops because the farming in the area was unprofitable, and many farmers had moved to the city of Rochester to work in factories. The countryside seemed the same. Of course she told the story of her father, Matt Donahee, and the bear. The children were especially interested because they'd never known their grandfather. They looked for bears.

The train sounded its loud whistle several times before coming to a stop in the town of Yates. The Donahees were the only passengers to debark the train. The stationmaster told them the train whistle could be heard at Shadigee, and the number of whistles signaled that they had customers. Shadigee would send a motor coach for them. Fifteen minutes later, a dark green motor coach pulled up to the train station. The driver got out and yelled, "Shadigee Hotel!"

He was looking at the Donahee family because they were the only ones there. He was friendly and put their luggage in the coach. The ride to the lake had changed from Lydia's last visit, and she had to guess where the bear had scared the farmer's horse. The children were excited. Lydia forgot about her chant of "I see the lake!" until the children started the same chant she and her brother had sung years ago.

The lake was calm and inviting. The hotel was warm and friendly, with a huge open porch to sit on and watch the lake. There was no boating activity at the Yates Pier, but there were several horse-and-buggies and men fishing off the pier. Margaret and Odessa spent time with the children while Lydia enjoyed a rocking chair on the front porch.

Hunter never had leisure time and did not know what to do with his time. He sat with Aunt Lydia on the front porch and puffed on a new Cook's cigar, a brand he'd never heard of before. There were other guests at the hotel. A family came outside in swimsuits and ran to the lake. Hunter's children followed with

Margaret and Odessa close by. Hunter went inside, put on his old pants, and followed his family to the water's edge.

Ross had taught his children to swim at an early age. Uncle Zachariah had taught Hunter how to swim in Lake Ontario. Lydia told Hunter that learning to swim was for their safety. Megan complained that the water was too cold and that the rocks hurt her feet. Luke went right in with Odessa holding on to his hand. Odessa enjoyed getting wet. William wanted to go out in the deep water with his father, but Margaret held his hand and kept him close to shore. Hunter had no shirt on, and Margaret eyed his farmer's build when he came in to get little William and take him out farther. Margaret thought an afternoon nap might be nice.

Lydia came down, took her shoes off, and walked with her feet in the water. They enjoyed the beach very much. Hunter kept a keen eye on all and remembered his Red Cross training. He realized how much he missed his social activities. The children could have stayed in the water all day, but it was time to get dressed for supper.

They were seated in the dining room, when a salesman from S. A. Cook came in to the front desk. He sold cigars and candy that were displayed at a counter at the front desk. After listening to the talented salesman, Hunter excused himself and went to say hello to the man. His name was Jacob Kern. He spent ten minutes talking with Hunter before he left for his next customer. Hunter came back to the dining room just as their food came to the table.

Margaret asked who the man was, and Hunter just said he was an interesting and talented salesperson. After dinner, the children wanted to go back in the water. Margaret told them they had to wait an hour after eating before they could go in the water. Hunter took the boys for a walk on the pier. Hunter talked to many fishermen and found that they were farmers catching food to feed their families.

Odessa and Aunt Lydia took Megan to a roller-skating rink on the other side of the pier. Megan tried on a pair of roller skates and learned to skate with her aunts holding her hands. Before long, she was skating by herself. Margaret sat in a rocking chair on the front porch of the hotel. She could not remember the last time she'd felt so comfortable and relaxed.

They went back to their rooms and changed to go into the water. Odessa and Lydia came out wearing bathing suits. They played in the water until the sun was about to set. They all went to the front porch, wrapped in towels, and watched the most beautiful colors of pink and purple as the sun settled under the horizon. Hunter asked the children whether they could hear the sizzle when the sun settled in the water.

The children and women went to bed and fell asleep fast. Hunter went to the bar and had a few drinks with some other men staying at the hotel. The man who'd picked them up at the train station was tending bar. He told Hunter he was going to Medina in the morning to get supplies for the hotel. Hunter asked to go with him.

They all had a good night's sleep, except Hunter. He had something on his mind. He told Margaret he was going to Medina with the hotel manager. Margaret agreed reluctantly. Hunter put on his good suit and left. The hotel manager dropped Hunter off at the S. A. Cook Wholesale Company and agreed to pick him up at Skip's Diner on Center Street. Hunter loved the quaint village of Medina and accepted a job as a salesman when it was offered to him. Hunter would begin selling for Cook's in two weeks.

His next stop was to see a Realtor on Main Street. Hunter bought a house on Erie Street, close to the Buffalo, Lockport, and Buffalo Railway station. Hunter went to the Central Bank on Main Street. He signed the papers for a home mortgage. He would have to get his savings from his bank in Rochester and come back to make the arrangements. Hunter went to the diner and ordered a cup of coffee. The Shadigee manager came in and had a cup of coffee with him. They left for the lake.

Margaret was sitting on the beach, while Odessa and Aunt Lydia were in the water with the children. Hunter did not stop to change his clothes. He walked right to the beach and sat next to his wife. A moment of silence passed before Margret asked, "So are you going to tell me what you did in Medina?"

"I got a new job and bought a house."

Hunter whispered so no one else could hear what he told Margaret. Margaret acted as if she had not heard him at first. It took a minute for her to understand the gravity of his statement. Margaret had never been to Medina. Hunter explained that Medina was similar to Brockport but had more businesses and was much quieter.

"You bought a house?"

Margaret finally got the gist of what Hunter told her. Hunter whispered that he wanted to tell his sister and aunt later. Hunter couldn't tell whether Margaret was happy or angry that he had not included her in his decision. Margaret asked to be the one to tell Odessa and Lydia. Hunter agreed.

Hunter took the children for a walk along the beach, except for William, whom he carried. Megan talked about her morning at the roller-skating rink and how much fun it had been. Luke was collecting pieces of driftwood. They were smooth and rounded from being in the water but obviously had been part of something at one time—maybe a treasure ship, Hunter thought. The sun was getting close to the horizon, so Hunter turned back to the hotel.

Margaret, Odessa, and Lydia were sitting in a row of rocking chairs on the hotel porch. Hunter noticed they all had hankies and were wiping their tears. Margaret had told Odessa and Lydia the news about moving to Medina. Hunter took the children inside and ordered ice cream for them. He left them in the dining room and went back to the porch. Odessa said she was happy for them, but she would miss the children terribly. Hunter fought back tears and reminded his sister and Lydia that Medina was a quick trolley ride away and that he and his family would see them often.

Hunter remembered his promise to his grandma Jade. He sat with Margaret while Odessa and Lydia watched the sunset with the children. The new house had electric lights, indoor plumbing, and three bedrooms. The cost of the house was $3,000, which was about half what a similar house in Rochester cost. In addition to three bedrooms for them and the children, it had a kitchen table that would seat the whole family and a dining room that could be made into a bedroom for Big Mike.

Margaret started to get excited about having her own house again and asked whether it had room for a garden. Hunter said it had room for a small garden in the backyard, between the house and the woods. They watched the sunset in silence. Hunter told Margaret that Medina was only ten miles from there.

"I love the lake and hope we come here often." Margaret said.

Hunter slept well that night. The next morning, he was up early. He borrowed some bamboo fishing poles and took the children fishing on the pier. Margaret came with him to keep an eye on the children. Luke caught the first fish. It was a large white perch, but Luke landed it by himself. William was too small to concentrate on catching a fish. He sat with Megan until her fishing pole bobbed up and down. Megan caught a small jack perch and made Hunter let it go. She stopped fishing because she didn't want to hurt the fish.

The sky filled with dark clouds, so Hunter and Margaret took the children back to the hotel. They got there just as a loud clap of thunder shook the rafters on the porch. They sat on the porch and watched the lightning get closer. Margaret thought the storm coming across the lake was intriguing and different from the storms that came to Rochester. Hunter took the fish they'd caught to the cook, who promised to serve it to them for lunch. Hunter returned to his family on the safety of the front porch.

A giant gray cloud looked puffy on the top, while underneath, a wall of violent gray water plummeted toward the lake. Between the storm and the safety of the porch were sunshine and calm water. It was pleasant on the porch. In front of the storm, which was headed for the Shadigee Hotel, winds picked up, and large swells started rolling loudly to shore.

It was fun to watch the storm as it headed toward the hotel. Lydia and Odessa were smart enough to get out of their chairs and go inside, where other guests were watching through the windows. The wind came first and brought leaves and other small debris. Margaret grabbed William, declaring it was time to go inside. Megan and Luke protested, but when the rain came sideways, they followed their mother inside, and Hunter made sure all were safe.

In a moment, the children and Hunter were soaking wet. The storm battered the front of the hotel, and nothing could be seen through the thick rain. A minute passed, and so did the storm. The storm came from the northwest, where Toronto could be seen from the upstairs of the hotel on a clear night. The storm moved back to the northeast and away from shore. People went outside to watch it move away.

The waves were gigantic and roared like a beast as they broke along the shore. The shimmering silver Lake Ontario turned brown, with whitecaps decorating the tops of waves. The sun came back to the sky as the darkness moved farther away. The air was heavy, and breathing was awkward. The lake was beautiful but showed that it could be dangerous. The children wanted to go play in the waves. Margaret denied their request because she was worried the waves would carry them away. Hunter agreed.

The sun managed to take the humidity away after a while, but the waves on the lake grew larger, while the whitecaps became scarce, except for along the shore, where waves met land. A large ship that had been far out on the lake was still there but closer to Toronto than before the storm. People walked closer to the shore and studied the shoreline, as if they might find a sunken treasure washed ashore. It was time for lunch.

Megan refused to eat the fish because she thought it was cruel to kill and eat it. She had chicken instead. Hunter thought about the farm and how much Megan liked the live chickens that gave her eggs. He felt like telling her that the chicken she was eating used to be alive, but he loved her innocence and kept quiet. Odessa and Lydia talked about other storms they had seen but agreed that this was a pretty storm both before and after.

That night, the sound of the rolling waves lulled Hunter to sleep. Morning brought a plethora of birds singing different strains of an orchestrated harmony of nature. A large buck was drinking water from the big waves on the shoreline. White seagulls swooped into the water to catch small fish, offering amusement to the children. The rumbling of the motor coach pulling up to the roadside entrance of the hotel signaled that it was time to leave. Hunter loaded the travel bags onto the back of the coach.

No one ever wanted to leave the Shadigee Hotel, and that was true for Hunter and his family. When he got in the coach, William turned to look at the lake and said, "Bye-bye, lake."

The children never stopped talking about Shadigee. Hunter looked at Margaret and asked her if now was a good time. She knew what he meant and agreed. Hunter got the children's attention and told them he was happy his children liked Shadigee and wanted to go back. "Close to Shadigee is a town called Medina. Would you like to go there sometime?"

"Of course."

The children agreed. Hunter told them that was good because they were going to move there in two weeks. The children were excited until Lydia could no longer hold back her tears. The children did not understand why Aunt Lydia and Odessa could not come with them. Hunter explained as best as he could. During the next two weeks, everyone got used to the idea of leaving Aunt Lydia's house and moving to Medina. Aunt Lydia and Odessa talked about traveling together more so they could see more fun and beautiful places around the Rochester area. Hunter gave notice to a disappointed Mr. Michaels.

With two large, well-packed Likly's trunks, made by the company Lydia and Odessa worked for, Hunter, Margaret, and their children boarded the trolley and headed away from Rochester to Medina. Big Mike was there to see them off. He promised to visit soon. The children were excited on the trolley as they passed towns on the way. Margaret was familiar with Brockport and liked the town. She hoped Medina was as pleasant as Brockport was.

Towns seemed to get smaller as the trolley moved west. They went through Holly, Brockville, Huberton, and then Albion. The next stop was Medina. The trolley followed the south side of the Erie Canal, and the ride provided beautiful scenery. Margaret saw a tall church steeple ahead, then another, and still another. There were four tall church steeples reaching above the trees toward the sky. Hunter said, "That's Medina."

"It must be a wonderful town with so many churches," Margaret said.

"It is."

The children got excited as they got close to town. The trolley made a stop across from the Episcopal church on Center Street. Margaret admitted it was a gorgeous church, but she wanted to know where the Catholic church was. Hunter pointed up in the air and farther west and told Margaret she would see it soon. The children wanted to get off the trolley and see their new home. Hunter had to tell them there were two more stops in Medina; theirs was the last stop.

At the next corner, the trolley turned north onto Main Street. Margaret loved the variety of stores, shops, and businesses that decorated Main Street. People exited the trolley, but no one got on. The next stop was Erie Street. The trolley stopped, and the Donahee family got off. Hunter struggled with the two big trunks and all the small bags. Erie Street was a beautiful paved dead-end street with a half dozen houses between the trolley and Center Street. The smell of flowers filled the air. No one was there to help with the trunks. Hunter could not keep Margaret and the children from running down the street to see their new home. It was 150 yards from the station.

MEDINA

Hunter carried what he could and left the two large trunks by the trolley station. The house was unlocked, and by the time Hunter got there, his family was running around the house in amazement. The house had electric lights and running hot and cold water. A coal furnace for winter heat was in the basement. There was no outhouse and no need for one. The big backyard merged into a wooded area full of colorful singing birds. Hunter found Margaret on the back porch, smelling the summer flowers in the air.

"Do you hear that?" she said.

Hunter listened to all the faint and distant sounds. "Hear what?"

"A cow mooing."

Hunter listened and heard, way off in the distance, the faint moo of a cow or cows.

"We're near the country but not in the country. I love it," Margaret said.

Hunter left to go back to get the big trunks he'd left at the station. He had to drag them to the house one at a time. The street was quiet, and there was no one around to help. It was hot outside, and it took Hunter a long time to get the trunks to the house. He maneuvered the first trunk inside and went back for the other trunk. Upstairs was the bathroom, with a modern toilet and a bathtub. There were three small bedrooms and a small room in the back.

Margaret assigned Luke and William to one bedroom and Megan to another, while she and Hunter took the larger bedroom in the front. They'd save the extra room downstairs for her father, Big Mike, when he visited. There were beds in all of the bedrooms. The large bedroom had a view of evergreen trees across the street. The family was hungry.

Hunter suggested they walk downtown. It was a half mile from their home to Main Street. Hunter carried William most of the way, while Margaret, Megan, and Luke walked ahead of him on Center Street. They found a cozy little diner to eat lunch at. Hunter gave Margaret ten dollars to go to the downtown stores. Hunter ate his lunch fast and told Margaret and the children he had something to do and would find them on Main Street in about an hour.

Margaret had never had so much money to spend, but she was frugal. They stopped at a men and boys' clothing store and bought new Sunday clothes for Luke and William. She said she would pick them up on her way home, and the store set them aside for her. Next, they went to Medina Dry Goods and bought a dress for Megan. Then Margaret bought herself a new dress. Margaret felt guilty for spending almost half of the ten dollars already. Still, there were more shops to visit.

Margaret walked down Main Street, talking to friendly people and enjoying the town. The children were excited when a trolley came down Main Street. Behind the trolley was a new green-and-black car that turned into a parking spot right in front of them. The children looked at the shiny new car as Margaret proclaimed, "Hunter!"

Twenty-five years ago, Hunter had worked hard for two years while intending to buy a bicycle. However, there had always been something more important to do with his money, and he'd never owned a bicycle. If he could have bought a tractor on the farm in Kansas, he could have made more money. While living with his aunt Lydia and Odessa, Hunter had saved almost all his income. He would have had to struggle to buy a house in Rochester. The house in Medina was half the price of houses he'd considered in Rochester. He'd taken out a small mortgage on the house so he would not be strapped for money. He'd had enough money left to buy the Chevrolet Superior. He would have to use his own car for work at S. A. Cook Wholesale.

Hunter loaded up the family and picked up Margret's packages. They stopped at the grocery store to buy food for the house. Margaret was amazed at the products that were made or canned right there in Medina. She bought a jar of sweet pickles made at a local factory, Heinz Foods, for the children. The people in the store were friendly. There was room inside the back door for all the packages and groceries. The three children sat in the backseat. Margaret liked sitting in front with her husband.

On the way home from the store, Hunter drove the family around their new hometown. He drove past the S. A. Cook furniture factory and had to explain the difference between the Cook Furniture Company and Cook Wholesale. Seeley A. Cook had started the wholesale company first. To enhance sales, he'd made pieces of furniture for cigar customers when they'd saved enough cigar bands. So many people had wanted the furniture that he'd started a second company to make furniture. Both companies had grown larger.

The children weren't that interested in their father's story until he told them that separating the businesses had allowed the wholesale company to start selling candy as well. He drove down East Avenue by the big red building that housed S. A. Cook Wholesale Company, and the children wanted to go inside. Hunter persuaded the children to forget about the candy by driving to a playground and Saint Mary's Church on West Avenue. The school that Megan would attend was behind the church, on Eagle Street. Hunter took his family to their new home in the new car in the new town. Then he told them he had to go to work to let Mr. Menke know he was settled and ready for work.

Hunter left his happy family at home and went to the warehouse that housed the S. A. Cook Wholesale Company. He walked in the front door and saw half a dozen employees unloading a boxcar that was parked on the tracks behind the warehouse. Hunter joined in, carrying product from the boxcar to the warehouse. No one seemed to notice that he was a stranger, but it was obvious they appreciated the help. When the boxcar was unloaded, Joseph Menke came out of an office and introduced Mr. Donahee, their new salesman, to the workers. Hunter Donahee knew he would enjoy working with such fine men.

Mr. Menke took Hunter into the office and explained pricing to him. Hunter understood well the concept of a retail price, a wholesale price, and the manufacturer's pricing. A box of nickel Hershey chocolate bars had twenty-four candy bars in a box. Twenty-four times five cents was $1.20. Cook's sold the box for eighty-five cents, providing a thirty-five-cent profit for the retailer.

Mr. Menke told Hunter he would work inside the warehouse for his first week to learn the products and pricing. Then he would be ready to start selling in the southeast territory. That territory included Batavia to Churchville and back on the south side of the Erie Canal. Mr. Menke then asked Hunter how his family liked Medina and their new home. Hunter was pleased at his boss's sincerity regarding his family's happiness.

Hunter was ready to start work right away, but Mr. Menke suggested he take the rest of Friday and the weekend to explore Medina with his family. Monday would come soon enough. Mr. Menke stated that Seeley A. Cook was a community-minded man who served as president of the village and encouraged all his employees to be active in the community. Hunter saw great opportunity.

Reluctantly, Hunter left Cook's. On his way home, Hunter realized what a grand opportunity Mr. Menke had afforded him and his family. Hunter drove down Center Street and marveled at the big homes with well-manicured lawns and flower gardens along the way. He turned right onto Erie Street, toward his house. He backed into the driveway so that he could load his family and head out to explore the area around Medina.

Luke and William were playing in the backyard, and they came running to meet their father. Hunter picked up both boys and carried them inside. Megan was watching Margaret, who was standing on a chair in the kitchen. She was taking down the curtains to wash them. She was pleasantly surprised to see Hunter home so early. Hunter put the boys down and told them to go back outside to play. Megan went with them.

Margaret had busied herself cleaning the new home and unpacking their trunks. "It looks more like home, doesn't it?" she said.

"Needs something before it can be home."

Margaret looked surprised at Hunter's comment. Hunter looked out the back window and told Margaret the children were fine. He took Margaret's hand and led her upstairs. Margaret knew what was on his mind. A half hour later, Hunter was about to fall asleep, when a loud tugboat's deep whistle stirred him. He looked at Margaret and said, "Let's go watch the boat go under the lift bridge."

He jumped to his feet, fixed his clothes, and ran down to get the children. They were in the front yard, looking north toward the trolley station at the end of the street. The Erie Barge Canal was a hundred yards past the trolley. They could see the big red tugboat moving slowly toward downtown. Hunter had them in the automobile when Margaret came out the front door. Hunter walked her around and opened the door to help her inside and show his sons what a gentleman did. They drove out of the driveway in a hurry.

There were sixteen lift bridges on the Erie Canal, and thirteen of them were on the western part of the canal, where the land was relatively flat. Medina was the center of that area. Hunter turned east onto Center Street and drove a few blocks to Prospect Street, where he turned left toward the canal. The massive steel bridge was moving up. Hunter got there in time to see the tugboat push the barge under the bridge. They all got out of the car and watched until the bridge came back down to the road.

They got back in the Chevrolet and drove over the bridge. Hunter wasn't sure where he was taking his family as he headed north on the gravel road. He knew that ten miles ahead was Shadigee, but he did not want to drive the hour it would take to get there. Hunter and his family just enjoyed riding in the automobile and looking at the countryside. The road ran along Oak Orchard Creek. Hunter was about to stop the car to take the children to see the creek, when he saw a sign ahead: Elm Park. He continued on to the park.

Elm Park was located two miles north of Medina, on North Gravel Road. Hunter pulled in, and the children opened the back doors of the car to get out.

"Close those doors," Margaret said.

Hunter looked at her.

"You don't open the door until your father determines that it is safe to get out," she said.

Hunter parked next to two trucks. He turned his head and looked behind his automobile before he opened his door. He got out, walked around to Margaret's door, and opened it for her. He saw the excitement on his children's faces as they glared at him, waiting for the signal. After Margaret was out of the automobile, Hunter said, "You can get out now."

The back doors opened, and the children jumped out with excitement. There was no entrance gate like the one at Ontario Beach, where one had to pay a fee to enter. In fact, there were no fences or barriers. The park was green with elm, oak, and maple trees. Down a hill were swings and a small merry-go-round that had four horses and a baby elephant for the children to sit on and ride. The merry-go-round was not running, but a few other children were on the swings and a slide. Megan, Luke, and little William joined them.

A bridge that arched in the middle crossed Oak Orchard Creek and led to a baseball field on the other side. Margaret sat on a bench. Hunter noticed the printing on the side of the bench: Sweat Foundry, Medina, New York. Hunter joined his wife on the bench. He put his arm around Margaret and told her he loved her. Margaret said, "I love our home in this new town."

Hunter was happy, but his thoughts were on his new job. He couldn't wait to start dealing with these generous country people. A man came over the bridge and walked up to Hunter and his wife. Hunter stood and introduced himself. The man told Hunter he collected the fees for the park and was getting ready for the Elks' clam bake on Saturday. He told Hunter to enjoy the park for free. He did not have time to collect money now. Hunter thanked him and watched him go to one of the trucks.

The man got a rake, shovel, and wood box filled with sand from his truck. It was a lot for the man to carry. Hunter excused himself from Margaret and helped the man carry his load over the bridge. Margaret was thankful to have such a gracious husband but missed having him sit next to her. A woman came over the bridge and sat next to Margaret. They introduced themselves and became instant friends. Mary Law was the mother of some of the other children. She welcomed Margaret to Medina and said she lived on the dirt road west of Eire Street. It was called Beach Dive. Her children often played in the woods behind Margaret's new house.

Mary's husband worked in a sandstone quarry and was a member of the Elks Club. They talked about the Medina schools and stores. Mary gave Margaret several recommendations for her shopping. The women hardly noticed that it was getting darker. Between their sentences, they would look at the children playing and count their children. The men were coming across the bridge.

Hunter was carrying his jacket and looked dirty and sweaty. He was talking and laughing with the other men. He passed by the women with hardly an acknowledgment. Hunter put his load in the back of one of the trucks and put his jacket in the Chevrolet, but he took a cigar out of the pocket first. The men came back down the hill and walked over to a structure that had a paddle wheel attached. The man who'd talked to Hunter earlier reached down and moved some levers.

The whole area lit up with white electric lights strung throughout the trees. The children cheered and got off the swings and slide. They went to the merry-go-round. Five at a time went round and round before the merry-go-round stopped to change passengers. Little William was two years old and climbed into the elephant's seat with Megan's help. Luke was on a bright red horse, while Megan rode a cream-colored horse with a long brown wooden mane.

One of the men came to Margaret and Mary and told them, "It's your turn." Margaret thought she was too big for the merry-go-round, but Mary told her that their ride was different. She led her to a bench that seemed to hang from a tree next to the bridge. Mary told Margaret she would go first. She sat on the bench, which was only large enough for one person. The bench started to move and took Mary up in the air and halfway across the creek, when it stopped. Margaret didn't see the other bench stop where Mary had gotten on.

"Your turn," Mary said.

Margaret reluctantly sat on the bench. It took off and followed Mary high up in the trees and over the river. Margaret was tense and hung on tightly until she saw the view of the baseball field. It was bright green with brown baselines and all lit up. The ball field had cornfields all around it. It was beautiful and reminded Margaret of the farm. The moving bench went slowly enough that a person could walk off it when it met the ground by the baseball field. Mary stayed on the bench, and so did Margaret. They passed each other going in opposite directions back over the creek. Margaret thought it was like being a bird with the freedom to fly. She felt like singing.

Margaret watched Mary step off and away by taking the hand of the man who'd turned the ride on. Then it was her turn. Margaret thought it would be hard to get off but was pleasantly surprised when it wasn't. The children watched in amazement as their mothers got off the strange ride. They wanted to go, but the man told them the ride was for mothers only. The ride was for women to get to the other side without having to cross the bridge. Children had to cross with their fathers. The man felt that everything was ready for the next day and turned off the water-powered electric generator. Everything got quiet and dark.

Hunter was not ready to just turn around and go back to town, so he drove north to an intersection and turned right onto a dirt road. The road went about a mile and ended at Horan Road. Hunter turned right again, figuring the road would take him back to Medina. Horan Road was a dirt road that wound around some and went over a hill. The lights in Medina were a combination of gas and electric lights. The streets were lit by gas, and the stores had electric lights. A hand-dug lake called Glenwood Lake sat behind Boxwood Cemetery on Gravel Road. Horan Road passed along the other side of the lake and Oak Orchard River. At the north end of the lake was an electric power-generating plant that powered Medina. A large, dangerous-looking waterfall was just north of the canal on Oak Orchard Creek. Farther upstream, the creek went through a culvert that ran under the Erie Canal. On the south side of the canal was a wide area in the creek with little current. That was the place where the Red Cross gave swimming lessons.

Hunter went over a high single-lane steel bridge and into the town of Medina. The children were tired. Hunter drove home and put the automobile in the driveway. He had to carry little William to bed. Luke and Megan went straight to bed without having to be told. Margaret was about to spend her first night in her new home. With the children sound asleep, Hunter took Margaret outside, and they sat on the front porch.

The birds quieted, except for a great horned owl asking, "Who? Who?" in the woods behind the house. A doe and her two fawns walked down the street. The sun sank somewhere past the woods in the back of the house. A cool breeze relaxed Margaret's face and made her feel comfortable. The front porch had room for rocking chairs like the ones at Shadigee. With everything Margaret had, she felt guilty because she still wanted a rocking chair for her front porch.

Margaret had loved the farm, but the uncertainty and poverty of farmers had made her ready to leave the farm. Aunt Lydia's house was small and crowded, and they'd stayed there since before William was born. She missed Lydia and Odessa, even though she'd only left them that morning. Medina was the most wonderful place Margaret had ever been, and she was excited to make it her home.

Saturday morning, while Margaret was making coffee and deciding what to fix for breakfast, she heard a knock on her side door. The main door was open, with a screen door in place to keep the bugs out and let the air in. Margaret looked down the short stairway and saw a man wearing all white. He looked at her and said, "Milkman."

Margaret went down the stairs, remembering that Mary Law had said she was going to send him over. The milkman asked Margaret how much milk she used. Margaret was thinking about breakfast and told the milkman she didn't know.

"How many children, and what ages?"

"Three, ages two, four, and six."

"How about two quarts today and Monday? I don't come on Sundays."

Margaret told the milkman that was fine. She was not used to making such decisions. Margaret accepted the two quart bottles of milk. It was cold. Margaret realized she did not have ice in her icebox. The milkman walked to his truck, brought a small chunk of ice to Margaret, and told her the ice ought to last the day. Margaret thanked the milkman.

"I know the ice man from the ice sprayer. If you like, I'll send him over."

"That would be wonderful. How much do I owe you?"

"I collect every Friday. I'll leave your invoice with the milk on Thursday."

The children heard the milkman drive away and came running downstairs, asking Margaret where they were going to go that day. Margaret told them that when their father got out of bed, he would decide. Hunter had finally fallen asleep after thinking about all he was doing. Megan and Luke whispered to William to go wake up their father while they distracted their mother. He did.

William woke his father up. Hunter had had a good night's sleep and was thankful. The cold milk went well with some raspberry muffins for breakfast. Margaret had not had much time to cook. After the milkman had left, their new neighbor, Judge Skinner, and his wife had brought the muffins over as a housewarming gift. Hunter sent Luke and William outside to play with Megan while he decided on the activities for the day. Margaret was busy cleaning the icebox to keep the milk fresh and cold.

Luke and William walked across the street to watch the construction of a new house on the corner. Hunter decided to spend less money and take the children for a walk around town, or at least around his corner of the town. He walked over to get the boys and met the owner and builder of the brick house. His name was William Gallagher, and he owned a construction company that was paving the roads in the area. Hunter took the boys home to get Margaret and Megan so they could begin their adventure.

Hunter took them down West Center Street to Catherine Street. They walked by the Medina School and on to Eagle Street, where they walked east to Saint Mary's School and Church. The school was open, with nuns washing windows. Hunter remained suspicious of the mind-reading nuns because of his school experiences. One of the nuns saw the Donahee family looking at the school. She came out and introduced herself as Sister Kathleen.

Sister Kathleen taught first grade and would be Megan's teacher. Sister Kathleen took Megan and her family into the school and showed Megan her classroom. The parish priest was in the school. He was also the principal of the school. He signed Hunter up as a member of Saint Mary's Church. Megan liked the nuns and was looking forward to seeing them in church the next day.

The Donahee family left to continue on their walk toward downtown. They stopped to watch the trolley go by. After it passed, they were ready to continue their walk, when they realized little William was not with them. He'd been there before the trolley had passed by only seconds earlier, but now he was gone. Margaret got panicky.

Margaret took Megan and walked back toward the school, looking for William. Hunter took Luke and followed the trolley. They asked people along the way whether they'd seen a two-year-old boy. They joined in the search. William couldn't walk that fast, so they turned and headed for downtown. Margaret was beside herself, and Megan was scared because her mother was scared.

Hunter met a fireman, who alerted the fire company. It was a long half hour before William showed up riding on a fire truck and having a grand time. William was ringing the fire bell. Margaret was relieved. The volunteer fireman took Megan and Margaret and went searching for Hunter. Hunter was on his way to Main Street when the firemen found him and Luke. They put the Donahee family in the fire truck and rode around, announcing that little William had been found. The fire truck took them home. Hunter was embarrassed.

William was given a whipping and sent to his room. The family festivities were done for the day. Hunter got in his automobile and went to thank the firemen. Hunter had been in town for one day and was already well known but not for the right reasons. He was determined to change the way people thought of him.

The next day, the family dressed for church. They ate a grand breakfast because Margaret had had time to cook all afternoon on Saturday. They drove to church, and Margaret never let go of William. Sunday's sermon was about when the prodigal son came home. The priest seemed to be looking at William while he delivered his sermon. People greeted Hunter and his family and welcomed them to the congregation. Hunter was more relaxed after Mass.

LOST BOYS

Hunter did manage to change his reputation. His wife was happy and active in Medina. Margaret hosted social functions and joined the Catholic Daughters of America, for which she chaired a bowling night. Hunter became active in the church as well. He joined the Knights of Columbus and the Elks and became a familiar voice at political meetings.

One Saturday each month, Hunter took the family on the trolley to Charlotte to visit with Aunt Lydia and Odessa. They were always happy to see the children and often got news about St. Mary's Church that could lead to stories in their *Catholic Journal*. Lydia and Odessa volunteered time to the Catholic paper as editors and sometimes writers.

Lydia Smith and Odessa Donahee had become well known for their dedication to the Catholic church and to Rochester. Their popularity as a social voice provided them several opportunities to attend social functions in or around the city. Lydia and Odessa had pictures of fascinating trips and events, but they wanted to hear about how Hunter's family was getting along. Megan, Luke, and William especially liked their aunts because they were genuinely interested in their lives and listened to their stories about life in Medina.

Their visits were getting shorter, as Hunter was often in a hurry to get back to Medina for some sort of function. That Saturday night, Hunter was meeting with a gentleman from Lockport to work out the details to start a Boy Scout troop sponsored by St. Mary's Church. Hunter believed the Boy Scouts of America built leadership and community pride in young boys.

He believed boys who were involved in the scouting program would become better men. Hunter wanted his boys to have every opportunity to be successful. Putting boys in a wilderness environment with proper adult supervision was a way to instill confidence in them.

That spring, Boy Scout Troop 29 had its first campout off Bates Road, in back of the Conservation Club on the northeast side of Medina. The old sandstone quarry had flooded and made an excellent swimming hole. Twelve boys and three adults, along with Scoutmaster Donahee, planned the event for a Saturday and Sunday, with the campout ending with a hike to St. Mary's Church, where the boys would attend Mass together in their scout uniforms.

The adults checked for safety and let the boys plan where and how their overnight shelters would be constructed. An area was selected for a latrine, and the boys dug a hole. A campfire would provide a source for cooking. The boys roasted hot dogs on sticks for lunch and used a big cast-iron pot to make a stew for dinner. After dinner and cleanup, Hunter took the boys on a nature walk to identify birds, animals, and plants.

The scouts followed deer and other animal paths, which often led to water. They were in a thicket of trees, when Hunter asked, "How do we get back to the camp?" Hunter knew, but he let the boys lead the way. The boys decided they'd not seen the sun above the horizon, so they must have been going east. They followed the sun, which was on the western horizon and in the opposite direction of the camp. The sun was getting closer to the horizon, and the boys were getting tired. Even Hunter began to wonder how far they had gone.

The scouts were getting scared, as it was starting to get dark in the thickening woods. Hunter was getting worried as well, but he felt certain the boys would exit the woods on Horan Road, just north of the canal, and it would be an easy hike along the canal back to camp. It seemed the boys had been heading west through thick woods and bushes for hours, when they came to a quarry filled with water. On the south side, a path led to the northwest. Hunter did not have to suggest the scouts follow the path. They were happy to be on a dirt path that was easy to walk on.

A few feet from where the path started, the boys stopped. A giant, slithering black water moccasin blocked the path.

"Is it poisonous?" one boy asked.

"It's big," said another.

"It's coming after us."

Hunter picked up a stick and used it to fling the snake toward the quarry. He explained, "The black moccasin is poisonous, and it is aggressive." Hunter agreed that was a big one.

The boys automatically got behind Hunter as he led the way down the path for about a hundred yards. The road was a welcome sight. Hunter had worried about a possible newspaper headline reading, "Scoutmaster Disappeared with Twelve Scouts: Never Found." Now his confidence returned. The boys chose to go north on the road, but Hunter showed them the church steeples rising above the trees.

"Medina is that way, so which direction should we go?" Hunter said.

"South," the scouts declared in unison.

Five minutes later, they saw the canal and followed its shore back to the camp. The other two adults had the campfire going. Seeing the glow from the campfire, the boys found the path to the camp. The other adults asked Hunter why he'd waited until dark to return.

"We were having fun," he said.

The scouts started talking about all the things they'd seen, including the black water moccasin. The scouts' fears were gone in the safety of the camp. They slept well that night. Morning was pleasantly cool as the sun rose, and the scouts woke. Hunter was up before the boys, and he put a kettle of water on the fire. He cooked strips of bacon in a large frying pan while another adult got eggs ready to cook in the bacon grease. The scouts toasted thick slices of homemade bread with their hot dog sticks.

Cleaning up the campsite was an important task. They carefully extinguished the campfire after scrubbing the cooking utensils clean. They cleared the area of any trash and covered the latrine with dirt. Hunter led the scouts and three adult helpers to the canal and followed the canal past Horan Road, where Medina Falls roared far below the canal. The falls were on Oak Orchard Creek, right after the creek passed under the Erie Canal. On the left side of the falls was another power plant that generated electricity for part of the town of Medina.

They were at the wide bend in the canal. On the other side of the canal was a view of the backs of the stores on Main Street. Hunter led them around the bend and over the high bridge that took them to the intersection of Main Street and Eagle Street. The scouts stopped on the bridge and could see far down Main Street to the south. To the north was a big factory that rested between the canal and Commercial Street, where the trolley tracks were in the middle of the street. A block away to the west sat St. Mary's.

The walk to the school behind St. Mary's Church was pleasant. The scouts put their camping equipment in the basement of the school, where Margaret and other women were preparing a brunch for after Mass. Margaret forewarned Hunter that he smelled like a campfire. The boys got cleaned up as best as they could and went to church, where they sat as a group for Mass. Luke and William were the youngest boys in the scout troop at that time. After Mass, other boys were interested in becoming Boy Scouts. Troop 29 grew.

Margaret drove the Chevrolet to church with Megan. After Mass, the Women of Saint Mary's had coffee and cakes for the parishioners. The scouts were there to greet people and have milk and cake together. Hunter told Margaret he and the boys would wait for her so they could all ride home together. Margaret told Hunter to walk home with the boys because they smelled too bad to get in the automobile. Hunter and the boys were tired as they headed home from their adventurous weekend. Hunter wanted to take a nap.

Big Mike stayed in Hamlin, working on the farm. He would show up from time to time to see Margaret and the children. Just as Hunter closed his tired eyes, the familiar pounding on the door signified Big Mike's arrival. William and Luke answered the door. Big Mike was sober. He usually was on Sunday mornings. Luke and William were tired but came running when they heard their grandpa knock on the door. The boys talked about the camping trip. Hunter remained asleep in his chair.

Big Mike took the boys down the street to the trolley station and left Hunter home asleep in his chair. Margaret and Megan came home from church. They saw Big Mike and the boys. Megan got out of the automobile and ran to join them. Margaret went inside and found Hunter asleep in his chair. She let him sleep and put her church apron and goods away. She sat on the front porch and talked to a neighbor who was walking by.

The women watched an airplane fly overhead. Margaret figured it was the flier McDarmott, who came to Medina from Leroy. He'd been at the Walsh House last April, speaking about flying and trying to entice men to learn to fly. When Big Mike came back with the children, William was excited about the airplane. Big Mike sat with Margaret on the porch and talked for a while until a farm truck pulled into the driveway behind the Chevrolet. Big Mike said goodbye to Margaret and then went behind the house and said goodbye to his grandchildren. He got in the truck and left. Margaret never knew when he was coming or how long he would stay. She loved her father very much and wished she could see more of him.

Margaret went inside to find that the truck had woken Hunter. "Did you have a nice visit with my father?"

"He's here?"

"Was. He just left."

Hunter was glad it had been a short visit, because on his longer visits, Big Mike would go to O'Brien's tavern and drink too much. Then Big Mike would get in a fight, which embarrassed Hunter. The children were playing in the woods behind the house. Hunter told Margaret he was going to Curvin's Newsroom to buy the paper. The day's New York Times would be there. It amazed Hunter that the paper came by train to Rochester, was loaded on the trolley to Medina, and arrived the same day. Hunter wanted to read the economics section, which was sure to have more bad news about the stock market and the nation's economy.

Hunter hollered out the back door, and the children came running. They liked to go with him to Curvin's because they each got to spend a penny on candy. Hunter loaded the children into the Chevrolet and left Margaret home to fix lunch. Hunter did not invest in the stock market, as his sister and Aunt Lydia did, but the market interested him and helped him in his sales for Cook's.

Hunter took his newspaper and children home. The children knew better than to bother him while he was reading his Sunday paper. Hunter could not believe how fast stock prices had risen since last week. Stock brokers speculated that stocks would continue rising. Food prices were going down, and that concerned Hunter because he was familiar with the production of and farming for food.

The Diana Theater was showing a talking movie called *Sal of Singapore*. Hunter took Margaret and the children to the movie theater that afternoon. After the movie, Hunter made the children tell him what was good or bad in the movie. The movie was a film with silent actors, with Jack Holt narrating the film. Megan thought the parents of the deserted baby should have been found because they would want their baby back. Hunter accepted her synopsis as good and thoughtful. Luke liked the ship and crew in the movie and determined that shipping was a hard life because daddies were away from home too long. Hunter agreed with Luke that it would be hard to leave his children for such a long time. William wanted to know why Singapore Sal was angry and unhappy until the end of the show. Hunter told William that a woman needed a good man to take care of her and that all men weren't good.

"Like you, Daddy?" William said.

Margaret chuckled and confirmed, "Your daddy is a fine man."

Hunter did not share his opinion that a movie should not have such delicate subject matter. He kept his opinion to himself for the time being.

In August, Hunter organized a Boy Scout banquet to give recognition to the scouts who'd completed certain requirements. Margaret and the other mothers prepared the food in the basement of St. Mary's School. Megan had fun waitressing for the event. She was pleasantly surprised when her name was in the newspaper for her service to the scouts. Newspapers reported on community-minded people and the good things they achieved.

In September of 1929, William was six and excited to start

school. Luke was in the second grade, and Megan was ten years old and in the fourth grade at Saint Mary's School. They walked to and from school. The first day, Margaret walked with the children. She walked home alone. She could not remember having a day all to herself.

Margaret kept busy while the children went to school. The following year, Margaret became a chairperson for the Catholic Daughters of America's bowling social. Two years after that, Margaret became the vice president of an organization called the Mount Carmel Guild. The organizations she was involved in did work to better the community by having functions, such as a sewing club that Margaret chaired in 1932.

Hunter became more active with the Boy Scouts, Knights of Columbus, and the community. He continued selling for S. A. Cook Wholesale. Hunter read the newspaper every day. His belief that the stocks of companies could not have increased as much as they had during the Roaring Twenties proved true. The United States was in the midst of the Great Depression. Large companies closed. The Rochester, Lockport, and Buffalo Railroad closed and no longer came to Medina. Investors traded working capital for gold, causing banks to fail, and the federal government increased interest rates. The value of the dollar plummeted.

Franklin D. Roosevelt was elected president in 1932, but his New Deal had yet to fix the nation's economic crises. Financial stress occurred in countries all over the world. People lost jobs, homes, and farms. Medina lost a couple of businesses that had been sold to large conglomerates. Individuals who tightened their belts and continued doing business owned most industries in Medina, and those individuals survived the Great Depression. New Deal advertisements offered consumers ways to take advantage of opportunities to buy goods while prices were low. Times changed.

In the spring of 1934, Big Mike knocked on Hunter's front door. Hunter recognized the knock and let William answer the door. Big Mike stood in the rain, soaking wet and travel worn. William brought him inside. Big Mike announced that he was working on a farm just outside of Medina. He set his old worn-out canvas bag that held all of his belongings on the floor and said, "I'm moving in."

NEW BEGINNINGS

Hunter was not excited to have Big Mike move in with him. Margaret was happy because she missed her father. The children liked Big Mike because he was kind to them. Big Mike did three things well: he worked hard, drank much, and loved a good fight. Big Mike taught Luke and William how to box. The boys practiced on each other but with sportsmanship. They never hurt each other.

A week after Big Mike moved in, Hunter came home after the children had left for school. Hunter coaxed Margaret into the automobile to go for a short ride. He left Erie Street and drove three blocks before turning left onto Ann Street and into the drive of a grand old West Center Street house. He parked in front of a large two-story barn and walked Margaret around the house and up the stairs of the large wrap-around porch to the front door.

Hunter opened the door without knocking and held it for Margaret so she could walk inside. She did. The living room was huge, with bay windows on two walls. The staircase going up was grand and wide. There were also two downstairs bedrooms, a dining room that could seat twelve, a den, and a kitchen. Humming in the kitchen sat a brand-new Kelvinator refrigerator. Margaret went to the refrigerator and opened the door to feel the cold air.

"Oh, Hunter, I would love to have a refrigerator."

"It comes with the house."

Margaret was puzzled but only for a moment. Hunter

explained that he'd paid off the mortgage on Erie Street five years ago and had been saving ever since.

Upstairs, the house was set up for another apartment. Margaret saw the large rooms and told Hunter the boys could have their own rooms. The house was only a block away from Megan's high school. Hunter took Margaret home and went back to work. Margaret could think of nothing other than the new house. Three days later, a young schoolteacher and his wife came to the Erie Street house to look at it. They loved the house and the quietness of the dead-end street. Two weeks later, they moved in, and the Donahees moved to their new big house on West Center Street.

Big Mike had a room on the first floor, across from Hunter and Margaret's room. The children had their own bedrooms and bathroom upstairs. Hunter, with Big Mike's help, installed a speed bag in the barn. The talented boys got good at punching the bag. So did Megan. None was as good as Big Mike. Big Mike went to work every day, and he took to carrying a pint of whiskey in his back pocket.

On weekends, Big Mike liked to go to the local taverns. Such was the case one particular Saturday night. O'Brien's Tavern was next to the police station. Big Mike was inside drinking, until he found three obnoxious men who needed to be taught a lesson in etiquette. A patron ran next door to the police station. The police were no match for Big Mike either.

A battered policeman knocked on Hunter's door at midnight. Hunter woke and went to get Big Mike. Big Mike refused to come home and even threatened to fight Hunter. William heard the commotion at home, and concerned for his grandpa, he walked to O'Brien's. Big Mike behaved when he saw William come inside the bar. William looked at the battered people and his father. He walked up to his grandpa and asked, "Grandpa, will you walk me home?"

Big Mike put a friendly hand on William's shoulder and left the bar with him. Big Mike drank and fought for fun, and he would never hurt his grandson. Hunter stayed to clean up the bar and smooth things over with the police. The police respected Big Mike because he fought fair and would take on many men at one time. They told Hunter they would be ready for Big Mike the next time. They thought they were ready.

A month later, when Big Mike entered O'Brien's, the barkeep sent a messenger next door to warn the police that Big Mike was back. The police rounded up ten tough officers, firemen, and citizens. When the inevitable brawl broke out, the police and their friends would make Big Mike sleep his binge off in a jail cell.

At one o'clock in the morning, the same battered policeman who'd come to see Hunter last month knocked on Hunter's door. Hunter told him to wait a minute while he got dressed. The policeman said, "Can I just take William with me?"

Hunter understood why the officer wanted William and agreed. William was already coming down the stairs. The policeman gave William a ride in the police car to get his grandpa. When William brought his grandpa out of the bar, the policeman offered them a ride home. They accepted the ride. Hunter was waiting, and it was a good thing. Big Mike had fallen asleep in the policeman's car. It was a big job to get Big Mike out of the car. Hunter suggested they leave him in the barn because it would be easier than carrying him into the house. There was an old horse stall that was cleaned up. Hunter had William get one of the Boy Scout camping cots and put it in the horse stall. They got Big Mike on the cot. He was sleeping soundly.

The officer closed the sliding door, which had iron bars in

the window, and smiled. "That's as close to a jail cell as we'll ever get him."

Hunter thanked the policeman and took William inside to go back to bed.

That event repeated itself every other month for the next year. Big Mike never lost a fight, missed work, or mistreated his daughter or grandchildren. After picking apples in the fall of 1936, Big Mike sat next to a tree and took a small sip of his whiskey. His heart gave out, and he died in the orchard. Big Mike had a big funeral. Margaret and the children greeted mourners. Many visitors told the family how much Big Mike had helped them when times were bad. Hunter realized where Margaret got her generosity and her community-mindedness. Big Mike had been a tough man who made the world a better place.

Hunter's children honored Big Mike by trying to be as kind as he'd been. Megan finished high school with honors and was accepted to St. Joseph's School of Business in Buffalo. Megan went to stay with her aunts Odessa and Lydia for a week before Christmas. Hunter taught his children that family and community were important. Luke and William played football for the high school. Sports built social skills. They boxed on the boxing team. Hunter's boys were good athletes. They were active in the community. William became homeroom president, while Luke took up acting in community plays.

Hunter's sales at S. A. Cook Wholesale were good, but the company restructured with a group of owners. Jacob Kern moved to Lockport and started a candy distribution business. Hunter was offered a job as an engineer for William Gallagher's construction company. Hunter left Cook's and began work as an engineer, paving roads and building a bridge on Route 18 north of Albion, near Point Breeze.

That summer, Luke, age fifteen, and William, age twelve,

worked with their father at the bridge site. One of their tasks was to carry a bucket to a farmhouse and bring cool water back for the men working on the bridge. It was a long walk to the farm, and it took the two of them to carry the heavy pail back without spilling too much water. The other workers would drink the water, and the process would start over again.

Luke and William were happy when school started, because they could play football. William was quarterback for the high school team. Luke was a fast runner. Margaret was busy with the teacher-parent association to make sure the students of Medina High School got the best education possible. The Donahee family was well known, in a good way, in Medina.

On an unusually hot Saturday afternoon in September, Luke, William, and some friends went to the quarry on Ryan Street to swim. The top of the quarry was thirty-five feet above the water. Luke and William were excellent swimmers. When he dove off the cliff, William displayed a graceful form that made it clear why people called the maneuver a swan dive. Other boys tried to match him.

A buddy named Edward tried to match William's dive but concentrated too much on the form and misjudged the distance to the deep water. The boys had to run and jump to clear the cliff. Edward did not run and jump far enough. He hit the side of the cliff feet first and was pushed out to deep water. He landed on his belly and sank.

Luke and William were climbing up the cliff to dive again when they saw Edward's tumble to the bottom. Luke and William hit the water at the same time. Edward rose to the surface as the boys searched for him on the bottom. They finally found him on the surface. He was laughing on the far side of the quarry.

"Try to beat that form," Edward said.

William and Luke were both surprised and angry to find him in good shape, but as they got close, they realized he was not in such good condition. His belly was bleeding from tiny little cuts caused by the belly flop. He'd cut his feet on the side of the cliff, and he had blood dripping from his ear. He had to swim to the other side of the quarry to climb up the cliff, but from where he was, there was a long path that made it up to Glenwood Avenue.

In the Boy Scouts, Luke and William's father had trained them in first aid. The boys checked Edward over and decided he should not climb the cliff. The long path was the way to go. Edward stood up and fell back down. Luke and William had to use the scout-carry technique to carry Edward up the path and to the road. At the top of the road, they told Edward they would go find help. Edward jumped to his feet and said, "I'll race you!"

Luke and William were both angry and glad at the same time. Edward had faked being dizzy from his injuries to make the brothers carry him. William and Edward were the same age, and William had been worried that Edward would not be able to play football. Edward was a tough football player, and the team needed him. Edward enjoyed playing practical jokes, and William and Luke vowed to get even.

When Luke graduated from high school and Megan finished college, Hunter decided to start his own family business and left Gallagher's Construction. He traded his old Chevrolet for a two-year-old Elgin panel van he could use in the business. He used the barn behind the house as a warehouse and store. Megan took care of the office work and the store, while Luke and Hunter took to the road. Donahee Specialties sold restaurant supplies, including pickles, popcorn, and potato chips. Hunter got a telephone, which opened the business to the world. The number for the business was 635.

Hunter enjoyed selling again. He built a route with Luke and turned the customers over to Luke. Hunter found a second truck for sale. He bought it and started another route. Luke traveled the north side of Medina, while Hunter went south. Adding Dad's Root Beer and Queeno Pop expanded and diversified the product list. The business was growing when William started eleventh grade in the fall of 1940.

While William's family was busy working, he started his junior year in high school. William planned on having fun that year. It was a time to study, work, and play sports. August was the beginning of football practice. William was proud to be elected team captain. He played a rough tackle. William was getting tougher and reminded his mother of a sober Big Mike. William's friends were always welcome at his home. Teammates would often discuss football strategies and do homework at the Donahees' kitchen table. The Donahee boys' good looks and athletic acumen made them popular.

William learned to be a viable part of the community from Boy Scout activities. He was active in school as well. He often joined others to make school a better or more fun experience. William liked to box for the boxing team because it proved the better of two competing men. Hunter's children worked to make their father happy. They succeeded. News of the war in the Pacific and in Europe escalated from 1939 to the present summer of 1941. William was thinking about school and football when he started his senior year at Medina High School in September 1941. He was sure it was going to be a good year.

William was proud of his father when Hunter started a political career by being elected trustee on the Medina Village Board in March 1941. William knew his father could easily sell himself as a political candidate, and his reason for entering politics was solely to make Medina a great and prosperous village to live in. William believed that his father was thinking about his and his siblings' futures as well as the economic security of the village. By the time school started in September, William's father had proven that he had a future in the leadership of Medina.

Three months later, the Japanese bombed Pearl Harbor. The bombing reverberated across the county, exploding emotions of country pride and courage. On December 8, that pride and courage drove William Donahee and several of his friends to the National Guard unit down the street from the high school. They joined Company F of the 108th infantry. The boys—or men, as they believed themselves to be—were doing what they thought was expected of an American man.

The men left for Fort McClellan in Alabama by train. They returned on December 10 on a furlough but had to leave after Christmas to report back to McClellan by January 1. It would be William's last time with his family for many years. William received a letter telling him that Luke had joined the navy. William's father was left to run Donahee Specialties with only Megan's help.

Many of the young men in William's unit shared his youthful pride and sense of indestructability. William, like many soldiers, got a tattoo on his forearm. Before leaving Fort McClellan, William and four other close friends from Medina who'd joined Company F had a scroll with the first letter of their last names inscribed. One by one, William's friends were killed in battle. William was devastated. He was stationed in the South Pacific on Japanese-inhabited islands.

William saw several Americans killed by Japanese who moved about in underground tunnels. Thinking he was the last of his group of friends to inevitably get killed, he volunteered as a tunnel rat. William believed he could save many lives as a tunnel rat. He would find the Japanese tunnels and go inside to find the Japanese fighters. William followed a Japanese soldier down a dark tunnel. The Japanese knew William was behind him and fired his rifle toward William, hitting him in the shoulder twice. William completed his underground mission, killing the Japanese soldier, and made it to the surface. William was in bad shape and thought he was about to join his friends as another casualty of war.

William received medical attention and was sent to the island of Molokai in the Hawaiian Islands to recover from his injuries. Because his injuries were to the upper torso, his legs were good. Every day for the six-month recovery time, William and another American soldier took turns climbing a mountain to establish a Japanese submarine lookout. William was on top of the beautiful island mountain, when he spotted a Japanese submarine heading toward the island of Oahu. William was scared because a Japanese submarine could do severe damage to the naval base in Honolulu on Oahu.

William excitedly ran down the dirt path that led from the mountaintop to the small village below. A radio was hidden in a hut in the small village. William used the radio to call in the sighting. He was instructed to go back up the mountain and keep looking. It normally took an hour to maneuver the path to the top of the mountain. William made record time, running up the path in thirty minutes. He saw several airplanes between his mountain and Oahu. Two ships left Honolulu and disappeared over the horizon to the northwest. The planes turned to little dots and then vanished, following the ships.

Sergeant Rosas came to the top of the mountain early to relieve William. Rosas had heard about the sighting and wanted to see what was going on. Normally, the lookouts would split the day, with one arriving on the mountaintop at dawn and staying until the other arrived in the afternoon. The other would stay from one o'clock until dusk. There was no need to man the lookout at night, because they would not be able to see a submarine in the dark.

William stayed with Rosas until two in the afternoon. There was no more excitement, so William made his way down the mountain to the village. Most of the men were out fishing every day, so women and children occupied the small village when William returned from his watch. William enjoyed his time in the village.

William's shoulder was sore. He'd lost a lot of weight and wore only a pair of short pants and no shoes. William and Rosas did not wear their army uniforms on the island. To gain strength, William would race the boys to the tops of coconut trees to pluck ripe coconuts. The boys would wait for William because he made chores fun. The village women would make crafty novelties to send to Honolulu to sell for money. The younger women would dive into the ocean to gather seashells for jewelry.

After two months, William's shoulder had healed well enough that he could join the younger women in the ocean. William became proficient at staying underwater for long periods of time and finding many valuable seashells. William felt at home in the village, working with the women and caring for the children. All the women and children would run to the beach when the men came in with their catches of fish. The men and their women would celebrate a safe return from the sea by greeting each other with a loving embrace. Often, the single men would find single women who were willing to greet them with hugs.

That afternoon, William was looking at the catch with the children. With everyone in the village watching, an old fisherman walked up to William and gave him a hug. The entire population of the village laughed. William laughed too, but he realized that the men thought of him as one of the women.

William introduced the men to the rough-and-tough game of American football. He gained the tough island men's respect. The women showed William how to make necklaces and bracelets with the shells he gathered by tying and stuffing a string into each shell. William got good at making the jewelry and always donated his jewelry to the village to sell. A young village girl named Alanah asked William whether he had a girlfriend back home. When he told her no, she returned a necklace to William and said in bad English, "For your mother."

William wrapped up the necklace and put it in a box to send home for his mother. The next time the supply boat came to the island, William mailed the necklace with a letter describing how beautiful Hawaii was. William and Rosas slept in the radio tent at night and talked about how much they liked the island. William wanted to stay there forever.

William watched the supply ship make its way to the island. Normally, the ship was at the beach for a few minutes and then left. This time, the ship stayed on the beach. William wondered why the ship stayed, when he heard Rosas and two other voices coming up the path. Rosas and William were being replaced. The island soldiers were going back to the war after six months in paradise.

The supply boat was waiting for William and Rosas. The islanders were sad to see them go. They brought gifts for the soldiers, including William's favorite fruit: lemons. Alanah, the young woman William had enjoyed diving with, gave him another necklace and a bracelet she'd made from her shells. William's uniform was too large because he'd lost so much weight while blending in with the villagers. Duty called, and William's feelings did not matter. He was a patriotic man. William courageously left Molokai to go back to fight.

Two days later, William was with his old unit on a different

Pacific island. The loss of men who'd died in skirmishes while he was gone saddened him. William did what he was good at: he chased the enemy down the dark holes hidden all over the Pacific islands. William often looked at his tattoo and figured he would be the last of the group to die. He fought with no fear.

The tunnels became more sophisticated, with turnaround spots, intersections, hiding places, and ammunition storage holes. William caught up to an enemy soldier in such a tunnel and used his knife so that others would not know he was coming. William could hardly squeeze over the dead soldier to continue through the tunnel. The blood of the corpse provided a lubricant, allowing William to move on. Strange voices ahead alerted William to an underground meeting area. William couldn't count how many Japanese there were, but he guessed there were several. William quietly took a grenade out and pulled the pin.

William planned on tossing the grenade into the group and backing away. It was difficult to move backward uphill while confined in the tunnel. The Japanese voices became loud and fast. They knew an American tunnel rat was coming. Bullets hit the ground in front of William's face, kicking up dirt and stones into his face. The sound hurt his hearing until he heard nothing. William tossed the grenade and emptied his rifle. He thought it was his turn when the grenade exploded ahead of him. The tunnel collapsed around William, and he could no longer breathe. The grenade must have exploded in an underground ammunition bunker, causing stored explosives to massively blow up.

William's squad above the surface figured William had set off the explosion. They looked for William to emerge from the ground somewhere. He did not. Two of the American soldiers climbed into the crater caused by the explosion. They found the remains of several Japanese bodies and much debris in the hole.

One of the soldiers recognized the slight edge of an American helmet protruding under the butt of a Japanese gun embedded in the ground. He dug out the helmet. Written inside was the name William Donahee.

"Here!" the soldier yelled, and help came to dig the ground around the spot where the helmet had been found. The blackened barrel of William's M1 carbine came first. The men dug fast and found William's hands still on the gun. He'd never had time to back away. They got to his hands and pulled. The dirt was loose, and they freed William's limp body from the grave. William had a pulse.

About a hundred feet away, a grassy trapdoor opened. William's squad was close and hit the Japanese soldier with the butt of a rifle. They took him prisoner and put dynamite in the hole he'd come out of. Sergeant Callahan was working to revive William when they brought the prisoner over. The Japanese soldiers seemed cruel, but they were dedicated soldiers. The squad found another trapdoor and dynamited the door.

The explosion seemed to shock William into consciousness. The Japanese soldier looked at William as if he recognized him. The prisoner spoke something in Japanese in a clear voice and language that no one understood. What the prisoner did next shocked the American soldiers: he snapped to attention and saluted William. The salute was an obvious sign of respect. Part of William understood that the Japanese were fighting a war against the United States and its allies to survive. For a moment, William respected the fierce killer as a man with strong convictions. William closed his eyes.

WAR SOUVENIRS

William caused a dozen enemy soldiers to die that day. He felt bad but understood the war. The explosives had been extensive and intended to do much damage to American troops. While digging the crater out, the soldiers found a radio that might have brought Japanese air support. William's squad had caught an important prisoner and caused dramatic damage to the enemy's strategy. William was taken to a medical tent, where he was treated and released a day later. William partially recovered in a few days. William's ears rang for a week, making life and even sleep difficult.

William was terrified to go back underground, and no one would have blamed him if he had not gone. He was moving through a field on the other side of the island, when he heard a gunshot. His buddy five feet away went down with a bullet in the chest. William saw the trapdoor close and went after the Japanese guerilla. William opened the trapdoor and dove in headfirst. Two minutes later, gunfire could be heard under the ground. The American soldiers saw a trapdoor open fifty feet from the one William had dived into. They pointed their guns at the hole, but no one fired. William emerged in great pain. He'd been shot.

"I got him," William said.

William was conscious but bleeding badly. He'd been shot in the other shoulder. William received first aid and was sent to a medical unit. The bullet was removed, and William was patched up. William had muscle damage that needed time to heal. He was assigned to submarine watch again. He couldn't believe his luck.

That afternoon, William met members of a marine unit that was sent to Iwo Jima to replace the American tunnel rats with flamethrowers that filled the tunnels with oxygen-depriving fire. The marines also had a weapon called a corkscrew that William had never seen demonstrated.

William was left on the same beach he'd left in the fall of 1943. He received a warm welcome from the people in the village. Alanah gave William a hug. The old man who'd hugged William a year ago saw Alanah give William the hug and shrugged and laughed. William ate fresh pineapple, fish, and lemon juice with the villagers. The two soldiers who were already there stayed to themselves and ate the rations the army had left for them.

The current soldiers wore their uniforms every day. They had been on Molokai for seven months and were only cordial with the villagers. They were happy to have another sub watcher with them. They had not seen a submarine the whole time they'd been there. They had been spending the fifteen hours of daylight on the mountain together. At first, they'd taken turns, but they'd had trouble staying awake. They wanted to set up a schedule in which two men were on the mountain at a time. William knew it wasn't necessary, but he went along with the other soldiers.

A month later, the supply boat brought supplies for William and took the other two soldiers back to the war. They had fully recovered from their wounds. William gave his supplies to the villagers. He found an abundance of canned food and other rations that the other soldiers had left behind. Their supplies went to the villagers as well. William was given orders to be on the mountaintop for nine hours a day. He could choose the nine hours as long as they varied and were in daylight. He had to radio when he left for the mountaintop.

William had healed enough to start diving for seashells by the time he was the only watcher on the island. William was tired of the war and hoped it would end soon. He performed his watch duties diligently. Often, the children would climb the mountain to see what William did. William made a game to see who could find the fishing boats. Sometimes they could not find them until the boats came into view as little dots on the sea.

William worked with the women and dove for seashells when he wasn't on top of the mountain. Alanah and William became close. Sometimes Alanah would climb the mountain with William to work on her English. William was twenty-one years old, and he wished he could stay on Molokai with Alanah. He fought the urge to get too close to Alanah, because he knew he would have to leave her again.

George Jones from West Virginia came on the supply boat when William had been on the island for three months. Corporal Jones was quick to fit in with the villagers. He was on the island for all of fifteen minutes before he cut the legs off a pair of fatigue pants to match William's island attire. George was not interested in working with the women as William did. He wanted to go fishing with the men.

George had been badly wounded in his leg and chest. It took William an hour to walk up the path to the top of the mountain, while George, because of his injuries, struggled for two hours to get to the top. William agreed that George would be better off fishing with the men. George was happy and turned out to be a good fisherman. There were no orders to extend the time on top of the mountain to more than the nine hours William was doing, so he kept doing the nine hours. William was happy spending time helping the village women and children.

When William had been on Molokai for six months, he figured the supply ship would take him back to his unit any day. William's heart sank when the supply boat came in December. The captain gave William his orders to go back to his unit. They were dated January 1945. William had one more month on the island.

William knew he was in love with Alanah, but his Catholic upbringing prevented him from acting on his feelings. Alanah would have had to convert to Catholicism, and William saw too many differences in her Hawaiian beliefs. The only promise William made to Alanah was that when he left soon, he would never forget her. The month passed slowly as the love quandary gnawed at William. William never saw a submarine during his second tour on Molokai.

William saw the supply boat coming when he was on top of the mountain. He hurried down the mountain, put his uniform on, packed his duffel bag, and looked for Alanah. She was nowhere to be found. The villagers saw William off, and Alanah's mother was in tears when she hugged him goodbye. William stood on the beach, looking to see Alanah one more time. The boat captain asked, "Are you coming?"

"Yes, sir."

William stood on the bow of the boat as it backed away. He followed the deck on the side of the boat as it turned around. Alanah came from somewhere in the trees. William could tell she was sobbing. He wanted to jump into the water and swim to her as she ran into the water. The last thing William heard was "Take me with you!"

The boat sped away with William on it. William went back to his unit to find many changes. The marines had come to the island and were thrashing the enemy. Marine and navy Corsair fighter planes provided support that saved the lives of many army and marine soldiers. The war was still going on, and William was in the thick of the fight.

HOME

William received a letter from home letting him know that his brother, Luke, was doing well on the USS *Hornet*. Luke was also in the Pacific. Sugar prices had risen so high that the soda pop Hunter sold had not been available for years during the war. Now he was getting some shipments with limited quantities. William believed his father needed help with Donahee Specialties. William was ready to go home when the war ended. The European war ended on May 8 with the surrender of Germany. Three months later, Japan surrendered. The war was over.

William arrived home in October 1945, and Luke came home shortly after. Hunter was ready for them to go right to work for Donahee Specialties. He made the boys feel needed, and their work habits were needed to make Donahee Specialties survive and prosper. William, Luke, and Hunter moved the business from his barn to a better location on Center Street. Hunter installed a telephone. The phone number was 6.

William wrote several letters to Alanah in Hawaii, but she never answered any of them. William and Luke had been teenagers when they'd left for the war. One thing they missed from their youth was playing football. The Donahee brothers and some friends made time to plan a semipro team for Medina. Other than playing football, the Donahees worked. Luke and William split up the sales route their father had worked during the war. Margaret and Megan worked inside the new warehouse on East Center Street.

Luke worked the old northern route, while William worked the southern towns. William loved selling and getting new customers. Luke was steady and maintained customers while increasing sales. Donahee Specialties advertised in the *Medina Tribune* for new sales drivers. The company hired a new salesman, trained him, and bought a new truck. William gave the new salesman his best area. William built up another area and hired another salesman. Donahee Specialties continued the process, and by the end of 1946, they had seven trucks on the road.

The Donahees' business grew, as did the nation's economy after the war. By the summer of 1947, Luke and William took some time off on weekends to build their father and mother a cottage on the shore of Lake Ontario. Hunter and his family had always loved the lake. It reminded Luke of the USS *Hornet*, and William would look at the lake and think of Hawaii. Luke was doing what he'd done before the war, but he enjoyed building the cottage. He was good with his hands. William enjoyed a youthful wildness.

William bought a Harley-Davidson motorcycle. His boyhood friend Edward bought one as well. They rode together when they weren't working and drank too much alcohol. The cottage was completed by the time summer was halfway over. Donahee Specialties had a problem. However, growing pains were a good problem to have. The company had grown fast, and the facility was too small. In the fall, they bought a larger building on East Avenue. Luke spent more time working on the building and the equipment used to package the popcorn and potato chips.

William took over the northern territory and started building more sales routes. After work, he played football or rode his motorcycle. He and Ed were out riding their motorcycles one day, when they stopped at Curvin's Newsroom for ice cream. William's eye caught a pretty girl in the soda shop. Her name was Donna. William brashly asked her, "Would you like to go out with me?"

William was wild, tough, and popular. He spent his time working. He was shocked when Donna said yes.

William provided a time and date and left with Ed. William and Ed had some GI educational benefits and decided to use the funds to learn to fly airplanes. William took his first lesson at Medina Airport. He did not trust that the plane would fly. William taxied the plane up and down the runway, learning to use his feet to steer the Piper Cub while it was on the ground. His flight instructor told him to pull the throttle all the way back and go straight down the runway. The tail wheel of the plane rose up as the Piper moved faster down the runway. Following instructions, William eased the stick back, feeling his stomach sink. The nose of the airplane pointed slightly upward. Trees at the end of the runway were getting closer.

William held the stick firmly as the plane left the ground. William looked at the trees ahead as they got closer, but soon the trees were of no concern, because the horizon above the trees appeared. William relaxed as the airplane cleared the trees. He thought briefly about his time in a tunnel and felt that experience had been the opposite of flying freely in the sky. The instructor had him make turns and learn to maneuver the plane. Then William had to line up with the runway. He was ready to land the airplane, but the instructor told him to relax and watch the instructor land.

William's first flight was exhilarating. He eagerly made an appointment for his next lesson. Riding the motorcycle after William's flight required an adjustment. He rode the motorcycle too fast. His exuberant driving made him think of the wind on top of his Molokai mountain and of Alanah. He headed for the highest cliff he knew in the area.

Culvert Road was the only place on the Erie Canal where a road passed underneath the canal. William liked the echoing roar of his motorcycle as he went through the culvert. On the northwest side of the culvert, a lane took William out to a shooting range. Behind the targets, a dirt cliff rose high above the shooting area. The high cliff prevented stray bullets from hitting animals or worse, because the bullets buried themselves in the dirt of the cliff. Ed saw William ride through Medina and tried to catch him, but William was driving too fast. Ed caught up to William while he sat looking at the rifle range.

"What're you up to?" Ed said.

"Watch and see."

William cranked his spark suppresser over, cranked his wrist to put gas in the carburetor, and kicked the starter. The machine roared. William slammed the shift lever to first gear with his left hand and let his foot off the clutch. The motorcycle lurched forward toward the wall of dirt, accelerating faster. Ed must have thought William had gone crazy. The motorcycle got to the bottom of the hill and started up at the base. William seemed to be going straight up into the sky. The motorcycle started slowing down, and William thought he would tumble down the hill with the motorcycle on top of him. William barely made it to the top of the cliff and rolled forward without falling back down. He turned the motorcycle around and looked over the cliff. He expected to see Ed at the bottom of the range, where he'd left him, but Ed was not there. A flash of steel and rubber appeared next to William. Ed had seen him make it up the hill, so of course, he'd had to try it.

The motorcyclists followed a tree line around and down the hill and back to the range. They watched each other barely make it up the hill. After a half dozen rides up the hill, they were ready to go back down along the path they were making.

"Ready?" William said.

"Yes, sir."

Ed turned around and started driving to the path, when he caught William out of the corner of his eye. William went over the cliff, motorcycle and all. Ed got off his motorcycle and ran to the edge of the cliff. He could hear the motorcycle's engine; it was slowly getting farther away. Finally, William showed up riding away from the base of the cliff. He'd ridden the motorcycle down the cliff and survived. Ed was determined to do anything he was dared to do or saw someone else do, but not that day. He got on his motorcycle and rode the path down to meet William.

As he rode away with Ed, William's thoughts of Alanah vanished. He was thinking about his date with Donna. Donna worked for the Buffalo Niagara Electronics Corporation. William went home to get cleaned up before his date. He had to make a good impression with Donna's father before she could go out with him. William thought of his grandfather watching over his mother and father while they were courting. It hadn't been proper for a man and a woman to be left alone without a chaperone in those days. William had been a gentleman the whole time he was in Hawaii, for such protocol on Molokai did not exist. He would remain a gentleman on his date.

William wasn't sure what he was going to do that night with Donna. Luke had taken a girl bowling and said they had fun. Megan suggested taking her to a movie and then out for an ice cream soda. William took her for a motorcycle ride. They ended up at a high school football game. William figured that watching football was the next best thing to playing the game. William had fun at the football game, as did those around him who listened to his commentary on the game.

William took Donna home after the game. She told him she'd enjoyed the game and riding on the motorcycle. William had had a good time, but he always had fun. When he got home, Megan asked William how his date was.

"Great."

"Where'd you take her?"

"A football game."

"You idiot."

Megan and William discussed how a polite girl would tell someone she'd had fun even though she had not. Megan told William that Donna would probably never want to see him again.

William decided to listen to Megan and plan a movie and a meal if Donna would go out with him again. William asked Donna out and was happy when she said yes. Per Megan's advice, he took her to a romantic movie. William found it boring, but he could tell Donna was happy. After the movie, William was going to take Donna to the Sandhurst Inn on the corner of Bates Road and East Center Street for a nice dinner.

A group of William's football buddies were across the street from the theater, going to O'Brien and Kelly's Bar. Ed was among them, and he invited William and Donna to join them for drinks inside O'Brien and Kelly's. Donna looked at William's eyes and saw that he would like to join his buddies.

"Sounds like fun to go in for one drink," she said.

William was happy with Donna's comment, and without thinking, he took her inside for a drink. William knew every restaurateur and bartender in the area from his work selling restaurant supplies and bar snacks. William knew everyone in the bar and had conversations as he introduced Donna to several people. After three hours, Donna told William she was hungry. He thought about eating at O'Brien and Kelly's but remembered the advice Megan had given him: to take Donna to a nice restaurant.

William rode the motorcycle with Donna on the back to the Sandhurst. The restaurant stopped serving dinner at eight in the evening, and it was a quarter hour past. However, William got special treatment because he knew the owner. William and Donna were the only ones in the dining room. They had an excellent, romantic dinner, and the special treatment impressed Donna.

William liked Donna, but just as important to William, his friends liked her too. William saw much of Donna. She even came to his football games to watch him play and cheer him on. There was one problem: Donna was a Baptist, and William could only get serious with another Catholic. William's friends often congregated at his house, and those who had girlfriends would bring them along. William brought Donna home while his friends were visiting. William's mother blurted out to Donna that she should go to church with William and the family on Sunday. Margret said, "It is possible to convert to Catholicism."

On Christmas 1947, the Donahee family filled a whole pew row in church. Hunter sat by the aisle so he could get up to pass the collection plate. Margaret sat next to him with Megan and her boyfriend, Austin Brown, who was a prominent chicken farmer. On their right were Luke and William with their friends Penny and Donna. Donna enjoyed the congregation. Margaret introduced her to several parishioners, most of whom she already knew. Donna met the priest, and with Margaret's persuasion, they discussed converting to Catholicism.

Hunter, Megan, and the boys were busy on New Year's Eve, taking inventory at Donahee Specialties. The inventory determined how economically successful their year had been. They made plans to go the Knights of Columbus with their significant others to celebrate the beginning of 1948. None of the Donahees owned a car, so Hunter drove the delivery truck to round up the family and their dates after they'd finished the inventory. Several happy events were coming in the following year. Sadly, the year 1948 would bring heartbreak as well.

CHANGE IS THE ONLY CERTAINTY

H unter had promised his grandmother Jade Donahee that he would never marry a woman and make her his slave wife. Hunter had married Margaret for love. She was fifty-seven years old and still the most beautiful woman he'd ever seen. He still had a physical hunger for her. Margaret had worked in the fields on the Kansas farm and taken care of a household of seven, plus her father, when they'd crammed into Aunt Lydia and Odessa's house. Hunter had brought Margaret to Medina in 1925, and every year, her life got better.

Margaret was looking forward to her children getting married and giving her grandchildren. Margaret was active in the community but really looked forward to her women's card group that met twice a month. Margaret had a big house and wanted to fill it with grandchildren. Her children were in love, and she believed some weddings were going to increase her family size soon. Margaret felt tired and lay down in bed. Her heart stopped. Margaret died contemplating her family's future.

William was in Olcott when a customer told him she'd received a telephone call asking her to have William call the office. She handed William her phone. A voice asked for the number, and William replied, "Medina number six." Hunter, Luke, and Megan were not in the shop. An employee told William to hurry back as quickly as possible. The worker would not tell William why he had to hurry back. William finished with his customer and left for Medina.

William could only speculate as to what the problem was while he drove the truck quickly down back roads to the shop.

He thought maybe his brother had gotten hurt while working on the building or equipment. Maybe his father had had an accident of some kind. Maybe there'd been a fire in the shop. William had to pass the Donahee home on his way to the plant. There were two Donahee Specialties trucks parked at his house, and he saw several people on the front porch. William saw the bewildered look on his father's face as he ran up the steps to his father.

"Your mother died," Hunter said.

William stood with the same blank stare his father had. Megan came to William, sobbing uncontrollably. She held William and seemed to need him to keep her standing upright. William fought hard to be a man and not cry. He did so by refusing to believe his mother was gone. Two firemen brought Margaret out on a stretcher to put her in the ambulance. She was covered with a blanket. William walked over and had the firemen wait while he folded the blanket away from her face. William could no longer deny what he had been told. It was a snowy, cold Friday in February 1948.

Three days later, St. Mary's Church was full for the funeral mass. Margaret O'Reilly Donahee had been a well-known and well-liked member of the Medina community. She certainly had been loved by her family. Lydia and Odessa came from Rochester and stayed with Hunter and the children. They were the reason Hunter made it through the tragic time. William and Luke were strong men, and they never let anyone see them cry. William had seen a lot of his friends die in the war, but losing his mother had been unexpected. Margaret was buried in Medina at St. Mary's Cemetery, in the town and church she'd loved so much.

William Donahee and his family missed their mother very much every day that year. Luke married Penny in May. Megan married Austin Brown in July and had a reception for the family at the Maple Crest Inn, one of Donahee Specialties' good customers.

William sold his motorcycle and bought Donna a wedding ring. They were married on Donna's birthday in August.

Hunter buried his grief by keeping busy in the community. He became the grand knight of the Medina Knights of Columbus. Medina needed a new source of water. With the best water source in the world ten miles away, Hunter wanted to get water from Lyndonville, north of Medina. The other option was to pipe water from the Niagara River fifty miles to the west. Hunter believed that common sense would prevail, and clean water would come from Lake Ontario. Hunter decided to run for the office of state senator.

Hunter received the Democratic nomination from Orleans County and from the Lockport Democratic Committee. The water project was part of the campaign. Hunter campaigned hard, leaving Luke and William to run Donahee Specialties. The senate race pitted common sense against individual economics. Hunter was devastated when economics won. Bringing water from the Niagara River was more expensive than piping better-quality water from Lake Ontario. The Niagara water system created more jobs at a high cost, and that lost the senate race for Hunter.

William and Luke noticed how heartbroken their father was and decided never to get involved with politics. However, they would always support their father in his political ventures. Luke and William dedicated their time to working at Donahee Specialties. Megan worked part-time for the family business, because she was busy with her husband on their chicken farm. Megan started delivering fresh eggs to homes in Medina.

Luke bought a parcel of land on Erie Street to build a house on in 1949. Luke had heard stories about his grandfather Ross Donahee and how he'd built his own house with help from friends and family. After building the lake cottage for his father, he thought he could handle building a nice house for Penny and himself. He and Penny lived with Hunter, William, and Donna in the West Center house.

Luke went to work every morning and got the factory work started. Then he worked on his house. William was busy working while Luke worked on building his house. Luke was happy his brother stayed at work, because William would try to make a miscut board work, while Luke would cut the board perfectly. Luke wanted his house to be built perfectly. Building a house was a much bigger job than Luke had expected. He was busy seven days a week.

William was managing a sales force of seven, when one of the trucks was involved in an accident with a car. The truck was not damaged, but the car needed work. The family in the car was from New Jersey and needed a place to stay while their car was being fixed. William took them to stay at Hunter's cottage while they waited for their car to be repaired. The New Jersey family told William that staying at the Donahee cottage was the best part of their trip.

Hunter, Luke, and William did not own an automobile, so they shared a delivery truck to grocery shop. The family was close, but William managed to get Donna pregnant despite the lack of privacy in the crowded house. Megan was also pregnant. William's father was looking forward to grandchildren. William missed sharing the news of grandchildren with his mother, Margaret. Keeping busy was an antidote to sadness. William's father kept busy in organizations and at Donahee Specialties. William built up the business's sales.

Megan gave birth to a son in June. She named him after her grandfather. Michael Brown was Hunter's first grandchild. A second grandchild was born two weeks later when William and Donna had a baby girl. They named her after William's mother, Margaret. Luke was busy working on his house, when they found a good used potato chip cooker.

Luke had to stop working on his house to set up the automatic cooking machine. By September, Donahee Specialties was making their own brand of chips: Donahee's Potato Chips. They made their own product line of popcorn and their favorite caramel popcorn. They were fine-tuning the equipment when, in November, Hunter transferred ownership of Donahee Specialties to William and Luke.

Luke went back to work on his house. While living at the family homestead, both Penny and Donna got pregnant. Megan was also expecting her second child. The family had a productive year in 1950, as both the Donahees' business and families grew. Luke and Penny had their first baby, a girl they named Hannah. William and Donna had another girl and named her Catherine. Megan's second baby was a girl with red hair and freckles named Scarlett.

Hunter spent as much time as he could at the lake cottage, where he met a woman named Ivy. He enjoyed her company and married her in November of 1950. Six adults and three babies filled the Donahee home. Luke worked hard to finish his house. In 1951, the house was finished, and Luke, Penny, and Hannah moved into their new home. Luke had built a perfect house. It was beautiful.

William, Donna, and their two children still lived with Hunter and Ivy. Donna was expecting a third child. William was looking for a house to buy. The next street leaving town west from Erie Street was called Beach Drive. On the south side of Center Street, the road was paved and well developed. The side going north was a dead-end dirt street with two houses on it. The woods behind the Beach Drive house that William liked were the same woods he'd played in as a child. He thought it would be a good place to raise children. The house was close to his father and even closer to Luke.

William bought the house on Beach Drive in the summer of 1951, and the family moved in while Donna was very pregnant with their third child. William had two daughters and was hoping for a son. Hunter was hoping for a grandson to carry on the Donahee name. In September, Donna went to the hospital and had a difficult breech birth. Peter William Donahee was born, and his mother was already mad at him for the difficult birth. William and Donna agreed to call him Pete.

Medina was a progressive community near the richest city, Rochester, in the wealthiest state in the most powerful nation in the world. Hunter saw new opportunities for the future and for his sons and grandson. Hunter would secure a political position that assured that Medina and his heirs would have every opportunity to succeed in such a great country.

Hunter looked at the handsome baby and thought about his family. Hunter's grandfather Mathew Donahee had left Ireland and come to America. He'd taken risks and taken advantage of opportunities. He'd met and married Hunter's grandmother, who'd been an abolitionist and women's rights advocate. Grandma Jade had been nontraditional. She'd been the one who demanded that Hunter never treat a wife like a slave. Their children, Hunter's father and uncles, had worked hard to provide for their families. They'd been good, complacent men who'd taken few risks that would affect the security of their families. Even though Ross had been willing to go fisticuffs with a bear to protect young Hunter, he'd been complacent like Hunter's children.

Hunter had become a big risk taker when he'd tried farming, selling, engineering, and starting a business for his sons. Hunter's loyalties were to his family, community, and business. Luke and

William had taken risks in the war, in sports, and for fun, but they'd ended their risk taking when they'd started their own families. Hunter felt his sons were going to live satisfying yet complacent lives. Hunter expected greatness from his grandsons. He decided to run for Orleans County sheriff the year after Pete was born. Hunter lost the election but continued helping people in town and in civic organizations.

William supported his father's political activities with pride. Donna had two miscarriages after Pete was born. Finally, in 1955, she gave birth to another son and named him Patrick. A year later, Tristan Hunter Donahee was born. William's father had his legacy and watched closely to see what kind of men his grandsons would become. William had to raise his family well.

At the time Tristan was born, Hunter was running for mayor of Medina and found a good opportunity to involve his grandson Pete in the process. A local appliance store owner took advantage of the first television coming to Medina. He installed a television with an antenna on the roof of the Medina Elks Club in the S. A. Cook Building on Main Street. Channel 2 from Buffalo, New York, was granted the right to increase the power of their broadcast station. The power-change time was advertised, and local dignitaries were invited to see the first television in Medina. Hunter took Pete with him. A *Medina Journal* photographer took Pete's photo while he was sitting on his grandfather's shoulders and watching the lighted box called a television. William displayed that newspaper article on his desk for years.

Pete was ready for first grade at St. Mary's School. The school was not ready for Pete. William and Donna had to produce Pete's birth certificate for him to start school. The name on Pete's birth certificate was wrong. It said his name was William Peter instead of Peter William. Pete was confused when his teachers called him William. Pete Donahee, which his father insisted was his name despite the name on the birth certificate, knew his name was Pete. He believed his teachers were the ones who were wrong.

While Pete was in first grade, William bought Donna an old Plymouth car to use to take the children to school and go shopping. The car also provided transport to summer swimming lessons at the conservation club's quarry in the summers. Pete got good grades in first grade and was pleased with all the As on his report card. He and his sisters gave their mother their report cards in the car. Pete's mother told him he'd failed.

Pete argued with his mother and asked how he could have failed with straight As. Donna told Pete he'd gotten the As because the nuns liked him, but some people were made for school, and some were made to work. Pete's mother told him, "You are too stupid for school and will have to be a worker."

Pete was a devastated six-year-old boy. He took every opportunity to go to work with William after that and never talked about the fact that he was stupid. Patrick and Tristan started school and did better than fine. Patrick was a straight-A student and Donna's favorite son. Pete did not try to do well in school, and he became the troublemaking student every teacher dreaded. However, Pete did become useful at Donahee Specialties.

THE GOOD, THE BAD, AND
THE TALENTED

William worked fifteen hours a day but always came home to take his family to St. Mary's Church on Sundays. On Sunday afternoons, William and Donna would take the children on an outing. One of those outings took the family to the Allegheny Mountains. While visiting a forest ranger fire tower, William decided to take his three sons on a trail hike. A map showed trails that ranged from two to twenty-five miles. William decided to take the short two-mile trail. Donna stayed back with the girls.

William followed the trail markers along the trail through the wooded mountains. Pete was eight years old, Patrick was four, and Tristan was only three. William figured the hike would take under an hour if they walked slowly, and he believed his boys would enjoy and could handle the short hike. Two hours later, William was getting worried, and Tristan was tired. William had to carry Tristan, while Pete stayed with Patrick.

The hikers looked for trail markers and found yellow markers on the trees, indicating they were on the trail. William tried to hide his fear that they were lost. After five hours, they came to a power line cleared for fifty feet on each side. They were near the top of the mountain but could see far down the power lines. They could not hear any cars, which would have signaled a highway nearby. A yellow marker depicted where the trail went into the woods on the other side of the power line. William chose to remain on the trail.

Donna was worried and alerted the forest ranger to William

and the boys' failure to return. She showed the ranger where William had started the trail. The ranger determined that William had taken the twenty-five-mile yellow trail instead of the two-mile blue trail. Rangers started a search. They gave Donna a map and told her the spots where the trail came close to the road. She left in the car to see whether William and the boys had made it to the road.

The sounds in the woods changed as dusk approached. William was thinking about starting a fire and waiting until morning, when he saw a bear following them in the woods. He kept going. Pete practiced carrying a wounded victim by taking Tristan from his father. William carried Patrick. William wondered how to fight off a bear. They came to another power-line path, and William decided to stay in the clearing. Pete thought he heard traffic on a highway below the mountain.

The mountain was steep, and William was too exhausted to try going down the mountain, because they would not make it back up. They stayed there and listened for the traffic. They heard a car horn honk several times in the distance. There was a highway down the hill. William brought the tired boys to the bottom of the mountain, where a road signified civilization. He figured the fire station was south. He put the boys beside him away from the road and got ready to hitchhike. The first car that came by was Donna.

She drove back to the ranger station to tell them she'd found the lost hikers. The tall, smiling ranger gave each boy a hiking insignia, and the Donahees left for the ride home. The boys slept in the back of the family station wagon. William and Donna took turns driving. He was too tired to drive.

The next family outing was to the Rochester Zoo and to visit Aunt Lydia and Aunt Odessa. Pete really liked his great-aunts, even though he felt he was too old to be called Little Petey. Pete's aunts were fancy city women and always very formal.

Hunter had gotten his start in Medina by working as a salesman for S. A Cook Wholesale Company. He'd left when the company changed ownership, and he'd gotten a new opportunity to work as an engineer for Gallagher Construction. The former company eventually changed its name to Cook Wholesale, and the last surviving owner put the business up for sale. Hunter saw this as an opportunity and talked his sons into buying the business in 1959. Luke was apt at running Donahee Specialties while William's sales ability made him a good candidate for taking the helm at Cook's. William and Luke bought the business.

The Donahee brothers formed a partnership, with Luke and William owning both businesses equally. The businesses complemented each other. William found that he could make more money by buying merchandise smartly. He wrote letters and built relationships with factory representatives to buy directly from factories. Both businesses flourished. Both men worked long hours to ensure their industry knowledge and expertise.

When Hunter had moved to Medina in 1925, he'd promised to go back to Rochester to visit his sister Odessa and his aunt Lydia as often as possible. He rode the trolley every three months from Medina to see his appreciative sister and aunt. The trolley stopped running during the Great Depression in 1933, and the trips became occasional, but he still went at least twice a year. After the war, Hunter and his grown children took turns visiting their kind and interesting aunts. In 1961, Aunt Lydia and Aunt Odessa died six months apart. They were buried in Sepulchre Cemetery in a group with Donahee ancestors. Pete wished he'd gotten to know them better.

THE BAD SON

Pete got by with little effort in school, but he became useful in working for his father. Pete felt special when he would get up at four in the morning and walk to work. Often, Pete felt as if he were the only one awake in Medina, besides his father and the baker from the doughnut shop. Pete worked until he had to leave for school. Pete loved to read books. He enjoyed any book with a car on the cover. In ninth grade, Pete had to do a book report each month. His English teacher graded his work by giving him an F for mechanics, an F for grammar, and an A for content. Pete hadn't gotten an A since he'd failed first grade.

Pete's English teacher asked to see him after school. He was used to staying after school for fighting or acting up in class. Pete went after school to see his teacher. He was surprised that he was not in trouble. She told him he could not turn in any more book reports on books about racecars. She handed him an old, well-used copy of *Wuthering Heights* and told him to do his next book report on that book.

Pete read the book and put in his book report his negative feelings about how boring the book was and why it had not caught his interest. If nothing else, Pete was truthful. The teacher wrote his usual grade on the paper and wrote a note asking him what his next book would be. Pete found a copy of *Tarzan of the Apes* and read it. There were several movies and even comic books about Tarzan, but none of them were as good as Edgar Rice Burroughs's book. Pete learned to love books and started to read voraciously.

Most people read books or watched movies egocentrically—they associated themselves with a main character. Pete read that

Burroughs had written *Tarzan* while sitting at his kitchen table and had never gone to Africa. Pete started reading allocentrically— he pictured the writer working at a kitchen table or some other place. Pete took a date to a Tarzan movie. His allocentric view of the movie provided an interesting conversation about where the camera was located and how many people were around each scene. Obviously, there was a whole different story than the one seen on the movie screen. Pete became a socially interesting person.

Pete's father was always disappointed with Pete's report card. Pete was a D-average student doing merely enough to get by in school. But something troubled Pete. He often got high marks on Regents exams. Pete did sloppy and careless homework but seemed to have gained knowledge in his classes. Pete would carry a book with him and read it while concealing it in a textbook so that his teachers thought he was paying attention.

In tenth grade, Pete's English teacher handed out a book on the first day called *Joy in the Morning*. Pete read in bed, as he often did, until late in the evening or early in the morning. Pete finished the book that night and got up to go to work at four in the morning. Pete liked the book and was eager to talk about it in English class. Pete was disappointed when the English teacher told the class not to read the whole book, because they would read and discuss only ten pages at a time. Pete had already read the book and moved on to other books. He could not remember enough specifics of the ten pages being discussed in class and did not participate in the class discussions.

By eleventh grade, Pete had started thinking that he wasn't stupid, and he tried to change his bad school habits. It was difficult to become studious, and Pete's bad reputation negated his efforts to win the trust of the teachers. William told Pete that college would be a waste because he would do well in business.

When William told Pete that college was for people who could not make it in the real world, William's eyes looked down at the tattoo with the initials of his four friends who'd died bravely in World War II. Pete wanted to go to college to study marine biology. William told Pete that the only thing he could do with a degree in marine biology was stay in school. Pete accepted that insight.

Pete's family always had dinner together. The day before report cards came out, a discussion of anticipated grades developed during dinner. Patrick was concerned that he might get a B in one of his subjects. That was unusual for Patrick, who always received straight As. It was Pete's turn to report his anticipated grades. Pete told his father that he could get all As but would be ashamed of what he would have to do to get them. Pete's father told Pete, "Prove it."

The next morning, report cards were handed out in homeroom. The students were called one by one to the teacher's desk so the teacher could write the grade on the report card and comment to the student. Pete took his report full of Ds from previous semesters to the teacher and asked for an A. Pete pleaded because he was trying so hard to be a better student. Only one teacher refused to give Pete an A.

A good friend of William's was a math teacher at Pete's school. Pete never had him for a teacher except for one day when he filled in for Pete's geometry teacher. Pete came to life with his father's good friend teaching the class. Pete correctly answered any question the substitute teacher asked. Pete was a D-average student who liked math. He earned a 100 percent on his geometry final exam. The teacher told William that Pete was one of the smartest students he'd ever had in school.

At dinner the night the Donahee children brought their report cards home, each child handed the report card to William one at a time. Patrick was relieved that he had not gotten the B, and his straight-A report card remained consistent. Pete was last to report.

"Sorry, Dad. My gym teacher would not give me an A."

William looked shocked when he saw the nearly perfect report card, and he asked Pete why he hadn't gotten these good grades the whole time. Pete was still embarrassed because his mother thought he was mentally challenged. He just mumbled, "Because I shouldn't have to beg for my grades."

That summer, Pete started his own business while still working for his father in the mornings. When young, Pete had gone to bars to sell snacks with his father. He remembered the putrid smell of stale beer and whatever else was spilled on the floors. One of Pete's friends got a job cleaning the Green Front Tavern in the mornings. He told Pete that he had to mix hot water with soap and soak the floor. Then he put concentrated orange juice in hot water to mop and eliminate the smell.

Pete experimented and talked to different bar owners to find a cleaner that would mask the smell. He came up with a formula that worked. He started a business, mixing the formula in his grandfather Hunter's barn. Donahee's and Cook Wholesale distributed the floor cleaner to their customers. The product was good, and the business was growing. Pete was not old enough to drive and could not handle the business. A cleaning supply distributor contacted Pete and bought the business for $500. Pete was a success, and William was happy. Hunter was pleased.

A year later, Hunter called William to come get him because he didn't feel well. William took Pete with him. Hunter was waiting in his front porch rocking chair. He was having trouble breathing. William helped Hunter down the steps. He had Pete drive the truck up the front lawn. Pete was only fifteen and did not have a license to drive. Pete drove to the hospital with

William and his grandfather in the back of the truck. Hunter went to a nursing home in Gasport and died shortly after. After a magnificently exciting life, Hunter was buried next to Margaret in Saint Mary's Cemetery.

Pete was getting ready to start his senior year in high school. A small group of parents came to talk to William and Pete about a problem their sons had in school. Their sons had been expelled from school for fighting with a teacher. They explained that every year, a specific teacher would start a fight with a particular student. The student would be expelled. The normal sequence was the fight, expulsion, and then the military. Two of their sons had been killed in the Vietnam War. The parents agreed that the teacher would likely pick Pete as his next victim. They were there to warn Pete.

Pete was ready. The teacher called him up to the front of class one day and punched him in the face. Someone else had made a noise, but the teacher had targeted Pete. Pete did not punch the teacher back. He just smiled, walked to the door, and opened it to leave.

"Where do you think you're going?" the teacher asked.

"I'll see you after school."

The teacher looked scared. Pete went to the principal's office and explained what had happened, and he said that after classes, he would go fight the teacher. The principal told Pete that if he did, he would be expelled. Pete suggested he call the police. The principal reiterated that if Pete did that, he would be expelled. Pete went to Cook's and asked his father for a full-time job, but he explained that he needed to leave at two thirty to take care of something. William told Pete to grab a broom.

An hour later, William came to Pete and asked for an explanation. Pete told the truth. William went back into his office and out the front door. Later, the school secretary told Pete what his father had done.

William walked into the school office and asked for the principal. The secretary told William that the principal was busy as she glanced at his office door. William walked into the office and asked the two men, "Which one of you is the principal?"

One man pointed to the other, who sat behind a desk. William put his hands on each side of the desk and said, "I am Pete Donahee's father, and if my son can't fight his battles, I'll fight them for him. And I'll start with you."

William's powerful hands flipped the principal's desk up against the wall, and William was two inches from the principal's face. The high school principal wet his pants. William did not have to touch the coward. The principal told William that if Pete did not fight the teacher or call the police, he could graduate with the credits he'd already earned. Pete had to come back by two o'clock with his decision. That would give the principal time to go home and change his pants.

William came back to Pete and explained the deal the principal had made. Pete left at two. Pete thought the deal was unacceptable because he had done nothing wrong. He went right to the teacher's classroom, ready to fight. The principal was teaching the class because the teacher had had to leave early. The teacher had chosen a tough student to fight, because he'd thought he could get away with scaring the student from fighting because of the consequences. The teacher was not strong or tough. He had so-called small man's disease and was a bully.

Pete figured he would wait until the next day to fight the teacher, but the opportunity never came. The teacher stayed away from school. Pete's first class was English, and they had a quiz in class. After class, the teacher asked Pete to see her. She put a grade on Pete's quiz, told Pete it was his final exam, and said he should not come back to class. Every teacher did the same, except for one who offered to teach Pete and let him finish the class at the teacher's home. It was class club day, when students met after school to join clubs. Pete and anyone with him were asked to leave the meetings and not come back. Pete knew his school days were over.

Pete went back to the business teacher, the one who'd offered to let him take classes in his house, and asked if he could take the book home and come in for the final. Pete needed the class to get a second major. The business teacher agreed. Then Pete went to the principal with a note he'd written. He said he would not come back to school if the principal put the note where everyone could see it. The principal read the note: "Anyone who has trouble with Mr. Babylon, call the number below, and Pete Donahee will beat the daylights out of the teacher for you." Pete's phone number was on the bottom of the note.

After reading the note, the principal opened his desk drawer and took out some keys. Pete followed him to the school entrance, where he opened the trophy case and put the note on display.

"How's that?" the principal asked.

Surprisingly, Pete was satisfied. Occasionally, Pete would go back to the school to make sure the note was still there. The note remained displayed in the trophy case until Mr. Babylon retired, when Pete's children were in school. Pete appreciated his father's support and knew that it came from trust, because William Donahee had raised his children to tell the truth. Pete would teach his children to tell the truth. Pete learned that some people, such as his business teacher, had integrity, while others were self-centered and lazy. Pete vowed to maintain the integrity that his father had taught him.

A week later, Pete turned eighteen, and he signed up for the US Army Reserve. Pete worked for his father at Cook Wholesale while he waited to go active. Pete proudly voted for Richard Nixon that November. Pete felt like an adult. William could not give Pete any permanent work, because he was going to leave for active duty at any time. Normally, a new army recruit would go on active duty within a month.

Pete worked at the weekend reserve drills as a company clerk. A year later, Pete's active-duty file was found behind a filing cabinet. Pete received his orders a week later. Three days before he left for active duty, Pete's girlfriend told him she was pregnant.

THE GOOD SON

Patrick Donahee earned great grades. Like William, Patrick was class president in high school. William was staunch and believed that men worked hard and didn't ever cry or show fear. Those men didn't play musical instruments. Donna was a buffer between William's staunchness and the importance of learning. William bragged that he'd never finished high school, although he'd passed his high school diploma exam while in the army, and he'd become successful. That did not mean William was not intelligent. William was a talented chess player and found common ground with Patrick's intellect while playing the game.

Patrick was controversial and an intelligent negotiator even at a young age. He challenged William about his beliefs. Aunt Lydia, Odessa, and William's great-grandmother had challenged society's norms. Hunter had improved on society with masculine common sense, and that was expected of the men in the Donahee family. Patrick was different. He had the strength of the Donahee men and the kindness and willpower of the women who supported those men. When Pete got married, Patrick used his hard-earned money to buy a cooking stove for Pete and his wife. Patrick worked hard to accomplish his goals, yet he had the generous compassion that the Donahee women contributed to the family. Patrick was perfect.

Jade and Trina had been attracted to the Donahee men because they had strong, big arms, which meant they would be able to work hard and be good providers. Margaret had been attracted to Hunter because his sales suit had been like a uniform, which signified steady income. Donna was in love with William, and the fact that William was successful in a growing business meant that he too would be a good provider. Patrick was a good athlete. Girls Patrick's age wanted college graduates because they would be good providers.

Patrick wanted to become a lawyer because an episode of *Perry Mason* had inspired him. Patrick was adamant about going to college, and with constant badgering from Donna, William agreed to send Patrick to college. It was not easy. William had to work hard to pay for a college tuition that he felt was unnecessary because Patrick could be successful in business.

Pete's oldest sister, Jade, attended practical nursing school in Rochester and then worked to pay for her registered nursing program. Catherine, who was William's favorite child because her kindness and generosity reminded William of his mother, went to college to become a schoolteacher. William believed Catherine would be an excellent teacher. William believed college was for men who were unfit for the military or, worse yet, cowardly. Patrick was an athletic man with the ability to do anything and succeed. It took great courage for Patrick to stand up to his father and argue the benefit of his going to college.

William caught Pete sneaking off to take college classes and was saddened. He agreed to send his second son, Patrick, to college. Often, when Patrick's college tuition was due, William would have to lay off workers to pay the bill. Pete was working for William at the time and was put on salary so he would not get too much overtime. It was common for William and Pete to work more than a hundred hours each in a week when others were laid off from working at Cook's. It was a struggle for Patrick as well because he had to work and barely had enough food to eat while he was studying law.

William could not have been prouder the day Patrick hung his shingle out for his law practice in Medina.

THE TALENTED SON

Tristan did not get the great grades that Patrick got, though he certainly got better grades than Pete. Tristan had many friends and partied with them often. Tristan had fun but did his schoolwork well enough to do better than just get by. Tristan was an above-average scholar and, pleasingly to William, a good worker.

Tristan graduated from Medina High School and wanted to go to college to become a police officer. When Tristan asked William to let him go to college, William struggled to pay Patrick's tuition. William asked Tristan to wait a semester because he did not have an extra $500 to pay Tristan's tuition.

That night, Tristan told William, "Don't worry about my tuition, because I joined the navy today."

William's heart broke because he'd let his youngest son down. Tristan was perfect for the business because he had Hunter's personality and likeability. Four years later, Tristan proved his talented ability to be a salesman. After the navy, Tristan went to work with Luke at Donahee Specialties. Tristan was given a sales route that was performing poorly.

Tristan built the route up so that he was making a big commission. Luke had not seen such a good salesman since William had built up the business before they'd bought Cook's. Luke expected Tristan to work like his father did. When Tristan built up a route, Luke would put a new salesman on the route and give Tristan a route that needed or had the potential to be built up.

Luke did not realize that William was his partner when he

built up routes years ago. Luke and William were partners and made the same money. Luke thought of Tristan as a partner like William was, but did not think about fair compensation for Tristan whom worked hard to make money and felt punished when he succeeded, because he was paid a commission based on his efforts and then moved to an unprofitable route. Tristan left the family business and worked for another firm in Medina. Eventually, Tristan became a corrections officer and happily retired while he was still a young man.

A common thread for the Donahee brothers, sisters, and cousins is that they can be proud of each other. The people who marry into such a family are blessed with tradition that drives a person's loyalty and goodness. New generations provide growth as viable citizens in society. The new generations of Donahees will achieve success. Their success stories might be short or lifelong. They will have commonalities with their grandparents. Humility negates greatness while it endures fame.

EPILOGUE

Pete got married on a weekend leave from the army and had two children before his wife left him. At twenty years old, Pete bought a business and a house. He married a second time. Pete had two more children before his second wife left him. He married a third time and gained a stepson. Pete's third wife was the only woman who truly loved him. Pete was always a good provider, but he failed at being a good father, because society negated Pete's efforts to raise his children properly.

Pete and his brothers maintained a high degree of integrity. Pete had a successful social and political life. He was elected as a village trustee, as his grandfather had been forty years prior. Pete was president of the Niagara Frontier Association of Village Officials. He was active in social organizations as well. The Donahee integrity had contributed to the successes of Matt Donahee's ancestors.

Pete was successful in business. He took over the family business at twenty-eight years old. The Donahee philosophy of business was to provide a quality product at a fair price. Pete owned or operated retail stores, a logistics company, a service business for scuba divers, and an Internet business. The business environment changed before Pete's children were ready to start their adult lives. Pete discouraged them from joining the family business. After working in, running, or owning the family business for nearly half a century, Pete closed the business.

Pete constantly tried to prove his intelligence. He got his pilot's license, progressed to an instrument pilot, and earned his commercial license. Pete started scuba diving at fourteen years old. He took courses to become a professional diver, a boat captain, and a scuba instructor. Pete took college classes several times but could never dedicate the time to completing a degree. At thirty-six years old, Pete quit his job at the family business and signed up for college to become a history teacher. That did not work out, so Pete bought the business, and the business grew. When Pete was fifty, his children were grown, and Pete started college again. He went to college full-time. There are 168 hours in a week. Pete worked eighty hours and dedicated forty hours to college. That left him with forty-eight hours a week to sleep, eat, and do homework. It took four and a half years for Pete to earn a master's degree.

Pete's first job in academia was teaching scuba diving. Pete tried to get a full-time job teaching and had to leave home to secure a full-time position. Pete earned his doctoral degree and became a college professor and, finally, a dean. Pete was happy, believing he could improve the lives of the next generation. Pete retired from academia and worked as a scuba diver in Florida. Pete had five children, a dozen grandchildren, and half a dozen great-grandchildren.

Patrick stayed in his own law office for only one year before political aspirations led him to become the district attorney. He later became the county judge until he retired. Patrick married once and had three children. All Patrick's children received extensive college educations. His oldest son followed in Patrick's footsteps and became a lawyer. Patrick had several grandchildren.

Tristan retired from the correctional facility and performed hard labor better than today's young workers. He married twice and had a stepson. After retirement, Tristan learned the violin. He was known to play with his brother Patrick.

The children of the proud Donahee brothers each will have

his or her own saga to write in a few years. Will they be like their grandfathers? One thing is for certain: times will change, but the attributes of the characters in this story will survive as long as decency is required in society and sacrifice is demanded to make the world a better place.

AFTERWORD

Some of the historic dates or years were changed to fit this story. While all people have ancestors, many of those people do not know the fantastic stories their ancestors could tell. This story is a small reminder that there is always more to a life than what is known. The title, *A Man like His Grandfather*, hints that men and women become like their grandparents because they don't want the heartaches their parents had. Thus, every other generation has similar attributes. The men in this story were typically driven to obey social norms, and they taught their children the importance of strict behavior. The women in their lives demonstrated the kindness that provided happiness to their children. Happiness and social normality must always be in balance.

Printed in the United States
By Bookmasters